RANGE REBEL AND CODE OF THE GUN

Two Full Length Western Novels

GORDON D. SHIRREFFS

WOLFPACK
PUBLISHING
— EST 2013 —

Range Rebel and Code of the Gun
Paperback Edition
Copyright © 2023 (As Revised) Gordon D. Shirreffs

Wolfpack Publishing
9850 S. Maryland Parkway, Suite A-5 #323
Las Vegas, Nevada 89183

wolfpackpublishing.com

Paperback ISBN 978-1-63977-317-6
eBook ISBN 978-1-63977-316-9

RANGE REBEL AND CODE OF THE GUN

RANGE REBEL

CHAPTER ONE

The dawn rain had ceased its steady drum tapping on the taut canvas fly. For a time, the wind thrashed the wet branches of the tall pines and then it died away. Dave Yeamans listened to the quiet drip of the rain and the last soughing of the wind as it whispered through the leaves. His fire had gone out during the night. Dave closed his eyes, fighting against sleep. A subtle warning seemed to come to him. He raised his head. It was too darned quiet to suit him. He threw back his tarp and blankets and scratched his armpits, yawning widely. "Damn but it's cold," he said sourly. Winter was on its way to the Mogollons.

Dave knelt by the fireplace and began to shave splinters. Suddenly his head snapped up. He threw himself backward and scrabbled for his Spencer. He levered home a round and poked his head out from beneath the fly, cursing as icy water dribbled down his back. The woods were quiet again, as they always were after a rain, but something had moved in the wet brush.

A gun flatted off from behind a tree. The slug ripped through the taut canvas of the fly. "Drop that carbeen!" called a man. "There's four of us out here, hombre! Calf rope! Grab those fuzzy ears!"

Dave's finger tightened on the trigger. There was a lot of movement in the brush. They could make his tarp look like a sieve and the slugs would ricochet from the rock formation against which he had situated his camp. He lowered the repeater to his blankets and slowly raised his hands.

"Go get his shooting irons, Mort!" the same voice called out. "I got a bead on his belly!"

The brush rustled and a lean man trotted toward the shelter holding a Henry rifle at hip level. He brushed past Dave and snatched up the Spencer and Dave's gun belt, heavy with a converted cap-and-ball Colt and a Bowie. "All right, Dan!" he yelled. "He's dehorned!"

Three men came out of the brush. The rain glistened on their ponchos. One of them was broad enough to make two of Dave. He had tied a gaudy scarf about his battered black hat and knotted it below his blocky chin. His face seemed hewed from the very rock of the mountains about them. "Get a fire going, Shorty," he said. He looked at Dave. "Where's the coffee?"

Dave jerked a thumb toward his fiber morral in which he carried his food. "Can I put my pants on?" he asked.

"Ain't polite to stand there without 'em," said Shorty with a grin as he pawed into the morral.

Dave limped to his clothing and pulled on his trousers. "What's the idea?" he asked over his shoulder.

"Listen to him!" said Shorty as he prepared the coffee. "Innocent as all hell, ain't he?"

The big man looked at the fourth man. "Mick," he said quietly, "look for a running iron."

Dave had a scaly feeling as he watched the man look through his gear. He was some kind of a breed. His flat face was deeply pitted by smallpox scars. His eyes were a startling light blue in contrast to the mahogany color of his face.

The man named Dan squatted by the fireplace and watched Shorty light the splinters.

"Name?" he asked over a broad shoulder.

"Yeamans. Dave Yeamans."

"Business?"

"Hunter."

The big man sucked at a tooth. "Sho? I'm Dan Edrick. Run the Lazy E spread down in the valley. Ain't heard of no hunters up here other than local boys."

"You have now."

"Yeah." Edrick scratched in his short beard. "Texas man?"

"Brazos country."

"How long you been around here?"

"A month or so."

"How long in Arizona Territory?"

"Couple of years." Dave limped to his bed and got his pipe and tobacco pouch.

"Rebel, eh?"

Dave slowly turned. "I was a Confederate soldier, if that's what you mean."

Edrick shrugged. He glanced at Dave's legs. "Wounded?"

Dave nodded.

"What regiment?"

"Fifth Texas. Hood's Division."

"No running iron," said Mick in a flat voice.

"Don't mean nothing," said Edrick, "A smart sticky looper would have cached it." He watched Dave light his pipe. "Maybe you were wounded at Chancellorsville?"

Dave shook his head. "Longstreet's First Corps was at Suffolk at that time."

"Where were you wounded?"

"Chickamauga."

Shorty spat. "Damned liar," he said, "That was Braxton Bragg's battle. If he lies about the war, he'll lie about anything, Dan."

Edrick ignored the short man. "So you were a Hood man and was wounded in a battle fought by Bragg?"

Shorty fed the fire. "We got rope, Dan. Let's string him up. Only man around here who can't give a good account of hisself."

Edrick grunted. "What the hell you know about the war, Shorty? You sat on your dead rump in Arkansas stealing chickens and playing soldier. The man is right."

"Chickamauga!" snorted Shorty.

Edrick nodded. "Old Pete Longstreet was detached from the Army of Northern Virginia in September of 1863 to join Bragg. Hood was in Longstreet's First Corps. The Fifth Texas was at Chickamauga."

"Sho?" asked Shorty. He glanced at Dave. "I'm sorry, Limpy."

Dave flushed. He puffed at his pipe. Mort was squatting at the back of the shelter. His rifle covered Dave. Mick Ochoa was cleaning his long fingernails with a slim Mexican *cuchillo*. His eyes constantly studied Dave from beneath his eyebrows.

Dave tamped his pipe. "Why did you jump me, Edrick?"

Edrick smiled. "We've lost over three hundred head in the last month. We can track them into the canyon country south of this place and then they vanish. All the local ranchers are looking for strangers. God help 'em if they can't account for themselves."

"Like me, eh?" asked Dave.

"Yeah," said Shorty, "Like you." He left the shelter and returned carrying tin cups.

Dave rubbed his bristly jaw. "I'm only a hunter," he said quietly. "I sell game to the ranchers and to the soldiers patrolling south of here."

"Not much in it, is there?" asked Mort.

"No," admitted Dave, "but it pays for salt and bacon, cartridges and tobacco. Besides, I like it up here."

Edrick eyed Dave. "Like a lone wolf. Like a steer that won't lie with the herd. An outlier."

"Is it a crime for a man to like to live alone and hunt?" asked Dave.

"No, unless he's hunting other people's stock."

Dave waved a hand. "You find any here?"

"We didn't expect to find any...here."

Shorty filled the cups. "What'll we do with him, Dan?"

"Don't be in a rush. Maybe he's seen something."

Dave accepted a cup from Shorty. "I did hear some cattle a week or so ago, along the crick five miles south of here."

"We were probably trailing them. We don't get much farther than the crick."

Dave sipped the strong brew. "That's all I know."

Edrick rolled a smoke and passed the makings to Ochoa. "How well do you know this country?"

"Better than most men. I hunted up here two years ago. Wintered up here. Damn near froze to death."

"Yeah," said Edrick, "you musta." He drained his coffee cup. "Let's vamoose, boys."

The three men glanced at Dave and then at Edrick. "What about him?" asked Shorty with a grin.

"We'll let him hunt."

"A rope is better," said Shorty.

"*Si! Si!*" said Ochoa.

Edrick gripped Dave's hand in a powerful grip and thrust his cigarette tip into the pipe bowl. His gray eyes looked up into Dave's. "Bloodthirsty bastards, ain't they?"

"Man ain't done nothing we can prove," said Mort.

Edrick released Dave's hand. It was a little numb from the crushing grip. "Shorty always was a fast man with a rope. Around a cow or a man. Mick Ochoa is near as bad. I'll tell you about him, Davie. Irish mother. Father was half Mex and half Yaqui. Best tracker in the country. Now, Yeamans: you can stay up here, but *don't try to leave!* Mick can trail a ghost. I ain't sure you're in on this sticky looping, but if you are..." Edrick spat. "Mick will know. Next time we won't be so damned formal. *Adios,* Rebel!"

Dave watched them file out of the clearing. "Still think we oughta string him up," said Shorty. "Teach a lesson to these damn rustlers."

"Shut up!" said Edrick. "You talk too damn much for a little man!"

Dave heard them plow through the wet brush. Moments later, he heard the dull thud of hoofs on the soft earth. Even after they were gone, he seemed to see the Cheshire Cat grin of Shorty and the flat eyes of Mick Ochoa. Time for Dave Yeamans to vamoose. He struck his camp swiftly. There wasn't much gear. Four years of war had taught him to travel with a minimum of gear. Winter was coming on and he had a hankering to hit the trail south into Sonora. He made up cantle and pommel packs and got his rangy clay bank from the sheltered meadow near the stream. The sun was hardly over the mountains when he kneed the horse onto the trail. "Time to cut, Brazos," he said, "we ain't welcome here."

The sun was well up when Dave reached the bottom of the rough trail. Time and time again he turned in his saddle to study the silent woods behind him. There was no sign of life other than a hunting hawk floating on outstretched pinions high overhead. Damn them! It had been a good camp. It was always so. Every time he settled in a good place something like this happened. The five years since the war had filled Arizona with drifters, war veterans, men on the run, settlers and rustlers. Everyone regarded strangers with suspicion. Many a man had danced a reel on thin air because he couldn't explain why he was in a certain part of the country at a certain time.

Dave caught the pungent odor of woodsmoke as he crossed a shallow valley. There was a low log building backed against a slope. Beneath an overhanging rock formation were other outbuildings. A horse whinnied from a peeled-pole corral as Dave neared the house. A door banged open, and a woman came out beneath the ramada, shading her eyes to study Dave. She went inside the house.

Dave was dismounting by the gate when the woman reappeared. A heavy Sharps rifle was in her slim brown hands. "Stand where you are!" she called out clearly. "Who are you? What do you want?"

Dave swore under his breath. "Women too," he said to Brazos. He placed his hands atop his battered hat. "Wayfarer!" he called out. "Passing through! I need coffee and salt!"

"Come closer then!"

Dave walked toward the house. He raised his eyebrows when he caught a good look at her. Not more than twenty or so. Honey-colored hair, braided smoothly, with the sunbeams seemingly tangled in it. Gray eyes. A mouth too wide for beauty, but pretty enough to a man who spent most of his time in the company of a clay bank. "The name is Dave Yeamans," he said.

"Where are you from?"

"Texas, ma'am." Dave smiled.

She shook her head impatiently. "I mean just now!"

Dave jerked his head. "North of here. In the woods near that bald butte. I'm heading south now. Sonora way."

She eyed him closely. "Did you see anyone up there?"

"Four men."

"Who?"

"Man by the name of Dan Edrick. Three others; Mort, Shorty and Mick Ochoa."

She raised her head. "The Lazy E corrida."

"Yes."

"You're sure you saw no one else?"

Dave shook his head.

She looked up at the mountains. "My father is up there somewhere. John Waite. I'm Leslie Waite."

Dave waggled his finger. "Can I take my hands down now?"

She nodded but the Sharps was centered on his belly. "What's your business here?"

"Here it comes again," said Dave with a sigh.

"What do you mean?"

"Nothing, ma'am, nothing at all. I'm a hunter. Stay in the mountains most of the time. An outlier I've been called."

She looked up and down his shabby clothing. "Saddle tramp would be more like it, wouldn't it?"

Dave flushed. "I pay my own way."

"You're sure you didn't see my father? About as tall as you. Gray hair and eyes. Riding a bayo coyote mare."

"No, ma'am."

She bit her lip and looked uncertainly past Dave. Despite the heavy weapon in her hands, she suddenly seemed like a lost child looking for her parents. "Two of the boys went after him at dawn. He was due back last night. I haven't seen the boys."

Dave rubbed his jaw. "Seems as though there's a lot of rustling going on hereabouts. Maybe he's found something."

She grounded her rifle. "Maybe I can trust you," she said. "If you'll go and look for him, I'll fill a sack with supplies for you."

Dave was about to refuse when he saw the look in her eyes. She was worried sick. "All right, Miss Waite," he said. "Which way do I look?"

"Ride back the way you came. There's a fork in the trail a mile back. Take it to the right. Toward Shadow Valley. He might be somewhere about there."

Dave walked back to his horse. "You can forget about the supplies, ma'am," he said over his shoulder, "but I'd admire to have a real home-cooked meal when I get back with him."

"You bring him back and you'll get the meal and the supplies."

———

DAVE FOLLOWED the trail to the fork and turned off. He reached a narrow valley, dark and damp, shielded from the sun by a knife-edged ridge. He turned up the collar of his sheepskin coat against the chill. "Into the valley of death," he said wryly.

Brazos gave the first sign. He whinnied sharply. A moment later he shied and blowed, dancing nervously to one side. Dave freed his Spencer and rested it across his thighs. He studied the wet brush. Something scraped against a tree to his right. He peered into the shadows. A darker shadow moved. Dave's eyes grew accustomed to the dimness. Cold sweat trickled down his sides. A man was hanging from a tree limb, swaying gently in the cool wind that crept down the valley. Dave dismounted and pushed his way through the brush.

He gripped an ankle and turned the body. The staring eyes were gray. The bare head was covered with gray hair, shot with white. Despite the contorted face Dave knew the man must be John Waite, for the girl was a picture of him. "For God's sake," Dave said softly. He stepped back and stumbled over something lying in the wet grass. It was a running iron. The brand was an odd one. "Three diamonds?" said Dave. "No. Maybe Double W."

Dave whistled for Brazos. The clay bank was nervous. Dave stood up on his saddle and cut the dead man down. He hoisted John Waite across Brazos' withers and tied the ankles and wrists together beneath the horse. He thrust the running iron through the straps of his pommel pack and led the clay bank back to the trail. "It was the valley of death," he said. "How in hellsfire will I break this news to that girl?"

Hoofs thudded on the trail as Dave neared the fork.

Before Dave could lead Brazos into the brush two riders appeared. One of them threw down on Dave, but Dave's Spencer covered the man's belly. "Put up that cutter," he said quietly, "I've been choused enough for today."

The man slid his Colt into its sheath. "For God's sake, Kelly," he said over his shoulder, "it's old man Waite!" Kelly kneed his horse forward. He eyed Dave. "What happened?"

"I found him strung up in Shadow Valley."

Kelly circled his horse on the forehand. "That's it, Carl," he said nervously. "I been expecting trouble. Let's pull leather."

Dave cocked the Spencer. "Wait," he said, "are you men from the Waite ranch?"

"Yeah," said Carl. "Why?"

"Miss Waite said you were looking for her father."

"We've found him, stranger," said Kelly. "Let's go, Carl! We're dusting outa here before we get one of them hemp neckties!" He set the steel to his bay and was off down the trail before Dave could speak again. Carl followed his partner. In a few minutes even the steady drumming of the hoofs was gone. Dave shrugged. He led the clay bank on and halted him in a motte of scrub trees near the ranch.

The girl had been watching for him, for she hurried from the house and met Dave near the fence. "Is it him?" she asked.

Dave took off his hat and nodded.

"How did they do it?" she asked.

Dave looked down at the ground.

"How did they do it?" she almost screamed.

She ran to the horse and looked into her father's face. "Oh God," she breathed. "Not by the rope."

Dave wanted to leave. She turned. "Who did it?"

"I don't know. I found him in Shadow Valley. That running iron was in the grass at his feet. I met Carl and Kelly. They pulled out."

"Yes," she said scornfully. "It would be like them to do just that. Just as the others did."

"Why would they do it?" he asked. "Hang him, I mean."

She shrugged. "You're a stranger here. For months there has been a plague of rustling. Every man eyes his neighbor with suspicion. We bought this place months ago. Dan Edrick accused Dad of rustling. Mick Ochoa had found three Lazy E steers with our stock in Cup Valley. Edrick made a lot of talk about it."

"Do you think Edrick had him hanged?"

"Who knows? It could have been other ranchers, but Edrick was the most outspoken."

Dave placed a hand on her shoulder. "Go to the house," he said. "I'll lay him out."

She shook her head. "There is a little burial plot up the slope behind the ranch houses. Dig his grave please."

Dave watched her walk straight-backed to the house. He led the clay bank to the barn and got a shovel. There was an uneasiness in Dave borne of the morning's events.

Edrick had warned him not to leave the country. Even now the iced eyes of the breed might be watching the ranch.

On a slope behind the ranch houses was a small cemetery plot. Three white headboards shone in the sun. "Amos Pearce," read Dave aloud from the first one, "killed by Tontos, 1868. Rest in peace." He looked at the others. "Jared Pearce. Nine years old. Died of fever. 1869. Gone from this earth to his reward in Heaven. Jonce Pearce. Killed by his horse. 1870. Our loss is Heaven's gain." Dave shoved back his hat and set the shovel against the grass, driving it deep with a hard push of his foot.

As Dave cut back the thick turf, he thought of the many other graves he had dug. From Elthan's Landing, the blooding of famed Hood's Texans, through Gaines Mill, Freeman's Ford, Groveton, Second Manassas,

Sharpsburg, Gettysburg and Chickamauga. He had buried his cousin Cad at Gaines Mill. He had buried his brother Jim at a forgotten spot in the rain on the retreat from Gettysburg. When he had come back to the Brazos country after a long siege in hospital in Tennessee, his uncle Mark had shown him the graves of his father and mother, killed by guerillas the last month of the war. No wonder he was an outlier, a man who sought the solitudes, a man who had no kith nor kin, now that Uncle Mark had died in Texas. The war had taken a sixteen-year-old boy into its red folds and spewed out a partially crippled man four years later. It had seared a hatred for the ceaseless conflict of man against man deep into Dave's soul.

The girl came slowly up the slope as Dave finished the grave. Dave lowered the body to the ground and watched her as she wrapped the corpse in a blanket and then wrapped canvas tightly over that. Dave wiped the sweat from his face. "You ought to lay him out until the law gets here," he advised.

She looked up quickly. "Law? What law? There is none! Bury him! I'm the only one to mourn or avenge him!" she said bitterly.

Dave carried the body to the grave and lowered it. He looked at the girl. "All right?" he asked.

She was dry-eyed. "Yes."

Dave hesitated. "Maybe a few words from the Good Book?" he suggested.

"Bury him," she said quietly. "God knows he was a good and honest man."

The clods began to fall. She watched him as he finished filling the grave and then got rocks to cover the mound. He bowed his head for a moment and said a soft prayer for the man he had never known. When he looked up she was almost at the house. He picked up the spade and led Brazos down the slope. Something winked from a bald butte across the valley. He was willing to bet Brazos against a platter of hog belly that someone was watching the ranch through field glasses. He'd better move on.

She was waiting for him beneath the ramada that shaded the front of the sturdy log house. She had a sack in her slim hands. "Your salt and coffee," she said. Her eyes met his steadily. "Are you looking for work?"

"No."

She raised her head. "I'm alone now. Carl and Kelly were the last of the men who worked here. There are fifty steers in Cup Valley."

"Alone?"

"Mack Muir is with them. He's a friend of my father. He promised to take care of them until Dad came back." The loneliness in her voice swayed Dave. "I'll stay awhile," he said. "Until you get help, that is."

"It may be a long time," she said quietly.

CHAPTER TWO

The odor of cooking drifted invitingly out to Dave as he finished feeding Brazos and turned him loose in the corral. Dave took his field glasses from their case and stepped into the barn, away from the bright sunlight which would reflect from them. They were good glasses, German made, captured from a Yank officer at Gettysburg. Dave could pick out each rock and clump of brush on the bald butte bordering the valley to the east. The sun glinted from something. There was a furtive movement. Dave picked out the impassive face of the breed, Mick Ochoa. The breed settled again, studying the ranch through his glasses.

Leslie came from the house. Her face was flushed from the heat of the kitchen. She wiped her hands on her apron. "It's ready," she said. She looked curiously at the glasses.

Dave handed her the glasses. "Look up that bald butte."

"Skull Butte?" She studied the rock formation. "There's a man up there. Why, it's Mick Ochoa!"

"Why is he watching the ranch?"

"He could be watching you, Dave. He must have seen us at the cemetery."

"Edrick still thinks I had something to do with the rustling."

She handed him the glasses and tilted her head to one side. "And have you?"

Dave cased the glasses. "No," he said quietly.

"Yet you were heading out after meeting him."

Dave smiled. "I usually do as I please."

"Dan Edrick runs this part of the territory or tries to."

"So? He won't run me." He took her arm and walked her toward the house. "Let's give Mick something to report."

She had set a fine table. Venison, small potatoes, corn bread, coffee and apple pie. She did not fill her own plate but sat watching Dave eat. "I envy you in a way," she said. "Free as a bird, traveling when and where you will."

He grinned. "Going hungry. Getting lost. Shot at by bronco Apaches."

"Have you never wanted to settle down?"

Dave applied himself to the cornbread. "Yes, but somehow the same things happen. Men always pick sides for a fight. A man has to join one side or the other."

"Not necessarily."

He shook his head. "It's the way of the world. My father left Kansas because of the Free Soilers. We never owned a slave nor grew cotton. We were never great on the question of State's Rights. Yet my brother, my cousin and I enlisted, because we believed in our new state of Texas. Cousin Cad died at Gaines Mill. Brother Jim died of wounds received at Gettysburg. I got a Minie ball in my left leg at Chickamauga. I came home to find that my father and mother had been murdered by guerillas who claimed to be Southern partisans. It seems as though my father had some fine mules they wanted." Dave shoved back his plate. "May I smoke?"

She nodded and watched him fill his pipe. Dave lit up. "Reconstruction was the same thing all over. Some

Confederates joined the scalawags and carpetbaggers. Others left Texas and went into Mexico to fight with Maximilian, or against him, with Benito Juarez. I couldn't see any of it. I decided to stay by myself, see the west, and avoid other men's fights."

"You speak as though you've had an education."

"My mother was a schoolteacher from Illinois. My father was a lawyer from Kentucky. My elder brother Jim made me keep at my books while in camp. Seems odd now. Fighting bloody battles, killing men, and then sitting down beside the bivouac fires to study."

She refilled his coffee cup. "Now you're entangled again."

"No, I'm helping a woman who is alone."

Her eyes held his. "Then you must still believe in fighting."

"I believe in helping a woman, Leslie. There is a difference."

She shrugged. "I will not leave this valley. My father bought this ranch from Mrs. Pearce. Her husband defended this house against Tontos and was killed. Her youngest son died of fever during a hard winter. Her eldest son was killed by his own horse. Now Dad has been lynched fighting for his own land and cattle. There has been too much blood already spent to hold this land, but I intend to stay right here."

Dave leaned back in his chair. "One woman? You'll need help. Do you have money?"

"Enough to keep going."

"You'll need good men, handy with guns."

"Men are afraid to work for the small ranchers. You saw what happened with Carl and Kelly. They were good men, honest men, but the threat of a rope drove them away."

"Your father was suspected of rustling. They won't leave you alone. Your stock will be driven off. Perhaps they'll burn you out. Anyone who tries to work for you will be driven away or killed. Is it worth it?"

She placed her elbows on the table and clasped her hands, resting her chin on them. There was no fear in her gray eyes. "When did you think the Confederate cause was lost, Dave?"

"After Gettysburg. We had lost too many good officers and the pick of the men. The blockade was strangling Confederate commerce."

She nodded. "Yet you fought on. If you hadn't been wounded at Chickamauga would you have fought on until Appomattox?"

He tamped down his tobacco. "Yes," he said softly.

"Then perhaps you can understand why I will not leave. This is my home. My father's name has been disgraced. I'm the last of my line, as you are, and *I will not leave!*"

Dave stood up. "Then God help you." He turned. His hunter's hearing had brought the faint thud of hoofs to him. "Someone is coming. There might be trouble."

She smiled as she stood up. "You were the one who was trying to avoid entanglements with other men." She walked into the living room.

Dave eyed her full figure and honey-colored hair. "With men?" he asked himself aloud.

She turned. "What did you say?"

He flushed. "Nothing. Who is it?"

"Dan Edrick. Shorty Ganoe. Mort Hastings."

Dave slipped out the back door and got his Spencer. He twirled the cylinder of his long-barreled Colt and returned it to its holster. He came around the side of the house just as Leslie stepped out beneath the ramada. "I have the Sharps just inside the door," she said.

Edrick glanced at Dave with no surprise as he drew rein near the gate. "Where's your Pa?" he asked Leslie.

Leslie stepped out into the sunlight. Shorty rested his

forearms on the saddle horn and eyed her appreciatively. "We buried him two hours ago," said Leslie.

"Sho? I'm right sorry to hear that. Took sudden-like, was he?"

She shook her head. "This gentleman found him lynched in Shadow Valley."

Edrick shoved back his hat. "Well, I'll be damned," he said. "Beggin' your pardon, Miss Leslie."

Dave eyed the big man. He seemed genuinely surprised, but the man was evidently a good actor.

"Who did it?" asked Edrick.

Leslie held back a stray wisp of hair. "We don't know, but we'll find out, Mister Edrick."

"We?" Edrick glanced at Dave. "He throw in with you?"

"He's helping me until I can get more men."

Edrick scratched his jaw. "Lemme see. I can loan you a couple of the boys for a time. Always ready to help out. That's Dan Edrick's way, Miss Leslie."

"We'll make out."

Shorty shifted in his saddle and grinned at Dave. "Limpy cut hisself into a nice deal," he said.

Dave colored. He moved the Spencer a little. "As Dan said earlier today, Shorty, you talk too damned much for a little man."

Shorty paled. His right hand dropped onto his thigh, near his Colt. Dave grinned. "Go ahead," he said. "This morning you had three hombres to back your play, Shorty. Against an unarmed man. Go ahead. Draw that cutter. I'll slide a slug up underneath your scaly hide so fast you'll die wearing that damned grin of yours."

Shorty glanced uneasily at Mort. Mort kneed his horse away from the little man. "You been talking war," he said, "don't look to me for help. I think he can do it."

Dave looked steadily into the pale eyes of Shorty Ganoe. Shorty looked away. Edrick spat. "What happened to you since this morning, Yeamans? You were a hell of a lot less argumentative then." Edrick cupped his chin in his right hand and glanced at Leslie and then back at Dave. "Sho?" he said, "I might have figgered that out."

Leslie Waite raised a slim hand. "What is it you want?" she asked.

Edrick waved a hand to the south. "Me and the boys is making what you might call a routine check. I'd like to look at the stock in Cup Valley."

Leslie raised her chin. "Why do you ask me? You didn't ask Dad when you sent Mick Ochoa there."

Edrick's eyes were veiled. "He did find three Lazy E cows there, didn't he?"

"How many of our steers are in amongst yours?"

Edrick smiled. "A few. No more. I'll have the boys bring them over."

She leaned forward a little. "You can look at my stock, but Mr. Yeamans will go with you."

Shorty raised his eyes. "Mr. Yeamans," he murmured.

"I'll get my cayuse," said Dave.

As Dave walked back to the corral, he heard Edrick speak angrily. "You keep prodding that maverick, Shorty, and he'll turn on you yet."

"I wish he would," said the little man. "I sure wish he would!"

Leslie called Dave aside as he returned. "Let them look all they want, Dave. Don't start any trouble, but don't let them start any either. Mack is a good man. He had already agreed to stand by Dad and me until this trouble was over."

Dave nodded as he sheathed his Spencer. "If anything serious happens you must ride down to Pebble Crick south of the canyon country. Ask for Captain Dwyre. He'll help you. He has a company of cavalrymen bivouacked there."

She placed a hand on his arm. "Take anything from

them rather than fight. Shorty Ganoe is a killer for all his smiling."

Dave doffed his battered gray hat. "I've done some killing myself, ma'am." He looked into her eyes, and for the first time in six years he began to suspect he might have a real purpose in life, after all. He mounted Brazos. "See you later, Miss Leslie," he said, and rode to join the three Lazy E men.

Edrick set a fast pace down the valley. He waved a thick arm, encompassing the valley. "One of the best spots in the whole damned Mogollon country, Yeamans. Plenty water. Fine grass. Protected by them ridges. I can see where Miss Leslie would want to keep it. I tried to buy out Missus Pearce, but she just wouldn't do business with me."

Shorty rolled a smoke. "She never did like the Lazy E," he said.

Edrick scowled at the little man. "I was always a friend to them Pearces," he said.

"Shore. Shore." Shorty grinned.

After a two-mile ride they reached a narrow opening between two rugged buttes. "Cup Valley," said Dan. "Part of the Waite layout. Best place in these mountains for keeping stock."

The entrance wound in an S shape, rose up a slope, and opened out into a small valley, more of a box canyon, that was almost circular in shape. Cattle were scattered across the grassy floor. The sun glinted on a dammed pool fed by a winding stream. Smoke drifted up from a line shack set in a motte of pines. A man came out of the shack as they approached. "Mack Muir," said Mort Hastings.

Muir was a well-built man with a fine head of red hair. His blue eyes studied the horsemen. "Hello, Dan," he said easily, "Mort. Shorty."

Edrick nodded. "This is Dave Yeamans. Working for Miss Waite."

"So? Miss Waite? She doing the hiring now?"

Edrick leaned on his saddle horn. "John was strung up in Shadow Valley this morning, or last night, by some unknowns."

Muir paled. "Not John!"

"We'd like to get our hands on the killers. John never was no rustler."

"You're damned right he wasn't! You looking for the killers now?"

Edrick shifted a little. "Not now. We got business here."

Muir's eyes narrowed. "Nothing in here but Double W cows and a few of mine."

"We'll look anyway. Go ahead, Shorty."

Shorty and Mort cantered off. Muir rested big hands on his hips. "Still running the show, eh, Dan?"

Edrick held out his hands, palms upward. "Just a routine check, Mack."

"I've got coffee heating," said Muir. "Come in and set a spell."

Dave followed Edrick into the shack and sat down. Muir filled the cups. "Leslie planning to stay on, Dan?"

"Looks like it. I'll buy her out any day."

"Yeah," said Muir dryly, "I'll just bet you will."

"What's riling you?"

Muir sat down. "Everything. I've lost thirty head of stock. Three of my boys quit last week. I've got two left. The way things are going I won't have a *vaquero* left. Who's behind this rustling, Dan?"

Edrick shrugged. "Half a dozen of us ranchers been combing these mountains asking questions. I've lost three hundred head. I've heard tell we're up against some of them Mex rustlers from over in the Blue River country. But we ain't seen any of them." He sipped his coffee. "Some say it's the 'Paches. But what the hell would 'Paches do with all them cows? They ain't stockmen. Besides, they'd rather eat a cayuse or sweet mule meat.

Me and the boys scouted the whole northern end and only came up with Yeamans here. He ain't nothing but an outlier, hunting for a living."

Muir glanced at Dave. "How come you suddenly settle down to work for Miss Leslie?"

Edrick leaned forward. "Now ain't that a helluva question to ask a good looking hombre like Yeamans when a fine looking filly like Miss Leslie, smooth in the flank and slender in the pasterns, who ain't been roped yet, is all alone?"

Muir reddened. Dave seemed to feel a subtle warning emanate from the rancher. Beneath the surface of the blue eyes was a hard icy core. "That true, Yeamans?" asked Muir.

Dave shook his head, but the lie was in his teeth. "I was warned to stay around this country by our mutual friend, Mister Edrick. Claims he'll send Mick Ochoa chousing after me if I pull out."

Edrick coughed. "Now that ain't exactly true! I just said he'd watch you to make sure you ain't mixed up in any sticky looping!"

Muir glanced through the window. He stood up. "Damn them," he said. "They got ten cows."

Edrick yawned. "Must be mine then."

"The hell you say!" Muir turned to snatch up a Henry rifle which leaned against the wall. Edrick moved easily for all his bulk. His six-shooter was out and pressed against Muir's back. "Now, Mack," he said softly, "we'll look into this legal like. Let go of that repeater."

Muir placed the gun against the wall. He turned slowly. "Someday," he said between his teeth, "someday."

Edrick twirled his cutter on a big forefinger and deftly holstered it. "Come on," he said, "we'll check them brands."

Dave followed them. Shorty drew rein. "Ten of 'em, Dan," he said.

Muir looked at the steers. "Those aren't Lazy E brands," he said.

"Sho," said Edrick. "But they ain't Double W or Bar M either. They're Lazy L."

Muir spat. "I bought them from Lem Linter over on Cache Creek," he said quickly, "just a week ago."

"Damned liar," said Shorty.

"What do you mean, Ganoe?" snapped Muir.

Shorty leaned forward and spoke in a flat voice. "I been working up a small herd for my old age. Dan's been allowing me to let 'em run with his herd. My brand is Lazy L. Yuh see: my middle name is Lawrence. Used a Lazy L brand for Lawrence. Nice handle, ain't it?"

Muir glanced back at the shack.

"Don't move, Mack," said Edrick quietly. "You're damned lucky you're getting away with the loss of only ten cows. Lem wasn't nothing but a damned rustler. Got them cows from my herd. Maybe you ain't heard what happened to Lem? Somebody shot him through the back of the head. Used a Sharps. Why, you'd have hardly recognized him from the mess that slug made outa his face."

"Something terrible," murmured Shorty with a solemn nod.

Edrick mounted. "You coming, Yeamans?"

Dave shook his head.

"Maybe he don't like it, Dan," said Shorty. "He's got itchy fingers and two shooting irons."

"Take them," said Dave, "I work for Miss Waite. Those steers haven't her brand. I work for the Double W. Remember, Shorty?"

Shorty grinned. "How can I forget. Why, hell! If we wanted to check that whole damned herd close enough, we'd have a chance of finding some blotted brands. That Double W iron sure could mess up an honest man's brand."

Dave felt rage rise from the depths of his soul. He drew a checkrein on it. Those three hardcases wouldn't hesitate to throw down on him if he made a false move. He might get one of them if he was lucky. He watched Shorty and Mort drive the ten steers toward the valley entrance. Edrick followed the small herd without looking back. Dave looked at Muir. "Well?" he asked.

Muir's tanned face had gone white with suppressed rage. "Damn them! I've got a mind to throw a few Henry slugs after them."

"What about Lem Linter?"

"Linter was slick, it's true. No one ever knew much about him. It's possible he stole the steers and then disposed of them to me. What riles me is Edrick and his cute tricks. Shorty with a small herd of his own. The Lazy L! Don't you get it?"

Dave nodded. "A short, straight iron could easily burn in two horizontal bars and make a Lazy L brand into a Lazy E."

"Keno! Tell Leslie I'll stay here until she can get a man to relieve me. What's the story on John?"

Dave told the redhead. Muir rubbed his jaw. "I knew they were hot after him. He told me just a week ago that someone tried to drygulch him."

"Maybe he was mixed up in something?"

Muir came close to Dave. "Look, Yeamans! John was my best friend, and well, at one time Leslie and I had an understanding. Don't ever talk like that about John if you want my friendship."

"I'm sorry, Muir."

Muir rolled a smoke. "How is it that you started working for Leslie?"

"She needs help."

"I would have given her all she wanted," said Muir softly.

"I'll be heading back," said Dave. "Any message?"

Muir lit up, his eyes held Dave's over the flare of the lucifer. "Just one. Not for her. For you. She's my woman,

Yeamans. We'd have a difference of opinion, but she's going to be my woman. Guide yourself accordingly."

Dave mounted Brazos. "See you," he said and touched the clay bank's flanks with his heels. He glanced back as he reached the exit from the canyon. Muir was looking at him. He did not wave.

CHAPTER THREE

Leslie Waite listened quietly as Dave told her what had happened at Cup Valley. "It's Edrick's way," she said when he had finished.

"Is that all of your stock at Cup Valley?"

"Yes."

"It's not much of a herd for a ranch as big as this."

"Dad was planning to buy more stock. I have the money to do so now, but the way things are going on I just won't risk it. Besides, I need men to work for me. They just won't work for the smaller ranchers now."

Dave filled his pipe. "The thing that bothers me is where the missing stock can be. You just can't hide hundreds of steers as you would a stolen horse. They have to have water and grazing."

"It's a big country," she said, "much of it unexplored."

"How much stock have you lost since this rustling started?"

"Over a hundred head."

Dave whistled. "You've lost a hundred. Edrick claims to have lost three hundred. Muir has lost about thirty. That's four hundred and thirty alone, not counting the losses suffered by other ranchers."

Leslie walked around the side of the house and looked at the encircling mountains. "Somehow I still think they are hidden around here in some secret valley or canyon."

"It's possible."

She turned. "I wonder why I trust you so. I know very little about you, other than what you've told me, Dave."

He grinned. "I know very little about you, Leslie."

She smiled. "Fair enough. Will you stay here while I drive into Deep Spring for supplies? Dad meant to bring some back."

"I'll go."

She shook her head. "Deep Spring doesn't exactly welcome strangers these days. Edrick and his type run the town. Frank Andrews was badly beaten one time when some of the Lazy E corrida claimed he was mixed up in rustling. Frank fought back. If it hadn't been for Dad, they would have maimed him."

Dave walked toward the corral. "I'll hitch up the team. Make out a list of necessaries. If I'm to work for you, I'll do what's expected of me."

She eyed him as he walked away. "All right. But don't look for trouble. Get in and out of there as fast as you can."

Dave hitched a pair of mules to a light wagon and placed his Spencer beneath the seat. He drove to the front of the house, and she handed him a list. "If you get into any trouble you can rely on Cass Simmons. He runs the general store. Follow the valley road four miles south to a junction. Turn left and follow the creek road four miles into Deep Spring." She placed a hand on his arm. "Dave, be careful."

"I will," he promised. He touched up the team and drove off. Oddly enough he felt as though her hand was still on his arm and even glanced down foolishly to see. The touch was that vivid. "Damned fool," he said aloud. "You were the one who wanted peace and quiet. The outlier! Now look at you, you damned jackass, going shopping for a woman!"

The trip was uneventful, and Dave made it in good time. Deep Spring nestled in a steep-sided valley, a double line of false fronted stores and houses on each side of the main street. The buildings were warped and weathered by the heavy winter rains and snows. A shallow rushing creek brawled over the smooth stones of its bed behind the eastern row of buildings. Scattered throughout the town were more durable structures of native rock. Dave tethered the team outside of the biggest of these. A sign identified it as Cass Simmons Deep Spring Emporium. As Dave stepped up on the splintered boardwalk, he saw Mick Ochoa standing whittling in front of a saloon grandly named The Star of The West. The breed sheathed his knife and disappeared into the saloon.

Dave entered the store. It was an orderly wilderness of stacked sacks, boxes, kegs and tubs. Harness, saddles, and other gear hung from pegs set into the walls. Pots, pans, skillets, spiders and other culinary equipment hung from wires stretched from wall to wall. A bald-headed man with a beak of a nose was opening a packing case at the rear of the store.

"I'm Dave Yeamans," said Dave. "Working for the Double W. Miss Leslie sent me in for supplies."

The storekeeper turned slowly and looked at Dave over his spectacles. "So? You working for John?"

"No. I said Miss Leslie."

"Yeah. I know. Didn't know she was setting up independent from her Pa."

"John Waite is dead, Mister Simmons."

The storekeeper dropped his hammer. "You don't mean it!"

"It's true."

The eyes peered at Dave again, measuring him. "Yes. I believe you. When did he die and how?"

"I found his body this morning, hanging in Shadow Valley."

"You ain't suggesting that John committed suicide?"

"I didn't know him. I'd say he was lynched." Simmons glanced past Dave. "Keep a checkrein on your tongue in this town, young man. John was my good friend. I knew he'd end up murdered, one way or another. It didn't surprise me none to hear you say so. John Waite was afraid of no man. Whoever killed him knew he was a man that had to be killed."

"He was afraid of no man? Meaning Dan Edrick?" Simmons nervously wiped his hands on his apron. "For a stranger you seem to know a helluva lot, Mister Yeamans."

"I've met Edrick and his hardcases."

Simmons took the list from Dave's hand. "Can't hardly imagine John being dead. Leslie planning to keep the place?"

"Yes."

"Who's working for her?"

"Me."

"Yeah. I know. But who else?"

"No one. Mack Muir plans to help her."

"What about Carl Hobie and Mike Kelly?"

"Quit when I brought John's body back."

"That figures." Simmons went behind the counter and scanned the list, but now and then, as Dave looked about, he knew the storekeeper was studying him over the top of his spectacles.

"I wanted to get the sheriff," said Dave, "but Leslie said not to bother. Maybe I'd better see him while I'm here."

Simmons rubbed his jaw. "You know who he is? No, of course you don't, or you would have known why she didn't bother to bring him in on the case."

"Who is it?"

"Name of Edrick. Bart Edrick. Dan's younger brother."

Dave whistled. "Then the law is part of the Edrick spread?"

Simmons nodded. "Now I ain't saying Dan Edrick did have anything to do with John's death, but if he did, Bart wouldn't do anything about it. If he didn't have anything to do with John's death, Bart still wouldn't make much of an effort. This country is full of hardcases. Men who wouldn't hesitate to even tangle horns with the Edricks if they thought Bart was getting too nosy. Dan wouldn't like that."

Dave leaned forward. "So what do we do? Bury a man who was hung by unknowns and forget about it? How far back has this country slipped in the scale of civilization?"

Simmons placed both hands flat on the scarred counter. "The Dark Ages. If I didn't have every dime I own invested in this place I would have pulled out long ago. I admire your nerve in working for Leslie, but you've showed more guts than brains, sonny. Dan Edrick wants the Double W spread and he's aiming to get it, too. He's scared off every man who's worked for them since they bought the place."

Dave walked to the door. "I'm going to see Sheriff Edrick," he said.

"You won't get anywhere," warned Simmons.

"I'd just like to hear what he has to say."

Dave stopped on the boardwalk and rolled a smoke. There were only a few people on the street. Half a block away was a small frame building with a star-shaped sign labeled Sheriff's Office. Dave lit up and walked toward it. He opened the door. A thin-faced man was seated at a littered desk carving a linked chain from a single piece of wood. "Are you the sheriff?" asked Dave.

The thin man grinned. "Hell no! I ain't got any connections. I'm the jack-of-all-trades around here. Jailor, clerk, swamper, and errand boy. Name of Tom Finney. What can I do for you?"

"Where's Sheriff Edrick?"

"Over to the Star of The West. You can't miss Bart Edrick. Wears the biggest and brightest star in Arizona."

Dave nodded. He crossed the street and pushed through the batwings of the saloon. Shorty Ganoe and Mick Ochoa were seated at a table. A big-bodied man wearing a white hat stood at the bar talking with another man. A polished star was pinned to his black coat. There was no doubt that he was an Edrick, for he had the same blocky build as Dan, but the forcefulness of Dan didn't seem to emanate from the sheriff.

Dave stopped in front of the big man. "I'm Dave Yeamans," he said, "I work for Miss Waite out at the Double W. I've come to report the death of John Waite."

Edrick worked his cigar from one side of his mouth to the other and spoke around it. "What happened?"

"I found him early this morning. Strung up in Shadow Valley."

The hard eyes studied Dave. "Suicide, eh?"

"I don't know," said Dave quietly. "It could have been murder just as well."

Edrick took his cigar from his mouth and studied it. "Where's the body?"

"I buried it in the ranch cemetery."

Edrick slapped a big hand flat on the bar making the glasses jump. "What? That's illegal! Shoulda been held for an inquest."

"It was Miss Waite's wish."

"That so? She oughta know better."

"We can dig it up."

Edrick grimaced. "Too late now, ain't it?"

"I've seen 'em dug up lots later, Edrick."

Edrick scratched his chin. "Waal, I'm due over to Little Forks on an investigation. I'll send Tom Finney, my deppity."

Shorty laughed and shoved back his hat. He seemed to be enjoying himself immensely. Edrick frowned. Dave threw down his cigarette. "I think it's your job, Sheriff Edrick," he said quietly.

Edrick tilted his big head to one side. "So? You telling me how to run my office?"

"You must have a lot of murders around here to act so damned casual like about it."

"Now listen here! You ain't even from around these parts! You pay taxes? Have a home? Land? Cattle? No! You ain't nothing but a drifter. I heard about you from some of the Lazy E boys."

"A fine recommendation."

Edrick leaned forward. "You ain't above suspicion, hombre. Hiding in the mountains like a damned 'Pache. Claiming to be a hunter. Hawww! No money in that. Just you watch what you say to an officer of the law," he blustered.

Dave stepped back and glanced at Ganoe and Ochoa. "I can see what Miss Waite meant when she said there was no law around here."

Edrick scowled. "Damn you! I heard you was a troublemaker." He slid his beefy hand inside his coat and half drew a nickel-plated Colt. "Now eat them words! Pronto!" Dave laughed. "I don't think you've got the guts to draw that shiny cutter, Edrick. Chew on those words yourself." Dave turned on a heel and pushed through the batwings. He heard Edrick's voice. "Shorty! Mick! Get moving!"

Dave crossed over to the store. He walked up to the counter. "You were right," he said.

Simmons nodded. "Big bag of wind. Looks enough like Dan to be his twin, but it's like comparing a grass snake to a diamondback." He heaved two sacks up on the counter. "Here's your stuff. I'll add it on to the bill." He hesitated. "You'd better pull out pronto if you had words with Bart. Bart lets others do his fighting. Had trouble with Frank Andrews once and Frank slapped him across the face with his hat. Bart sent some of the boys after him. Damned near crippled Frank and spoiled his looks for life. John Waite stepped in and stopped the massacre."

Dave carried his sacks to the door. He pushed through it and turned to say goodbye. Something hooked under his right leg and he went down hard, spilling potatoes, cans and other articles into the muddy street. Dave looked up into the grinning face of Shorty Ganoe.

Shorty spat. "Lookit him, Mick," he said. "Shopping for the Waite filly. You do the maid's work too, Limpy?"

Dave stood up. His temper was doing a slow burn. He glanced at the breed. Ochoa was leaning against the front of the store paring his fingernails with his long-bladed *cuchillo*. Men stopped to watch the three of them. Cass Simmons came to the door. "Get going, Dave," he said.

Dave picked up the articles and placed them in the new sack Simmons held out. "Wipe 'em off!" jeered Shorty. "That Waite filly allus was fussy about things. Too damned bad she ain't so fussy about men."

Dave turned and drove in hard like an uncoiling spring. His left caught Shorty alongside the jaw and his right smashed just above the big belt buckle. Shorty rebounded from the wall into a vicious right that snapped his head back. He reeled and fell from the boardwalk into the mud of the street. He clawed for his Colt but Dave's six-gun cleared leather first. He moved the muzzle back and forth in an arc covering both Lazy E men. "Throw that cutter into the street," he told Shorty.

Shorty threw aside the Colt. He wiped the blood from his battered face. "I ain't done with you," he said thinly. Dave holstered his Colt and unbuckled his gun belt, "Come on then," he said.

Shorty plunged in. Four hard blows sent Dave up against the wagon. He rolled sideways and met a smashing jab to the mouth. A tooth cracked. He covered up with elbows and forearms and danced back. Shorty grinned. He came in fast, weaving and ducking like a belt winner. He threw punches like a small-sized triphammer until Dave straightened him with a left and threw a right hook that caught the smaller man off balance. Shorty fell over a board and lay flat on his back, his mouth working and hate shining from his eyes.

"Had enough?" asked Dave softly. His chest rose and fell, and he could feel waves of pain pouring up his weak leg.

"Yeah. Yeah. You win."

Dave turned to get his gun belt. Shorty uncoiled like a bull whip. He whirled Dave about and hit him with a hard one-two. Dave went down striking his head against a wagon wheel. He shook his head, trying to get up as Shorty raised a boot, poising the cruel spur to rake Dave. Dave rolled sideways, gripped the ankle, felt the spur rip through the flesh of his forearm, and then heaved up hard, forcing himself to stand up. Shorty thudded to the ground and Dave dropped atop him, punishing him with short blows to the face. They thrashed through the mud to the center of the street and Shorty broke free. He was up first and booted Dave alongside the head. Ochoa yawned. He walked slowly toward Dave, slipping the knife into its sheath.

Dave tried to get up but was helpless, watching the breed and the grinning little man close in on him.

"Tough hombre, eh?" asked Shorty. He laughed. "Well, we ain't done with you."

Cass Simmons reached back inside the store and swung up a sawed-off, double-barreled Greener, sweeping both hammers back with his left hand. "Get back, Ochoa!" he called out. "I got Blue Whistlers with split wads in here and a nervous trigger finger. Get back! They can settle this alone."

Ochoa spat and leaned against a post. Men ringed Shorty and Dave. Dave got up to meet a fast rush by the little man. Dave clinched and whirled Shorty around. A knee came up into his groin. He doubled up and had his head snapped back by a vicious uppercut. Down he went again. Shorty snatched up a splintered billet of wood. It swished over Dave's head. Back it came again glancing from his right cheekbone. The splinters lanced cruelly into his flesh. He warded off another blow with his right arm, went underneath the billet and hit Shorty a smashing blow in the gut. Shorty dropped the billet and gripped his belly, staggering down the alleyway toward the bank of the creek, gasping for breath.

Dave followed the little man, weaving back and forth, but with an unholy desire in his mind to close with the grinning puncher and end it all. Shorty turned and raised his hands to defend himself. Dave closed in, hit hard with both fists, sending Ganoe off balance, and then followed through with a perfectly timed right hook that drove Shorty back into the creek. Dave walked toward the struggling man. "Damn you," spluttered Shorty, "I'll cut you down for this!"

Dave stepped into the cold water and gripped Shorty by the front of the shirt with his left hand. He slapped the puncher hard across the face three times and sent him down, flat on his back beneath the rushing water. Shorty came up in time to meet a boot that smashed him under for the last time. Dave leaned against the side of the store as two men jumped into the water and dragged the sodden, unconscious man to the bank. Blood trickled from Dave's mouth. He picked a ragged splinter from his cheek and blew on his abraded knuckles. He limped back to the wagon and buckled on his gun belt, watching Ochoa through half closed eyes. "Tough hombre," said Ochoa softly. "Whang leather and steel, eh? Maybe Mick Ochoa will try you some day."

Dave picked up his hat and climbed wearily up to the wagon box. Simmons handed him the reins. "Get going," he said. "You blew the lid off the pot for sure. You're a real huckleberry, Yeamans. You value your life from now on, you'll drop off them groceries and keep moving. Fast!"

Dave slapped the reins on the rumps of the mules. "I'll deliver the groceries," he said quietly, "and what's more I'll stay to eat them." He drove the wagon out into the middle of the street and did not look back.

CHAPTER FOUR

It was after dusk when Dave arrived at the ranch. He had stopped at the creek and washed carefully but no water would conceal the welt on the side of his face nor his fat lip. Two horses were tethered to the fence. Dave grimaced as he eased his leg from the wagon. He'd feel a hell of a lot sorer in the morning.

The door of the house swung open flooding Dave with yellow lamplight. Two men stood behind Leslie staring curiously at Dave. "Good news," she said. "I've hired two men."

Dave limped into the house. One of the men was an old-timer, bowlegged and burned by the sun. He held out a hand, eyeing Dave's face curiously. "Hollis," he said, "Monte Hollis. Useta work for John years ago down in the Sulphur Springs country. Me and Jesse here was over in Deep Springs yestiddy and heard John was needing some hands."

Dave liked him instantly. Jesse was almost a kid until you looked into the hard dark eyes. He was too damned good looking. His clothing was of good quality. But it was the two low slung holsters, hanging from a broad, ornately carved buscadero belt, that warned Dave. "This is Jesse Vidal," said Hollis. "Runs with me. A good hand."

"Howdy," said Jesse. "You look like you've been in a brawl."

Leslie looked closely at Dave. "Were you in a fight?"

"Yes. Had a run in with Bart Edrick. He put two of his boys on me, Leslie."

"I know Bart won't fight," she said scornfully.

"No," said Dave, "but Shorty Ganoe can, and did. For a little man he's packed gunpowder with a short fuse. I'm lucky I licked him."

"You've got a cutter," said Vidal quickly.

Dave nodded. "Yeah. And I would have been cut down if I had tried to use it. Mick Ochoa was standing not ten feet away with his knife in his hand."

"Shorty won't let a licking rest lightly," said Leslie. "I warned you to be careful and avoid trouble. You disobeyed my orders!"

Dave eyed her. "Maybe I work for you, Miss Leslie, but orders or no, I'm not going to be choused by a grinning ape like Shorty."

"We're in enough trouble now!"

Dave turned slowly. "You asked me to work here," he said quietly. "Maybe you'd like me to quit?"

"Take it easy," said Monte.

Jesse inspected his slim hands. "Shoulda used the cutter," he said. "More permanent."

"Shut up," said Monte.

Leslie bit her lip. "I'll forget what happened," she said quietly, "but hereafter, you'll listen to my orders or else take your pay and leave."

"We'll see," said Dave. "You can't turn the other cheek to those men."

Dave unloaded the wagon and then went to the bunkhouse after unhitching the team. Warbags lay on two of the bunks. Dave peeled off his shirt and went outside to wash. Jesse Vidal lounged around the side of the bunkhouse. "You sure don't know how to talk to a lady," he observed.

Dave dried his face. "You teaching me manners?" he asked.

Jesse took the makings from his pocket and rolled a smoke. "Where I come from a man don't talk that way to a lady," he said as he lit up.

Dave pegged the kid then. Two-gun man. Phony gentleman. Looking for more six-gun notches. Dave combed his hair. "I don't know where you come from, Vidal, and personally I don't care," he said, "but you mind your own business. There's enough trouble around here as it is."

Vidal flipped away his smoke. "Meaning?"

Dave placed his hands on his lean hips. "I've been choused from dawn up until now. I'm not in a mood to take any more."

There was a tenseness about Vidal now. His lips drew back. "I killed a man in Tucson for less than what you've said, Yeamans."

Dave rolled up his eyes. "My God," he said sadly, "what have I done to deserve this?"

Jess paled. He held out his slim hands. "I ain't going to shoot," he promised, "but you try to outdraw me. I figure you ought to know how good I am."

Dave grinned. "I'll take your word for it. I never draw on an empty stomach."

Monte came around the side of the house and glanced quickly from one to the other of them. "Miss Leslie wants some water, Jesse," he said.

Jesse smiled. "All right, Monte." He looked coldly at Dave and then walked away.

"What the hell is going on?" asked Monte of Dave.

"Your friend didn't like the way I talked to Miss Leslie."

"Chihuahua! The kid has a hair trigger temper. A good man but seems to think he can outdraw and outshoot any man in the west."

"He might get his chance around here," said Dave

dryly. "There are a few hombres around here who think the same way he does."

Monte leaned against the wall. "Play along with him," he said. "Met Ben Thompson and Wes Hardin once. Ain't never been the same since then."

"You get him aside and tell him we haven't got time to be battling amongst ourselves."

"You don't scare easy, Yeamans."

"I've been shot at and missed and shot at and hit. I went to war when I was sixteen and was twenty when it was over."

Monte nodded. "Yeah, I know what you mean. But there's a new breed of man growing up now, Dave. Can't find enough fighting the usual way. Have to look for more."

"Bloodthirsty bastards."

Monte shook his head. "Not exactly. They want to be recognized as big men. They want to draw a cutter faster than anyone else they meet. Seems to be the only way they can prove they are big men."

Dave spat. "Then some day they find themselves facing a better man than they are. It never fails."

Monte shrugged. "I guess so. Miss Leslie wants Jesse and I to ride south of the canyon country and bring back about forty-fifty cows."

"When do you leave?"

"Tomorrow."

"How long you figuring on being gone?"

"Give us a day to go south. A day or so to pick out the cows and three days to get them back."

"Fair enough. I'll meet you at the creek in six days."

"You expect trouble?"

"I don't know. Make damned sure you get a bill of sale."

"Yeah. I know what you mean."

They all ate in the big cheery kitchen that night. Dave was quiet. Monte talked a lot, but it was Jesse Vidal who stole the show. He paid a great deal of attention to Leslie, displaying better manners than most cowpokes. Dave thought he must come from a better family than the average punchers. Dave and Monte left the kitchen, but Jesse gallantly volunteered to dry the dishes. Monte sat down on the bench outside of the bunkhouse and rolled a smoke. "Jesse sure has taken to that girl," he said.

"She's lonely, Monte."

"Maybe Jesse is cutting you out?"

Dave shook his head. "I stayed here to help her. I'm in no mood to get tangled with skirts. I'm heading south to Sonora as soon as I can get away."

"You expect gunplay around here?"

"Yes. Things are shaping up damned ugly."

Hoofs drummed on the valley road. Dave stood up. "Let's see who it is."

"One hoss."

Dave and Monte walked to the front of the house. Mack Muir drew rein at the gate, swung down and tethered his horse. "Leslie around, Yeamans?" he asked.

"In the house."

Muir glanced at Monte. "Who's this?"

"Monte Hollis. Worked for John some years ago. Signed on with Miss Leslie today."

"Bueno! See you later." Muir walked into the house.

Monte puffed at his cigarette. "Miss Leslie's gentleman friend?"

"I guess so. He won't like finding Jesse in the house."

"No more than Jesse will like him horning in."

"I hope the kid doesn't start trouble."

"He won't in front of her."

They sat down on the bench. They could see the three people in the brightly lit kitchen. Muir had a set look on his face. Shortly after Muir had entered the house, Jesse sauntered out and squatted beside Monte. He fashioned a smoke. "Who's the redhead, Yeamans?" he asked.

"Mack Muir."

"Yeah. Yeah. I know the name. But who is he?"

"He has a small ranch not far from here. Been helping Miss Leslie."

Jesse lit his smoke. "He sweet on her?"

Dave shrugged. "I guess so."

"Push you out?"

Dave flushed. Monte glanced at Jesse. "Shut up," he said. "You get too damned nosy at times."

Jesse laughed. "Just figuring out the deal. No harm in that is there?"

"No."

Jesse looked at the house. "He don't like me," he said softly.

"Can't understand that," said Dave dryly. "I take it you don't like him."

Jesse turned quickly. "No," he said flatly, "I don't."

"He's a friend. We need friends."

"I can do enough shooting for three men."

Dave leaned back against the bunkhouse. "There's more to this deal than shooting, Vidal."

Monte nodded. "We'd best turn in, Kid. We got a long ride tomorrow."

Jesse looked at the house. "I'll wait awhile," he said.

Monte shrugged and went into the bunkhouse. Dave filled his pipe. Jesse sat on the bench, thrust out his long legs and looked at his fine, figured boots. "Nice place here, Yeamans. Plenty grazing and good water. A man could make out well here if he stocked the place."

"It's one of the best spots in this country."

Jesse eyed him slyly. "Maybe you had it in your mind to try for this place?"

Dave stood up. He was determined not to let this smart kid trigger his temper. "I'm going to bed," he said.

Jesse leaned back. "So long as you aren't interested in this place, I guess you don't care whether or not I make a play for it."

"You might get more than you bargained for."

"Oh, hell! Running a ranch wouldn't be any chore for me, Yeamans."

Dave went into the dark bunkhouse and sat down on his bed. He pulled off his boots. Monte stirred. "Cocky, ain't he?" he said in a low voice.

"I wish to hell you'da come alone, Monte."

"The kid and I been traveling together. Onct he helped me outa a shooting down Nogales way. I ain't forgot it."

Dave peeled off his shirt and walked to a window. He could make out the dim figure of Leslie and Mack Muir near the front gate. Mack kissed her and left. The steady drumming of hoofs drifted back from the valley road. A hopeless feeling came over Dave as he stood there. Then he saw Jesse Vidal walking toward Leslie. They began to talk. She looked up into his handsome face. Dave dropped on his bunk.

Monte got up and padded to the window. "He's at it again," he said. "Damned fool over a filly."

"He's good looking," said Dave quietly. "He's got a lot of guts if he doesn't get killed showing off."

Monte dropped on his bunk and lit a smoke. His wise eyes studied Dave over the flare of the lucifer. "He'll make a good man someday."

"I hope so."

Monte lay back. Dave could see the lined face as Monte puffed on the cigarette. "Seems to me you like that girl a lot more than you let on, Dave."

"Maybe I do."

"You sure as hell don't show it."

"I'm a slow man with the ladies, Monte."

Monte snorted. "She likes you."

"Sure likes to ride me."

"You sure don't know wimmen. They allus ride hell outa a man they like. Seems as though they hunt around for the man closest to the ideal they got, then they hogtie him, marry him, and then spend the rest of their lives making him miserable trying to make him over into their ideal. Which they never succeed in."

"You sound like you know something about it."

Monte laughed. "Been married twice. Couldn't live with either one of them."

The door opened and Jesse came in. He dropped on his bunk fully clothed. Dave looked at him through the dimness. Jesse rolled onto his side. "How we fixed for dinero, Monte?" he asked.

"Couple of hundred, kid."

"Not much, is it?"

"You blew a lot of it down to Globe playing faro."

"Yeah. Dammit. I sure could use it now."

Dave closed his eyes. The kid was making a big play for Leslie. It wouldn't set well with Mack Muir and it sure as hell didn't set well with Dave Yeamans.

CHAPTER FIVE

It was almost noon of the day that Monte Hollis and Jesse Vidal had left for the new cattle when Dave heard a noise from the south, as though a boy had swiftly dragged a stick along the pales of a picket fence. Leslie came out of the house. "What was that, Dave?" Dave was saddling Brazos. "Thunder maybe." He had heard that sound too many times in the sixties to mistake it. Gunfire and plenty of it. He swung up on the clay bank and rode toward Leslie. "I'm taking a pasear down to Cup Valley."

Her eyes were grave. "That was shooting, wasn't it?"

He nodded. "Stay here at the house." He spurred Brazos out toward the road and then turned south, riding fast.

It wasn't until he was within half a mile of Cup Valley that he saw the swirling cloud of dust pour out of the valley entrance. The muffled bellowing of steers came to him. The sun flashed on metal. A rifle flatted off. A rider came out of the dust, sinking the steel into his horse. He turned once and fired and then came on toward Dave. Dave freed his Spencer and levered home a round. The cattle had been turned south and were pouring down the valley. The horseman hammered up and raised his Colt.

Dave cursed and turned Brazos away, leveling his Spencer. "I'm from the Double!" yelled Dave.

The puncher drew rein. "I'm Cooper Jones! One of Mack Muir's *vaqueros!* Mack left me and Billy Free with the steers! Billy has been downed!"

Dave spurred Brazos toward the herd. "What happened?" he yelled.

"Damned if I believe what I seen!" yelled back Jones. "Me and Billy was in the line shack rustling some grub when a coupla slugs came right through the boards! Then we heard someone chousing the cows! We run outside and Billy got it right through the head with a rifle slug! I lit outa the valley ahead of the cows to get help! They's four men chousin' the herd!"

A masked man pulled away from the herd and fired his rifle twice. Dave let drive a shot. The man jerked, gripped his left shoulder and turned his horse into the pall of dust. Another masked man came up out of a hollow and fired. The slug whipped over Dave's head. Cooper Jones holstered his Colt and freed his Henry rifle, but a rifle spat flame from a motte of scrub trees and Jones' horse skidded to a halt and went over, catapulting the Bar M puncher to the ground. He lay still.

Dave fired rapidly but the steers had a good running start and masked men wove in and out of the dust like Comanches, driving hot lead back at Dave. Dave circled Brazos and dropped to the earth beside Jones, ground-reining Brazos. The steers were a quarter of a mile away now, making fast progress, filling the valley with the thunder of their hoofs and their hoarse bawling.

A horseman came out of the motte, riding fast, bent low in the saddle and Dave leveled on him and fired. The horseman cut back behind the trees and vanished from sight.

Dave eased Jones over on his back. Jones opened his eyes. Blood flowed from a gash on his forehead. He slowly drew up his legs and then lowered them again. "All busted...up," he said softly, "Jesus, I hit hard." He coughed and bright blood spewed on Dave.

Dave bent low over the injured man. "Did you recognize any of them?"

Jones coughed harshly. "Masked...they was." His eyes were clouded. He grinned feebly. "Fit all the way from... Bull Run to...Appomattox...and never...got...a scratch. Funny...ain't it?"

Dave wiped the blood from Jones' face. "You recognize any of them?"

"Rile...Rile!" Jones' head sagged back, and he looked up at Dave with glazing eyes that did not see.

Dave looked south. There was nothing left to denote the passage of the herd but tattered layers of bitter dust and the trampled earth. Dave shoved back his hat and wiped the sweat from his face. There was a cold, hard core in him when he stood up. Up until this had happened, he had not been sure why he had stayed at the ranch. Now a bitter hate galled him. Men who would kill wantonly for a few head of cattle must be fought to the death.

Dave lifted the dead man and placed him across the saddle of his skittish horse. He led Brazos and the other horse into Cup Valley. Not one steer was left. A man lay sprawled in front of the shack. The wind stirred his fine blond hair. The bullet had killed him instantly. Billy Free gripped a large spoon in his right hand. A few beans were still stuck in the spoon bowl. Dave felt a sour taste in the back of his throat. He went into the shack and got a spade. The place reeked of burned beans. He took the pot from the stove and threw it out the window. He went outside and began to dig a common grave on a pleasant knoll which overlooked the waterhole. There was a sickness in him, coupled with the bitter hate.

Dave buried the two men and covered the grave with rocks. He took the two horses with him and rode back toward the ranch. Leslie was waiting for him. She saw the blood on his shirt. "What happened?" she asked in a low voice.

"Rustlers. They hit the valley when two of Muir's boys were getting some grub. Billy Free was killed instantly. Jones' horse was slightly wounded and fell, throwing Cooper Jones. Jones lived only a few minutes. The steers are gone."

Her hand went to her throat. *"Who* did it?"

Dave shrugged. "There must have been four or five of them. They were all masked. They drove the herd south toward the creek. I buried Free and Jones."

She bowed her head. "I wonder if it's worthwhile to stay and fight it out?"

Dave looked down the valley, pleasant in the bright sunlight. "I'm staying," he said, "if I have to fight alone."

Dave treated the wound on Jones' horse and turned both Bar M horses loose in the big corral. He went to the house. "I'm trailing those steers," he said to her.

"Alone? Wait for Monte and Jesse."

He shook his head. "They've got a good start now. I can't stop them, but I might learn something."

"Please stay! I'm about ready to quit this hopeless business."

He touched her face. "No. You said you'd stick it out. Let me see what I can do."

"I don't want you killed, too."

Dave smiled. "I'm hard to kill. I'll be careful." He opened the door. "Tell Muir to stay here when he comes back. I'll be back as quickly as I can. Incidentally do you know anyone around here by the name of Rile, or anything that sounds like Rile?"

She shook her head. "Why?"

"Jones mentioned the word, or name, before he died."

"There is no one around here to my knowledge with a name anything like that."

Dave rode south down the valley. It was mid-afternoon when he reached the end of the valley. The herd trail was plain to see. The cows had been driven across the swift-flowing creek. He followed the broad track. The trail led him up a high-walled canyon thickly grown with scrub trees and thorny brush. He rode slowly with his Spencer across his thighs. It was late in the afternoon when the trail finally petered out. The canyon floor was naked rock stretching out of sight with never a mark of the passage of cattle or horses on its barren surface. He followed the canyon to a place where several other canyons branched off. He tethered Brazos and entered one of the offshoots. It was a box canyon. No room for a herd in it.

The second canyon was bigger, and the floor was composed of sand and decomposed rock, but there was no sign of cattle. The third canyon was big and narrow, trending off to the west. It was choked with thick growths. He plodded on, eyeing the walls for signs of a lurking ambusher. Long shadows were creeping down the slopes when he saw some ruins high on a rocky slope, beneath a huge overhang, stained deep red by the smoke of many fires.

Dave worked his way up the slope. The dying sun colored the ancient buildings warm yellow and rose. Dave wondered how long they had been squatting there tenantless. He had seen other ruins in his solitary travels, but none as extensive as these. Many of the roofs had collapsed, filling the small interiors with rubble.

There was an air of intense, brooding loneliness about the place.

Dave walked along a sort of terrace in front of the buildings. It was as quiet as the grave. He looked down into the silent canyon. There was no sign of life. Now and then he looked back over his shoulder as though expecting to see someone watching him. He had experienced that eerie sensation before while poking about old ruins. He saw crude letters cut into the adobe of a building. He read them aloud. "Jeb Gregg. Lost in here.

1858. God help me. No water. No food. Apaches around."

Dave looked into the nearest dwelling and recoiled in surprise. A skeleton, partially clothed in dusty rags, lay in a corner of the littered room. A rusty rifle leaned in a corner. "Jeb Gregg," said Dave. He took off his hat. He limped down the slope and looked back at the ruins. Maybe he was the first man to penetrate there since Jeb Gregg had done so twelve years before. If Dave kept on being an outlier, he could expect such a lonely fate. He shivered a little as he walked quickly to his horse.

Dave turned north after he mounted Brazos. Where in God's name could those cattle have been spirited to? It was too dark to explore further. Yet he planned to follow the main canyon to its end someday.

It was dark with the promise of a faint moon when he reached the Double W. The yellow lights of the house showed through the darkness. The door swung open as Dave turned into the gate, and Mack Muir came to meet him. "What did you learn?" he asked.

Dave shook his head wearily as he dismounted. "I trailed them south, beyond the creek into a long canyon. The canyon branched into three off-shoots. No trace of the cows after I reached a rocky area. It's just as though them damned cows sprouted wings and flew over the walls."

"You were in Twelve Mile Canyon. It opens into Bitter Creek Canyon. Maybe they were driven down there."

"No, the trail just vanished."

"How the hell could it?" demanded Muir.

Dave rolled a smoke. "I don't know."

"You couldn't have looked very hard!"

Dave lit his smoke and eyed the angry man. "I did my best while you were bellying up to a bar in Deep Spring. Besides, I don't work for you, Muir."

Muir dropped his hand to his Colt. "I don't like your lip, Yeamans!"

Dave smiled thinly. "Then don't rile me. Was Edrick in town?"

"Yes!"

"Shorty? Mort? Ochoa?"

"All but Mort."

"How many *vaqueros* in Edrick's corrida?"

"Fifteen or twenty. He has a big spread beyond town and has some grazing land south of here."

Dave shoved back his hat. "Then he wasn't in on it. Unless he has some hands working for him we don't know about."

Muir turned back toward the house. "I haven't got a goddamned cow left! What the hell am I going to do?"

"You aren't alone in that. Miss Waite hasn't exactly got a cattle kingdom here."

"When will those two new hands be back?"

"Hollis and Vidal? Couple of days."

"If they do come back!"

Dave remembered how Vidal had looked at Leslie. "They'll be back all right."

"You game to look for those rustled cows?"

"What else is there to do around here?"

Dave led Brazos to the corral and unsaddled him, rubbing him down carefully. He washed himself and then tapped on the kitchen door. Leslie was at the stove as Dave opened the door. Her face was flushed. She looked angrily at Muir and then adjusted a stray wisp of hair. She set a plate for Dave, and he sat down to eat. It was damned obvious that Muir had been interrupted in the pleasant game of love. Dave told them the story as he ate. "I still think it's hopeless to keep on," she said as he finished.

Muir slapped a hand on the table. "We'll keep on," he said.

Dave filled his pipe, and surreptitiously watched the

feisty redhead. Not once had Muir mentioned the loss of his two *vaqueros*. There was a cold core in the man, for all his fiery temperament.

Dave went out to the bunkhouse and cleaned his Spencer. Now and then he looked toward the house. Neither of them was in sight. There was a small green flame of jealousy in Dave, although Leslie had never given him any encouragement. He worked slowly on the repeater, a job he always liked to do, for handling the weapon had always given him a feeling of satisfaction. He polished the metal and wiped the stock with a linseed rag. He slid it into its sheath and then filled his pipe, going outside to sit on the bench next to the bunkhouse door. The new moon gilded the tips of the darkened peaks. Now and then the wind brought the murmur of voices to him from the front porch.

Dave was dozing a little when he heard the crisp sound of flesh meeting flesh. Angry voices broke out. Dave placed his pipe on the bench and sauntered toward the front of the house. Leslie was standing near the porch rail. Mack Muir was at the foot of the steps, hat in hand. "If that's the way you feel," he said, "maybe I'd better pull out of this mess and take care of my own affairs!"

She shrugged. "You made your so-called deal with my father," she said angrily. "It gives you no privileges with me, Mack!"

"You always thought well of me."

"Can't you realize what has happened? My father has been murdered. I can't think clearly on any other subject now."

Muir put on his hat. "I'll give you time, Leslie."

Dave turned to go. Muir walked toward him as Leslie went into the house. "Were you listening?" he demanded.

"I heard an argument."

"Keep your nose out of my business, Yeamans."

Dave grinned. "You sure are on the prod this evening."

"I have a right to be!"

"Then go home and cool off."

Muir flushed. He glanced at the house. The living room and kitchen lights were out. "Maybe you're waiting for me to leave?" he suggested.

Dave yawned. "I'm going to bed, if that's what you mean."

Muir spat. "If I thought you were figuring on cutting Leslie out from me, I'd gun you down."

"Don't start anything you don't intend to finish," said Dave softly.

Muir's right hand drove down toward his gun butt. Dave stepped in close, gripped Muir's gun wrist with his left hand, and drew his own Colt. He prodded the redhead in his lean gut. "You see?" he asked quietly. He released Muir's wrist and stepped back, sheathing his Colt.

Muir was still gripping his cutter. For a moment he eyed Dave and then he turned away. "She's waiting for you," he said, "like a damned Globe hurdy-gurdy girl."

Dave gripped Muir's shoulder, whirled him about and dropped him with a solid right to the jaw. Dave looked down at the redhead. "She's a lady," he said. "Maybe you're not used to ladies. Either mind your manners or keep away from her!"

Muir got up slowly wiping a trickle of blood from the corner of his mouth. He backed away, eyeing Dave and then turned quickly, striding to his horse. He mounted the black and sank the hooks in viciously. The hoofs drummed on the hard road.

Leslie came out on the porch. "Did something happen between you and Mack?" she asked.

Dave walked to the foot of the steps. She was wearing a white robe over her nightdress. Dave caught the faint fragrance of lilac. "No," he lied.

She came down to the foot of the steps. "He worries me at times," she said.

"What was this deal he mentioned?"

"He and father were talking of pooling their resources. At the time they planned it, I was engaged to Mack. He expected too much from me on the strength of the engagement and I broke it off."

"That explains a lot of things, Leslie."

She looked toward the road. "He has changed a lot," she said quietly.

Dave shifted a little as she came closer to him. He placed a hand on hers where it rested on the stair rail. "Don't worry about him," he said. "He talks a lot." She did not move away. Dave took her by the shoulders. She pulled away a little and then raised her face. Dave bent and kissed her. She slipped her arms about his neck. Her warm softness pressed against him. Wild thoughts roared through his mind and then she turned away and was gone into the house. He heard her bedroom door close and a moment later the light went out.

Dave touched his mouth, still warm from her lips. "Well, I'll be damned," he said.

CHAPTER SIX

In the days that followed, Dave kept in the saddle as much as possible, acquainting himself with the ranch area. Leslie showed no indication that anything unusual had happened. She cooked and served his meals, talked to him about ranch business, and kept herself busy. Beyond that, there was nothing. The day Monte Hollis and Jesse Vidal were due back from the south with the new cattle, Dave rode down to meet them. There had been no visitors at the ranch.

Dave found Hollis and Vidal at the creek, watering the new cattle after their thirsty trip through Twelve Mile Canyon. Most of them were butterball Herefords with a few crosses, black-and-whites, and several Durhams. Monte showed Dave the bill of sale. "We won't have any trouble," he said. "Bought the best we could get from Jimmy Mansfield, and no one had better question his honesty or Jim will come up here as wild as a Nueces longhorn."

Vidal sat his fine trigueno, one leg hooked about his pommel. "How's Leslie?" he asked.

"Fine. Just fine. She's damned anxious to get these critters bedded down at the ranch."

"Maybe she's anxious to see me, Yeamans."

"No accounting for tastes," said Dave dryly.

Vidal flushed and looked at Monte. Monte grinned. "We'd better cajole these cows north," he suggested.

They got the herd in motion. As they approached the wide entrance to the valley, they saw six horsemen angle toward them out of a motte. Dave spurred to the front of the herd. There was no mistaking Shorty Ganoe at the head of the horsemen. He drew rein and grinned at Dave with his battered face as though nothing had ever happened between them. "See you got some cows," he said pleasantly.

"Yeah," said Dave, "you got a sharp eye, Ganoe." The other men were a tough-looking lot, but none of them were familiar except Mort Hastings who sat his horse off to one side. Monte rode up as Shorty rolled a smoke. "Where'd you get the butterballs?" asked Shorty.

"Jim Mansfield," said Mort. He looked at Dave. "Let's keep moving."

Shorty glanced back at his men. "We're out checking again," he said as he lit up. "Seems as though Dan has lost twenty more head the last few days."

Dave waved a hand at the herd. "You can see Mansfield's brand," he said. "Monte has a bill of sale."

"Do tell?" said Shorty. He looked back at his *vaqueros.* "Eddie! Slim! Joe! Take a gander at them cows!"

Vidal cantered up. He eyed the three men riding alongside the herd. "What the hell is this?" he demanded.

"Just a routine check, as Dan always says," said Shorty easily. "Who's this hombre, Yeamans?"

"Jesse Vidal."

"You gonna let 'em look?" asked Jesse of Dave.

Dave shrugged. "It makes them happy," he said. "They haven't got enough to do at the Lazy E."

"Damned if I'll let 'em!" Vidal slapped slim hands down on his twin Colts. They came up swiftly, cocked and centered on Ganoe. "You tell them hombres to get back where they belong, you!"

Shorty was gutty. He did not move. His eyes were cold as a sidewinder's. "You hiring gunslingers now, Yeamans?"

"Miss Waite does the hiring," said Dave. "Put up those cutters, Vidal!"

Jesse spat. "If you haven't got the guts to stop them, I have!"

Shorty shifted a little and held out a hand toward his three men. They halted and watched the slim kid with the six-guns. "Yeamans has guts all right," said Shorty. "You got no call to draw them plow-handles."

Vidal smiled. "No one goes near that herd."

Shorty shrugged. "Regular hard case, eh? All right. Let's ride, boys. Maybe we'll talk about this some other time, sonny."

"Draw, if you've got the guts," said Jesse.

Shorty smiled. "Why, I ain't no gunman!"

Monte rode toward the back of the herd to get it into motion. Shorty circled his horse on the forehand. Fifty yards from the herd one of the men drew a six-gun. It flashed. Jesse moved swiftly. Dave slapped his hat across the twin sixes. One of them roared, spurting dust from the hard earth. The Lazy E men sank the steel into their mounts. Jesse cursed and turned toward Dave. Dave drew and cocked his Colt. "Damn you," said Vidal.

Dave kneed his horse close to the kid. "We've got enough trouble without you acting like Ben Thompson, Vidal!"

Jesse spurred his horse. He set off at a dead run for the retreating cowpokes. He fired a Colt and then drew rein, fighting the *trigueno* as it reared and plunged. One of the Lazy E men yelled and gripped his left shoulder, bending over with the pain of the slug which had holed him. Shorty waved his men on, and they raised a cloud of dust as they rode down a slope out of sight.

Jesse turned his horse and hammered up beside Dave.

Jesse's face was white and set. "You ever do that again," he grated, "and I'll gun you in half!"

Monte Hollis rode in between them. "Goddammit!" he roared, "You wanta spook them cows? Dave is right, Jesse! We got enough trouble without you flashing them six-shooters!"

For a moment Jesse eyed Dave, then he cross-pin-wheeled, flipping the twin Colts into the air and letting them smack into opposite hands. He rolled them and jammed them down into their sheaths, the while his hard eyes never left Dave's.

"*Sta bueno,*" he said softly, and spurred his horse toward the herd.

"He could have started a real ruckus," said Dave.

Monte rolled a smoke and flipped the makings to Dave. "All he's done since we left is talk about that girl," he said. He lit up. "He seems to think he's all the protection she's got."

"One of those men got hit hard," Dave said. "It'll start more trouble."

"Let's chouse the herd."

"We'll keep them near the ranch house. We'll take no chances on Cup Valley until we get more vaqueros."

Monte laughed. "More men for fifty butterballs?"

"Yes, if we have to. Once we show these longloopers that we can keep what we have, we'll be safe enough with a larger herd."

"I hope you're right, Davie. I just hope you're right!"

They drove the herd to the ranch and quartered them on a gentle slope above the buildings. Monte stayed with them. Dave went to the house to report the safe arrival of the herd. Jesse made tracks for the bunkhouse to clean off the trail dust.

Leslie was waiting for Dave in the big living room.

"I was worried," she said. "I'd rather lose those cattle than have one of you hurt."

"We'll keep them near here. Can you afford to hire a few more men?"

She smiled. "Why? We might be able to use a cook."

"We have to protect what we have."

"It would only bring on more shooting. I'd rather stay just as we are for a time."

Dave nodded. "As you wish."

"Was there any trouble at all?"

Dave hesitated. "Ganoe showed up with five Lazy E *vaqueros.* They let us pass."

She studied him. "You're sure there was no trouble?"

"No trouble."

She came closer to him. "You've been a great help, Dave," she said softly.

Dave took her in his arms. She seemed to expect it. He kissed her. He looked over her shoulder. There was a quick movement at one of the side windows. He tilted her head back. "Don't worry about anything," he said. "We'll make a go of the Double W."

She turned away. "Dad could have used you. He fought on practically alone."

"Someday we'll find out who murdered him."

She leaned forward and brushed her lips across his. "I know," she said. "I've got to get dinner now. Anything you'd like?"

He touched his lips. "I've had my dinner," he said. He opened the door. "Has Mack Muir been around?"

"No. It seems as though I have hurt his feelings, Dave."

"We can manage without him." Dave stepped down from the porch and rounded the house. Jesse Vidal was seated on the bunkhouse bench polishing his six-shooters. His dark eyes studied Dave for a fraction of a second and then he went on with his work, but in that short time Dave had a feeling as though a diamondback had been gauging him for the strike.

It was after dark when the beating of hoofs on the

valley road came to Dave. He walked down toward the fence, easing his Colt in its holster. Jesse was in the kitchen helping Leslie with the dishes. Half a dozen men drew rein at the gate. Bart Edrick swung down and came toward Dave, glancing back over his shoulder to see if his men were right behind him. Shorty Ganoe was watching Dave with slitted eyes. A tall, slim puncher was hunched in his saddle, his left arm in a sling.

"What can I do for you, Sheriff Edrick?" asked Dave.

Edrick jerked a thumb toward the injured man. "One of the Lazy E boys, Slim Edwards there, was plugged by you or one of your boys this afternoon. I've come to arrest the man what did it."

Ganoe slid from his horse. "It was Yeamans," he said. "I seen him draw his Colt."

"You're a damned liar," said Dave.

Edrick eyed the house. "Who's in there?" he asked.

"Miss Waite and Jesse Vidal, one of the new hands."

"Who's with them cows?"

"Monte Hollis."

"Get 'em both. Wait! Joe, you get Hollis."

Jesse and Leslie came down from the house and stopped behind Dave. In a few minutes Monte rode down the slope alone. "I left him to watch the steers," he said to Dave.

Edrick sucked at a tooth. "Now," he said importantly, "who done the shooting?"

"They shot first," said Monte quickly.

"Sho?" said Edrick. "What did they shoot at?"

"Damned if I know."

Edrick glanced at Jesse. "What'd you see?"

Jesse glanced at Dave. "Yeamans chew on me to keep me from going after the Lazy E boys. Then he threw a shot after them to keep them moving."

"He's lying," said Dave.

Ganoe nodded. "The kid is right. I seen Yeamans shoot toward us."

Dave felt icy cold. Leslie looked closely at him. "You saw what happened, Monte," he said. "Tell them."

Monte rubbed his lean jaw and looked at the ground. "Like I said, I ain't sure. But I seen you with a smoking Colt in your hand, Dave."

Edrick shifted a little. "You'll have to come with me then, Yeamans. I got a warrant here."

"Yeamans said he wasn't going to be choused no more by the Lazy E corrida," volunteered Jesse quickly. "I tried to calm him down, but he was on the prod."

Edrick held out a hand. "I'll take that Colt," he said.

Dave drew his Colt and handed it to the peace officer. He looked at Jesse. "We'll settle this soon," he said coldly.

Jesse raised his brows. "I only told them what you said!"

Dave gripped Monte by the arm. "Tell them the truth, Hollis!"

Monte pulled away. "I already said what I know."

"Get his hoss," said Edrick. Monte went to the corral and got the clay bank. Leslie came over to Dave. "You lied to me," she said. "You, the one who is against shootings."

"Before God, Leslie, I didn't do it!"

She turned and walked to the house. "Let's go," said Edrick. Dave mounted. Two men rode in behind Dave. The wounded man bent his head in pain and held his smashed shoulder. Dave wondered why they had taken him on a long night ride in his condition. They rode south on the valley road. They knew he was the one to fear. It was a neat way of getting rid of him. He wondered if he would ever see the inside of the Deep Spring juzgado. It would be easy to shoot him in the back and then swear he had tried to escape. *Ley del fuego,* as practiced by the gentle Mexican cousins along the border. Let a man escape and then shoot him down.

They rode swiftly, saying nothing. Dave wondered when it would happen. His chances for a break were slim.

It wasn't until they reached the Deep Spring road that he saw his chance. The road skirted the brawling creek. On the far bank was thick brush. The moon was faint in the east. Edrick drew rein and looked back. "Shorty!" he called.

Shorty spurred forward. They spoke in low voices, glancing at Dave.

Dave shifted in his saddle. The man behind him was rolling a smoke. Dave sank the steel into Brazos and gave out with a piercing rebel yell. The man behind him cursed. The clay bank was into the stream before the first gun split the air with its report. A slug whipped through the brim of Dave's hat. The clay bank struggled up the far shore. Guns twinkled in the darkness. Slugs cut through the brush. "After him!" yelled Edrick.

The clay bank crashed through the brush. Dave shielded his face with an arm. He sank his spurs in deep. Brazos plunged down a slope. Guns rattled on. Water splashed high as the first men hit the stream. Dave turned the clay bank down a slope and then up a rise. For a moment he was in the open. A slug hit his left heel, numbing his leg. Then the clay bank was in the clear, racing across a meadow. Dave looked back. Four men reached the far side of the open area. Guns flashed. Brazos hit a narrow trail and stretched out.

Hoofs drummed on the earth behind Dave. He set the clay bank at a steep slope, topped it, and plunged down the far side in a rattle of gravel. To his left was the shadowy mouth of a canyon and he turned the horse into it, praying that it wasn't a box. Men yelled through the darkness. Hoofs thudded past the canyon's mouth. Dave led the clay bank south, threading his way through the thick brush. In half an hour there were no sounds from behind him. The moon was well up when he stopped for a breather. It was as quiet as the grave.

Dave swung up on Brazos and rode south. He needed a gun, for now he was an outlaw, a *ladino*. Bart Edrick wouldn't rest until he had rounded up Dave. Jesse Vidal had neatly placed Dave where he wanted him; on the run, suspected even by the woman he loved. It left a clear field for the jealous kid. In a way Dave was well out of it, but there was an inborn stubbornness in him. He was an outlier again, destined to play a lone hand. Very well, he'd play the lone wolf. It was his way.

CHAPTER SEVEN

It was close to midnight when Dave dismounted from Brazos in an arroyo that sloped down toward the ranch buildings. A dry wind swept mournfully through the valley and rustled the leaves of the cottonwoods. A rectangle of yellow light revealed a window of the bunkhouse. Dave set off afoot. There was a chance that some of Bart Edrick's men had come back to the ranch to wait for him. He stopped at the far side of the corral and studied the area. There wasn't a strange horse in the corral. Dave skirted a shed and stopped close behind the bunkhouse. He flattened himself against the wall and peered into the building. Jesse Vidal was seated at the table playing solitaire. Monte Hollis was lying on his bunk smoking his battered pipe.

For a time, there was nothing but the soft slap of cards on the table and then Vidal spoke. "We'll run those cows down to Cup Valley in the morning. You can stay there with them, Monte."

Monte grunted. "One of us oughta be with those critters right now."

"Hell with it! Ain't no one gonna bother them. Not with me around, they ain't."

"Shore. Shore."

"Well, they ain't!"

"What are you going to do tomorrow?"

"Try to round up a few men. Edrick is gonna have the damnedest hassle on his hands he ever saw if he tangles with me."

"Yeah." Monte tamped his tobacco. "What do you think they'll do with Yeamans?"

"Who cares? He's nothing but a saddle tramp who thinks he's the pure quill."

"He had the Edrick riled all right. It'd be easy for them to bushwhack him and then say he tried to escape."

"So?"

Monte relit his pipe. "He wasn't a bad hombre. I'm sorry I helped cold-deck him."

Jesse slapped his cards down hard. "Look! He riled me! Jesse Vidal! I aim to be a big man around these parts. This spread has possibilities. Leslie can't help but like a real *buscadero* like me. I had to get rid of him!"

Monte placed his hands behind his head and looked up at the ceiling. "Yeah, but you'll have your hands full now. Edrick wants this ranch. Mack Muir is riled about Leslie. Yeamans, if he gets away, will come agunnin' for yuh."

Jesse spat. "I'll get some good boys to back me up. Muir don't worry me none. Yeamans hasn't got the guts to stand up to me."

"I wouldn't copper that bet."

"You talk like you like him."

Monte sat up. "Dammit! I do. He's a good man. Besides, even if he didn't see it, I think Miss Waite likes him."

Jesse's handsome face worked. "Damn you! Don't ever say that again!"

"You never could face the truth about yourself, Jesse. You think you're the fastest man with a horse, the fastest man with a Colt, the greatest ladykiller in the west."

Jesse stood up and placed his hands on his lean hips. "You saying I ain't?"

Monte groaned. "Take it easy. I was just trying to warn you that there may be a few more men with the same claims."

"Let 'em come!"

"They will."

Jesse approached the older man. "Listen to me! You helped put Yeamans out of the way because I told you to."

Monte looked up angrily. "Yeah! Yeah! But I couldn't look him in the eye."

Jesse grinned. "Maybe you'd like to ride into town with me and tell Edrick that Yeamans is innocent? Go ahead. I won't stop you."

Monte looked away. "You've got too much on me, Jesse. You know damned well I got to ride the *rio* with you."

Jesse leaned close to the older man. "You're damned right you do! Just remember what I know about you." The kid peeled off his shirt and unbuckled his heavy gun belt, hanging them at the head of his bunk. He got ready for bed and put out the lamp. Dave could see the soft glow of Monte's pipe, lighting the worried face. He had wondered why Monte had turned against him. Dave faded around the corner of the bunkhouse and went into the shed. He sat down on a box, wishing for a smoke, but fearing to light one. It would take time for Vidal and Hollis to get to sleep.

The moon was on the wane when Dave pulled off his boots and padded back to the bunkhouse. His Spencer was racked on the wall beside his bunk. He stopped at the window which was closest to his bunk. He could hear the quiet breathing of both men. He reached in the window and gripped his Spencer, easing it slowly out through the opening. He needed a six-gun too, for Edrick had taken his Colt. For a moment a perverse imp whispered in his ear, urging him to take one or both of Vidal's matched forty-fours, but it might raise Vidal's temperature still more against him.

Dave walked to the house. He had seen several handguns hanging on a wall of the living room. He placed his Spencer in the shrubbery and went in through an open window. The house was quiet. Leslie's bedroom door was ajar. He looked in. She was asleep, the faint rays of the moon revealing her unbound hair. He eyed her for a moment, fighting down another urging from the imp, and then he went back to the living room.

He passed by two cap-and-ball Colts and a converted Remington and looked at a pair of Starrs. He had captured one from a Union sergeant at Gettysburg and had carried it until it had been stolen from him. He slid it into his holster and helped himself to cartridges from a desk drawer. A sudden movement in the bedroom sent him out of the window.

There was a soft footfall in the living room. Leslie looked about the dim room, opened the front door and looked out and then went back to her room. Dave almost called out to her and then thought better of it. There was a job of work to be done before he returned to the Double W and cleared himself with her.

Dave returned to Brazos and sat for a time in the saddle as he rolled and lit a smoke, eyeing the sleeping ranch, and then he touched Brazos with his spurs, riding south down the valley.

Dave stopped at the line shack in Cup Valley and scrounged the blankets, cooking utensils, and whatever food he could find. He found a big canteen and filled it while he watered Brazos at the pool, glancing up now and then at the big common grave on the knoll. He left the valley and rode south again, heading for Twelve Mile Canyon. The mystery of the lost cattle trail still gripped him. If Twelve Mile had been used to chouse rustled cattle through, it would be used again. There was no better place for him to hole up in.

Dave rode to the canyon where he had found the cliff-dwelling ruins. He worked his way to the far end of it, under an overhanging wall of rock. Perched high under the dome was a little cliff-dwelling, with a narrow footpath going up to it. He placed his gear at the foot of the path and then picketed Brazos in an off-shoot of the canyon. He carried his gear up the crumbling trail to the small dwelling. He inspected it by candlelight. It was still in solid shape and empty of debris. He made his bed and placed himself on it, falling asleep almost instantly.

During the night the wind increased, shifting from the east to the north. Dave awoke. The faint sound of bawling cattle had come to him in his sleep. "You're getting as skittish as a Johnny Raw recruit," he accused himself, and then went back asleep again.

The sun shining through the T-shaped doorway of the dwelling awakened Dave. He pulled on his boots and walked out onto the small terrace in front of the building. The canyon brooded in the early morning sun. A hunting hawk hung almost motionless on outstretched pinions and then suddenly glided off before the morning wind. Dave ate a cold breakfast, hooked his canteen to his belt and then plodded off down the canyon carrying his rifle. The sun shone on the smooth face of the larger cliff-dwelling to his left. "Hope you slept well, Jeb!" called out Dave as he looked up at the room where Jeb Gregg's skeleton lay in the dignity of death.

Dave was almost at the entrance to Ruins Canyon when he saw the pile of cow dung. He knelt beside it, raking through it with a mesquite stick. It crumbled readily. It had been there some time, probably from a *ladino* or a stray. He walked into Twelve Mile and headed south. He missed the easy, mile-eating gait of Brazos, but it would be easier for him to hide while traveling afoot. It was close to noon when he called a halt. The heat beat down into the great trough. He had seen no signs of human life or cattle tracks. He started back and eyed a place where a great fault split the canyon wall. The talus slope was steep but could be climbed. He worked his way up it. It was after two o'clock when he reached the top and sat down in the dubious shade of an outcropping to roll a smoke and take a drink. Jumbled country was to the east, with great upheavals of rock studded with scrub trees and thorny brush. A thin thread of smoke, miles to the east, was raveled by the wind. Somewhere in the area, he was sure, there must be a place where a great many steers could be hidden. But it was a hell of a big enterprise for one man to uncover.

He started along the lip of the canyon, picking his way through masses of shattered rock and thick brush. Sweat worked through his clothing and soaked it. His throat was harsh and dry when at last he reached a place close to Ruins Canyon. He rested again, scanning the country. The sun flashed from something down in Twelve Mile Canyon. He shaded his field glasses with his hat and focused them on the canyon. A lone horseman was riding slowly south along the littered floor of the canyon. The glasses picked out the hatchet face of Mick Ochoa. Dave cursed. That human bloodhound was probably on his trail. The breed rode to the mouth of Ruins Canyon. He dismounted and studied the ground, for all the world like a questing hound. It was too long a shot for the stubby Spencer, although Dave was almost tempted to send down a lead calling card.

The breed led his horse out of sight. Dave waited for him to reappear from behind a huge, naked shoulder of rock. Ochoa did not appear. Dave felt cold sweat work down his sides. Ochoa had either gone into Ruins Canyon or was waiting down there for some purpose of his own. Dave cased his glasses and plodded on to the rim of Ruins Canyon after two detours. It took him an hour and a half to reach the crumbling brink. There was no sign of life in the great trough. Ochoa was not in sight.

Dave looked back. It would be after dark by the time he reached the place where he had ascended. He decided to look for a place to work his way down into the canyon. He made a sling from his scarf for the Spencer and slung the weapon across his back. The going was easy at first, but by the time he had reached the bottom he had lost a spur, some of the skin from one hand and the skin from both knees. He sat down for a time, panting from his exertions. The canyon was still devoid of life. Shadows were beginning to form at the west end of the canyon. As he walked toward his hideout, he stopped short and then darted into the brush. There was a fresh pile of horse droppings in an open area amongst the mesquite. Dave cut through the brush toward the offshoot. Brazos neighed a welcome. The picket line had not been broken. Dave watered Brazos from his hat. There was no doubt in Dave's mind that Mick Ochoa had been in Ruins Canyon.

Dave went up to his cool hideout and ate, stretching out on his blankets for a rest. He had a long, hard ride ahead of him that night. It was dark when he awoke. A cold wind searched through the canyon. He went down to the clay bank. As he mounted, he seemed to hear something borne to him on the moaning wind. A low noise which he couldn't identify. He rode into Twelve Mile and north until he reached the creek where he watered Brazos. The creek road was silvered by the rising moon as he rode east. The moon was full up when he reached a point half a mile from Deep Spring. He picketed Brazos in a brushy draw and left his Spencer in its sheath.

Dave followed the creek until he saw the first buildings of the town. He walked along the dark street which bordered the rushing creek. The lights were on in the back room of Cass Simmons' General Store. He worked his way up the side of the building until he could see the front. The store was dark. He went to the back and peered into a window. Cass Simmons was working at a littered roll-top desk. Dave bent down and spoke through the partly open window. "Cass! Cass Simmons!"

Cass started. "Who is it?"

"Dave Yeamans. Let me in."

Simmons cursed. He opened the door and came outside to close the shutter over the window. Dave walked into the office. Cass locked the door behind him. "You damned idiot!" he said. "Bart Edrick and his men are lookin' all over for you."

Dave sat down. "They won't think of looking for me here."

Simmons took a bottle and filled two glasses. "No, but don't stretch your luck. Where you headin' for?"

"I'm sticking around here."

"You're loco! Bad enough you had to larrup Shorty Ganoe, but you have to wing one of Edrick's other boys too."

"I didn't do it, Cass."

"So? That ain't the way I heard it."

Dave told the storekeeper what had happened. Simmons nodded. "Vidal was in here today, stockin' up. Said he was thinkin' of hirin' half a dozen good gunslingers. I told him to just keep out of a range war. The silly bastard laughed at me! I'm worried about Leslie, Dave."

Dave downed his drink and allowed Cass to refill the glass. "Vidal is a troublemaker."

"You're tellin' me? He swaggered up and down Front Street like he was waitin' for trouble to start."

"He'll get it."

Simmons wiped his mouth. "Slim Edwards is dyin'."

"Who's he?"

"The man you were supposed to have winged. Doc Yarrow says it's pneumonia."

Dave felt a ball of ice form in his gut. "They'll have a murder warrant out for me soon then."

Simmons tapped Dave's knee with a bony finger. "You won't have a chance better'n a snowball in hell when Edrick's boys get after you. Any time a Lazy E man has been killed the man who done it never reached the calabozo. Sort of an unwritten law of the Lazy E corrida. Why don'tcha pull out of this country?"

Dave emptied his glass and rolled a smoke. "I don't aim to be cajoled out of here."

"You'll end up with a hole in your back or like a cottonwood blossom hangin' from a hemp stem!"

Dave eyed the older man. "Maybe."

"Why are you stickin'?"

Dave lit his smoke. "I don't like to see Leslie Waite run out of here by Edrick. And I don't like Jesse Vidal! He fired the shot that hit Edwards. He and Hollis made it look like I did it, to get me off the Double W. I broke away from Bart Edrick because I knew damned well I'd never reach the juzgado here in Deep Spring unless I was slung over a horse with lead weighting me down considerable."

Simmons leaned back in his chair and lit a cigarillo. "I don't know why I trust you, Yeamans, but you strike me right. That larrupin' you gave Shorty Ganoe did my heart good. You ain't no lone wolf workin' against these boys."

"So? I've been damned lonely so far."

Simmons got up and padded to the front of the dark store. He came back into the office and unlocked the door to peer up and down the dark half street behind the store. He sat down and drew his chair closer to Dave's. "For some time, some of the smaller ranchers and a few of the bigger ranchers have been workin' to uncover this rustlin' ring. We hired a stock detective to watch Edrick."

"We?"

Simmons nodded. "I've got money invested in several small spreads. Besides Deep Spring business has been hurt by these *ladinos* around here. A lot of ranchers who do business with me are talkin' of sellin' out. I'll go under if they do. I need their business. Anyway, we have a man watchin' Dan Edrick."

"Who?"

"You know him. Mort Hastings."

"Well, I'll be damned!"

"A good man. Worked for Pinkerton in Wyoming and Colorado."

Dave refilled his glass. The rye was good. "Has he uncovered anything yet?"

"Not much. If Dan Edrick is mixed up in the rustlin', he's managed to keep his trail pretty well covered up."

"Who else could it be?"

Simmons shrugged. "Damned if we know! All we do know is that a helluva lot of cows are missin'. We estimate between five hundred and a thousand beefs are gone."

"Where could they dispose of them?"

"You have me there. None of them have showed up within miles of here. Leads us to think they never left the country."

Dave nodded. "I'm with you on that."

Simmons puffed at his smoke. "As long as you're stubborn as an old mossyhorn, and won't hightail outa here, you might as well do some good. You want to work for the Association?"

Dave scratched his bristly jaw. "I'd rather work alone."

"What chance have you got workin' like a damned lobo? Throw in with us. You'll need all the help you can get."

Dave shrugged. "It's a deal then. What do you want me to do?"

"Stay hidden. Poke about. As soon as you get a lead let me know."

"How about Hastings?"

"I'll tip him off."

"Can he be trusted?"

"Absolutely."

"Is he still working with the Lazy E?"

"Yes."

Dave watched the storekeeper fill the glasses. "Damned odd he hasn't learned anything out at the Lazy E."

"If Dan Edrick is mixed up in the sticky loopin' he's as slick as a greased pig about it."

Dave drained his glass. "I'll get out of here now."

"Where can we reach you?"

"Leave any messages under the west end of the bridge where the valley road joins the creek road. Don't mention my name."

"I wasn't born yesterday."

Dave drew out his Starr. "Get me some cartridges for this. A box of Spencer .56/56. Bacon, flour, canned food, embalmed beef, tobacco, coffee and salt. You have any good rope?"

"All you want."

"*Sta bueno!* About one hundred and fifty feet strong enough to hold a man."

Simmons bustled about the dark shop and then came back with a full sack. He slipped in a bottle of rye. "For the night chill," he said.

"Make out a bill."

Cass gripped Dave's shoulders with a long arm. "It's on me, Davie."

"Thanks then. I'll be on my way."

Simmons doused the light. "Be careful," he said seriously. "This is a damned dangerous business."

Dave grinned in the darkness. "Nothing new for me, Cass. I was a scout for the Fifth Texas." Dave picked up his sack and faded into the shadows.

CHAPTER EIGHT

In the week that followed Dave's visit to Cass Simmons he managed to explore some of the most confusing, tangled country he had ever encountered. Masses of fallen rock, fields of shintangle brush, sedge and shinnery, box canyons and trails that ended abruptly. He floundered through piles of bone-gray flood wood and many times was forced to backtrail for miles to extricate himself from the jungle of shattered rock and huge naked ridges that thrust rough shoulders out of the very earth itself. His beard grew and his clothing was tattered. Once he had a hard fall from a rock face and lay stunned for half an hour. He put the rope to good use. At the end of the week, he had learned nothing while his body felt like a herd of *ladinos* had trampled it.

He rested for a full day in his hideout, mulling over everything that had transpired to date. There were no real clues. He had almost fallen asleep when something came to him as though the soft voice of a dead man had spoken over his shoulder. The voice of Cooper Jones who had died when the masked longloopers had taken the herd from Cup Valley. "Rile...Rile...Rile," the voice seemed to breathe hollowly. He turned quickly but he was alone. Dave sat up and filled his pipe. It was the only word, or name, that had been mentioned so far as having something to do with the rustling. Everything else had been shrouded in shadowy mystery.

Dave propped himself against the wall. "Rile might have been Riley," he mused. "A slim lead, but it's the only one we have so far. I'll be damned if I can find any trace of cattle in this malpais jungle!" Dave pulled on his paper-thin boots and picked up his Spencer. He went down, saddled Brazos and headed the clay bank north down Twelve Mile.

There was a faint light from the old moon when Dave reached the bridge. He snapped a lucifer on his thumb and inspected the underside of the old bridge. He touched a fold of oil cloth. He unwrapped it. There was a fold of paper in it. He went back into the deep brush and lit another match, reading softly from the paper.

"Jesse Vidal is now foreman of the Double W. Has hired three hardcases; Jonce Wilde, Tom Bowman, Chili Vegas, Double W stocking up on cattle. Double W corrida has had a brush with small number of masked men who tried to stampede small herd near ranch. Dan Edrick and some of the Lazy E corrida plan to scout Twelve Mile Canyon area soon. Slim Edwards died of pneumonia brought on by wound. Warrant for murder against you issued by Sheriff Bart Edrick. Mick Ochoa and Shorty Ganoe haven't been around Lazy E. No trace of missing cattle as yet."

Dave tore off a piece of the paper and wrote a message.

Anyone by the name of Rile, or Riley, known to you? Possibly Lazy E man. Important. No trace of cattle found as yet.

Dave folded it in the oilcloth and took it back to the bridge. He mounted Brazos and rode toward the Double W.

Dave left Brazos at the mouth of Cup Valley and went in on foot. The bitter odor of woodsmoke came to him as he entered the valley. There was a small herd bedded on a nearby slope. Dave walked back into the bigger valley. He led Brazos for a time and then rode toward the ranch. He hid the clay bank in the same arroyo he had used the night he had stolen the guns from the ranch. As he neared the ranch, he shook off a driving impulse to see Leslie. He dropped behind a rock outcropping and studied the ranch. There were quite a few horses in the corral. A small group of steers was on the slope beyond the buildings. Dave snaked forward, trailing his Spencer. He was within a hundred yards of the house when the butt struck a rock. The sharp sound carried clearly on the night air.

Dave lay still for a time and then raised his head. A rifle flashed in the darkness near a shed. The slug bounced from a rock ten feet from Dave and sang thinly through the air. He rolled down a slope as the bunkhouse door banged open. A man yelled something which Dave could not make out. He trotted back toward Brazos. The rifle spat again.

Dave mounted Brazos and urged him toward the road. Hoofs clashed on the hard earth behind him. Dave struck his one spur against Brazos and took off, jumping up a lot of dust. Men yelled and a rifle flatted off in the darkness. The rangy clay bank split the wind. Dave looked back, making out the shadowy forms of two men racing after him. He levered a round into the repeater and snapped a shot behind him. He fired again, sheathed the Spencer, and looked back. He had slowed them down. Dave grinned. He rode hard, letting Brazos full out. He cut off the road, topped a low ridge and shot down the slope to draw rein in a small motte where he waited until he heard the hammering hoofs go back on the valley road.

Dave dismounted and led the clay bank south,

keeping away from the valley road. He heard the two men ride back toward the Double W. There was a faint suggestion of the false dawn in the eastern sky as he entered Twelve Mile Canyon. He was bone-weary as he reached Ruins Canyon, picketed Brazos, and climbed slowly to his hideout. Vidal was prepared for a range war all right. Part of the false dawn in the eastern sky as he entered Twelve at the ranch; riflemen on watch at the ranch for any intruders. Dave pulled off his boots and thoughtfully rubbed his feet. He could raise hell with Vidal's plans, if he had any desire to give the Double W trouble, but he wasn't fighting against Leslie, Jesse Vidal was his huckleberry.

Dave slept until the sun was well up and then cooked and ate a big breakfast. He looked out of his hideout after he had doused his fire. He swore and jumped for his rifle, cocking it, and eyeing the lone horseman who slowly picked his way across the brushy floor of the canyon, scanning the high walls. Dave uncased his glasses and focused them on the rider. The lean, serious face of Mort Hastings swam into view. There was no one else in the canyon.

Dave's natural suspicion kept him undecided what to do until he realized he must trust someone. He hadn't done any good working alone. He stepped out on the terrace and waved his hat. Mort moved like a well-oiled machine. He was off his horse in a flash, slapping the bay's rump and jerking his rifle out. He dropped into the brush as the bay trotted away. Dave grinned. The stock detective wasn't taking any chances either. The sun glinted on field glasses in the brush. Dave took off his hat and waved his hand. Hastings stood up and waved back, then walked to his horse and rode to the foot of the trail where he met Dave. Dave smiled. "How'd you find me?" he asked.

"I had a feeling you were in here somewhere. Why didn't you tell Cass where you were hiding?"

"Why take chances?"

"Yeah, but I wanted to talk to you."

Dave pointed to the offshoot. "Take your cayuse in there. I'll heat the coffee up in my mansion."

When Hastings came into the dwelling he looked around in appreciation. "Very snug. Ghosts bother you?"

"Not yet."

"I might be uncomfortable in here. I've got too much imagination."

Dave filled the cups and handed one to Hastings. He studied the agent as he drank. Hastings was long of face and nose, with a pair of keen gray eyes. A drooping dragoon mustache hung over his wide mouth. A stag-butted Colt was hung at his left side for a cross-arm draw. It was his rifle that interested Dave. It was a Sharps, but shorter than the issue Sharps. Yet it was longer than the issue carbine. Dave took the heavy weapon in his hands. "Special job?" he asked.

Hastings shook his head. "U.S. issue. 1862. It had a thirty-inch barrel but I had it cut down to twenty-six inches. Makes it easier to handle on a horse. It's still four inches longer than the issue carbine though."

"Most men carry repeaters now. Henrys or Spencers."

Hastings drained his cup. "I've always had good luck with the Sharps."

Dave leaned the rifle against the wall. "What's up?" he asked.

"Mick Ochoa came in last night. Reported something to Dan Edrick. I didn't get a chance to hear what it was. Did you get my message all right?"

"Yes. I left an answer. Didn't you get it?"

"No. I came by there on the way here and looked. Nothing there."

Dave felt cold sweat break out on him. "Maybe Cass got it."

"I hope to God he did!"

"Do you know of a man named Rile, or Riley, or something like that?"

"Not on the Lazy E. I can't think of anyone by that name around here."

"Cooper Jones mentioned the word, or name, before he died."

Hastings rolled a smoke. "I'll check into it. What are your plans?"

"I've been trying to find traces of the missing cattle. No luck so far."

Hastings lit his smoke. "One thing you can be sure of, they come through Twelve Mile wherever they end up."

"I haven't seen any around here."

Hastings shrugged. "They do though. That's all I know."

"You're sure Edrick isn't mixed up in this? You must have learned something."

Hastings shook his head. "Edrick spends most of his time looking for rustlers. By God, if he is doing the rustling, he's the slickest one I ever seen."

"Has Jesse Vidal caused any trouble?"

Hastings grinned. "The two-gun man? Some of his *vaqueros* have taken pot shots at cowpokes wandering near the Double W. I happen to know the men he hired. Chili Vegas was mixed up with the Blue River gang at one time. Bowman and Wilde are Texas hardcases from the Pecos country. Vidal must be trying to start a range war."

"Where is Shorty Ganoe?"

Hastings shrugged. "He's been gone for a few days."

"How'd you get away from the Lazy E?"

"Dan let me go to get some venison. He's partial to it."

"You might have been followed!"

"I wasn't born yesterday. I backtracked a few times. No one followed me."

Dave looked out of the doorway. "Still, it's dangerous. If they find out who you are you won't have a chance."

Hastings refilled his coffee cup. "Maybe you don't understand why I took this stock detective job. I like this country. Got a wife and two kids back in Colorado pining to join me out here. I figured I could help break tip this rustling crowd and then bring my family out here and get a small spread. Damned if a man can do it the way things are now."

Dave nodded. "I know what you mean. I think I stayed on for the same reason."

Hastings eyed Dave. "I remember the first time I saw you. You were an outlier then."

Dave grinned as he looked about his hideout. "Looks like I still am."

"What really made you change your mind, Yeamans?" asked Hastings curiously.

"I'll tell you the truth. I cut John Waite down in Shadow Canyon. He was an honest man. Leslie Waite didn't run away. She stayed to fight it out."

"Yeah. Sure is a nice girl, that Leslie."

"Who strung up Waite?"

"*¿Quién sabe?* It's mixed up with the rest of the mystery. I'll tell you one thing though, whoever did it won't get a chance to brag about it if I can line my sights on him."

Dave put out the fire. "You'd better dust the trail. Edrick might come poking up Twelve Mile."

"I'm not worried. He's down south."

"Just the same you had better move on."

Hastings picked up his Sharps and started down the trail. "Don't leave any more messages at the bridge," he warned.

"I'll bring information to Cass."

"It's dangerous for you to come into Deep Spring."

"We'll take that chance."

Hastings reached the bottom of the trail. "Look!" he called back. Dust was spiraling up from the canyon entrance. Through the veil they could see five mounted men.

Dave cursed. "Come back up," he called. He reached in and got his Spencer. They were neatly trapped.

CHAPTER NINE

Hastings ducked into the dwelling and peered through the window. Dave stepped back into the shadows. Shorty Ganoe, Mick Ochoa and three others were nearing the dwelling. Ganoe thrust up an arm and halted his men. He rode up behind a huge boulder and looked over the top of it. "You! Yeamans!" he called out. "Come on outa there! Calf rope! You ain't got a chance!"

"They know you been hiding in here," said Mort.

Dave spat. "I'll bet Ochoa knew it before. He was scouting in here."

Ganoe waved his Henry rifle. "We'll blow you outa there, Yeamans! Five against one! Grab your ears! Come on down now!"

"They don't know you're here, Mort," said Dave.

"What'll we do?"

"I'm not going there. That's a safe bet."

Ganoe's men scattered through the brush. One of them led the horses away into shelter. Ganoe peered around the boulder. "You coming or do we come up there and get you?"

Dave sighted his Spencer. He squeezed off. Powder smoke swirled back into the room. Shorty cursed and dived into the brush. Dave laughed. "Next one will be through your pin head!" he yelled.

Rifles sparkled in the brush. Slugs thudded against the ancient dwelling. A bullet whipped through the doorway and ricocheted from the back wall. Dave dropped to the floor. "We'll have to drive them off so you can get outa here," he said. "If they spot you the jig will be up."

Hastings fondled his Sharps. "Let me take a shot at them."

"Hell no! Hold your fire! That cannon will let them know I ain't alone."

Shorty's boys kept up a steady fire. Slugs slashed through the brush and slapped against the walls. A slug flattened itself against the inner wall and careened off to hit Mort's shoulder. Mort cursed. "Bruised me," he said.

Dave pulled at his lower lip. "Those ricochets will play hell with us."

"We can't leave."

Dave eyed the south wall. There was a walled-up doorway in it. "Start picking out that mortar. There's a room beyond this one. Sealed up. There's heavy brush at the far end of the building. We might be able to get down the slope under cover of it."

"So? We still can't get out of the canyon."

"We can play hell with them in the brush."

Hastings drew out his sheath knife and went to work. Dave fired now and then and was rewarded with a yelp of pain from one of the besiegers. Smoke rifted in the wind. Hastings loosened a rock and pried another from the wall. Bullets pattered steadily against the walls and screamed off into space. Hastings battered at the remaining rocks with one of those he had removed from the doorway. "Enough room to squeeze through," he said.

"Take a looksee in there."

Hastings crawled through. "For God's sake," he said.

Dave fired twice and then poked his head through the

new doorway. Hastings lit a match. "Look," he said quietly.

Four skeletons lay on the floor amidst a litter of pots, matting, animal bones and piles of maize. "Looks like the ancients left them buried here when they left the canyon," said Dave. He crawled in. He lit a match and eyed the east wall. The outline of the T-shaped door effected by the ancients showed clearly on the wall. "This door is shielded by brush outside," he said. "Bust through, *amigo*. I'll keep our little friends from getting lonely out there."

Dave went back into the first room and fired at a man running across an open space. The man hit the dirt and disappeared. Hastings worked at the wall. Powdery dust drifted into the first room. Hastings coughed. "It's open. You were right. Brush in front of it," he called through to Dave.

"Keno," said Dave. He settled down and waited for a clear shot. One of the horses moved up out of the hollow. The horse-holder dragged at the bridle reins. Dave aimed fine and slid a slug across the horse's rump. The horse screamed like a frightened woman and jerked the reins free. It set off at a dead run. A trickle of blood ran down its flank. The other horses stampeded after the first one. Ganoe cursed loud enough to set the echoes flying.

Dave grinned as he reloaded. He crawled into the other room. Hastings was already out on the narrow terrace, lying behind the brush. "Long drop here," he said over his shoulder.

Dave reached back into the first room and got his rope. Hastings made one end fast to a rock and slid down to the floor of the canyon. Dave lowered the Sharps and Spencer, and then followed them. He peered through the brush.

"I think I winged him!" yelled one of the men watching the dwelling.

Hastings capped his Sharps and crawled down the

slope, lying flat in the mesquite. He slid his rifle forward. "Shall we make a break for it, Dave?" he asked.

"Too many of them. You game to flush 'em?"

"Sure."

Dave pointed down the slope. "Work your way over there. When I open fire see if you can drop one of them."

Hastings vanished, trailing his Sharps. Dave fired four rounds. A man stood up to change position. The big Sharps boomed. The heavy slug dropped the man like a calf with a lasso around his forelegs. Dave changed his fire toward Shorty. Shorty hit the dirt and crawled out of sight. Hastings shifted position and fired again. The slug smashed the Henry rifle from Mick Ochoa's hands.

"They's two of them!" yelled Shorty. "Fall back!"

Dave and Mort worked like a team of questing hounds. They fired and then moved to fire again. The canyon was alive with hollow echoes of the firing. The four men darted into a hollow, opened up a heavy fire, and then fell back again. Twigs, cut by the leaden missives, drifted down about Dave and Mort.

The four men broke for it at last, legging it clumsily in their high-heeled boots. Dave and Mort quirt them on with hungry slugs. There was a moiling of dust as they caught their horses and pulled leather for Twelve Mile.

Hastings dropped beside Dave and wiped his sweat-beaded face. "Just like a skirmish line, Dave."

"You must have been a damned good skirmisher," said Dave as he fed cartridges into the butt-gate of his Spencer. "Army of Northern Virginia?"

Hastings shook his head. "No."

"Army of Tennessee?"

Hastings slapped the butt of his heavy rifle. "Army of the Potomac. Berdan's First Regiment of United States Sharpshooters."

"A Goddamned blue-belly!"

Hastings laughed. "You rebel bastard!"

Dave handed Mort the makings. "You were opposite the Fifth Texas at Gettysburg."

"Sorry if I caused you any trouble."

"Not me personally. Quite a few of the boys of the Fifth got your calling cards though."

Hastings lit up. "Seems funny to be fighting beside a Johnny Reb."

"Yeah." Dave looked down the canyon. "You lie low while I take a pasear down there. They might be forted up for us. Wouldn't do for them to see you."

Hastings went to look at the horses while Dave scouted the canyon. The man who Mort shot lay on his back, dirty hands gripping the front of his bloody shirt. The heavy slug had killed him almost instantly.

There was no sign of Ganoe and his men at the canyon entrance. Dave trotted back to Mort. "Go ahead. Be careful. Play dumb if they see you."

Hastings led up his horse and thrust out a big hand. "You're a good man in a pinch, Dave."

"No more than you. Get moving. I'll cover you if they show up again."

Mort Hastings left the canyon. Dave went to his hideout and loaded his gear onto Brazos. There was no time to waste. He rode from the brooding canyon, leaving the dead man in the silent company of Jeb Gregg and the ancients.

CHAPTER TEN

Dave cached his gear in a cleft of Twelve Mile. The gnawing loneliness in him had been somehow eased by the visit of Mort Hastings. Yankee or not, the stock detective was all right. A good man and a first-class fighter. A sort of crusader, thought Dave, trying to make a home for his family and other families by bringing law and order to the Mogollon country. The odds they were facing were high. One slip and Mort Hastings would never see his wife and kids again. It brought thoughts of Leslie to Dave. It was late afternoon. He had to see her.

Luck played with Dave that day. On his way toward the Double W, he saw a streamer of yellow dust rise on the valley road. He studied it with his field glasses. It was a buckboard, driven by Monte Ellis. Leslie sat beside him. The glasses brought her face close to Dave. There was a sadness about her. Dave feasted his eyes on her until the buckboard turned off on the creek road, heading for Deep Spring.

Dave kept to the timber on the south back of the creek and then picketed Brazos in the woods opposite the town. He crossed on the footbridge west of town and stopped in the shelter of a tumble-down shed at the edge of town. The town was lit up and the tinny banging of an off-key piano came to him from the Star of the West.

Hipshot ponies dozed at the hitching racks. Buckboards and spring wagons lined the dusty street. Dave suddenly realized it was Saturday night.

Dave skirted the backs of the buildings which edged the rushing creek. There was a continual hum of voices from the crowded main street. It was a poor time to come to Deep Spring, but the sight of Leslie had cast the die. Dave stopped out of sight in a doorway and tested the Starr, spinning the cylinder and testing the trigger pull by holding back the hammer to keep it from striking a cartridge. It was a heavy weapon, weighing almost three pounds, with a six-inch barrel. The grip was a little awkward for one used to the finely designed butt of the Colt. But the Starr could be fired single as well as double action, by using the small rear trigger instead of the big front one. Dave slid it into his sheath and walked to the rear of Simmons' Store.

The old man would be busy that night. Dave eased through the back door into the unlit rear office. He peered into the store. It was crowded and Cass had two extra clerks. Cass himself was talking with Leslie Waite.

Cass came toward the rear of the store and Dave stepped back. "I keep the dress patterns back here, Leslie!" called Cass. "Be with you in a shake." Cass came into the office and Dave clamped a hand over Simmons' mouth. "It's Yeamans," he said softly.

Dave released his hold. "For Christ's sake," said Cass, "you scared the wax outa me!"

"I didn't want any noise."

Cass shut the door behind him and went to a cabinet. "Where the hell is Mort Hastings?" he asked over his shoulder.

"I saw him this morning. We had a ruckus with Shorty Ganoe and some of the Lazy E boys."

Cass took some paper patterns from the cabinet.

"Yeah. It's all over town. Shorty was deputized by Bart Edrick to get you."

"They found me."

"Who killed Charley Mitchell?"

"The man with Shorty? Mort dropped him with his Sharps."

"It's tallied against you."

Dave shrugged. "One more doesn't make any difference."

Cass gripped the door handle. "I got to get these patterns to Leslie."

"Tell her I want to see her."

"You been eatin' jimpson weed?"

"I've got to talk to her!"

"All right! All right!" Cass said testily, "but make it short." He left the office.

Dave watched Cass speak with Leslie. She glanced at the office door and then at the customers. Cass raised his voice. "Got more patterns back there, Leslie, if these ain't what you want. Take a looksee, if you like."

For a moment she hesitated and then she came back to the office and closed the door behind her. Dave lit the harp lamp. Her eyes were cold as she looked at him. "Well?" she asked.

"You still believe I shot Edwards, don't you?"

"I don't know what to believe."

Dave came close to her. The lilac fragrance came faintly to him. "I swear it wasn't me."

"Monte wouldn't lie to me. He said you did it."

Dave shook his head. "Jesse Vidal has something on Monte. He forced him to bear witness against me."

She sat down and looked at his tattered clothing and bearded face. "Where have you been?"

"Hiding out."

"They say you killed another man today."

"No."

She looked away. "Why do you lie? You were alone

when the posse trapped you. You fought back. Charlie Mitchell was killed."

"Won't you believe me? I had nothing to do with either of those killings."

"You were alone today when the posse found you!" she said angrily. "Who else could have done it?" Dave turned away.

"You didn't answer me. Who was with you if you didn't kill Charlie?"

"I can't say. What's more, don't tell anyone I wasn't alone."

She stood up. "Witnesses say you shot Edwards and yet you deny it. You say you didn't kill Mitchell, and yet you can't say who did. Can't you see why I have no faith in you?" Dave shrugged. Someone had been working on her. "I hired you, thinking you were different from the rest of these kill-crazy men around here. You have killed two men and are known as a Double W man. Do you see where that places me?"

"I see where it places me."

"Why don't you give yourself up?"

"Here? To Bart Edrick? I'd be lynched or shot down before I had a chance to clear myself."

"Then run away and hide!"

Dave gripped her by the arms. "Remember what you said to me when we buried your father? I'll tell you! 'Law? What law? There is none!'"

She bowed her head. "I want to believe you, Dave."

"Jesse Vidal is no good. He'll bring trouble to the Double W."

"He has fought for me."

"Yes! For his own ends. Even Monte Hollis was forced to testify against me. Those men Jesse hired for you. Do you know who they are?"

"They work hard."

"Chili Vegas ran with the Blue River gang, the worst set of owlhooters in Arizona. Bowman and Wilde are the same brand as Vegas. You'll have a range war on your hands. It will be to the death! All because Vidal wants you and the Double W, and I think he's done his work well so far!"

She lashed out at him, striking him hard across the mouth. Dave drew her close. "I had nothing to do with those two killings. You must believe me."

Cass Simmons came to the door. "Look out," he said in a low voice, "Mack Muir just came into the store."

Dave stepped back. "Don't say anything about me to him, Leslie."

"Why not? He's a friend. You said you were innocent."

"I have no friends." Dave stepped behind a projecting wall cabinet. Mack Muir came into the office and closed the door behind him. "One of the clerks said you were back here, Leslie."

"I'm looking at some patterns."

"I haven't had a chance to talk with you. Why won't you let me come and see you?"

She turned quickly. "I never stopped you."

"That's not what Hollis says."

"I never told him I wouldn't see you!"

Muir flushed. "Then it must be that damned two-gun Vidal that told him to tell me! He takes too much on himself." He came close to Leslie. "I could have helped you more than he has."

"I lost cattle when you were helping me. Two of your men were killed. Since Jesse has been foreman, we've managed to keep what we have."

Muir laughed. "You credit Vidal with that? I still think Yeamans has something to do with the rustling. There hasn't been much of it since he disappeared."

"He has his faults but he's no rustler."

"Why do you defend him? Why did you hire Vidal? I was willing to share your troubles, to protect you. Your father always wanted us to get married."

Cass Simmons opened the door. "Monte is here, Leslie." He glanced at the cabinet behind which Dave was standing.

Muir turned to the storekeeper. "I've been telling Leslie she should have worked with me instead of drifters like Yeamans and Vidal. What do you think, Cass?"

Simmons shrugged. "Yeamans was a good man."

"Him? A murderer?"

"I only met him once, Mack. I still don't think he's a killer."

"Why are you defending him?"

Simmons tilted his head to one side. "Why? Because I didn't see him kill anyone."

"That's proof?"

"Listen, Mack: I wasn't there when Slim Edwards was wounded, and I didn't see Charlie Mitchell get it either, but when it comes to takin' the word of men like Shorty Ganoe and Mick Ochoa, I'd stick with Yeamans any day."

"Monte Hollis said Dave shot at Slim."

Cass snorted. "Him? He's scared to death of Vidal. He'd say anything Vidal told him to."

Leslie walked to the door. "I'm leaving," she said quietly. "Maybe Cass is right. I don't know. I do know that the men I have at the Double W are protecting my property. I intend to keep them working for me!" She left the office.

Muir lit a cigar and looked at Cass. "Why are you actually backing Yeamans?" he said.

"I said I never seen him kill anyone."

Muir blew out the match. "You've never liked me, have you, Cass?"

Simmons shifted his feet. "I've known men I liked a lot more."

"There are times when you act damned mysterious. What are you hiding?"

Simmons pointed to the door. "Get out," he said quietly. "Vamoose! You've pestered that girl a long time and now you're startin' in on me. I've got work to do. Vamoose!"

Muir stepped in close and gripped Cass by the front of his long apron. "Damn you! I bet you've helped turn her against me!"

"Let go of me! You can't bully me, Muir!"

Muir slapped Cass hard across the face. Simmons struck out with a bony fist and hit Muir over the right eye. "Damn you!" grated the redhead. He let go of the shirt and sledged Cass backed against the cabinet behind which Dave was standing. Dave stepped out. "That's enough, Muir," he said. "Unless you want a little tougher fight on your hands."

Muir jumped back, dropping the cigar from his mouth. "Yeamans! You were here all the time!"

"Get out," said Dave.

"Maybe you'd like a taste of what I gave Cass?"

Cass wiped the blood from his chin. "Try it," he said. "He'll rawhide you good."

Muir went into a crouch. His right hand slid inside his coat and whipped out, cocking a short-barreled Colt. "Don't move," he warned. "Bart Edrick will be glad to see you, Yeamans."

Dave leaned against the wall. "So? I didn't think you'd do a good turn for Edrick."

"There's a reward out for you."

Simmons nodded. "Yeah. But just put up that cutter, Muir. You won't turn Dave in. You'll get out of Deep Spring and forget you ever saw him here."

"Yeah?"

Cass leveled a long forefinger at Muir. "I say Dave never shot Edwards nor killed Mitchell. I ain't the only one around here that thinks so either. People around here are gettin' a bellyful of the Edricks and their type. One of these days they'll pay for what they done. You aim to stay in this country. You think people will forget what you did if you turn Dave in?"

Muir looked back and forth between the two of them. "You're bluffing, Simmons."

"Yeah? What about Leslie Waite? She likes Dave. Supposin' you turn him in, and he gets a rope or a bullet? What little chance you got with her now would be shot. Put up that gun, you fool! Get out of here and keep your mouth shut!"

Muir hesitated. Cass had set him to thinking. He lowered the stingy gun. "All right," he said. "I ain't one to condemn a man." He left the office.

Cass turned to Dave. "Pull leather," he said. "The town is full of Lazy E men. They're gettin' likkered up. Dan Edrick is in the Star of the West playin' with a noose. They're lookin' for you."

Dave doused the light. "Someone took the message I left at the bridge."

"For God's sake! Who took it?"

"Damned if I know. Mort told me."

"Lay low for a while until I can talk to Mort. I wish he'd come in and report."

Dave stepped out into the darkness of the alleyway. The door closed behind him. He reached the end of the next building before some subtle sense seemed to warn him. He stopped in a doorway. He could hear little above the rushing of the creek. A drunken shout carried to him on the wind. He placed his hand on his Starr and moved on. He turned. Someone had moved in the darkness behind him.

A man stepped out into a lighter area. "There he is!" he yelled. A pistol spat flame. Dave darted around a corner. A gun flashed fifty feet from him. The slug smashed into the wall inches from his head. He dropped flat and rolled over to the edge of the creek, drawing and cocking the big Starr.

"Damn him!" a familiar voice shouted from the shadows. "He can't have gone very far!" It was Shorty Ganoe.

Dave slid below the edge of the creek bank and lay

with his legs in the cold water. Boots slapped the hard earth. Two men rushed toward him. Dave fired twice over their heads. They broke for cover. Dave crawled over the rough stones of the bank ripping his knees. A gun spoke from a doorway and Dave's slug crossed the path of the other missile, striking the wood of a building. Guns rattled farther down the bank. Dave crawled out of the cold water. A slug plucked at his hat brim. He reached a doorway and backed into it. Feet thudded against the earth. A man stopped in front of Dave, holding a pistol, warily looking up and down the street.

Dave reached out with his left arm and quickly encircled the thick neck, ramming the muzzle of his six-shooter into the man's back. "Quiet," he said, "or I'll break your spine with lead."

"For Christ's sake," the man choked out. "Don't shoot, Yeamans!" It was Dan Edrick.

Dave screwed the muzzle in tight. "Call out to them," he ordered. "Tell them I'll kill you before they can move a foot. Quickly now! You and I are going to take a little pasear." Dave eased his throttling hold.

"You Lazy E men!" roared Dan. "Hold your fire! He's got me cold-decked!"

"Break away, Boss!" yelled Shorty. "Give us a shot, Dan!"

"Goddamn you! Hold your fire! He'll kill me!"

Dave shoved the big man out into the open. He pushed him toward the end of the building. "Drop your pistol," he said.

Edrick dropped the six-gun. "Don't shoot," he husked.

"I hear you had a rope ready for me."

"You killed two of my boys."

"I had nothing to do with it, Edrick."

"Sho? You aim to kill me too?"

Dave shoved him into a deep doorway. A horse was tethered ten feet away. "No," he said. "I'm no killer and never was. But I've got half a mind to live up to my reputation."

"How'd you get mixed up in this anyway?"

"I cut John Waite down, Edrick. You're a handy man with a rope. How does it feel to have a cocked .44 in the middle of your back? One squeeze of my finger and you'll join John Waite."

"Before God, I had nothing to do with it! I liked John."

"Yeah. You liked his cows and ranch better though."

"Sure. Sure. I liked the Double W. But I never strung him up."

"You lie!"

Boots grated down the alleyway. "Stay back, men!" called Edrick. "He'll kill me!"

Dave eyed the horse. It was a long shot, but he might make a break for it.

"Surrender," said Dan hoarsely. "I'll see that you get a fair deal."

"Shut up!"

"Damn you! Shoot then! Cut another notch on your six-gun! I had nothing to do with John's death!"

Dave peered out of the doorway. Two men were in the shadows at the end of the building. Dave stepped back and swung hard with the Starr, buffaloing Dan Edrick just above his right ear. Dan crumpled to the ground. Dave eased down toward the horse, untying the reins. He slapped it hard on the rump with his hat and then dropped below the edge of the creek bank. The horse set off with drumming hoofs.

"There he goes!" yelled Shorty.

Pistols blasted orange flame.

Dave cursed as the cold water soaked his ragged trousers.

"Get the hosses!" yelled Shorty. "I'll look for Dan."

Dave worked back into the cold water. The stream was about four feet deep. He let the swift current work him down to a cluster of willows on the far bank. He crawled from the water shivering like a scared pup. His gimp leg ached like the very devil. He hobbled along until he found Brazos. "How the hell did Edrick know I was in town?" he bitterly asked himself. A hard thought struck him. "Leslie? No. It couldn't be!" He spat and began to reload his six-shooter.

Brazos whinnied as Dave mounted him. Dave headed west along the south bank of the creek through the dark timber. The fat was in the fire now, and hell was to pay.

CHAPTER ELEVEN

There was a spit of rain in the wind as Dave led Brazos through the shintangle brush and scrub trees to the place where he had cached his gear. Now and then a shaft of forked lightning lanced through the darkness illuminating with an eerie glow the stark cliffs above Dave. He passed a slope crested with taller trees and caught a faint movement out of the corner of his eye. He turned swiftly, slapped Brazos on the rump and jerked his Spencer free from its sheath. Dave stepped behind a chest-high boulder and rested the repeater atop it. It was utterly dark. Rain began to patter on the dry leaves banked against the boulder. Dave wet his lips and slit his eyes, trying to probe the Stygian darkness. There was a darker shadow in amongst the trees. Dave dropped to his knees and skirted the boulder, inching along until he was close to the swaying trees.

The rain was steadier now. Dave got to his feet as thunder rolled like the beating of ox-hide drums and lightning exploded to the south. Dave looked up into the staring contorted face of Mort Hastings. The stock detective's body hung from a stout branch, his feet a few inches from the ground. Then the lightning died away leaving Dave sick to his gut with the sour taste of bile flooding his throat. He leaned his Spencer against a tree and slowly drew out his sheath knife. He cut the body down, catching it as it fell. He whistled for Brazos. The clay bank came up the slope. Brazos shied and blowed as he caught the odor of the dead man. Dave spoke to him quietly and then lifted Mort's body across the saddle, lashing it swiftly. He stumbled over something and picked up Mort's Sharps. The barrel had been smashed across a rock. Dave led Brazos away from the place of execution as the rain sluiced steadily down.

There was a cave not far from where Dave had cached his gear. He untied the body and dragged it into the cave, covering it with his tarp. Dave sat down and rolled a smoke, listening to the steady patter of the rain. Someone had found out who Hastings actually was. Dave had learned nothing from the agent. He was right back where he had started. He thought of Mort's wife and kids back in Colorado, waiting for word from the quiet man they loved. Mort Hastings had died for law and order as surely as if he had been wearing the badge.

Dave led Brazos under an overhang of rock and picketed him. Dave wrapped himself in blankets and poncho and lay for a long time looking up into the blackness before he fell asleep, five feet from the dead man. It was nothing new to him. He had lain amongst a pile of the dead in the woods at Chickamauga listening to the razorbacks worry the human clay, unable to move because of his shattered leg, and praying for death before the hogs got at him.

In the cold gray light of dawn Dave made his fire from dry wood he found wedged in the back of the cave from some flash flood of the past. He raised his first cup to his lips. A rifle crashed in the wet brush and the cup was snatched from him by an invisible hand, splattering him with hot jamoka. He hit the ground half-blinded by the hot liquid and instinctively grabbed for his Spencer. The echo of the first shot had hardly died away when the rifle spoke again. Brazos jerked back, ripping his picket pin from the wet earth. A worm of blood ran down his flank as he galloped up the canyon. Dave cursed, rubbing a filthy sleeve over his eyes.

He raised the repeater and flattened himself again as a slug caromed off the low ledge of rock in front of the cave. He rolled over to the side of the cave where a wall of rock thrust itself out man-high. He eyed the canyon. There was no sign of life in the wet brush. A thin layer of gun smoke drifted on the wind. There was a furtive movement farther up the wooded slope opposite the cave. Dave snapped a shot into the brush and was rewarded with a muffled curse.

Minutes drifted by. The sun struggled up over the rim of the canyon. Mist rose from the wet brush and damp earth. A rifle barked up the slope and the slug ricocheted inches from Dave's face, lancing it with rock chips. Dave absentmindedly wiped the blood away without removing his gaze from the slope. As yet he had seen no one. Brazos stood on a knoll down the canyon, looking back toward the cave and whinnying plaintively. A horse with a Lazy E brand trotted out of the brush and headed toward Brazos to keep him company. Dave recognized it as Shorty Ganoe's mount.

There were at least two riflemen besieging the cave. Dave snapped a return shot as a puff of smoke blossomed amongst some ocotillo. He caught a glimpse of a hat bobbing about and sighted on it, squeezing off easily. The firing pin did not click. Dave levered in a fresh round and fired again. There was no report.

Dave shook the repeater. "Goddamned main spring is broken!" he said. "Of all the bastardly luck!"

Steady rifle fire peppered the rocks about the cave. One slug whipped into the body of Mort Hastings with the sound of a stick being smashed into mud. "Can't hurt him anymore," said Dave dryly. He glanced at the battered Sharps which he had brought into the cave. It would have saved the day.

The sun rose higher, filling the canyon with steamy air. The last two shots fired at Dave came from a range of about one hundred and fifty yards. He rested his Starr on the rock and fired twice.

"Ain't using his long gun, Mick!" yelled Shorty. "Bet he's outa cartridges!"

Bullets poured down the slope battering the rocks, keening off into space, or slapping into the back of the cave. "Move in, Mick!" yelled Shorty. "We got him treed!"

Dave looked at the useless Spencer. They could play holy smoking hell with him now, safely out of range. It would only be a matter of time before a mutilated slug would keyhole through him with terrible effect. Suddenly Dave looked at the Sharps. "I'll be dipped in sheep manure," he said. He crawled to the Sharps and carried it behind the rock, hooking his morral from where it lay beside his blankets. He took his buckskin bag of gun tools and replacement parts, dumping it on the floor of the cave. Now and then a slug sang into the cave.

Dave worked swiftly, stripping down the Spencer. The main spring fell out in two pieces. He worked swiftly at the Sharps, dropping the breechblock, stripping off the lock plate with fingers greased with the sweat of fear. He removed the Sharps' main spring by using his Spencer main spring vise. Sweat ran down his face and he dashed it aside impatiently. A rifle boomed close to the cave and whipped through the slack of his shirt. He set the clamped main spring into the Spencer against the pins and then released the spring vise.

"You think we got him?" called Shorty close to the cave.

"He ain't shooting!" the flat voice of Mick Ochoa called back.

"He's tricky as a mossyhorn!"

Dave felt his breath harsh in his throat. Thank God

Spencer, in developing the sturdy repeater which bore his name, had used the Sharps main spring in its construction. He put the Spencer together with practiced hands and fed cartridges into the butt-gate.

A slug smashed against the rocks and a shard went through the lobe of Dave's left ear. He levered a round into the Spencer and reloaded his Starr, placing it close at hand. Shorty Ganoe was standing waist-high in the brush with rifle at shoulder. Dave fired too quickly. Shorty leaped aside, lowering his rifle. Dave's next slug caught him fair in the gut, toppling him over like a half-filled sack of wheat. A slug skinned past Dave's head. The creasing shot sent him reeling to the back of the cave. Blood flowed down the right half of his head. He dropped the Spencer and went down on his knees, holding his throbbing skull. Gravel rattled outside of the cave. A shadow fell across the floor. Dave looked up into the thin, evil face of the breed, Mick Ochoa.

Ochoa leaned his Henry rifle against the side of the cave, eyeing the dropped Spencer and the Starr far out of Dave's reach. He drew his *cuchillo* and tested its edge against a dirty thumb. "Now," he said softly, "You will not escape this time, hombre." He came slowly forward, balancing easily on the balls of his feet, poising for a fatal thrust.

Dave tried to get up. He sank sideways. Ochoa hooked a boot under his side and rolled him over. Dave thrust out a weak right hand and gripped the breed's ankle, heaving up with the last reserves of strength. Ochoa cursed as he staggered back against the wall. Dave got to his feet, facing the knifer. The blade flicked out, drawing blood from Dave's left forearm. Dave darted for the Starr, but Ochoa was like a panther, smooth and sinuous as he cut Dave off from the six-gun and drew blood from Dave's left hand.

They circled slowly like wrestlers watching for an

opening. Dave's breath was harsh in his throat. Green, slavering fear seemed to fill his hazy mind.

"Afraid?" asked Ochoa. "It will be quick if I choose to make it so, hombre."

The blade flicked out. Dave drew back. Ochoa grinned evilly. He was like a cat playing lazily with a weakened mouse. "You will soon join our dead *amigo* there," he said jerking his head toward Mort Hastings.

Dave was back against the wall. Ochoa rushed him. Dave went low and the blade clicked against the rock. It ripped through Dave's shirt on the backhand blow. Ochoa whirled and came in fast. He tripped over Mort's legs. Dave snatched up the bent Sharps and whirled it over his head, bringing it down with all his strength. There was the sound of a dropped pumpkin as the heavy barrel connected solidly with the breed's skull. Ochoa sprawled back over Mort Hastings. Dave dropped the bloody Sharps and leaned against the wall, staring at the smashed head of the breed. He wiped the sweat from his face and flicked the blood from his hands. He stooped and picked up his Spencer. There was nothing to fear from the breed now.

Dave limped to the cave entrance.

"Mick," yelled Shorty from the brush, "did you get him?"

Dave faded into the brush and worked his way slowly, sweat greasing the rifle in his hands. Ganoe pulled himself to his feet, holding his gut. "Mick! Mick!" he yelled frantically.

Dave raised the Spencer slowly. There was no pity in him. Shorty jumped as the repeater bellowed. He ran awkwardly through the brush, looking back fearfully over his shoulder, screaming shrilly in his panic. He plunged out of sight in a wash. Dave sent a slug whining over the wash. Shorty staggered up the far bank and swung up on his horse, sinking the hooks home with a vicious smash.

The horse buckjumped and plunged through the thick brush.

Dave limped back to the cave and looked at Ochoa. "Thanks, Mort," he said quietly. He gathered his gear and placed it outside the cave. He worked slowly in the humid heat, piling rocks to seal the entrance. Brazos trotted as he finished.

Dave loaded Brazos. Ochoa's boots had been crusted with fine yellowed mud. There was no earth like that in the big canyon. As he rode up the silent canyon he wondered where he had seen mud like that. It wasn't until he was a mile from the cave that he remembered the soil in Ruins Canyon at the base of the cliff dwellings. That soil, if wet, would create such mud. "Probably looked for me there," he said.

Twelve Mile was empty of life when he rode into it. A wide cattle track showed in the wet earth. It had been a fairly large herd. He slid from Brazos and led him along, eyeing the trampled earth. He reached the rock area and was studying it when boots grated on rock. "Stand where you are! Don't move!" a man called out.

Dave turned slowly, raising his hands. A Mex eyed him from a screen of brush. A rifle was at hip level. "Boss!" the Mex called out.

Boots rattled on gravel and Jesse Vidal appeared. "Yeamans," he said. "Just as I thought. Get the boys, Chili. I'll cover him."

The Mexican disappeared into the brush. Vidal rounded behind Dave and jerked his Starr from its holster. "Set," he said, "you've got some talking to do."

Dave sat down on a rock and began to fashion a smoke. "What's on your mind, Vidal?"

"What are you doing in Twelve Mile?"

"Looking for a place to light."

"Who was with you?"

"I'm alone."

"You're a liar, too!"

"You talk tough with a six-gun in your hand."

Vidal spat. "I can handle three like you without a cutter!"

Dave grinned. "I'll talk about the weather."

"Where's our cows?"

"Hell of a ramrodder you are if you don't know where your cows are."

Vidal raised the Starr. "Listen! Just after midnight last night we lost twenty head. We trailed them this far. It's a cinch they didn't climb these walls. Where are they?"

Dave lit his smoke. "How should I know?"

"Why are you staying around this country? You've killed two men and will swing for it. Why didn't you pull out?"

Dave yawned. "You'd like that," he said, "seeing as how it was you, and not me, that killed Slim Edwards."

Vidal laughed. "You can't pin that on me. Hollis is my witness."

"I'll wring the truth out of him."

"You talk as though you were going to live to do it."

"I aim to."

Vidal rubbed his jaw with the muzzle of the Starr. "We'll see about that. Besides, even if you talk your way out of that one, you'd still have to answer for the killing of Charlie Mitchell. Shorty Ganoe and Mick Ochoa will swear you did it."

"That so?"

"Yeah! What chance do you have now?"

Dave thought of Mick Ochoa stiffening beside Mort Hastings in the sealed cave. At least he wouldn't be able to testify against anyone.

Two men came out of the brush followed by Chili Vegas. Jonce Wilde and Tom Bowman, thought Dave. The shorter of the two men spoke to Jesse. "We looked through that canyon with the ruins, Jess. Tracks all over but no cows, and no way to get 'em out of there!"

"Damn it, Tom! They must be somewhere around

here! There ain't been time for them to be driven out the south end of Twelve Mile."

Jonce shoved back his hat. "I still say they never left Twelve Mile. They're around here!"

"That's brilliant, Jonce," said Vidal sarcastically. "But where? They got wings maybe?"

Bowman looked at Dave. "Maybe he knows."

"He's not talking," said Jesse.

Chili Vegas grinned. "We make heem talk. Easy. You want me to show you, Boss?"

Vidal shook his head. "Not yet. We'll take him to Cup Valley and keep him there. No one will think of looking for him there. Too damned many people poking around in here. He might have friends. He must have, 'cause he couldn't run off all them cows by himself."

Dave mounted Brazos and they tied his ankles beneath the clay bank and lashed his wrists behind him. Vegas took Brazos' bridle reins and led the clay bank up the canyon. The day was warm and humid. As they passed Ruins Canyon, Dave saw the tracks leading into it. Where the hell were they? He was no closer to the solution than the first day he had become interested in solving the mystery.

It was noon when they reached Cup Valley. Dave was shoved into the shack and tied to a chair. Bowman and Vegas left the valley. Jonce Wilde heated beans and sow bosom atop the spit-scarred stove. Jesse filled his plate. "Give him some grub, Jonce," he said.

"Waste of food, ain't it?"

"Feed him, you bastard!"

Jonce spat on the floor and filled a plate. Dave's hands were untied to allow him to eat. Vidal gave him time for a smoke. Jonce left the shack. Vidal lit a cigar and leaned back in his chair against the wall. "You ready to talk now?" he asked.

"Like I said, I don't know anything about your missing cattle."

"Weren't you working with Mort Hastings?" Dave controlled his face. How had Vidal found out about Hastings?

"Well?"

"No."

"Hastings hasn't been around. Maybe he's with the missing cows?"

"You're doing the talking."

"I'm going to blow open this whole damned business before long. I'm gonna wring the truth outa you and Dan Edrick."

Dave grinned. "You'll have a gay time wringing anything out of Dan. How do you figure you'll make him talk? You'll find yourself hitched to a bolt of lightning."

Vidal spat. "I can handle him," he said loftily. "I'm building up a first-class corrida on the Double W."

"What about Leslie? It's her ranch. Maybe she doesn't want a range war?"

"I'm running that spread. She has to go along with Jesse Vidal."

"You sure rung yourself in solid. You get rid of me, hire a bunch of hard cases, and practically take over the Double W. You're due for a comeuppance, Vidal."

Jesse tapped the side of his head. "I'm smart, Yeamans. I know a good thing when I see it. I ain't going through life working for thirty per and found. I've got big ideas. Real big ideas. Once I marry Leslie, you'll see what I mean. I'll be a big man in the Mogollon country."

"Maybe she won't marry you."

Vidal's conceited face turned dark. "Yah? She will if she knows what's good for her."

"I'm sure she does," said Dave dryly.

Vidal hefted Dave's Starr. "Now, for the last time, will you talk?"

"I don't know anything."

Vidal cocked the big double-action and leveled it at Dave. To Dave the muzzle seemed twice as big as it really was. Vidal leaned forward. "I can kill you easy, Yeamans. I won't get held for it. You're wanted for two counts of murder. I can say you tried to escape, and I was forced to kill you. The odds are with me. Now you talk! You tell me what I want to know, and I'll free you, give you fifty gold eagles, your hoss and a chance to get out of the country."

Dave laughed. "You damned sidewinder! If I did know anything, and told you, I'd get lead instead of gold, and a free ride to hell instead of out of the country. You haven't got the guts to shoot me."

The Starr roared. The slug whispered past Dave's head and smashed into the wall. Vidal's cold eyes looked through the veil of acrid smoke. "The next time I'll aim to kill," he said.

A shadow moved across the window next to Vidal. The seamed, ugly face of Monte Hollis appeared. The old puncher placed a finger at his lips and shook his head. Dave looked at Vidal, stalling for time. "All right," he said. "The cows are hidden near Twelve Mile."

"Where?"

"A hidden canyon."

"Tell me how to get there."

Dave shook his head. "I'll have to guide you in."

"How many head in there?"

"Maybe five hundred."

Vidal nodded. "We'll go as soon as Jonce gets back."

The door was kicked open. Monte Hollis jumped behind the kid, pressing a cocked six-gun behind his ear. "Drop that cutter," he said.

The Starr hit the floor. Vidal's face was dead white. "You sneaky bastard," he said. "I'll kill you for this!"

Hollis tossed a case knife to Dave. He cut his ankles free and stood up, stretching. He picked up his Starr.

Hollis plucked Vidal's fancy matched six-shooters from their holsters. "Get your cayuse, Dave. First tie this hombre up."

Vidal's body shook as Dave lashed him. "You've signed your death warrants," he grated.

Monte spat. He threw the Colts out of the window. "Let's go, Dave."

They got their horses and rode out of the valley. Dave looked at the older man. "Why did you do it?" he asked.

Monte waved a hand. "I'm sick of that loco kid's windy talk. Ever since I got you in trouble I ain't been able to sleep, and an old bastard like me needs his sleep. I'll have to hightail it," he said. "He'll kill me."

"How did you know I was in Cup Valley?"

"Bowman came by the ranch. He told Miss Leslie."

"So?"

"I figgered they'd kill you."

"I'd like to see Leslie."

Monte shook his head. "She knew what I was doing. She told me to get you outa the country."

Dave drew rein. "She knew you were coming to help me?"

Monte looked at Dave in surprise. "Hell yes! It was her idea, sonny."

"Let's go back and cajole them off the Double W."

"Wait! Your time will come. Right now, we gotta lay low. Some of the Lazy E boys are in Shadow Valley. We heard they was heading for the Double W. This is no time to buck up against that corrida. Seems as though you killed Mick Ochoa. That right?"

"It was him or me, Monte."

"I believe that all right. But they won't!" They rode fast, crossing the creek, heading into the wilderness south of the watercourse. Dave glanced at the homely man with him. If Monte hadn't showed up, he would be lying dead with a slug between the eyes from his own gun.

CHAPTER TWELVE

Dave and Monte rode into a branch canyon, thickly grown with brush, north of Ruins Canyon a few miles. The nights had been getting colder and Dave knew they must break the mystery of the rustling before long, for they couldn't live in the open through the bitter winter which was to come. Monte proved to be a skilled woodsman, working swiftly to make a brush lean-to. A shallow trickling stream afforded them water. Dave dropped a forked horn buck for much needed meat. Monte skinned the deer and they roasted enough of the venison to keep them supplied with cold food for a few days.

When it was dark, they filled their pipes and sat in the lean-to before the embers of their fire. The faint new moon was making itself known. "It's a queer deal," commented Monte. "Hundreds of cows vanish like wind-driven smoke. You, probably with the cleanest hands of anyone around here, charged with three murders, two of which you didn't commit, and one in self-defense, hiding out in the brush like a *ladino*. Two men, working against the rustlers, meet up with Judge Lynch. It beats me, Davie."

Dave lit his pipe. "How about Vidal? Is he working the long loop?"

Monte shook his head. "Hell no! Not that he hasn't at one time or another, but he ain't mixed up in this mess. He wants the Double W."

"What does he have on you, Monty?"

Monte rubbed his nose with the stem of his pipe. "Long's we been throwed together I might as well tell you. I jumped a paymaster's ambulance down in the Sulphur Springs Valley last year. Got plumb away with ten thousand dollars. I was loco with drink and dead broke or I wouldn't have done such a crazy thing. I made for the border with troopers hot after me. I got scared when I sobered up. I sneaked into the office of a marshal in a little *placita* near the border of Sonora and left the money. Then I met Jesse in a cantina. I needed help to make it across the border. Jesse offered it." Monte looked into the dying fire.

"So?"

Monte shrugged. "I got drunk again and talked too much to Jesse. That night the marshal was shot to death and the money was taken. I was in a hell of a fix. I couldn't talk myself out of not having the money then. I might get pinned with the marshal's killing. Who'd believe a saddle tramp like me? Jesse got me safe over the border. I tried to shake him then, but it was no go. He kept with me. Somebody had to be his *amigo* and he picked on me. He had plenty of *dinero*. I was broke. We came across the border six months later. Coupla times I tried to drift away from the kid. He'll run his neck into a noose one of these days. But I never got a chance to vamoose. Ever' time I tried to break away he would mention the payroll robbery. What the hell could I do?"

Dave nodded. "He had the screws on you all right."

"Oh, he treated me okay. Seems as though he had to have one friend in the world, and he had to pick on me. Times he'd listen to me, other times I had to listen to him. He's generous as hell at times, but, like I said, he'll be strung up or shot down one of these days, and I'm getting too damned old for that kind of end."

"You ever found out who actually got that payroll money?"

Monte glanced over his shoulder as though someone was eavesdropping. "I think so."

"Maybe you could clear it up?"

Monte drew his blanket about his thin shoulders. "No," he said quietly.

Dave leaned forward. "You're hiding something, Monte. Maybe I can help you."

"Yeah. Maybe you can at that. I helped you get away from Jess for mor'n one reason. You got the guts to fight Jesse, Edrick and the rest of 'em."

"Keep talking."

Monte glanced over his shoulder again. He was badly frightened. "You mind I told yuh Jesse got me outa Arizona into Sonora?"

"Yes."

"Waal, there was only one man knew about me leaving that *dinero* in the marshal's office."

"Jesse?"

"Yeah. We made it into Mexico, like I said. Jess was always well heeled. Cutting up big with them brown senoritas. Playing monte for big stakes. Drinking the best. Riding the best caballos. I cadged offa him all the time I was down there, but he didn't mind. Oh, we lived, I tell yuh. Saw all the big towns. Chihuahua. Parral. Torreon. Durango. Didn't miss nothing. Allus wondered how come Jess wasn't broke. Jesse and me didn't turn a hand. Finally, Jess went broke too, or said he did. We came back across the border. Drifted up here. Jess liked the Double W. Liked Leslie too. Figgered he'd frame you, which he did. Goddamn me for a brassbound liar. Waal, about three days ago he wanted me to go south and get some more cows. He got the money from Leslie. I needed *dinero* to travel with. Broke as usual, that's Monte Hollis. Jess was in a hurry to go somewheres. Told me to get some *dinero* outa his warbag. I went to get it. Down at the bottom of the bag I finds a piece of paper all crumpled up. Part of it was missing. You know what it was?"

"How the hell should I know?"

Monte tapped Dave on the knee. "It was a paper binder the army uses to wrap paper money for different outfits. This was marked C Company, Third Cavalry, Fort Bowie."

"It figures, Monte."

"Now I ain't too bright. Wouldn't be a saddle bum if I was. But I begins to figger. Remember I said Jess was down on his luck when I runs into him. We get over the border and suddenly he's living like a *hidalgo* for months without doing a lick of honest work. On top of it, he was losing more money at faro and monte than he was winning!"

He killed the marshal and got the payroll."

"*Keno!*"

In the silence that followed, Dave thought of the slick kid who had worked the deal on Monte. It was like him. Slick as a wet saddle. Now all he had to do was soft talk Leslie, and take over the Double W.

Monte relit his pipe. "Now you know why I had to break away. One thing bothers me. Jesse won't ever forget what I did, Dave. He'll gun me down at sight."

"You can raise dust for the border again."

Monte shook his head. "No. I ain't never been much good. John Waite treated me square when I worked for him down south. I ain't about to sit tight and watch that swift-talking kid do that girl outa that fine spread. That's why I threw in with you. You've got the guts and brains to help her. I'll ride the rio with you until we get this settled."

Dave raised his head. He heard the faint sound of bellowing cattle. He stood up. "Listen!"

Monte dropped his blanket. "Cows!"

"Come on!" Dave snatched up his Spencer and trotted through the brush. Monte was right behind him. They went to the mouth of the canyon and looked out into big Twelve Mile Canyon. "Coming from the south," said Monte.

The moon was casting a faint light into the canyon. A cold wind searched through their clothing. Dave shivered. It was almost as though there were ghost cattle in the distance. "I've heard that sound before," he said.

Monte gripped Dave by the arm. "Hoss coming," he said.

They faded into the brush.

A lone horseman appeared, riding slowly, with his head raised as though listening to the phantom sound, too.

"Frank Andrews," whispered Monte. "Has a small spread near the Lazy E. He was up to the Double W a few days ago asking about some of his stray critters. Lost twenty head."

"Is he all right?"

"Miss Leslie sets a store by him. He hates the Edricks like jimpson weed."

Dave took a chance. "Andrews!" he called.

Andrews kneed his horse into the shadows. "Who is it?"

"Talk to him, Monte," said Dave.

Monte stood up on a rock. "It's Monte Hollis of the Double W! Come on over for a palaver!"

"Who's with you?"

"An *amigo!* Come on!"

Andrews slid from his horse and drew his Colt. He glanced keenly at Dave. "Yeamans! What the hell is this, Hollis?"

"Bring your cayuse in here. Where you heading?"

"After my cows. They must be in here somewheres."

Dave eyed the rancher. His face had been battered

badly at some time in his past and then Dave remembered the story about how Andrews had been beaten to a pulp by some of the Lazy E corrida and was saved by John Waite.

"We just heard some cows down the canyon," said Monte. "You ain't aiming to go down there alone, are yuh?"

Andrews eyed Dave. "Maybe. You're travelin' in bad company, Hollis."

"No. You can depend on Yeamans, Andrews."

"A *killer?* Not me, Monte."

Dave took another chance. "Cass Simmons trusts me, Andrews."

"So? What's that got to do with me?"

"I was working with Mort Hastings."

Andrews sheathed his Colt. "Then you knew about the association?"

"Yes."

"Where's Mort?"

"Dead. Strung up. Just as John Waite was done away with."

Andrews paled. "Well, I'll be damned! We wondered where he was."

"What's this all about?" asked Monte.

Dave headed for the hideout canyon. "Cass Simmons and some of the honest ranchers hired Mort to work as a stock detective. I agreed to work with Mort. Never had much of a chance."

Andrews turned and whistled sharply. "I wasn't alone," he said. "Had a friend trailin' behind me. He's all right."

Mack Muir urged his horse out of the shadows. "Hello, Yeamans," he said, "Monte."

Dave stepped back and looked quickly at Andrews. Andrews waved a hand. "Mack is in the association now. We asked him to join awhile back. He'll work with you, Yeamans."

Muir dismounted and held out a hand. "Let bygones be bygones, Dave. I'll admit my temper got hold of me a few times, but I've been in love with Leslie ever since she came here. Let's work together. After we settle this rustling, we can decide who's the man for her."

Dave gripped the proffered hand. It was hard to resist Mack Muir when he put on the charm. He was a good man, too and God knew they needed every reliable man they could get. "We've got coffee up at the hideout," he said.

The four men went to the lean-to. They squatted about the fire. Monte piled it with squaw wood and set the pot on a rock. Andrews lit a cigar. "I've traced cattle into this damned mare's nest of a country time after time and lost them. Mack claims they take them clear south some-wheres. Me, I think they never left this canyon country."

"Keno," said Dave, "I've done some trailing myself and can't see how they were ever driven out of this area."

Mack Muir waved a hand. "Maybe. But where are they?"

"It's a big country," observed Monte. "Helluva lot of canyons. Plenty grazing. Good water. You could hide thousands of critters in here and no one would know the difference."

"That was John Waite's theory," said Andrews. "Mort Hastings backed it up."

Dave filled his pipe. "We all know what happened to them."

"Dan Edrick is behind it all," said Mack Muir. "Slick as a greased hog."

"I wonder," said Andrews. "He's worked hard tryin' to put down the rustlin'."

"A front," said Muir. "He's got enough men to do the rustling while he gallops about like a ranger looking for long loopers, playing vigilante. Edrick is power crazy. What better set-up could he have? Plenty of men to do the dirty work. Bart to cover up for him. Gets rid of every man who gets in Dan's way. Waite, Hastings and Yeamans here."

"Jesse Vidal had something to do with me being put out of the way," said Dave quietly.

"Maybe he's in on it, too," said Andrews.

Monte shook his head. "I know better."

"We won't settle it by crying about it," said Muir as he accepted his cup of jamoka from Monte. "I've got a plan. Yeamans and Hollis can stay around Twelve Mile. Andrews, you can go back and tell Cass to call a meeting of the association. Get every man you can to stand by. Cass can have two or three of them stay down at the south end of Twelve Mile in case the cows are driven out that way. The next time cows are rustled we can plug up the north end with more men. Then, by God, we can sweep through this area like a dose of salts!"

"Sounds good," said Andrews. He sipped his coffee. "How can we lose?"

Dave puffed at his pipe. "One flaw, Mack. Supposing you do bottle both ends of Twelve Mile? You'll have every man in the association out in the field. That'll leave herds practically unguarded throughout this country. If the rustling ring is big enough, they can pick steers where they damned well please and run them somewhere else besides Twelve Mile."

Muir leaned forward. "Yeah! Let them pick 'em up! If we find the place they been hiding them in here they won't be able to run them out! Don't you see? We'll force them into the open that way!"

Andrews slapped his thigh. "By Godfrey! It's worth the risk of losin' more cows to find out where the lost ones are! He's right! I was always one for forcin' a fight."

"You'll get it," said Monte gloomily. Muir stood up. "We can win this war my way." He smashed his right fist into his left palm. "You men with me?"

Andrews nodded. Dave stood up. "Monte and I will do our part."

Andrews gripped Dave's hand. "Good luck," he said. "You can depend on Frank Andrews."

"I'll ride north with you, Frank," said Muir. "I'm going to keep an eye on Jesse Vidal at the Double W."

After the two ranchers left, Monte eyed Dave. "You ain't too happy about this, Dave."

Dave relit his pipe. "I was thinking of the bloodshed, Monte. No man is going to be safe around here until we corral the actual rustlers. I know one thing; we're getting out of this canyon right now!"

"Why? We got a snug spot right here."

Dave looked at the little man. "It was snug until someone besides us knew about it. I'm used to playing a lone hand, Monte. I aim to keep on playing that way until this thing is over."

Monte grinned. "What about me? You're not alone now."

Dave spat. "One slip outa you, old-timer, and I'll sic Jesse Vidal on you."

Monte laughed. "Yeah. Yeah, I know what you mean." They broke camp. Dave got the horses. He mounted and headed west up the canyon. "That ain't the way!" protested Monte. "Ain't we going by Twelve Mile?"

Dave turned and rested a hand on his cantle pack. "No, but I've got a feeling this canyon is a helluva lot bigger than we realized. We'll ride up it a piece. There's just enough light to see. We can camp up there and pull out before dawn if it's a box."

There was no other sound other than the occasional clatter of hoofs on the loose rock that littered the canyon floor. A cold wind poked inquisitive fingers through their clothing. A coyote lifted its melancholy howl far up the canyon. The wind shifted. Dave raised his head. He could have sworn he had heard the bellow of a steer.

CHAPTER THIRTEEN

The moon was high when Monte and Dave made their new camp deep in the narrow, winding canyon. A shallow stream trickled over the rounded stones of its bed in the center of the canyon. To the south was a sheer wall of cliff, broken up by faults and cracks in which brush and scrub trees struggled for a living. To the north, trending toward the valley where the Double W was located, was a chaotic mass of shattered rock formations, thickly studded with trees and brush. As Monte strung the tarp between two trees, Dave eyed the south wall of the canyon. He estimated the distance between the canyon and Ruins Canyon to be about three miles. "I'd like to climb up there, Monte," he said. "There must be mesa land between here and Ruins Canyon." "You could see a helluva lot of country up there."

"That was my thought. You game to try the climb?" Monte shrugged. "Now I don't rightly know. I ain't much for the mountain goat stuff."

"Maybe you'll feel like it in the morning."

Monte grinned. "A little sleep won't change my mind."

They bunked down for the night. Twice during the night, when the wind shifted, Dave stirred fitfully, and once he sat bolt upright. He could have sworn he had heard the faint bellowing of cattle.

In the morning, Monte still wouldn't try the cliff. "I'll back you in gunplay, Dave," he said as he made their breakfast, "but I ain't about to try that climb."

Dave took his coils of rope from his gear and tested them. "Fill my canteen, Monte," he said, "and dig out my field glasses."

"You're loco."

"Maybe, but we're not getting anywhere. I've heard steers bellowing around here half a dozen times at least, and unless they've got wings and are flying around here at night, they must be somewhere between here and Ruins Canyon."

Monte brought the canteen and glasses. He made up a packet of food. "I heard tell of the Ghost Steer of Val Verde down in the Big Bend country," he said. "Great big bastard. Pure white with shining silver horns. Any *vaquero* sees him is doomed to die."

"We're a long way from the Big Bend country."

"Yeah. But they's queer things around this country, too. I even heard tell of a camel galloping around in the desert with a skeleton strapped in the saddle, still wearing soldier clothes. Big red beast. Sure death to see him. Imagine that! A goddamned camel in Arizona."

Dave grinned. "Could be. Jeff Davis worked out some kind of a deal with camels back in '56. Landed at Indianola, Texas. They were brought out here to help open a new road. The war broke up the experiment and they were set adrift. Great rusty looking beast was seen now and then after the war. Carried a dead man on his back. Last I heard of that whopper was that the legs of the rider was all that was left of the skeleton. Still in the stirrups."

"Yuh see?" said Monte triumphantly.

Dave looked up at the cliff. "I don't expect to see a camel up there, nor any ghost steers."

"What do you want me to do?"

"Can you make it into Deep Spring to see Cass Simmons?"

"Why not?"

"*Bueno!* You tell him what you told me about Jesse Vidal. I want Leslie warned about him. Be damned careful." He looked up at the cliff again. "If anything happens to me, I want you to clear me on that Slim Edwards shooting. Write out a statement and give it to Cass if you're willing."

"I am. Anything else?"

"Ask Cass if he ever found out anything about an hombre named Riley or something like that."

"Riley? You mean old One-Eyed Riley?"

Dave turned quickly. "You know a man named Riley?"

"Used to. Rustler. Hoss thief. Tinhorn. Quite a salty hombre was old One-Eyed."

"Is he in this country?" Dave gripped Monte by the arm.

Monte spat. "Hell, not Old One-Eyed was stabbed to death in a hurdy-gurdy hall in Tucson two years ago. He told Big-Nosed Molly she had fingers like a bunch of bananas. Now Big-Nosed Molly didn't like that. It seems that..."

Dave shook his head. "Get going. That's not the same Riley." He grinned as he watched Monte saddle his horse. "You can tell me about Big-Nosed Molly and One-Eyed Riley when you get back."

Monte waved a hand. "If you get back, *amigo*. If you get back!"

Dave hooked his canteen to his belt and took off his one spur. He looped the coils of line over his shoulder and pushed his way through the brush until he reached the foot of the cliff at the bottom of a long angling fault that traversed the cliff face. He climbed over a pile of talus and worked his way up the fault. He was about one hundred feet up when he dared to look down. Monte was almost out of sight. Dave worked up another twenty feet and stopped to rest on a crumbling ledge. He made a running noose in one of his lines and cast it upward toward a projecting rock. It slithered back. He made it on the third try and drew it tight. The line was knotted at two-foot intervals for easy handholds. He rested for a time building up his nerve.

Dave spat on his hands and gripped the line. He worked up it, swinging his legs up above his body, planting his feet on the cliff face, and then pulling himself up. Sweat had soaked his ragged shirt by the time he reached the end of the line. He repeated the process until he was fifty feet from the lip of the cliff. He repeatedly cast the line until it drew taut. He rested, watching a hawk drift through the canyon, veering off when he saw Dave.

Dave coiled his remaining line over his shoulder and started up. Fifteen feet from the top he was swinging out over the void. The line gave a little. With a furious outburst of strength he swarmed up, gripping a stunted tree at the top just as the line parted. He crawled over the edge and lay still, his breath harsh in his throat. He opened and closed his chafed hands. "Monte was damned near right," he said, forcing himself to look down into the canyon. He shuddered a little. "Come to think of it, I have to go back down there too."

Dave sipped some water, coiled his lines, slung them over his shoulder and started south. It was a mesa, cut up by deep gullies, stippled with shintangle brush. Cat-claw, ocotillo and high-stalked pitahaya waved in the wind. Half a mile southward was a curious humped formation rising about two hundred feet above the plateau. Dave used it as a landmark. When he reached it, preparing to start his climb, he heard a dull buzzing noise at his feet. He jumped sideways, clattering down the rocky slope as the diamondback struck hard. Dave cursed. He picked up a rock, hefted it and then threw it with all his strength, driving the scaly monster back. The second rock broke the back of the writhing killer.

Dave worked his way to the top of the hump. He uncased his glasses and studied the country to the south. The mesa rose at a low angle toward Ruins Canyon which he could easily identify by a curiously colored cliff. Yet he could see no other canyon between him and Ruins Canyon. He studied the terrain until his eyes grew weary. He rolled a cigarette. "Must be someplace in here for cows," he said, "unless Monte is right and we're hearing phantoms." He lit the cigarette and leaned back against a rock, studying the horizon from beneath the brim of his battered hat.

Dave snatched the cigarette from his lips. Unless he was mistaken, he could make out a tendril of smoke drifting lazily up into the clear sky. It was between him and Ruins Canyon. He snatched up the glasses. It was smoke all right. He lined it up with a tall butte to the south and slid down the hump, striking off through the jungle of brush and rock.

The sun beat down, reflecting mercilessly from patches of naked rock. Dave reached the top of the slope just about noon. He stared in astonishment. "Well, I'll be double-damned," he said.

A vast canyon spread out before him. Far to the right was an escarpment, lit brightly by the sun. Rugged humps of rock thrust themselves out from the canyon walls. At the bottom, in stark contrast to the purplish red of the canyon slopes, was a winding trace of bright green, denoting the presence of a watercourse. The sun glinted on pools of water. To Dave's right, far below, was an area of rough reddish rock, bare of vegetation.

There was no trace of smoke now, and no sign of life in the canyon under his view. He looked over the edge and shook his head. It was a long drop down to the smooth talus slope below.

Dave sat there for a long time, scanning the canyon floor. It was too far below him to distinguish tracks or other signs of cattle. The south wall must be the barricade between this mysterious trough and Ruins Canyon. There was no other trace of smoke. He cased his glasses and started back toward the hideout canyon.

The trip down the canyon was enough to gray Dave's hair. He hit the bottom in a shower of gravel and sat down to wipe the sweat from his face. He limped toward the camp and stopped short as he saw a familiar bayo coyote mare with a Double W brand. Monte came out of the shelter. "Hi, Mountain Goat," he said with a wide grin.

"Whose cayuse?" asked Dave.

"Yuh got a visitor, *amigo*."

Leslie came out of the shelter. Her hair was smoothly braided, and her wide-brimmed hat hung at her back. "I had to see you, Dave," she said.

Dave came closer to her. "It's good to see you, but why did you come?" A long hunger was appeased as he looked down at her.

"I was in Deep Spring when Monte came in to see Cass. He told me about lying when Bart Edrick arrested you. I'm afraid, Dave. Jesse acts as though the Double W is already his. He wants me to give him a power of attorney. I refused and he sulked for a whole day. Those men of his frighten me. They seem anxious to start trouble."

"I warned you about him, Leslie."

She looked up at him with troubled eyes. "I should have listened to you. Most of my cattle are gone. Vidal and his men do very little except sit around and play cards. Mack Muir tried to see me, and they fired at him."

"We're working on the rustling," he said. "Until we clear it up, we'll have to wait to deal with him."

"He's dangerous. I had to steal away from the ranch

to see Cass. Jesse tries to keep me on the ranch. He has asked me to marry him every day since you left. What shall I do?"

"You can't stay here. Can't you stay with Cass and his wife?"

She shook her head. "He'd only come after me. He has told people that we're engaged. He talks constantly of what he plans to do with the Double W. Now that you and Monte are gone I have no one to turn to."

"She oughta stay with us," said Monte. "I know that skunk. She isn't safe there, Dave."

Dave looked at Monte. "What did you learn in town?"

"The association had their meeting. Some of the boys are on their way south to the end of the canyon. Some of them are standing by waiting for word to block the north end of Twelve Mile. Andrews will be in charge of them. All we can do is wait until more cows are rustled and then move in on them. What did you find upstairs?"

Dave glanced at the cliff. "I thought it was a mesa between here and Ruins Canyon. But, between here and Ruins, is another canyon trending to the west. Plenty of water and grazing in it. No cows. I saw some smoke, or thought I did. But there doesn't seem to be any entrance to the east, and possibly from the west."

Leslie shrugged. "Another dead end."

"You'd better start back, Leslie," said Dave.

"Let her stay, Dave," said Monte.

She looked eagerly at Dave.

Dave shook his head. "It's too rough and dangerous."

"Aw, let her stay, Dave," said Monte. "Anyways I'm tired of cooking."

Dave scratched his jaw. "All right then. But if anything happens you must head for Deep Spring. Cass will take care of you." He picked up his Spencer. "I'm going to scout along Twelve Mile."

She watched him as he saddled Brazos. Monte crawled into the shelter and brought out a shirt, trousers, a pair of boots and a set of spurs. He held them up to Dave. "I was getting ashamed to be seen with you, Dave."

"Thanks, *amigo*." Dave swung up on Brazos and rode away from the little camp.

Long shadows were creeping into Twelve Mile when Dave saw dust rising half a mile north of his position. He kneed Brazos in behind a rock ledge and loaded his Spencer. The beating of hoofs came toward him. One horseman rounded a bend in the canyon. He was about to pass Dave's position when Brazos stamped hard and neighed shrilly. The man turned. It was big Dan Edrick. He jerked his reins and spurred his bay into the brush on the far side of the canyon.

Minutes drifted past. Dave worked his way through the brush on foot. He saw Edrick's hat crown showing above the brush. He rounded behind it. "All right, Dan," he said. "The game is up. Come on out."

"Sure will, Yeamans," said Edrick from behind Dave. Dave whirled. Dan was standing hatless not ten feet away from him with leveled rifle. Dave cursed. He had been taken in by one of the oldest tricks in the book. "You try for a shot, Yeamans, and I'll let daylight through you."

Dave gripped his Spencer. Edrick grinned. "Still," he said, "I might miss, and you might drill me with that carbeen."

"It's possible."

"You're a cool one, Yeamans."

There was no other sound in the canyon except the occasional click of a rock as a horse moved.

"I'm alone, Yeamans," said Edrick. "I want to palaver with you."

"We've got a hell of a lot to talk about, Edrick."

Edrick lowered his rifle and eased the hammer down. "Sho? Maybe we can settle some things."

Dave leaned on his grounded Spencer. "Talk," he said.

Edrick took out the makings, rolled a smoke and

passed the makings to Dave. "You know I coulda strung you up the first time we met."

"You had nothing on me."

"Any stranger in this country is open to suspicion. Shorty Ganoe woulda strung you up if I hadn't stopped him."

"True enough."

Edrick lit his cigarette. "I never believed you shot Slim Edwards."

"Why?"

"You ain't the type."

"What about Charlie Mitchell?"

Edrick looked quickly at Dave. "Who did kill him?"

"Mort Hastings."

"I'll take your word on that."

"Why all the kindness?" asked Dave.

Edrick grinned. "I figgered you was a troublemaker. I wanted to buy the Double W. I still do, as a matter of fact, but I ain't one to war on wimmen, although I'd as like plug that bastard Vidal as look at him."

"I'm with you on that, Edrick."

"He cut in on the Waite filly, eh?"

"Never mind."

Edrick rubbed his right ear. "Lots of folks think I'm behind this rustling. Silly, ain't it? I got money. I got the best spread in this country. Useta have a fine big herd. All shot to hell now," he said ruefully. "However, here's why I wanted to palaver. I've thought a lot about you. You had the guts to face down my brother Bart with Ganoe and Ochoa backing him up. It took guts to teach Shorty a boxing lesson there in Deep Spring. It took more guts for you to stay around this country with the Lazy E and Jesse Vidal chousing you."

"Thanks for the sugar. Get to the point."

Edrick glanced keenly at Dave. "The thing that finally sold me on you was that night in Deep Spring when you coulda killed me by squeezing a finger. You gave me a fair deal although you damned near cracked my skull."

Dave puffed at his cigarette. "You've got a hard head, Dan, in more than one way."

"I agree. Another thing that made me change my mind was you being so thick with Cass Simmons. Now Cass is a cantankerous old vinegaroon, but he's honest, which is mor'n I can say for most of the people around Deep Spring. I got to figgering and thought to myself that Dave Yeamans may be just the man I want."

"Don't softsoap me, you old mossyhorn!"

Edrick waved a huge paw. "I ain't! Frankly, Dave, I'm in a hell of a mess. I'm losing money on this rustling deal. My boys ain't done a thing to clear it up. Bart ain't worth a continental. He's too busy polishing that star of his and making eyes at the young fillies in Deep Spring to worry about me. Me, who's paying the bills, and who engineered that job for him in the first place. I can't hardly get him to stick his fat rump on a saddle no more to go look for them sticky loopers."

"I thought Shorty was doing all the looking?"

Edrick rolled another smoke. "What happened when Shorty and Mick Ochoa trailed you down?"

"Let Shorty tell you."

"You killed Mick, didn't you?"

"It was him or me, Dan."

"Yeah, I can see where it woulda been."

"I thought Shorty was hit bad."

Edrick shrugged. "Your slug hit his belt buckle, knocked his wind out and gave him a helluva bruise."

"Maybe you'll stop sending men after me now."

Edrick lit his smoke. "I didn't send them after you that time. I didn't know a thing about it."

The wind rustled the brush. A bird chirped nervously. "Then who did?" asked Dave.

Edrick shrugged. "Maybe it was personal on their part. I don't know. I sent them after you once into Ruins

Canyon. But the time they ran you down had nothing to do with my orders."

"What do you want me to do?"

"Keep on as you are. But know this: I'm depending on you, like a lot of other people, to clean up this mess. You get information on these long loopers, and I'll back you with the whole damned Lazy E corrida. Fair enough?"

"I can't believe it."

Edrick thrust out a paw. "Remember the first day we met? At your camp? You said you was wounded at Chickamauga?"

"Yes."

"I knew you wasn't lying then. I was with the old Third Arkansas in your division for a time."

Dave gripped the big hand. "A damned good regiment, almost as good as the Fifth Texas."

"Sho? Maybe we can argue about it over a bottle of red-eye someday."

"Whenever you say."

"I been mighty high-handed, Dave. A man has to be to make his way around here, fighting Apaches, hoss thieves, weather and rustlers. But something happened to me when John Waite was strung up."

"Who did it, Dan?"

"*¿Quién sabe?* But if I find the bastard that did it, I'll cut him down like a sunflower!"

"Let me get first crack at him."

Edrick went to his horse. "I can't work with you in the open, Dave. You know why. I know all about Cass Simmons and his association. I knew Mort was in with them. I had nothing to do with his death either. But when the chips are down, and the shooting begins, you can depend on Daniel Armstrong Edrick, *amigo.*" Edrick mounted with a smash of leather and spurred the bay, riding north in the shadowy canyon.

Dave went to Brazos. He stroked the clay bank's mane. "Brazos, the older you get the more puzzled you get. You know, I actually believed that damned Arkansas rebel." He mounted and rode back toward the hideout canyon. The sun was almost gone, and a cool wind scouted through the dim canyon. An owl drifted high overhead on noiseless wings. A coyote raised its mournful cry up the canyon.

CHAPTER FOURTEEN

The hideout canyon was deep in shadowy darkness when Dave guided Brazos toward the camp. Now and then the wind carried the odor of the fire to him. Suddenly, he saw the embers of the fire, but there was a quietness about the place that warned him. He dismounted and stood in the brush eyeing the silent camp. The wind rose a little, fanning the fire which illuminated the interior of the shelter. It was empty.

Dave drew his Starr and walked slowly toward the camp. "Monte! Leslie!" he called. There was nothing but silence and the flickering fire.

A rock clicked against another. Dave dropped, thrusting out his Starr. A gun flamed. The bullet smashed into a stunted tree inches from Dave. Dave ripped out two shots. A man cursed. Another gun roared from behind the shelter. Dave rolled over, jumped to his feet and fired three times through the back of the shelter. There was a hoarse scream, and something thrashed in the brush.

A man ran through the brush. Dave snapped out his last shot. He dropped to the ground and crawled toward the base of the cliff. He crouched behind a rock and reloaded slowly, peering up the canyon. Boots grated on gravel. A horse whinnied. Suddenly there was a clatter of hoofs and a dark shape materialized moving swiftly toward the camp. A handgun was thrust past the horse's head. It flamed twice illuminating the hard face of Tom Bowman, the Double W hand. Dave fired from the ground. Bowman cursed. He slapped his horse on the flank with the barrel of his pistol. He sank in the hooks, leaning low as the pinto raced for the canyon entrance. Dave stood up, leveled the Starr across his left forearm and squeezed off. Bowman jerked upright, threw up his arms and slid sideways from the saddle into the brush. The pinto raced on, dragging Bowman by one foot twisted in the stirrup.

Dave ran toward the canyon entrance. Bowman was flung free from the excited horse. He crashed into a hollow. Dave walked up to him. He lit a lucifer. Bowman's head was out of shape. He stared unseeingly at Dave. Dave went back to the shelter. He pushed aside the brush which formed the back. Jonce Wilde lay in the brush. His hands were twisted in the bloody shirt front. He was dead.

"Dave! Dave Yeamans!" the voice came faintly from farther up the canyon.

Dave whirled and faded into the brush.

"Dave!" It was Monte Hollis.

Dave walked toward the sound of the voice. Monte was face down in the brush, his hands tied behind him. He moaned a little as Dave cut him loose and rolled him over. Dave lit a match. Monte had been thoroughly worked over. His swollen face was bloody. "Where's Leslie?" asked Dave.

"She got away. Vidal and that bastard Chili Vegas went after her."

Dave helped Monte to the camp and placed wood on the fire. He went to get Brazos and took the Spencer from its sheath. Monte rubbed his wrists and wiped some of the blood from his face. "They jumped us an hour ago. Vidal wanted you. I was sick thinking you'd walk into the trap. Chili worked me over whilst I was tied up."

Dave held Monte's head and looked at his battered face. "The yellow bastard!" he said.

Monte winced. "Busted some of my teeth. Damn him! I'll kill him for this!"

"You all right now?"

Monte spat blood. "It'll take more than that tinhorn to stop me. Give me a gun!"

"Take it easy."

"You get them two?"

"Yes."

"*Bueno!* They was going to bushwhack you. Vidal's orders."

"I'm going after Vidal."

"Not without me you ain't!"

"Somebody has to stay here."

Monte shook a fist. "Yeah. But what about Leslie?"

"I'll go. You stay here and watch for cattle."

"Save Vegas for me."

"If there's anything left you can have it."

Monte raised his head. "Listen!"

From Twelve Mile they heard the low thunder of many hoofs, broken by the bawling of cattle.

"Goddammit!" said Dave. "Here they come!" He snatched up his repeater and swung up on Brazos, spurring it through the dark canyon. Monte threw sand on the fire.

Bitter dust swirled into the canyon from Twelve Mile as Dave neared the canyon mouth. The herd was south of the hideout canyon now, traveling fast. Dave spurred Brazos, riding recklessly through the pall of dust. Suddenly, he saw two horsemen turning back toward him. A rifle flamed. He kneed Brazos into the brush. Slugs whispered through the darkness as the horsemen poured lead toward Dave. The herd was still moving swiftly.

The two riflemen vanished like phantoms into the dusty darkness.

Dave listened to the sound of the receding herd. There was the promise of a moon showing in the east. Dave led Brazos forward. Half a mile farther on he was met again by the rear guard. Slugs slapped against rocks. Again, he hit the dirt.

Dave waited half an hour and then advanced again. The canyon still was filled with the bitter odor of the dust. He left Brazos in a deep cleft and went forward afoot to hide in the brush at the entrance to Ruins Canyon. Dust drifted from the canyon. Dave heard the faint sound of beating hoofs and the bawling of cattle and then there was silence.

When the moon illuminated the canyon country Dave scouted into Ruins Canyon. The air was still thick with dust. But nowhere in the canyon was a single steer. Dave shoved back his hat. He rubbed his chin. Monte's ghost stories came back to him. He padded out into the open without thinking and cursed as a rifle flatted off, awakening the canyon echoes as the sound of the report slammed back and forth between the towering walls. Dave cursed as he backtracked. He needed help.

Monte was missing from the canyon when Dave returned. His horse was not picketed in the hollow. Dave headed north up Twelve Mile. The moon revealed three men riding hard toward him. "They're in here I tell yuh!" one of them yelled. It was Frank Andrews. Dave held up his Spencer. "Frank!" he called out. "It's Yeamans!"

Andrews drew his pistol. "Hell, you gave us a jolt, Dave!"

Dave drew rein beside them as they drew in their plunging mounts. "Carl Winters and George Gunther," said Andrews jerking his head at his two companions.

Dave pointed south. "The cows were driven into Ruins Canyon. Disappeared like *chisos!* I was choused out of there by rifle fire."

"Ain't no way outa Ruins," said Gunther suspiciously. "It's a box."

"Goddammit!" roared Dave. "I know it! But they went in there, I tell you!"

Andrews spat. "This beats all," he said in disgust. "You game to go after them?"

"You'll be bushwhacked."

"What can we do?"

"Are the others down at the south end of Twelve Mile?"

"They been campin' there a couple of days."

"*Bueno!* Sit tight here until I come back. If you go near Ruins watch yourself. It's a cinch they can't fly out of this country."

"We met Hollis near the creek," said Frank.

Dave nodded. "There's one thing I've got to do before I find those cows. See you." Dave spurred Brazos to the north.

Dave met Monte on the Deep Spring road an hour after he left Andrews. The puncher's horse was lathered. "I been to Deep Spring," he said. "Leslie is safe with Cass."

"Where's Vidal?"

"Damned if I know!"

"As long as she's all right we'd better go back and help Andrews."

They found Andrews and his two men half a mile from Ruins Canyon. "Damnedest thing I ever saw," he said. "We scouted Ruins. Tracks all over. No cows. You sure they didn't go south?"

"I know they didn't!" said Dave.

Andrews spat angrily. "What do we do now?"

Dave looked up at the moonlit canyon wall to the west. "Sit tight. I'm going up there and look into another canyon I discovered."

"How the hell could they get in there?"

Dave shrugged. "I'm willing to bet my clay bank against a plug of Horseshoe that there is a way in there."

"Then we'll go into Ruins and look for it."

"You'll get bushwhacked! Spot yourself near the canyon mouth and watch to see if anyone comes out. Gather them up if they do. Monte and I will take a looksee up there. Maybe we can flush those birds."

"You've got guts, Dave."

Monte whistled softly as he looked at the cliffs. "Waal, I might as well go through with it. Damned if I can get to like the idea though!"

They picketed their horses in the hideout canyon, got the ropes, and started the dangerous ascent. It was hard going in the darkness, for the moon did not light the hideout canyon south wall. Dave hooked his slung Spencer on a projecting rock, and it took Monte fifteen minutes to work up beside him and free it. They finally sprawled at the top, gasping for breath in the thin air. Monte closed his eyes. "I think I oughta get sick," he said.

Dave snatched up the ropes and set off at a fast pace across the moonlit mesa with Monte plodding after him. They reached the brink of the mysterious canyon. Some of it was in deep shadow, unlit as yet by the rising moon.

Dave lowered his lines. "You ain't going down there, are yuh?" demanded Monte.

Dave nodded.

"You ain't going alone, though damned if I cotton to the idea."

Dave gripped the line and worked his way down the rope. Halfway down he landed on a ledge. Monte struggled down beside him, cursing under his breath as he rubbed his lacerated hands on his pants.

It took them the better part of an hour to reach the bottom. They rested, inspecting their bruises and cuts. Monte stood up. "Listen!" he said.

A cow had bawled from somewhere in the darkness.

They skirted the base of the cliff, working west. Now and then the wind brought the sound of rushing water to them. The brush rustled. They had covered a good mile when Monte grunted. "Look," he said.

The moon had begun to light a level area on the far side of the creek. Cattle dotted the area. "Must be about five to six hundred head over there," said Dave. "We've run them to earth, Monte."

"Yeah. Yeah. But what do we do now? No hosses. Miles from anywhere," Monte spat.

"Look," said Dave quietly.

A spot of flame had licked up west of them.

"What is it?"

"Looked like it came from the top of a chimney. Someone is starting a fire down there." Dave walked west.

A horseman rode slowly past the herd. They could hear him singing. Dave and Monte faded into the brush and came out on a wide flat of rock. The moon revealed a rock house perched on a slope over a place where the creek had formed a deep pool. Four horses were tethered to a hitching rack. A door banged and a man was outlined in light. "I'll take a pasear into Ruins then, Shorty!" he called back.

Another man came to the door. "If you see Dan Edrick, take a shot at him." It was Shorty Ganoe. He looked back over his shoulder. "That okay with you, Bart?"

Dave and Monte could not hear the sheriff's reply. "Did you hear what I heard?" asked Dave.

"Jesus! Ganoe and Bart Edrick! Slick as a greased hog. Who woulda thought of it?"

"Neither one of them, I'll bet. They haven't got the brains. This clears Dan Edrick all right."

"What do we do now?"

"We could try to get Shorty and Bart."

"Maybe somebody else is in there?"

"Let's look." Dave glanced at the distant herd. The man who had left the cabin was riding east. "Wait. You follow him. See if you can find out how they get these cows in here. I'll watch the house."

"Keno!" Monte drifted off through the brush.

Dave inched forward. It took him a long time to get around behind the building. Now and then he could faintly hear voices. Shorty Ganoe had even fooled Dan Edrick, but it was beefy Bart Edrick who'd have to pay the piper's bill when Dan caught up with him. Dave cached his Spencer and worked down behind the house. He edged up to the wall and stopped near a window which was open a few inches.

"Who was that who was following us down the canyon?" asked Bart.

"One hombre," said Shorty. "Too dark to see who it was. Buck Casey scared him off with a few shots."

"I don't like it. You sure he didn't see where we drove the cows?"

"Hell, no!"

"He'd be better off if he was dead if he did," said a voice from the far side of the cabin.

Dave straightened up. The voice was vaguely familiar.

"Hell, Rileton!" said Shorty. "What's the difference now? We got enough steers to drive west now. We can lay low for a while until the pressure is off."

Rileton. Dave raised his head. Rile...Rileton. That was the name Cooper Jones had been trying to say to Dave. Dave bent to get a look into the cabin. His foot hit a pile of discarded tin cans. They clattered loudly. Dave ran lightly into the brush and slid down toward the deep pool.

The three men came out in front of the house with drawn six-guns. "What the hell was that?" demanded Edrick nervously.

Shorty walked behind the house and poked about in

the brush. "What the hell is this?" He picked up Dave's Spencer.

"Maybe it belongs to one of the boys?" said Edrick. Dave lay low. He could hear them walking about the house. "Say," said Shorty, "that nosy bastard Yeamans has a Spencer. None of our boys have."

"I knew there'd be trouble tonight!"

"Let's get to the herd," said Shorty. Dave saw the three of them mount and ride down the slope. Shorty was carrying the Spencer. A clump of brush cut them off from sight before Dave could see who the third man was.

Dave went to the house. The fire was flickering in an open fireplace. He jumped as a rifle crashed down near the herd. He slid down toward the pool and looked east. Dave followed the stream. Rifles flashed steadily. Dave started to run. They must have flushed Monte.

Something moved in the brush. Dave whipped out his double-action. Monte staggered through the shadows. He was gripping his left arm. "I got holed. I was close to the herd when I fell and dropped my Henry. The night hawk saw me and opened up. The rest of them are looking for me."

The horsemen were quartering through the brush trying to cut sign. Dave trotted through the brush followed by Monte. "My arm is busted, I think," said Hollis.

"What did you learn?"

"Up a slope is what looks like a big cave. Horseman rode in it and didn't come out. I followed him. Helluva draft pouring through the cave so it must open up somewheres. I'll bet it opens into Ruins Canyon."

"Yeah. But where?"

"Damned if I know."

The horsemen were on the far side of the herd by now. They sat their mounts with rifles across their thighs looking out across the moonlit brush. They started across the shallow stream. Monte cocked his Colt. "Hightail it. I'll stand them off."

"No." Dave eyed the herd. They were restless from the shooting. It was only a matter of time before Monte and Dave would be flushed. "Hide. Don't shoot unless they're right on top of you."

"What about you?"

"I aim to raise a little pure hell in this big hole." Dave trotted at a crouch until he was west of the milling herd. The grass was dry. He squatted and lit a lucifer, cupping it against the west wind. He applied it to a dry bush. The flame flickered and then flared up.

"What the hell is that?" yelled Shorty.

Dave fanned the flame with his hat. Dave raced away from it, giving out a wild rebel yell. He ran the big Starr dry. The roaring shots echoed from the canyon walls. The wall of flame moved toward the excited herd. They began to move toward the four horsemen. Then the herd began to run. The men opened fire at Dave, but he slid into a hollow and reloaded his Starr. Dave held up the handgun and ripped out six more shots like the ripping of heavy cloth. The herd was spooked. They took off at a steady run for the east end of the canyon, straight toward the four men.

"Stampede!" one of them yelled. They sank in the hooks and cut across the front of the moving herd. The sound was like muttering thunder. The herd closed in on the hard-riding men. One of them went down as his horse stumbled and fell. The steers flowed over him, stifling a last agonized scream. The other three men lashed their horses toward the darkness of the cave, up a long rocky slope. One of them cut sideways to clear the herd. He crashed through the shallows of the stream but was engulfed by the herd. The last two men plowed up the loose rock of the slope, making hard going. One horse pitched forward. The man slid from the saddle and tried to reach the sheer wall of the canyon, scrabbling desperately for a hold but the mass of cattle crushed him against the wall. The last man buck-jumped his horse up the slope, slid from the saddle, gripped a stunted tree growing from the cliff wall and pulled himself up over the thrashing horns as the herd poured beneath him. Then everything was blotted out in a pall of thick dust.

Dave reloaded. He was a little sick as he realized what he had done, but there would have been short shrift for Monte and himself if they had tracked them down. One of them had possibly avoided a horrible death.

Dave found Monte seated on a rock. He looked up at Dave and shook his head. "Gawd," he said, "you did things to a turn."

Dave helped Monte to the cabin. He glanced back to see that the steers had vanished into the huge cave. "Sit tight here, Monte," he said. "I'm going to find that one man who I think got away."

Monte nodded as Dave helped him to a seat. "Where the hell did those cows go?"

"I aim to find out." Dave reloaded his pistol and left the cabin, walking at a fast pace through the moonlit brush.

CHAPTER FIFTEEN

Dave passed a curious blotch on the trampled earth and knew it for the first man who had gone down. A horse lay dead at the far side of the stream and a black hat floated in an eddy. It was Shorty Ganoe's horse. A scrap of bloody cloth hung across a rock. "Two down," said Dave.

The third man's big body was wedged into a cleft which cut into the cliff. It was shattered and bloody. Drops of blood dripped to the rocks beneath the battered corpse. The moon glinted on something bright. Dave picked it up. It was smashed but Dave knew it for Bart Edrick's big official star. Dave looked up at the body. "Anyway, Bart," he said, "you won't have to face your brother Dan."

The wind blew dust against Dave as he plodded up the rocky slope toward the cave. Moonlight filtered through the dust at the far end of the cave. Dave drew and cocked his Starr. There was a wall of the cave blocking his way. He placed a hand against it. It was masonry. He followed it for fifty feet and rounded a sagging corner. Ruins Canyon lay below him, bathed in silver moonlight. "I'll be damned," he said softly. He kicked a rock accidently. A gun spat flame. He hit the

ground and lay still. Something moved in one of the
doorways of the ruins. Dave fired twice and chipped
masonry.

Boots clattered on loose rock. A pistol flamed from a
small window. Dave rolled over and crawled behind the
long row of ruins. He eased through a doorway. The roof
of the room had fallen in, filling the floor area with dried
mud and crooked roof beams. Dave climbed the debris
and looked over the low wall. A shadow moved into
another room down the line. Dave snapped a shot, darted
through the rear door and padded along the back of the
line of ruins, under the great overhang of rock which
sheltered the dwellings. He eased into another room,
cracking his head against the low sagging roof. Dried
mud pattered about him as he crawled through a small
doorway into the next room.

Silence came, broken only by the dry patter of roof
adobe behind Dave. Suddenly the roof collapsed,
billowing the dust of ages toward him. Dave edged
toward the next door. A gun barked, chipping masonry.
He jumped through a back door and found himself in a
long natural passageway behind the dwellings. He soft
shoed behind the line of ruins through a litter of
potsherds and powdery animal bones.

Dave peered into a long room. A gun spat flame. The
slug picked at the brim of his battered hat. He fired twice
and then again as he saw a dim figure. Dave jumped back
into the passageway, ran to the next door and stepped in.
He raised his Starr as the man whirled. The Starr's
hammer clicked dryly. Dave pulled trigger again and then
realized he had run the big handgun dry.

"So," the dim figure said, "you haven't a chance now,
Yeamans."

Dave stared into the shadows. Moonlight shone on
Dave and pinned him stark against the back wall.

"Stand still!" The man moved out into the moonlight.
It was Mack Muir. He raised his Colt.

"What is this, Muir?" asked Dave as he raised his hands.

"The name is Rileton," he said quietly, "I use my mother's name around here."

"Then you ran the rustling deal?"

Rileton nodded. "Had everybody fooled until you blundered along." He jerked his head. "Who's out there in Ruins Canyon?"

"The men you stole cattle from."

"They just got a lot of them back."

"Yes."

Rileton leaned against a post. "I always knew it would be a showdown between us, Yeamans."

"You've got the aces. How did you work the rustling?"

"Easy enough. Shorty Ganoe helped me. Bart Edrick got a big split. Bart kept Dan busy on wild goose chases while we ran off his cows. John Waite trailed us in here once. He was going in for Bart Edrick when he died."

Cold sweat trickled down Dave's sides. "You did it."

Rileton smiled. "Yes. John told me he was cutting through Shadow Canyon to avoid the creek road. I got there ahead of him. Threw suspicion on everyone but me."

"You cold-gutted shark!"

"Mort Hastings got a dose of the same. I've lost the cattle but I'm in the clear. Bart and the boys can't talk. After I take care of you, I'll go back into the canyon and ride west. I'll show up later on, talk Leslie into marrying me, and end up owning my spread and the Double W too."

Dave shifted. Rileton stepped back. "Don't move! How do you want it? Belly or head?"

Dirt sifted down from the sagging roof. Rileton raised the Colt. Dave threw himself sideways just as the Colt roared. Dave hit a roof prop. The roof sagged. Rileton cursed. He fired again. The slug winged past Dave's head. He hit the post again with all his weight. Rileton was veiled in falling dust and mud. Then with a soft rush the heavy dried adobe poured down, engulfing Rileton, smashing him down under the debris. The earth stopped sliding. Dave coughed. He turned away and stepped into the back passage. He limped to the end of the building. He stepped out on the terrace.

A horseman leveled a Henry rifle down on the slope. "Calf rope!" he yelled. It was Frank Andrews.

"It's Yeamans!"

"Thank God! We've got the whole herd, Dave! Lazy E, Bar M, Lazy L, Double W, and my own Box A."

Dave wiped the sweat from his face. "Monte is back in the hidden canyon sporting a broken arm. Get me a horse."

Dave sat down and rolled a smoke with the last of his tobacco. It was all over. The rustling was, in any event. Yet he had a score to settle with Jesse Vidal of the two matched Colts. It wouldn't be easy. He lit the smoke and leaned back. He had traveled a bitch of a trail since the day Dan Edrick had surprised him in his hunting camp.

CHAPTER SIXTEEN

I t was close to dawn when Dave and Monte neared Deep Spring. Andrews and his men had penned the herd up in the hidden canyon. Monte's arm had been set and then Dave and Monte had ridden one horse to the hideout canyon to get their own horses. Dave had taken the time to put on the clean clothing Monte had brought him from Deep Spring. Monte, despite the battering he had undergone, was downright cheerful. "I feel better'n I have for years," he said. "Doing something honest?"

Monte grinned. "Yeah, now that you got the bad manners to bring it up."

"You were just a misguided boy, Monte."

"You expect to find Jesse in Deep Spring?"

"I'm going to see Leslie. I'll bet Jesse is around somewhere. If he is I'll straighten him out."

Monte shook his head. "He's sheer twinkling magic with the sixes, Dave. Not that you ain't a good man," he added hastily.

Dave turned up his collar against the cold wind. It was going to rain. "Maybe he won't get a chance to use his Colts," he said.

"I hope so. Just don't take any chances with him, Dave."

"I don't want any more killing, Monte. I've had a gutful of blood."

"Yeah. I'm looking forward to a nice quiet job of breaking up stampedes, taming wild hosses, or lassoing mountain lions."

The eastern sky was pale when they saw the first buildings of sleeping Deep Spring. They clattered over the plank bridge which spanned a branch of the creek. A big man stepped from a doorway and hurried toward them. There was a spit of rain in the cold wind as they drew near him. It was Dan Edrick. He looked up at Dave. "Well?" he asked quietly.

"It's all done," said Dave. "Some of your steers are with the herd we got back. Four of the rustlers are dead."

"By God, you did it! I wish I had been in on the kill!"

Dave glanced at Monte. "I'm glad you weren't."

Dan looked queerly at Dave. "What do you mean?"

"I've got bad news for you, Dan, depending on how you look at it."

"So?"

"Bart is dead."

"Who got him!"

Dave glanced at Monte again. Monte shrugged. "Tell him," he said.

Dave dismounted and offered Dan the makings. The big man rolled a smoke and lit it. "Shoot," he said as he filled his lungs with smoke.

Dave told him the whole story. He took the smashed badge from his pocket and gave it to Edrick.

Dan looked at the badge and then stowed it away. "Maybe it's just as well," he said quietly. "Ganoe was no good. Rileton, or Muir, was a slicker, but Bart, well, I been carrying him on my back for years." He looked at Dave. "You bury him?"

"Yeah. Decent. We said a few words. Cairned the grave."

"Thanks." Edrick hesitated. "One more thing, don't ever mention his name to me again. Understand?"

Dave nodded.

Edrick looked back over his shoulder. "I've been waiting for you. Vidal and that Mex *vaquero* of his been hanging around town all night. They been talking war. They tried to get Leslie Waite, but Cass Simmons forted up in his store with a loaded shotgun. Let's go get them."

Dave nodded. "Monte, you stay here. Dan will help me."

Monte spat. "Like hell! I'm going to be in on this showdown, busted wing and all!"

"I figured you would. Where are they, Dan?"

"They was in the Star of The West."

Dave looked at Monte. "Come on, *amigo.*"

Monte slid awkwardly from the saddle and freed his Colt. "Check this cutter, will you, Dan?"

Edrick twirled the cylinder of the six-gun. "All set." He handed it to Monte.

Dave drew his Starr and checked it. He slid it back into his sheath. He rolled two smokes and thrust one between Monte's lips. Dave hitched up his gun belt. "Let's go," he said.

They strode down the street in the gray light of dawn. The rain began to slide silently down, greasing the street. A wisp of bitter smoke trailed in front of them from some early riser's fire. A cock gave voice at the far end of town.

Dave glanced back. Big Dan Edrick was leading the two horses into shelter. He waved at them.

Their spurs jingled softly as they neared the big saloon. A door banged farther down the street and Tom Finney, Bart Edrick's deputy, came toward them. He stopped in front of them. "Where you goin'?" he asked.

"To flush some skunks," said Monte. "Names of Vidal and Vegas."

Finney shook his head. "No you ain't! I'm the law around here until Bart Edrick returns."

"Hell of a long time to wait," said Monte softly, "until Judgement Day."

"What the hell you talkin' about?"

"Bart is dead," said Dave. His eyes studied the silent saloon ahead of them.

Finney squared his shoulders. "Then I'm sheriff," he said importantly. "You get outa town!"

"Get out of the way," said Dave.

Finney tapped Dave on the chest. "I'll run you in for carryin' firearms in town."

Dave viciously backhanded the deputy, knocking him down. He stepped across the fallen man. Finney got up and scuttled for shelter.

The rain pattered steadily down. It was too damned quiet to suit Dave. The front door of the saloon swung slowly open. A lean man stepped out and stopped beneath the saloon awning. It was Jesse Vidal, rakish and handsome, wearing his twin Colts low and tied down. He leaned against a post as they stopped walking. "The two missionaries," he said with a sneer.

"Come to do some reforming," said Monte.

Vidal took a tailormade from his shirt pocket and lit it, eyeing them over the flare of the match. He placed the cigarette in the corner of his thin mouth. "How do you want it?" he asked. "One at a time or together?"

Dave glanced up the street. Vegas was not to be seen. "We'll give you a chance to pull out," he said. "Head out of here and keep going. Vamoose!"

Vidal laughed. "Hardcase," he said with a grin.

Monte cursed. He shoved Dave to one side with a shoulder thrust and raised his Colt. Vegas had rounded a corner of the saloon. Monte's six-gun spat flame and smoke. Vegas dropped his gun, looked queerly at them, walked a few uncertain steps out into the street where he pitched forward and lay still. The powder smoke drifted off before the wind.

Dave had never taken his eyes from Vidal. Jesse flipped his cigarette toward the dead man. "Never could take his time," he said. He eyed Dave.

Dave went for his Starr, but Vidal was a gun-swift. The twin Colts cleared leather, cocked and leveled before Dave's Starr was free of his holster. Cold sweat mingled with the rain on Dave's face.

Monte yelled. Vidal cursed and turned. Dave raced forward, driving home a jolting right to the lean jaw. Vidal twisted, dropping his right-hand Colt. He made the border shift quickly, tossing his left-hand Colt into his right hand, but Dave came up with a well-timed kick, sending the flashy six-gun clattering across the muddy street.

Dave stepped back.

Vidal raised his handsome head. "Go ahead," he said. "Shoot me down!"

Dave smiled. He threw his Starr down on the porch. He ripped a left into Vidal's gut. His right came up to meet the descending chin. Vidal's head snapped back. He bounced from a post and reeled out into the street. He raised his fists, but Dave was too fast, tired as he was. He speared Vidal with a left and jabbed in a vicious right which sent Vidal down flat on his back.

Vidal shook his head. "Let's settle this right, with guns," he said.

Dave shook his head. "There's been enough killing," he said. "Get up! I'll make a real man out of you, Vidal!"

Vidal came up on his feet. He sent Dave reeling with a right to the mouth. Blood flowed from the mashed lips. A left staggered him. The kid could hit like a maul. A right sprawled him in the mud.

Dave rolled away from a poised boot but the cruel spur raked his jaw. Dave gripped the ankle and upset the taller man. He rolled atop the raging kid. He battered at him with both fists. Vidal brought a knee up into Dave's groin and broke away. Dave forced himself up, covered his face with blocking elbows and weathered a flurry of hard blows.

Dave retreated, blocked a right and caught Vidal with a one-two that staggered him. He followed through with a left that smashed Vidal up against the side of a building. Vidal pulled away but Dave gripped his shoulder, spun him about and drove in a punch that sent Vidal down on his knees. Dave gripped him by the shirt front, dragged him to his feet and slapped the handsome, bloody face three times, shoving Vidal back to receive another one-two.

Vidal threw his shaking arms up in front of his face. He reeled back toward the rushing creek. Dave broke through the arms and let fly a blue norther that broke some of his knuckles. Vidal's pretty nose was askew through a spate of blood as he teetered at the edge of the rushing creek. Dave threw a haymaker which practically lifted the kid from the ground. He crashed back into the water and came up spluttering. "I've had enough!" he yelled.

Dave jumped into the stream and gripped him by the collar, forcing him to the bank. The kid covered his face with his hands.

Monte came toward them with cocked Colt. Half a dozen curious townsmen were standing in Front Street watching them. "Christ!" said Monte, "what a beating you gave him, Dave."

"I don't feel too good myself, Monte," said Dave dryly.

Monte eyed the battered kid. "Come on, Jesse," he said. "Outa the rain and into the calabozo. You've got some explaining to do about the death of a marshal and the stealing of an army payroll."

Vidal stumbled as he walked toward the jail. Blood dripped from his battered face.

Dave weaved a little as he headed for Simmons' store. His mouth was bleeding, and his right hand was beginning to swell. He was as bone tired as though he had just finished one of the long, forced marches during the war. But this time there was no Appomattox.

Leslie met him at the door of the store. She held him close. "I'm all bloody," he said.

She kissed him anyway. "I don't care," she said. "You've come back. You've come back at last!"

The rain sluiced down. It would be a hard winter, thought Dave as he held Leslie close. But the valley of the Double W was well sheltered, and he and Leslie would be, too. He was an outlier no longer.

CODE OF THE GUN

CHAPTER ONE

The wind was out of the east, driving a thin drizzle of fall rain against the buildings of Globe. Alec MacLean stepped out of the livery stable and paused under the shelter of the wooden awning to fashion a smoke. The big brown hands moved expertly to form the paper cylinder. Even white teeth held the drawstring of the tobacco sack as Alec drew the top together. He stowed the sack and lit the cigarette, scratching the farmer-boy match on a nailhead. The flickering light showed the lean face with deep-set grey eyes. The eyes steadied for a fraction of a second on the little man who leaned against the front of a rain-streaked building across the muddy street. It was the same nondescript individual who had followed Alec from the Silver King saloon twenty minutes before when Alec had stopped to ask directions to the law office of Attorney Andrew Barker.

Alec stepped out into the rain and turned up North Broad Street, heading for the trim row of cribs that lined the bed of rushing Pinal Creek. He knew the man was following him. Alec increased his pace, rounded a corner, and stepped into a doorway, freeing his hands from beneath his rain-slick poncho.

Feet squelched in the layer of pasty mud that covered the deserted street. The little man rounded the corner and looked uncertainly up the street. Alec moved like a great lean cat. He gripped the man's left shoulder, turned him quickly, and shot out a smashing right that dropped the other into the mud without a sound. Alec looked up and down the street before he hauled the man into the doorway. Then he stepped over the unconscious man and went back to North Broad, hurrying towards the two-story frame building that held Barker's office.

Yellow lamplight showed through the rain-streaked window. Alec peered in. A huge man was settled in a leather armchair, warming shaky hands at an open fire-place. Alec looked back down the street and then rapped on the door. Chair springs creaked musically. "Who is it?" a voice called out.

"MacLean!" The springs creaked again, and the door swung open. Alec brushed past the big man who stood looking at him and pulled down the window shade. He turned to look at Harley Forrest. "Well, Forrest," he said, "I'm here."

Forrest held out a palsied hand. Gone was the great strength of the cattle king. Alec felt as though he were holding the hand of a child. Forrest sat down in the great chair and jerked his head towards the desk. "Liquor over there," he said. "Get comfortable."

Alec shucked his poncho and held his dripping hat over the ash box. The firelight shone dully on the walnut butt of the Colt that hung high at his right side, the Missouri holster tilted forward for an easy draw. Alec unbuttoned his leather jacket and poured a drink from the square black bottle on the desk.

"How was Sonora?" asked Forrest.

"You didn't call me up here to Globe to ask me about Sonora, Harley," Alec said.

For a second the clear blue eyes of Harley Forrest

became frosty, and then he leaned forward to light his cigar with a paper spill. "No," he said. "Anyone see you?"

Alec sat down, eyeing the liquor in his glass. "Little man followed me out of the Silver King."

"Damn it! You should have come straight here!"

Alec grinned. "Stop shouting," he said. "How the hell should I know where this place was?"

Forrest puffed at his cigar. "Where is he now?"

Alec rubbed his bristly jaw. "Lying in the mud off North Broad, near the cribs."

"Did he see you?"

"He saw me. He didn't see who slugged him."

Forrest leaned back in his chair. "You still with the Arizona Rangers?"

Alec shook his head. "No. And if I was I wouldn't tell you."

"*Bueno!* I'll pay you two hundred a month for a job."

"I want no dirty deals, Forrest."

Harley Forrest flushed. "Damn you, Mac! You didn't lose any of your lip in the last few years."

Alec yawned. "You haven't lost any of your damned bossiness."

Forrest stroked back his mane of white hair with his right hand. "Ten years ago," he said, "I could have broken you in half across my knee. I could have outdrawn and outshot you."

Alec stood up. "Thanks for the liquor. I didn't come here to listen to an old man's tales of his virile youth."

Forrest waved a hand. "Sit down, you hot-headed maverick. This is business. Keep your opinions about me to yourself. I don't particularly like you, MacLean. Your past has some shadows in it that I don't like. But I need you."

"Speaking of shadows, they ever find out who dry-gulched Sim Pascoe on the East Verde fifteen years ago?" Forrest's big hands came together. For a moment Alec thought the palsy-ridden man would come at him despite his affliction.

"I'm sorry, Forrest," he said.

"All right. All right. If you stop shooting barbs into me, I'll tell you why I sent for you."

Alec nodded and refilled his glass. "Peace," he said with a grin.

Forrest leaned forward. "How long have you been gone from Arizona?"

"Two years."

"Where were you?"

"West Texas for a time. Central New Mexico. In Sonora for the last year or so."

"Things have changed in the Clear Creek country."

"So? You're no longer the king?"

"I'll be king up there for a long time to come!"

Alec leaned back in his chair and eyed the old man. Harley Forrest still had the framework of the man who had come into the Clear Creek country shortly after the Civil War, driving a mixed herd of grade Durhams and Texas cattle. Harley Forrest had fought Apaches, drought, flash floods, sticky loopers, and his own family to build up the well-known HF spread. His wife had been shot down in a short but bitter range war that had followed Forrest's peremptory seizure of a water hole he had no right to. His son, Willis, had died a hopeless cripple two years later from a stab wound suffered in a brawl over the same water hole. Alec knew, and all of the smaller ranchers in the Clear Creek country knew too, that Harley Forrest had all the water he needed on the HF spread, but because someone else had wanted that particular water hole, Forrest had fought for it.

Forrest warmed his shaking hands at the fire. "I want you to ask for a job on the HF."

"Not on your life! I've still got friends in the Clear Creek country."

The blue eyes studied Alec. "So? Who?"

"Cass Cronin. Bill Hoskins. Andy Fairweather."

Forrest puffed at his cigar. "Cass Cronin sold out a year ago. Bill Hoskins is lying in a Holbrook hospital with a slug in his back. Andy Fairweather was found three months ago shot through the head, near Bald Butte."

A ball of apprehension formed in Alec's stomach. "What's wrong up there, Harley?"

"That's why I sent for you. I want you to find out."

"Keep talking."

"I've lost over two hundred head of prime beef in the last six months. Hash Melrose, my foreman, was dry-gulched two months ago. Two of my water holes have been poisoned. Lost forty head that way."

"Your past sins coming home to roost?"

"Damn it, man! It's no joke! I'm being cornered. Rammed to the wall. Choused from morning to night. I need help!"

Alec rolled a smoke to conceal the thoughts in his eyes. The king was dying; long live the king. Harley Forrest had bulled his way through life, asking no favors, giving none. When King Forrest asked for help, Alec knew his kingdom was tottering to oblivion. "What do you want me to do, Harley?" he asked quietly as he lit up.

"Someone is working tooth and nail against me. I want you to find out who it is."

"So?"

"Consider yourself a stock detective."

"You mean thief killer, don't you?"

Forrest made a sideways gesture with his big right hand. "Call it what you will."

The rain slashed against the boards of the building. The harp lamp flickered in a strong draft that blew through the ill-fitting window frame. Forrest jerked his head towards the bottle and watched Alec fill two glasses. He clutched the glass. "Will you take the job?"

"No."

Forrest played his last card. "Ellen has come home from school, Alec."

Alec raised his head. It had been years since he had seen Ellen Forrest, Harley's granddaughter. She had been eighteen then, pretty as a young colt, with spirit to match. "The bait is no good, Harley," he said softly.

Forrest grunted as he sipped his liquor. The frosty blue eyes peered from beneath the shaggy eyebrows. "Your brother Parker has been sparking Ellen. Doing fine... with her, anyway."

The bolt struck home. Despite Alec's control, his jaw tightened, etching fine lines from the corner of his mouth. Park was his half-brother. They had the same mother, but Parker was the result of Amy MacLean's marriage to Sam Prince, a loose-jointed, big-mouthed cattleman from the Panhandle country. Alec touched the scar at the corner of his left eye. Sam Prince had damned near put the eye out in a drunken frenzy when Alec had been eighteen. Alec had knocked the man out with a billet from the wood box and had left home.

"When's the last time you saw Park?" asked Harley Forrest casually.

"Three years ago, at my mother's funeral."

Forrest nodded. "Sam Prince drifted off. Left the ranch to Parker. Parker sold out to Enos Strang. Got a nice sum for it."

"So? Probably went through it damned fast."

Forrest shook his head. "Parker is a good man with the cards. Gambles a lot in Holbrook. Makes quite a show for Ellen. You wouldn't know him, Alec."

Alec drained his glass. "When do I start?" he asked.

"Right away."

"When do we leave?"

"We? I'm staying here for a time under a doctor's care. You drift up to Clear Creek and ask for a job. Every month I'll have two hundred deposited here in Globe to your account."

Alec stood up. "Who do I look for?"

"You mean rustlers?"

"Yes."

"I don't know. It's a faint trail, Alec. You'll have to work alone."

Alec nodded. He put on his poncho and hat. He poured another drink and helped himself to a cigar from the box on the desk. "I'll leave before dawn," he said. "Who knew I was coming here?"

"Just me."

"I wonder who the little man I cold-decked was," Alec said thoughtfully.

"¿Quién sabe? Maybe just a local thug."

"Maybe." Alec walked to the door.

"One thing!" called out Harley Forrest over a broad shoulder. "Dance Ives and his cousin Pitzer have a spread in Cache Canyon. Thought you'd better know."

Alec looked at the old man. Years ago, he and Dance had fallen out over young Ellen Forrest. Dance and Pitzer had waylaid Alec and Park after a dance. Park had vanished into the night. Alec had badly damaged both opponents, but if Bill Hoskins hadn't interfered with drawn Colt, Alec would have been a cripple for life.

"Thanks," he said dryly. He opened the door and stepped out into the muddy street. He splashed across to the shelter of an awning and looked up and down the street. He could hear the tinny banging of a piano in a nearby saloon. There was no one in sight. He plodded to the livery stable; shoulders hunched against the cold rain.

Alec went into the livery stable and looked in on Spade, his rangy buckskin. The horse nickered as Alec absent-mindedly fed him a lump of sugar. "Long trail tomorrow, Spade," he said quietly. "Mind if I sleep here with you?"

Alec bedded down in the hay at the rear of the stable. He slid a hand inside his shirt and touched the place where his Arizona Ranger commission was sewn into the lining. The words of Captain Burton C. Mossman came back to him. Alec had reported into his chief upon receiving Harley Forrest's letter. "Go on up there and see what the old hellion wants," Mossman had said. "Do as you think best. There's the damnedest rash of rustling up in the Clear Creek country that ever struck Arizona. Six lawmen, including one Ranger, have been knocked off up there in the last six months. If you're crowded, show your commission, play the game below the table. Good luck, Alec."

Alec closed his eyes. The face of Ellen Forrest seemed to come to him so naturally that he opened his eyes to see if she were actually there. He saw nothing but the darkness of the stable. He fell asleep listening to the drumming of the cold rain on the metal roof.

CHAPTER TWO

Two days after Alec's meeting with Harley Forrest in Globe, he drew rein on the rimrock overlooking Clear Creek. To his right, the sharp-edged rimrock was almost a blood red in color. Below him spread the canyon of the Clear, with an irregular green line revealing the course of the shallow, winding creek. The steep slopes on each side of the watercourse were dun-colored, stippled with brush. To the right, as far as he could see, the canyon bent to the northeast to blend at last with the purple hogback of Saddle Mountain.

Spade cropped at the bare grass as Alec hooked a leg about his saddle horn and rolled a smoke. Despite his ticklish mission, it felt good to be home again. He liked the high country much better than the hot desert country close to the border where Captain Mossman had kept him busy. He smoked slowly, eyeing the huge trough before him. His father's old ranch was far to the northeast in the shadow of somber, brooding Saddle Mountain. A thin thread of smoke rose from somewhere far below him. He touched the buckskin into motion and let him pick his way down the rocky slope. Spade whinnied as he picked up the odor of the water.

The creek was shadowed with pines and aspen, throwing long shadows on the brown-tinted waters that purled over the rounded stones of its bed. Alec let the buckskin drink as he gathered squaw wood for a fire. Spade wandered off to graze as Alec smashed his coffee beans with the butt of his six-shooter and filled his coffee pot. He set the spider over the flames and filled it with hog belly. He readied a pot of beans and then relaxed against a fallen pine.

The bacon was sizzling when Alec heard the splashing noise further up the creek. He went to Spade and withdrew his .44-40 Winchester from its sheath, levered home a round, let down the hammer, and leaned the saddle gun against the log. The splashing grew louder, and a lone horseman appeared, riding up the center of the creek. He eyed Alec in surprise and kneed the dun up on the bank.

Alec looked up at the big man. "Howdy," he said easily.

The hard green eyes surveyed the camp area and then settled on Alec. "You alone?" the man asked.

"Looks like it, *amigo*."

The man grunted and slid from his dun. He tugged at the heavy dragoon mustache he affected. "Stranger, hey?"

"Passing through."

"That hog belly smells good."

"Set in. There's Mexican strawberries in the pot."

The big man squatted across the fire from Alec. He wore a stag-butted Colt at his left hip for a cross-arm draw. His eyes shifted to Spade. "Ain't no brand like that hereabouts," he ventured.

"New Mexico brand, friend."

"Oh." The big man scratched under his left armpit. "I'm Bert Jepson," he said. "Work for Dance Ives of the Lazy L."

"Alec MacLean. Saddle Tramp." Alec removed the

spider from the fire and shoved the bean pot into the embers. "Any work hereabouts?"

"Yeah. Some."

"What spread?"

"Best bet is the HF. They're always lookin' for hands."

"Thanks."

"Forget it."

Alec studied the big man as he went to his dun and got a plate and cup from his saddle roll. There was no reason for him to ride up the creek. There was a plainly seen, well-traveled trail winding through the trees. The handle of a running iron showed in the blanket roll as Jepson threw it on the ground.

Alec stirred the beans. "Whose range is this?"

"Part of the HF spread. Owned by Harley Forrest. Old Fire and Brimstone."

Alec nodded. "Thought it was."

"You know this country, then?"

"Used to live here. Over near Saddle Mountain. My father had the Bar M spread."

Jepson looked up slowly from the saddle roll. "You ain't Park Prince's brother, are you?"

"Half-brother."

The hard eyes half-closed. "How come you figure on working for the HF, then?"

"Did I say I was?"

Jepson squatted by the fire with his eating tools. "No. But you sure as hell ain't figurin' on working for Dance Ives, are yuh?"

"No. But what if I was?"

Jepson filled his plate with the hog belly. "I've heard Dance talk about yuh."

"Nothing complimentary, no doubt."

"No doubt," said Jepson dryly.

"Who's ramroddin' the HF spread?"

"Mustang Roberts."

"Don't know him."

"Texas man. Used to work over on the Little Colorado."

"He is looking for men?"

"Yeah. But I don't know whether he'd want Park Prince's brother working for him."

"So? Why?"

Jepson forked a mouthful of bacon and chewed nosily. He wiped the grease from his square chin. "He don't like Park, is all. Matter of fact, I don't know anyone around here who does. 'Cepting Ellen Forrest, Old Fire and Brimstone's granddaughter. She's soft on Park. Nice-looking filly. Slender in the pasterns and smooth in the flank, with no brand on her yet."

Alec ladled beans and bacon onto his plate. "What does Harley Forrest think of the deal?"

Jepson spat. "Ain't no one good enough for a Forrest, to hear him talk. The old man is down to Globe getting checked by a sawbones. The old bastard has the palsy."

They ate silently. Jepson scrubbed his utensils with creek sand and felt for his makings. He rolled a smoke and sat down on a rock, eyeing the Winchester. "You camping here tonight?"

"Figured to."

Jepson lit up, eyeing Alec over the flare of the match. "Be dark in about an hour. Mind if I bunk here? Left my damned grub bag back at the line camp. Been lookin' for strays."

"It's a free country, Jepson."

Jepson snorted. "Used to be."

"What do you mean?"

Jepson sprawled on the ground and folded his big arms across his chest. "Touchy as gunpowder these days. Old Forrest is hanging on to the choice grazing land. Got bob wire around his water holes. *His* water holes! Makes a cowman sick to his stomach."

"No range war going on, I hope. I had enough of that back in New Mexico."

Jepson shook his head. "Just a killing now and then. HF punchers ride their lines with ready rifles. Two of them together. God help a man who ain't got a real reason for being in this area. Like you, MacLean."

Alec grinned. "I've got a clean slate," he said.

Jepson grunted. He looked up the creek. "Yeah. I guess you have."

Hours later Alec awoke and looked across at Jepson. The big man was sound asleep, snoring with the energy of a steam engine. A pale moon hung low in the sky. The wind soughed gently through the pines. Alec lay for a long time looking up at the trees and then went back to sleep.

———

"Hey, you!" The voice crashed through the veil of sleep about Alec. He opened his eyes. The light of dawn filled the sky. Alec looked up into the muzzle of a Winchester. He sat up quickly. A squat man was looking at him. "Don't make any breaks, stranger," he said quietly. "I'd hate to riddle you with your own saddle gun."

Alec raised his hands. Another man was going through his gear. The man turned with a running iron in his big hands. "It's him," he said. The man had a long horsy face; his beak of a nose was bent to one side. He limped a little as he rounded the dead fire. Jepson had vanished. The horse-faced man jerked his head. "Make coffee, Joe," he said. He took the Winchester and eyed Alec. "Get outa them blankets, you goddam sticky looper!" There was an icy coldness in the drawling voice.

Alec threw back the blankets and pulled on his pants. He reached for his boots. "What the hell is this?" he asked.

"Listen to him," said the man named Joe as he prepared the coffee.

The horse-faced man spat. "What are you doin' on HF land?" he asked.

"Camping."

"Yeah. Yeah. But why here?"

Alec pulled on his boots, shivering with the damp cold of the dawn air. A veil of mist had settled over the murmuring creek. Where the hell was Jepson?

The horse-faced man held out the running iron. "This yours?"

"No."

Joe laughed. "Damned fool," he said over his shoulder.

"I'm Mustang Roberts, foreman of the HF spread," said the horse-faced man. "You're in a spot, mister."

"There was another man here," said Alec. "That's his iron."

"So? Who was he?"

"Said he was Bert Jepson of the Lazy L."

"Now, that's right interesting. Ever hear of him, Joe?"

Joe placed squaw wood on the fire and began to shave splinters. "Yeah. Bert quit a month ago. Left for the Blue River country before we could hang him for rustling."

There was an icy fear in Alec as he stood up. Roberts followed him with the muzzle of the Winchester. "Set, stranger," he said. "Name?"

"Alec MacLean."

"Sounds familiar."

Joe looked at Alec. "Where you been lately?"

"New Mexico."

Roberts spat. "Now, do tell! Where'd you get this iron?"

"A stranger camped here with me last night. That's his iron. Said he was Bert Jepson."

Roberts shifted. "Scout about a bit, Joe."

Joe placed the pot near the flames and walked up the creek. He came back in a few minutes. "No other cayuse was around here. No boot tracks excepting this hombre's."

Roberts eyed Alec. "Now what do you have to say?"

Alec shrugged. "He was here, all right. Must have erased his tracks. Big man, with green eyes and a hard face. Riding a dun with white stockings on the front legs."

Roberts leaned the Winchester against the log. Suddenly his right fist shot out. Alec went back over the log and hit hard; his wind knocked out. He tried to get up, but Roberts was over the log. A boot was poised over Alec's face, the cruel spur inches from his nose. "Now talk, damn you!"

Alec lay still. "It isn't my iron," he said. He gripped the ankle of the foreman and rolled sideways, throwing the tall man back over the log. He leaped to his feet and ran for his Winchester, but Joe was too fast. Joe gripped the saddle gun and held it at hip level. "Come on, you damned rustler," he said quietly. "It'd pleasure me to let daylight through you."

Roberts was pale beneath his tan when he got up. He touched the back of his head gingerly. Suddenly he closed in, backhanding Alec across the eyes. A fist slammed into his lean midsection. As he doubled over he was hit hard on the back of the neck. He folded over to meet a knee against his jaw. He fell heavily and a boot smashed his side. "That'll learn you," grated Roberts. "Get a rope, Joe. We'll take him back to the ranch."

The sun was tipping the eastern range when Alec was heaved up into his saddle. His wrists were lashed behind him and a stick was thrust under his arms. Roberts kicked out the fire. He looked up at Alec. "You might not see sundown tonight," he said coldly.

CHAPTER THREE

It was the middle of the morning when the trio of horsemen rode up from the creek bottom towards the ranch houses of the HF spread. It had been a long time since Alec had seen the whitewashed log buildings sprawled on the gentle slope of Juniper Canyon. Beyond the assembly of buildings, the canyon floor sloped up to a dead end more than a mile away. The castellated walls of the canyon were an odd conglomeration of strong hues—deep reds, light blues, medium greens, and browns. A mule bawled from a corral as the horsemen entered the road that led up to the ranch.

Alec eased his taut shoulder muscles. It would be an easy out to show them his Ranger commission, but the game wasn't that far advanced. Besides, there was a stubborn Scottish streak in Alec inherited from his Highland ancestors. Mossman depended on Alec. If the rustlers got wind that a Ranger had been sent into their country, they would be all the more cautious.

Roberts drew rein beside the big bunkhouse and slid from his saddle. Joe Vestal jerked his head at Alec. Alec threw a leg over the saddle and slid clumsily to the ground. Roberts took the Lazy L running iron from his saddle and made as if to slug Alec with it. Alec didn't move. Roberts grinned crookedly. "Hardcase, eh? We'll see how tough you are, *hombre,* when the noose tightens round your neck."

"Is there no law here?" asked Alec quietly.

"Yeah," said Roberts, "HF law. We don't need no star-wearers snooping around the Clear Creek country. We can take care of ourselves."

Two or three punchers eyed Alec as they went about their work. "Maybe we'd better tell Miss Ellen," said Joe Vestal.

"Why?" asked Roberts. "I don't take orders from her."

"Just the same, she won't like it."

Roberts spat. "Before God," he said in disgust, "coupla months ago you woulda backed me to the hilt. Now you're getting like the rest of these moon-faced cowpokes, shining up to her like *she* was the boss."

Joe shrugged. "She will be someday. The old man is failing."

Roberts threw the iron into the air and caught it. "*I'll* tell her, then. If this rustler makes a break you let daylight through him with his own gun."

"Keno," said Joe quietly.

Alec watched the tall foreman walk towards the ranch house. "All rawhide and steel, isn't he, Joe?"

Joe looked quickly at Alec. "Mustang? Yeah, I guess so."

"Popular with the boys, too, I'll bet."

"Him? Not so's you'd notice it."

"How does he get along with Old Man Forrest?"

"Well, enough. Old Fire and Brimstone likes 'em tough."

"Park Prince around here much?"

Joe lit a smoke and eyed Alec as he puffed at it. "Yeah. How'd you know?"

"He's my half-brother."

"You're joshin'!"

"No," Alec said. "We were kids on the Bar M. Sam

Prince was my stepfather. I left the ranch ten years ago and worked for Billy Hoskins for a while."

"Ellen won't like this."

"Neither will Old Man Forrest. Cut me loose, Joe."

Joe looked nervously at the house. "Maybe I'd better wait until Mustang gets back."

Alec looked the squat man in the eye. "Cut me loose."

Joe shrugged. He took out his case knife and cut the bonds. "I'm getting out of here," he said. "Mustang won't like this."

"I don't aim to make him change his mind. Put my Winchester in its scabbard."

"Sure. Sure. Say a good word for me to Miss Ellen."

"Yeah. Beat it now."

Joe led his horse to the corral and unsaddled it. He watched Alec between the bars of the peeled-pole corral. Alec kept the stick between his arms and leaned back against the side of the bunkhouse. Mustang came out of the house and walked easily over to Alec. "Come on, you," he said with a lopsided grin. "Miss Ellen says she'll see you."

"Cut me loose, Roberts."

"In a pig's eye."

Alec turned sideways, dropped his arms, and swung from the hip. His right fist caught the horse-faced man flush on the button. Roberts went down with a gasp. He came back on his feet and threw a looping right. Alec went under it and threw a left cross that connected solidly, sending Roberts down again. Roberts cursed and reached for his Colt. Alec kneed his jaw, tramped hard on the gun wrist with his left boot, and kicked the six-gun away as Roberts released it. Then he gripped the cursing foreman by the shirt front and pulled him to his feet. Someone came up behind him as he let go of the foreman and hooked home a right. Roberts went down hard, grunting for breath.

The foreman was dead game. He staggered to his

feet. Alec hit him in the gut. As he folded over he clipped him behind the ear with his right hand and rammed a knee under Roberts' face just as Mustang had done to him that morning in the creek bottom. Roberts went down, rolled over, and lay still. Blood flowed from his smashed nose.

"Stand where you are!" It was a woman's voice from behind Alec; a voice he hadn't heard for three years. He turned to look at Ellen Forrest.

She stood with hands planted on her slim hips. Anger blazed from her blue eyes, so like her father's. Her honey-colored hair held glints of sunlight in it.

"Hello, Ellen," said Alec. He slowly rubbed the knuckles of his right hand against his soiled shirt.

"Alec MacLean! What kind of show is this?"

Alec grinned. "Mustang gave me a lacing down in the creek bottom this morning. I just paid him back."

She had changed in three years, a magnificent change. The slim body had filled out in the proper places. The checked shirt rose over firm breasts. The young girl look had given way to that of a young woman in the greatest of all metamorphoses.

"Mustang said you had a Lazy L running-iron," she accused him.

Alec waved a hand. "I tried to tell him a man named Bert Jepson left it in my camp. He was so all-fixed anxious to catch a rustler he didn't believe me."

Mustang groaned. He opened his eyes and tenderly touched his nose. He stared stupidly at Alec and then jumped to his feet, reaching down to his empty holster. He cursed and turned to pick up the six-shooter. Alec let him reach it and then he jerked his .44-40 from its saddle scabbard, levering home a round by swinging the heavy gun up and down. "Go ahead," he said softly. "Blast off."

Roberts looked mad enough to do just what Alec said, but Ellen stepped between them. "Get cleaned up, Mustang," she ordered.

For a long moment, Mustang eyed Alec and then he sheathed his Colt and limped into the bunkhouse. Alec let down the hammer of his Winchester.

"Well," she said quietly. "This is some welcome-home committee you arranged for yourself."

Alec smiled. "Mustang arranged it."

"You were trespassing on HF land."

"Trespassing? I was passing through. Camped at that very spot many a time while hunting."

"Times have changed."

"So, I see," he said dryly.

"Why did you come back, Alec?"

"Looking for thirty a month and found."

"You didn't expect to find it here."

"Park sold the Bar M. I need a job."

She flushed. "Sam Prince left it to Parker."

"Nice of him, figuring it was my mother's property."

"You left home."

"Sam made it easy for me to do that."

"You've changed, Alec."

"Everything has changed, hasn't it? You. The HE. The whole country."

She brushed back a stray wisp of hair. "Come on up to the house. I want to talk with you. Do you still want a job?"

"I calculated on getting one here. That's out now."

"I can hire you, Alec."

He grinned. "After beating up the ramrod. No. I'll make out."

"Mustang is loyal to Dad. He tries hard."

"He'll get killed trying one of these days."

She shrugged. "You always were stubborn."

"And you never were?"

She turned on a heel. "Parker lives in town. Maybe he can talk some sense into you."

"Yeah," said Alec thoughtfully. "Maybe he can." He

watched her stride towards the house. She was a thoroughbred.

Alec sauntered over to the bunkhouse and walked in. Roberts was bathing his face. A skinny, long-legged puncher was standing anxiously beside the battered foreman. "He's here again, Mustang," he said.

Roberts turned. "What the hell do you want?" he barked.

"My six-gun."

For a moment, the foreman looked as though he were going to rash Alec. "It's in my saddlebag," he said. "When you get it, MacLean, head west, through the gate, and don't come back!"

Alec turned wordlessly and walked to the foreman's horse. He took his Colt from the saddlebag and slid it into his holster. A man was leaning against the fence behind the bunkhouse. As Alec slid his Winchester into its scabbard, the man moved quickly. Alec whirled and rested his hand on the butt of his Colt. The man stepped back in alarm. "Don't you draw on me," he said quickly. The dark eyes flicked from the Colt up to Alec's face.

Alec swung up on Spade and kneed him away from the fence. Two other men were watching him from the corral. One of them was Joe Vestal. Ellen Forrest was standing on the porch of the ranch house, looking down the slope at Alec. Alec shrugged and touched Spade with his spurs. He rode slowly to the valley road. To hell with Forrest and his two hundred a month. Alec had a job to do for the Arizona Rangers.

———

TONTO WELLS WAS at the junction of the valley road and the road that went through the pass to Holbrook. False-fronted buildings were mingled with the older stone buildings, thick-walled and loopholed, that had been built at the wells shortly after the close of the war. The east fork of the Clear meandered through a twisted valley. Alec rode over the plank bridge that spanned the chuckling stream and drew rein in front of the Juniper Saloon. Tonto Wells had grown somewhat in the years he had been away. There was a two-story hotel at the corner of Pine and Second, where the old Vegas corral had been. John Springer's General Emporium was housed in a new rambling building. Further up the street, the morning sun gleamed on the Congregational Church steeple. The old church had collapsed years before with the heavy weight of winter snow on its roof.

Alec tethered Spade and stepped up on the porch of the saloon, pausing to look up and down the muddy street. He pushed through the batwings and walked to the end of the bar. The bartender waddled down to him. "Your pleasure," he said.

"Hello, Baldy," said Alec.

Baldy Roscommon stared at Alec. "For God's sake," he said, "Alec MacLean!" He thrust out a fat moist hand. "Ain't seen you for a long spell, Alec."

"Been working in New Mexico, Baldy."

"That so? Well. Well."

"Rye," said Alec. He glanced at the thin man reading a newspaper at the end of the bar. A short puncher was asleep on a bench at the rear of the saloon.

Baldy slid a bottle and a glass in front of Alec. "You just visitin,' Alec?" he asked.

"Looking for work, Baldy."

"There's work, Alec. The HF is always lookin' for hands. Not that you'd work there, of course."

"I'm not particular anymore, Baldy."

"Down on your luck, son?"

Alec shook his head. "I've got some *dinero*. Seems as though I hit a bad streak in a faro game in Nogales and lost some of my stake. I've got enough to pay for beans and coffee for a spell."

Baldy leaned forward. "You need money, Alec, you

just ask old Baldy. You always was a good customer in the old days. I don't forget them things, Alec."

Alec raised his glass in salute and downed the liquor. "How's ranching these days?"

Baldy shook his head. "A mess. Rustlers, thicker than fleas on a hound dog. Itchy trigger fingers. There's been some shootings."

"Who's behind the rustling?"

Baldy glanced over his shoulder. "Some say it's Mexicans from around the Blue River country. Others say it's them Mormons from up around the Little Colorado. Now, I don't put no stock in that."

"So? You think it may be local men?"

"Me? I didn't say that," said Baldy hastily. He leaned forward again. "Be careful, Alec. Tonto Wells ain't like it used to be on Saturdays when the ranchers come in for supplies. In the old days, the boys would talk about cattle and grazing and suchlike, drink their liquor, get in a friendly fight or two, and then go home. Nowadays... Well, as I said, there's itchy trigger fingers now."

Alec refilled his glass. "Park in town?"

Baldy eyed Alec for a moment. "Yeah. He's in town."

"Where?"

"He don't come in here no more. Spends most of his time at the Tonto. Lives at the Bell House. That's the new hotel, corner of Second, where Bartolome Vegas used to have his corral."

Alec downed his drink and rolled a smoke. "Well, I'll see you, Baldy."

Baldy placed both hands flat on the bar. "Dance and Pitzer Ives still come in here, Alec. Thought you'd like to know."

"Thanks." Alec lit up and left the bar. He led Spade down the street to the Tonto and tethered him. He walked into the big saloon. Five men were in the place; two of them were playing cards at the back, two of them were at the bar, and the fifth man was seated at a rear table reading a newspaper. There was something familiar about him. Alec walked slowly back to the table, his spurs jingling musically. He stopped behind the huge white sombrero. "Hello, Park," he said quietly.

The man turned quickly, folding down the newspaper. He stared at Alec. "Alec! What are you doing here?"

"Came back for some money, Park." Alec straddled a chair and eyed his half-brother. Park had the dark hair of the Princes and the grey eyes of the MacLeans. There was a spoiled handsomeness about him. He was good-looking except for his mouth, which was almost petulant. He was twenty-four, four years younger than Alec. Alec eyed the fine broadcloth suit and the expensive sombrero. A gold chain, thick and long, crossed the front of the vest. A lodge emblem dangled from it. "You look like you're doing well, Park," observed Alec.

"I get by," said Park hastily. "Last I heard of you, you were working down in Sonora."

"I got tired of the desert."

Park signaled to the bartender. The man brought over a bottle and two glasses. Park filled them, studying Alec over the bottle. "I sold the ranch," he said. "To Enos Strang."

"How much did you get?"

"Not much."

"How much did you get?"

Park flushed. "Don't talk to me like that, Alec. I've got influence here in town. Yes, and in Holbrook, too."

"So? Where's my split, Park?"

Park downed his drink. "Pa left the place to me. We didn't know where the hell you were. You never wrote."

Alec laughed. "I should write to you two! Your old man damned near knocked my eye out ten years ago."

Park wiped his mouth and twitched his mustache. "Anyway, Ma left the ranch to Pa. Pa left it to me."

Alec yawned. "The prodigal returns for his portion. How much did you get?"

"Five thousand, no more."

Alec rested his chin on his folded arms and didn't take his eyes from his brother. "You always were a damned liar. That's why Sam hit me alongside the eye with that poker ten years ago. Because of what *you* did and didn't have the guts to tell him. You took that money out of the strongbox and spent it right here in Tonto Wells. He accused me, and you didn't tell the truth. Now... how much did you actually get?"

Park shoved the bottle towards Alec. "Fill up again," he invited. He leaned forward and spoke in a low voice. "Now listen, Alec. I've got some good prospects. I need money to keep up my end. If this thing pans out, I'll give you your split from the Bar M."

"Prospects? You mean Ellen Forrest, don't you?"

"How the hell did you know that?"

"I was up there this morning."

Park's mouth drew down. "She isn't interested in you anymore, Alec."

"I didn't say she was. What does Old Fire and Brimstone think of you and his granddaughter going together?"

"He's a shell of what he was. Full of palsy. Always doctoring. The HF spread needs a good business head to handle it. A strong hand."

"Like you?"

"Well, I do know my business, Alec. I haven't drifted off like you. I've got standing in this community!"

"My God," said Alec. He filled his glass. "Maybe you think you can stop all this rustling that's going on."

"So, you've heard about that, too."

Alec glanced up at Park. "It's all over Arizona."

Parker took a silver cigar case from an inner pocket and offered a cigar to Alec. Alec accepted one and lit up after biting off the end. Parker used a silver cigar clipper that was attached to the end of his gold chain. He puffed deeply. "I get them sent here from the East," he said with satisfaction. "Can't stand the ropes around here."

"What happened to Sam, Park?"

"My father?"

"Your father."

Park shrugged. "He left the ranch to me and went east. Last I heard of him, he'd died of pneumonia in Abilene."

Alec nodded. "Sam never did like ranching, did he? The money came too hard."

"I'm like him in that respect, Alec."

"I guess you are."

Parker glanced about the saloon and raised his voice. "Certainly, glad to see you again, Alec. I'll see what I can do to help you out. Maybe I can help you find a job in Holbrook."

Alec couldn't help grinning. It was just like Parker to make a big display of his generosity. "No," Alec said, "I'm figuring on staying right here in this area."

"Not many jobs open in Tonto Wells."

"I'm planning to work for one of the ranchers. I might even start a little spread of my own with the money you owe me."

Parker bit down savagely on his expensive cigar. "Keep your mouth shut about that," he grated. "I'll take care of you when the time comes."

Alec stood up. "I'll be around," he said.

Parker reached for his wallet. "I can let you have fifty on account," he said.

Alec shook his head. "I'll get by. See you later, Park."

Alec left the saloon and took the cigar from his mouth. He dropped it in the street and ground it out with his heel. Park hadn't changed much, despite his fine clothes and airs. He was still the grasping, conniving character he had always been. Alec wondered what Ellen Forrest saw in him. He looked down at his dusty trail clothes and rubbed the thick growth of his chin. "Maybe I ought to spruce up a bit myself," he said aloud.

A man stopped behind Alec. "You're Alec MacLean, aren't you?" he asked.

Alec turned to see a thin lath of a man, wearing shabby clothing that hung loosely from his gaunt frame. Deep-shadowed eyes studied Alec. "Yes," said Alec.

The man thrust out a thin hand. "Enos Strang. I bought the Bar M from your brother, MacLean."

"Glad to meet you, Strang. How does it go?"

Strang's Adam's apple traveled slowly up and down his corded neck. "Well, enough. Except for rustling. Hard to get hands these days. Too much shooting going on."

An idea came to Alec. "I'm looking for work, Enos."

The dark eyes lit up. "Say, I'd be glad to take you on, MacLean."

"I'd just as soon work on the old place as any."

Strang hesitated. "Howsomever, I don't pay as well as some of the other ranchers. Set a good table, though. My daughter Sophie cooks. Nice girl, Sophie. You'll like her, Alec. Nothing fancy, but she's wholesome. My boy Ike and I been running the place. Work is damned hard. Want to come out now?"

"Might as well." They walked to the end of the porch and Alec led Spade to Strang's buckboard, hitching the buckskin to the tailgate. Strang unwound the reins from the brake handle. "How does it feel to be home?"

"Good enough," said Alec as he fashioned a smoke. "I've learned plenty in my short time in Clear Creek country."

"What do you mean?"

"Nothing, Enos. Nothing at all."

Strang touched up the team of mules and they rode slowly out of town. Alec could have sworn he saw Parker Prince watching them over the top of the Tonto's batwings.

CHAPTER FOUR

The Bar M hadn't changed much in the three years since Alec had been there. The heavy log ranch house still stood in a niche below a spur of Saddle Mountain. The afternoon sun glinted on the dammed pool fed by an underground spring. Further up the canyon, the cattle dotted the grazing land that had been an asset of the Bar M. But a small cemetery beyond the ranch buildings took Alec's eye. He dropped from the buckboard. "I'll walk up to the cemetery, Enos," he said.

"Sure. Sure. We'll eat after the chores." Enos took a sack of supplies from the buckboard and watched Alec walk up the slope. He shook his head.

A young woman came out on the porch and shaded her eyes, watching Alec. "Who is it, Pa?" she called.

"Alec MacLean. Come back to Clear Creek."

"So? What's he doing here, Pa?"

"Going up to see his parents' graves, is all, Soph. Make a good meal. Alec is working for me now. You know what to do, girl."

She hurried into the house with a pleased look on her broad face. Before she started work in the kitchen she changed into a fresh gingham dress and tied a new apron about her thick waist, humming happily to herself.

Alec pushed open the sagging cemetery gate and stopped beside the two graves at the highest point of the graveyard. His father's grave was closest to the fence. Jim MacLean had been lost in a snowstorm when Alec had been just two years old. He had died three months later, still ailing. Amy MacLean had struggled for a short time, trying to keep up the ranch, and then had married Sam Prince, the big-mouthed drifter from the Panhandle country. Alec could not remember a time when Sam had been nice to Amy MacLean. Still, he had worked hard on the Bar M, keeping it up. Alec had started work early, much earlier than Parker had. Parker had been sickly as a small boy, and Amy, despite her growing dislike of Sam Prince, had always favored the youngest boy.

Alec placed a gaily striated stone on each of the graves and then left the small burial ground. There were four other graves off to one side. Three of them he knew. A drifter by the name of Mogollon, who had died of a rattlesnake bite. Benny Small, the old colored cook, who had died of a heart attack in the big ranch kitchen. George Eagle, a half-breed Navajo who had died of a fall from a half-broken mustang. The fourth grave was new. Alec looked over the fence. "August Freiser," he read aloud. "Born 1850. Died August 17, 1887. Killed by rustlers. Rest in Peace."

Alec walked to the back door of the ranch house. He tapped at the door.

"Do come in, Mr. MacLean," a young woman called out.

Alec took off his hat and entered the kitchen. Sophie Strang could be described only as dumpy. Everything about her was broad and solid, with the exception of her eyes and mouth. The eyes were small, and the mouth was tiny and pursed. "I'm Sophie Strang, Mr. MacLean," she simpered.

"You can call me Alec," he said.

"And I'm Sophie to you, Alec."

Alec looked about the familiar room. The big stove was the same, polished bright. The old waggle-tail clock still worked furiously. The table was set for four. The red-and-white checked tablecloth matched the pinned-back window curtains. His mother's small work table was close by the stove. Alec had patiently pegged it together himself when he was only twelve.

"Steak and hash browns," said Sophie, wiping her flushed face. "You like apple or peach pie?"

"Apple," said Alec absent-mindedly.

"Pa is in the living room."

Alec walked into the big living room. It was almost the same. His father's old Sharps hung over the fireplace. The Rogers group, "Wounded to the Rear," still sat on the small marble-topped table that had been his mother's pride. The chairs Jim MacLean had made of wood and cowhide still sat in the corners.

Enos Strang took his pipe from his mouth. "Set until supper, Alec," he said. "My boy Ike will soon be in. We always eat together, family and hands. I ain't one to put on airs."

Alec wandered about the big room, placing a hand on the slant-breeched Sharps. The Strangs were strangers in his father's house, although they had more right to be there than he did. There was no use in thinking about the Bar M except as a temporary place to work while he finished his job for the Rangers.

"Ready in a minute!" called Sophie from the kitchen.

"I'll go wash up," said Alec. He left by the front door, having no desire to run the gauntlet of Sophie's eyes.

A lanky young man was already washing up when Alec rounded the back of the house. He stared at Alec curiously, his wide mouth hanging open, showing uneven teeth with gaps between them. The colorless eyes surveyed Alec from top to bottom.

"Howdy," said Alec. "I'm Alec MacLean, working here at the Bar M now."

"Ike Strang." The lanky young man thrust out a damp hand.

Alec stripped off his shirt and began to wash. "How's business?" he asked over his shoulder.

"Pa don't like to talk about it."

"Why?"

"We ain't doing so well, that's why."

"Beef prices are good. You've got good grazing land and plenty of water."

"We *had* plenty of water."

"Run dry?"

Ike scratched under his arm. "No. The south water hole ain't ours no more."

Alec dried himself. "Since when? Didn't you buy it with the ranch?"

"We thought so. We found out different. Park says he didn't know it at the time, but the water hole was over the property line on the Lazy L."

"That's a damned lie! That water hole was always on Bar M land. Dad started the Bar M here because of that water hole."

"Yeah," said Ike gloomily. "That's what *we* thought. Anyways, we got to water the steers either here or down to the creek. It ain't no fun, short-handed as we are. Watching for them sticky loopers."

"It's bad, eh?"

Ike nodded. "Bad enough for Pa to want to pull out."

"How many hands do you have?"

"Just Emmett Adams. He's out at a line shack watching the rest of the cows we got. About sixty head."

Ike wandered sadly into the house. Alec watched the shadows creeping down behind the ranch. It was an idea, buying back the Bar M, but he'd have to get some money out of Park. A Ranger's pay of $120 a month didn't allow much saving. Still, he might make a deal with Enos. It was worth a try.

The meal was hell for Alec. Enos talked about

Sophie's virtues. Ike gloomily masticated his food as though eating loco weed. Sophie pressed titbits on Alec, and more than once she pushed her solid hips up against him as she waited on him.

Enos shoved back his plate and filled his pipe. "We'll have our coffee in the living room," he said.

Alec rolled a smoke, eyeing the taciturn ranch owner. Enos did everything with deliberation.

"What do you think of the place, Alec?"

"Looks in good shape."

"Ummm... I ain't running many head. Little over a hundred."

"You could easily handle five hundred."

Strang looked up. "I had three hundred last year."

"So?"

"Had more than a hundred run off. They killed one of my hands in the fight, and a slug through my leg. I'm always feelin' poorly because of it."

"Was Freiser the hand who was killed?"

"Yeah. Gus was a good hand. Three rustlers was cutting out part of the herd when me and Gus surprised them. Gus got killed right away, shot through the head. They dropped me next. Run off the cows."

"You identify any of them?"

"No," said Enos slowly. For a moment he looked as though he were going to elaborate and then he shook his head.

"You interested in selling the place?"

Enos jerked up his head. "Yes! You interested?"

"I could be."

"You got enough money?"

"What's the price?"

"I'll take eight thousand, which is a hell of a lot less than I paid for it."

"So?" Alec thought of his half-brother. Five thousand, he had said.

Enos eyed Alec. "How about it? You can pay me half

now and we can draw up papers. I'll go easy on you. Frankly, Alec, I want to go into some town and open a store. I'm willing to make good terms."

Alec puffed at his cigarette. "I may have some money coming, but I can't bank on it."

Enos felt his Adam's apple. He glanced at the kitchen. Alec was sure Sophie was listening behind the door. "Now, if you was to take an interest in Soph," said Enos, "I'd take you in as partner for about four thousand. Let you run the place. Maybe you could buy me out later, providing you was to take an interest in my daughter there."

"She's a fine young woman," said Alec uncomfortably.

"She ain't no fancy lady like some I could mention around here. Sensible and practical, like her dear mother."

"I'll bet," said Alec.

Strang looked quickly at Alec. "How about it?"

Alec stood up. "I'll think it over."

"Sure. Sure. I wouldn't want you to think I was selling my own daughter, Alec. You let me know tomorrow."

Alec walked out to the porch. The sun had died behind the western ranges. A cool wind blew up the canyon. Alec glanced back through a front window. Sophie was talking excitedly to her father. Alec walked to the bunkhouse. Ike was in the building, filling up his water bag.

"Where are you going, Ike?" asked Alec.

"Down to relieve Emmett. Emmett got a bad tooth. Has to go into town to get it yanked. I don't like going out to the creek. Too dangerous."

"How so?"

"Emmett got fired at twice last week. I don't think they was trying to get him. Just scare him."

Alec glanced at the house. He didn't want to be around the buxom Sophie and her anxious father too much. "I'll go," he said.

"Will you? By George, that's right nice of yuh. I'll tell Pa."

"Wait until I'm gone, Ike."

Alec led Spade out to the road and swung up, heading west along the dim trail that led to the creek. A coyote gave voice as he crested a rise and guided the buckskin down the far slope. Curiously enough, he felt as though he had never left the Bar M. He had made a mess out of getting the job at the HF, but he had never been keen on the idea. If he could get the Bar M back, he could help break up the rustlers in the Clear Creek country and become a rancher, which always had been his ambition. He began to whistle as the buckskin passed Lone Rock. It was good to be home.

CHAPTER FIVE

Alec drew rein on a rise overlooking the creek bottom. Steers dotted the grassy meadows between him and the rushing creek. Yellow lamplight showed from the line shack placed in a motte on a slight knoll backed up against a thicket. Alec rode down the rise. "Hello, the shack!" he called out.

The lamplight was gone almost instantly. A window banged up. "Stay where you are!" a muffled voice called. "I got a nervous trigger finger, stranger!"

"I'm Alec MacLean, Adams. Ike Strang sent me down to relieve you."

"Get off that hoss and come up here with your hands in the air! Grab your ears!"

Alec grinned. He slid from Spade and rested his hands atop his head and walked up to the line shack. "How's the tooth, Emmett?" asked Alec.

"Plumb hell!"

"Can I put my hands down now?"

"Just a minute." Feet grated on a wooden floor and the door eased open. A man came out of the building holding an old Henry rifle. "You come from the ranch?"

"Yeah."

"Sophie there?"

"Cooked supper less than an hour ago."

"What'd you have?"

"Steak and hash browns. Choice of apple or peach pie. Coffee and cookies."

"Yeah. That's all she knows how to cook. I guess you're all right. Come on in." The lamp went on again.

Alec saw a short man with his narrow face bound up with a bright bandanna. "God-damned tooth is killin' me," said Adams sourly. "I thought you was a rustler. Can't be too careful around here."

Alec rolled a smoke. "You'd better pull out," he said. "Maybe the dentist can take care of you tonight."

"Dentist, hell! Joe Schmidt, the blacksmith, can take care of me. Sets a cold chisel against the root, taps it with a hammer. Bingo! The fang is out. Just like that!"

Alec grinned as he watched the puncher gather his gear. "Any instructions?"

"Fence near the south water hole is busted. Damned if I know how it happened. I fixed it two days ago. Them Ives boys won't like it."

"Do tell."

Emmett looked up quickly. "Don't get funny with them boys, MacLean. They're mean as hell." He picked up his saddle and took it out to the shed, saddling his bay mare. Alec took his gear out to him. The short puncher reached down and gripped Alec's shoulder. "Don't pass in front of that window if you got the light on. Somebody's been shooting through the walls now and then. Never hurt nothing, but it's damned uncomfortable."

Alec nodded. He watched Adams ride up the rise and vanish. Alec took his blankets and made a bed in the thicket to one side where he could watch the front of the shack. He picketed Spade near the creek and took his rifle to the bed. He dropped on his blankets after levering home a round and half-cocking the hammer. He lay still, listening to the frogs at their nightly serenade. It would get colder before morning...

It was close to ten o'clock by Alec's watch when he heard the soft thud of hoofs. The lamp had died out an hour before. The moonlight silvered the weathered wood of the line shack. Alec lay low, sliding his Winchester forward.

Two horsemen appeared as if by magic on the rise and looked at the shack. Alec cocked the saddle gun. One of the horsemen raised a rifle. Alec let out half of his breath and cuddled his cheek next to the stock. The sights swam about and then settled on the barrel of the other rifle, the moon shining dully from the metal. Alec heard the horseman work the lever of his rifle. The rifle steadied. Alec squeezed off. The Winchester spat flame, the butt driving back into his shoulder. The big .44-40 slug sang off the other rifle, and there was a startled yell. The man dropped his rifle and shook his stinging hands. Then they were gone, setting the steel to their mounts.

Alec rolled down the slope and reloaded, listening to the echo of the Winchester die away up the canyon. There was the smell of bitter powder in the night air. Alec stood up and listened to the beat of the hoofs dying away on the creek trail. He padded forward and picked up the fallen rifle. It was a light Winchester. In the wood of the stock, the initials R. R. were deeply carved. Alec went back to his blankets and took his bed up along the creek to a deep thicket. He made his bed and crawled in. He didn't think he'd have any more visitors that night.

———

ALEC AWOKE BEFORE DAWN. There was a chill in the air. Tendrils of mist wove through the trees. Alec gathered his bedding and took it back to the line shack after hiding the light Winchester in the brush. He placed his own Winchester near the door and started a fire in the pot-bellied stove. The warmth felt good. He made bacon for breakfast and a pot of strong coffee, ate well, and then sat on the step of the shack for a quiet pipe. The sun was shining over the eastern range when he heard hoofbeats on the trail. "More visitors," he said aloud wryly.

Ike Strang guided his claybank towards the cabin. "Mornin,' Alec," he said sourly.

"What's up, Ike?"

"Dad wants you back at the ranch. He gave me holy hell, I tell you, for letting me send you out here."

"Why?"

Ike rubbed his lean jaw. "Sophie's been working on him. She has a hankering for you, Alec."

"So? She's a nice girl."

"Oh? Well, in a way."

"What do you mean?"

Ike flushed. "Pa's been trying to marry her off for the last two months. He's in a hurry."

"She's young enough to find a man."

Ike grinned. "Yeah. She found one. That's the trouble."

Alec relit his pipe and looked at the gangling young man. "What do you mean, Ike?"

Ike yawned. "Soph was out in the bushes with some hombre at the square dance down to Tonto Wells coupla months ago. Pa surprised them. The fella got away. Only Pa and Sophie are supposed to know she's in a family way."

"I'll be damned!"

"Yeah. That's why Pa's so all-fired anxious to marry her off. Soph don't hurry up and get her man, she'll start a scandal going."

"Maybe Pa ought to look for the man she was with."

Ike spat. "That's it. Soph said there was more than one of 'em."

"The same night?"

Ike flushed. "Yeah. And other nights, too. Makes a man sick to the stomach. His sister rolling around in the grass with anything wearing pants. I got a good mind to pull out. Always had a hankering to see California."

Alec puffed at his pipe. "Had two visitors last night, Ike. One of them was aiming at the shack when I shot his rifle out of his hands. Skirted out of here like flushed quail."

"Well, I'll be damned. Didn't I tell you?"

"Know anyone around here by the initials R. R.?"

"Can't think of anyone offhand."

"His rifle is over there in the brush. Initials carved in the stock. Why would they shoot at the line shack, Ike?"

"They got Pa scared to death. He wants to pull out. Whoever it is, keeps riding us, cutting fence, shooting near us, stealing cows, scaring off our help."

"Who do you think it is?"

Ike picked at his loose lower lip. "Could be the Ives boys. They always liked this spread. Could be some of the boys from the HF. They still want the whole damned valley. Old Fire and Brimstone does, that is. There might be others."

"Who?"

Ike looked strangely at Alec. "Your brother. I think he was always sorry he sold the ranch. I think he wants to get it back. He's got a reason."

"So?"

"He's been sparking Ellen Forrest. Wouldn't the Bar M make a nice wedding present to add to the HF?"

Alec nodded. Suddenly he stood up. "Someone coming," he said quietly.

Ike paled. "I'll go," he said.

"No. Stay here. I'll wait in the shack." Alec closed the door behind him and drew the drab curtains close together. Two men were riding rapidly towards the shack. Alec recognized Dance and Pitzer Ives. Dance was in the lead. He hadn't changed much, he was lean and handsome in a black sombrero, shirt, and trousers, fancy-stitched black-and-white boots, with two ivory-handled Colts attached to a wide *Buscadero* belt.

Pitzer Ives plainly showed his stupidity on his broad face. His thick muscles bulged against his huck shirt. He was a good running mate for Dance, for he did his younger cousin's bidding like a trained bear.

Dance drew in his white horse and leaned forward on his saddle horn. "You, Strang!" he called coldly.

Ike struggled clumsily to his feet. "Yes?"

"The fence near the south water hole is broken again. You been watering your cows there?"

"I got the whole damned creek to water cows in, Ives."

Dance spat. "Get down there and fix that fence or Pitzer will give you another thrashing like he gave you last month."

Ike flushed. He touched his jaw as though at the memory of Pitzer's rock-like fists. "Emmett fixed the fence coupla days ago."

"It's broken again."

"I'll fix it later."

"You'll fix it now!"

Ike thrust out his chin. "Damn you! I'll do it on my own time!"

Alec peered through the curtains at the gangling Ike. There *was* some spirit in him, after all. It took guts to face up to those two.

Dance spoke over his shoulder. "All right, Pitz." There was an expectant grin on his face as his big relative slid heavily to the ground and rolled up his sleeves, exposing his red undershirt. He spat on his hamlike hands and took two steps towards Ike. Ike glanced back at the shack.

Alec kicked open the door and stepped out beside the scared kid. "Hello, Dance," he said. "I see you have your trained bear with you."

Dance jerked his head. "MacLean! What the hell are you doing here?"

"Working for Enos Strang. Now, what's this about a beating?"

Pitzer growled deep in his thick throat. "I'll take 'em both, Dance. Just you watch."

Alec crouched a little. He swung back his right hand and brought it up and forward. When it came to hip level there was a cocked Colt in it, centered on Pitzer's thick middle. "Get back, Pitz," he said. "Dance is going to do the dirty work this time."

Dance stared. "Put up that shooter," he said uneasily. "You've got no right to draw on us."

Alec grinned. "Get off that cayuse, Ives. Unbuckle that gun belt, and you drop yours, Ike. Do you think you can take that fancy Dan?"

Ike slowly unbuckled his gun belt and dropped it. "I don't know," he said, "but I'd like to try."

Pitzer came forward, and Alec moved the Colt a little. "Where do you want it, Pitz? Belly or head?"

Pitz backed off. Dance dismounted and dropped his gun belt, facing the gangling Ike. Ike looked at Alec. "Now?" he asked.

"Now," said Alec.

Ike rushed in with flailing arms. Dance retreated, covered up, threw a short right that connected neatly, and dropped the clumsy kid. Ike got up, wiped the blood from his mouth, and went after Dance with a rush. Dance hit him three times. Ike bounced from the wall of the shack and went down.

Alec jerked his head. "He's yellow, Ike," he said. "All show and no bottom. Go after him."

Ike got up and thrust out his long arms awkwardly, circling the white-faced Ives. Dance measured Ike with a left and threw a looping right. To Ike's surprise, the blow swung over his head and his own awkward left smacked fair against Dance's jaw. Dance cursed and went back. Ike, flushed with success, rushed in to meet a stinging left that drove him back. Dance closed in, throwing a right hook that threw Ike against Alec. Alec shoved him back. Ike ran into a right jab that started a rush of blood from his nose. Ike shook his head. "I'm licked, Alec," he pleaded.

"Go after him."

"Kill him, Dance!" yelled Pitzer, eyeing Alec's Colt.

Dance shuffled forward, watching Ike like a hawk. He drove in vicious lefts and rights that shook Ike's head. Ike went down hard. Dance cursed, stepped in close, and booted Ike alongside the head. It happened too quickly for Alec to interfere. Ike groaned and covered his face with his arms. Dance was breathing harshly now, looking from Alec to Ike and back again. "Had enough?" he grated.

Ike lowered his arms and looked up at the dandy. "No," he said quietly, in a voice strange to him, "I ain't." Ike bounced to his feet and rushed Dance. His awkward blows were mostly misses, but those that landed hurt Dance. Dance retreated, driving in counterblows, but the balance of the scales had tipped. Ike seemed to feel nothing; his wild rage overcame his pain. His left caught Dance over the right eye. His right sank deep into Dance's lean gut. When Dance bent forward, Ike drove up a whistling upper-cut that connected with Dance's chin, skidded over his mouth, and ended up crashing under the nose. Dance folded up like a bag of rags and lay still.

Ike stepped back, breathing hard. He looked at Pitzer. "You want some?" he asked in a high cracked voice.

Alec laughed. "You've done enough damage to the Ives tribe. Get him out of here, Pitzer. Pronto!"

Pitzer shambled over to his damaged cousin and hoisted him over his saddle. He looked at Alec. "I'll get you, MacLean. I'll cripple you like I woulda done long ago if it hadn't been for Bill Hoskins. I won't forget this." He led both horses up the rise. Blood flowed from Dance's battered face and made bright droplets on the grass.

Ike looked at his skinned knuckles. "Never thought I could do it, Alec."

"Dance is yellow, kid."

"Yeah," said Ike soberly, "but what about Pitzer? He'll kill me!"

"You've got a gun. Besides, you wanted to see California. This is your chance if you don't want to face Pitzer."

Ike tenderly touched his battered face, "Yeah. So, it is. But I can't leave Pa."

Alec holstered his Colt. "Send Emmett down here when he gets back. Tell your father I'll make a deal with him. I'll get the money. You can pull out of here in a day or so."

Ike stood up. "What about Sophie?"

"Yeah, Ike. What about her?"

Ike shrugged. "Maybe she can find herself a man in California."

"I'm sure she can, Ike," said Alec dryly. He watched the kid swing up on his horse and spur it towards the trail. There would be no stopping Ike now.

It was late afternoon when Joe Vestal rode into the clearing. Alec rested his hand on his Colt. The squat cowpoke raised a hand in peace. "Wait a minute," he said. "I want to palaver with you."

There was a bandage beneath Vestal's black hat. "What happened to you?" asked Alec. "You fall up a tree?"

Vestal swung down. "No. Run into the barrel of Mustang's Colt. He knew I cut you loose. That was a hell of a beating you gave him, MacLean."

"About the same as he gave me."

Vestal squatted, accepted makings from Alec, and rolled a smoke. "I was up at the Strangs'," he said. "They told me you was down here. Is it true you're thinking of buying back this place?"

"I hope to."

Joe nodded. "How about a job?"

"Thought you were a loyal HF man."

Vestal spat and lit his smoke. "Mustang is a heller. He buffaloed me last night in the bunkhouse. I quit. You'll need a good man or two, Alec."

Alec rubbed his jaw. "You're sure Mustang didn't send you here?"

Vestal shook his head. He looked Alec in the eye. "When I went up to get my pay, Miss Ellen told me to look you up. She wants to see you tonight."

Alec leaned back against the wall. "I'll go."

Vestal inspected his smoke. "I passed the Ives boys. Dance looked like *he* fell up a tree. Who done it? You?"

"No. Ike Strang."

"You're bulling me!"

"So, help me. I was right here with a gun on Pitzer."

"Well, I'll be damned! Never thought the kid had it in him!"

"Neither did he."

Vestal touched the bandage below his hat. "I'd like to beat hell outa Mustang," he said.

"What's his first name, Joe?"

"Robert. Robert Roberts is his full handle. Why?"

"Just curious." Alec glanced towards the bottom where he had hidden the rifle dropped the night before. R. R.— Robert Roberts. "What kind of saddle gun does he carry?"

"Winchester seventy-three. Thirty-two-twenty."

Alec nodded. "Initials cut in the stock?"

"Yeah. Near the butt on the left-hand side. Why?"

"Nothing. I found it. I'll return it tonight."

Vestal looked at Alec queerly. "You're an odd number, MacLean."

"So, I've been told." Alec stood up. "Stay here, will

you? I'll pay you for the time. If I take over the Bar M you can work for me."

"Fair enough."

Alec went to the brush and saddled Spade. He slid the light Winchester into his scabbard and carried his .44-40 across his thighs as he rode towards the trail. He'd ram that damned Model 1873 straight down Mustang's throat when he saw him.

CHAPTER SIX

Alec turned Spade between the gate posts of the Bar M. The buckboard was standing out behind the ranch house piled high with boxes, bags, and miscellaneous articles. A ranch wagon was at the front door. Enos Strang hurried down the front steps, heaved a box into it, and ran back into the house. Out at the barn, Ike was gathering an armload of tools. Sophie came out of the kitchen, threw a clattering bag into the buckboard, and turned to go into the house. She stopped as she saw Alec.

Alec dismounted. The buxom Sophie ran over to him. "Oh, Alec," she gasped, "I'm glad to see you."

"What's up?"

"Pa is scared to death because of what happened between Ike and Dance."

Alec grinned. "Ike gave him a damned good beating."

"You know what you started? A feud! That's what!"

Alec rolled a smoke and eyed the frightened girl. "Your pa and Ike have guns. Emmett, Joe Vestal, and I will back them up."

She raised her eyebrows. "Oh, I ain't scared, Alec— long as *you're* around."

Enos Strang hurried round the side of the house. His

face grew dark as he saw Alec. "What the hell you mean by lettin' my boy fight them Ives boys?"

"Did you want to see Ike crippled for life? Pitzer would have got at Ike one way or another. I figured Ike might as well get some satisfaction out of whipping Dance."

Strang's Adam's apple bobbed. "Yeah. You're right. But Dance will cut Ike down like a sunflower. Listen, MacLean, I'm pulling out. Now. You agree to take care of Soph, and I'll let you have the ranch for five thousand."

"Oh, Pa!" said Sophie coquettishly.

"Sorry, Strang," Alec said.

Strang gripped thin hands together. "Make it four thousand?"

Alec flipped away his cigarette. "I'll pay you seven thousand. Three thousand down and the rest within the next five years."

"But what about Sophie?"

Alec rubbed his jaw. "That's your problem, Strang."

"She's a nice practical girl."

Alec glanced at the buxom, simpering young woman. "I'm sorry, Enos. I've got other plans."

Strang shrugged.

Sophie flushed. "Maybe I ain't good enough for you, Alec!"

Enos Strang bowed his shoulders. "No, Soph. You ain't. Get your things together." He looked at Alec. "I'll stop off in Tonto Wells. I'll talk to Lawyer Danby. You can deal with him. You're getting a good deal, Alec."

Alec looked about the tight set of buildings. "Yes, I am. Except for the Ives boys, the HF, and the rustlers."

Strang waved a hand and went back to his wagon. Alec walked up to the cemetery and leaned against the fence, looking down on the herd that dotted the canyon behind the ranch buildings. Maybe he was doing wrong. He didn't even know where the money would come from. Captain Mossman depended on him to break up the rustling activities. Still, for the first time in ten years, he felt as though he really belonged in the Clear Creek country. Harley Forrest might raise hell because Alec hadn't gone to work at the HF, but the circumstances of Alec's return to the Clear Creek area and his run-in with Mustang Roberts had canceled out his chances to work undercover on the HF spread. On his own ranch, he could have the time to get around with less suspicion of his activities.

Enos Strang mounted the seat of the ranch wagon and looked up the hill towards Alec. Alec started down, watching Sophie clamber up on the seat of the buckboard. Ike was riding his claybank and leading a sorrel. Enos looked nervously at the surrounding heights as Alec stopped by the wagon. "I ain't sorry to leave this damned country," he said. "Nice spread, but too much trouble around the Clear Creek country. You watch your back, Alec."

"I'll be all right."

Enos settled his hat. "Good luck to you, then." He touched up the team with his whip. Sophie slapped the reins on the rumps of the buckboard mules and drove past Alec with her head held high, the perfect picture of outraged womanhood.

Ike drew rein beside Alec. "I'm taking the ridge trail," he said, "so's I don't have to go through Tonto Wells. I want to thank you for backing up my play. I won't ever forget it," he solemnly promised. He looked at the straight-backed Sophie. "Lucky you didn't fall for that deal. Soph is a hellion once you get to know her. So long, Alec."

The dust settled slowly as Alec walked into the house. The Strangs had taken only the things they had brought with them. His mother's waggle-tail clock still swung back and forth furiously. Alec placed the half-full coffee pot on the stove and poked some wood into the fire. He sat down at the table. It was quiet, taking him back to the years when he had often sat at that very table, studying his lessons while his mother sat in her rocker near the stove knitting, occasionally asking him a question in her school-teacher's voice.

Spade nickered from behind the house. Alec got a cup from the shelf and walked towards the stove. There was a dull thud from the slopes behind the house. Glass shattered. Something smashed into the wall behind the stove. Alec hit the floor, instinctively whipping out his Colt as he dropped. The dull noise came again, and something crashed into the framing of a rear window.

Alec crawled into the living room and out onto the front porch. A rifle cracked flatly, and smoke drifted from behind a tree high up off the slope. The slug whipped into a post, inches from Alec's head. Spade neighed in terror. There were two riflemen, then. Alec rolled off the porch and crawled beneath it. The opening under the porch was one he had often used as a boy. He crawled to the far end and looked out the end opening up the hill. A rifle flatted off, and another window shattered into bits.

Alec eased out of the opening, crawled behind a fence, darted behind a shed, and worked his way into the barn. There was no more shooting. Spade trotted into the barn and Alec drew his .44-40 saddle gun from the scabbard and levered a cartridge into the chamber. He peered through a partly opened window at the back of the barn. A man ran at a crouch from a tree to drop behind a log.

Alec steadied the Winchester on the window sill, allowed a little windage, aimed high to compensate for shooting uphill, and squeezed off. Chips flew from the log. The man jumped up, gripping his face. Alec reloaded and fired again. The man jumped behind a tree. Another man broke from cover and crashed into some brush. The two of them legged it awkwardly up the slope followed by a whining slug from the big .44-40. Then they were gone.

"What the hell's all the fuss about?" The voice came from behind Alec.

Alec whirled, raising his rifle. Emmett Adams dodged behind a post. "For Pete's sake," he said. "Hell of a way to greet a man."

Alec lowered the rifle and shoved back his hat, letting the sweat run down his face. "You damned fool," he said. "I nearly holed you, Emmett."

Emmett stepped from behind the post. "I met Enos and his lovely daughter, Sophie, cutting the wind for Tonto Wells. What's up?"

Alec looked out of the window. A trace of dust showed on the heights. He spoke over his shoulder, telling Emmett of the sale of the ranch to him.

Emmett grunted. "Enos has had a bad time ever since he bought this place, what with trouble with them damned Ives boys, Sophie's trying to breed with every likkered-up cowpoke in the area, and rustlers stealin' him blind. What about me, Alec?"

"I need men."

"I'll stay."

Alec eyed the homely little man. "There'll be trouble."

"Always is, ain't there?"

"How's the tooth?"

Emmett fished in his vest pocket and brought out a great crooked tooth, still caked with blood. "Ain't that a bitch? After having that knocked out, I can lick my weight in wildcats."

"You may have to."

Adams carefully placed the tooth back in his pocket. "If I put that under my pillow tonight, I wonder if the good fairy will leave a bottle of red-rye for it."

Alec grinned. "I'll see to it. Frankly, Adams, I don't know you from a bale of hay."

The cowpoke drew out the makings and rolled a smoke. "Would it help any to tell you my brother Carl was dry-gulched three months ago on the HF spread? Thirty-two-twenty slug right between the eyes. Maybe you know now why I'm hanging around."

"So?"

Emmett lit up and eyed Alec over the flare of the lucifer. "Another thing. You still with the Rangers?"

A cold feeling came over Alec. "Me?"

"Yeah, you."

"Why do you ask?"

"I was down in Sonora last year. Met Burt Mossman in Nogales. Used to work for Burt over near San Marcial on the Rio Grande. Did undercover work for Pinkertons at the time. Burt asked me if I had seen you. You were working down near Nacozari on the Agustin Chacon case then."

"No use trying to fool you, then, is there, Emmett?"

"Hardly."

Alec accepted makings from Emmett. "You can do something for me, Emmett."

"Shoot."

"Pull out of here. Go to Snowflake. I want you to send a message over the old military telegraph down to Burt Mossman. This is the message: 'Unable to get work on HF. Have bought back Bar M. No progress so far on rustling. Have you any information on Robert Roberts, known as Mustang Roberts?'" Alec rolled a smoke. "Sign it with the numeral nine."

"I'd like to work with the Rangers," Emmett said.

"I'll vouch for you. Add your request in the telegram. I can swear you in. Get there fast. Wait for the answer. High-tail it back when you get it."

Emmett nodded. "I hate like hell leaving you here alone."

"I hired Joe Vestal this morning."

"Joe? He's an HF man!"

"He was until Mustang Roberts buffaloed him. Can he be trusted?"

"Damned if I know."

"All he knows is that I've taken back the Bar M."

"What about your brother?"

Alec eyed the little man. "What about him?"

"Maybe he won't like it."

"So?"

Emmett hesitated. "Well, I ain't one to talk, but Park gave Strang a rotten deal selling the Bar M without the south water hole. That always was Bar M property."

"Why do you think he said it was on Lazy L land?"

Adams wiped his sandy mustache both ways. "I ain't sure. He sure as hell don't get along with the Ives boys. To my way of thinking, he aims to get in on the HF now that Harley Forrest is ailing. Next move would be to crowd the Ives boys out. With the Lazy L range, the HF would be damned near as big as the Hashknife outfit."

Alec rubbed his jaw. "Sounds involved."

"The whole mess is."

"What about Bert Jepson?"

"Bert is supposed to be in the Blue River country."

Alec spat. "I saw him the first day I was back. He camped with me beside the Clear, left a Lazy L running iron in my gear. Mustang Roberts and Joe Vestal picked me up for sticky-looping. I swore Bert had left the iron and they said he had been in the Blue River country for a month."

Adams grunted. "Bert was as close to the Ives boys as a burr is to a saddle blanket. I'll bet he never was anywhere near the Blue."

"Well, get on the move. I'll be all right, Emmett."

Adams hesitated. "I won't be here tonight to wait for the good fairy," he said mournfully.

Alec laughed. "Come on," he said. "There's a bottle in the kitchen. It's yours. But damn it, don't go on a high lonesome and forget what you're supposed to do."

"Swear to God I won't."

Later Alec watched the little man ride from the

ranch, then walked up the steep hill behind the buildings. He found no empty hulls lying about. At the crest of the hill, he saw hoof marks in the soft earth. He shrugged and went back down the hill.

———

ALEC WAS BUSY THAT DAY. He went back to the creek and worked with Joe Vestal, driving the steers back to the canyon behind the ranch houses. It was after dark when they finished. Alec gave instructions to Joe. "I'm going to the HF," he said. "Don't stay in the house. Camp out up the canyon where you can see everything. There'll be a good moon tonight, so the chances of anyone trying to run off the cattle will be small. If they do, stay under cover and open fire with your saddle gun. If they come after you, don't try to fight it out. High-tail it back to the HF for me." "Keno," said Joe. "You can bank on me, boss." Alec mounted Spade and rode a dim trail south through the woods until he hit the creek, avoiding the well-traveled road. He drew rein at the gate of the HF. The big house was well lit. A thread of smoke crept down towards him from the big chimney, bringing with it the bitter smell of wood smoke. He kneed Spade into the ranch road. A dark figure rose from behind some brush. "Halt!" a voice barked. "Who is it?"

"Alec MacLean from the Bar M."

"Don't josh me, hombre. Enos Strang is the owner of the Bar M."

"He did until today. I've got an appointment with Miss Ellen."

"I guess it's all right. Pass on."

Alec shrugged. The HF was like a fortress in a time of war. He dismounted at the house and dropped Spade's reins. He slapped the dust from his clothing and walked up on the porch. He rapped on the door and heard the familiar voice of Ellen Forrest: "Come in!"

Alec opened the door and walked into the living room. Ellen was standing by the big fireplace wearing a simple blue dress that set off her hair. She smiled. "Alec! I'm glad you could come."

Alec looked about the room. A rack of rifles was beside the front door. Mounted sets of deer horns adorned the log walls. Ellen's piano was highly polished, reflecting the firelight on its dark surfaces. It had been a ninety-day wonder in the Clear Creek country when Harley Forrest had had it brought in for his young daughter years ago. The oil painting of Ellen's grandmother was over the fireplace. Below it, hanging from hooks, was the presentation saber given to Harley Forrest by the men of his regiment after the Civil War. There was an air of wealth in the big room, quite different from the simple rooms of the other ranchers in the Clear Creek country.

Ellen was watching Alec closely. "Have you recovered your composure after your experiences with Mustang?" she asked.

"I have. Has Mustang?"

"You've made a bitter enemy, Alec."

"I came home looking for peace. I found war."

"I can still hire you, Alec."

"No. I'm ranching again."

"So? Where?"

"I bought back the Bar M from Enos Strang."

Her hand went to her throat. "Does Parker know?"

"You know as well as I do that Parker and I haven't had much to do with each other in years. He sold the Bar M practically out from under me."

She flushed. "He said you had no interest in it."

"No? Other than the fact that *my* father built it. Fighting off Apaches, foul weather, and rustlers. It was left to my mother."

"Amy left it to Parker after Sam Prince left the country. Sam Prince has passed on. The property was Parker's."

Alec shrugged. "It's mine now. And Park will pay me my share of the money he got from Enos Strang."

She looked into the fire. "I should think brothers, even half-brothers, would try to get along when all the others here in the Clear Creek country are at each other's throats."

"Park and I were at each other's throats even as kids," said Alec dryly.

She turned. "Parker asked me to marry him, Alec."

"So? What did your grandfather have to say to that?"

"Grandfather says Parker has a business ability."

"He sure has."

"Parker is a gentleman," she said defensively.

Alec leaned against a table. "I remember a line from a book my mother had. "The lady doth protest too much.'"

She bit her lip. "Where were you the last three years? Wandering about the country, forgetting your friends, living like a tramp!"

"There was nothing here for me, Ellen."

Her blue eyes held his for a long moment and then she looked away. "I suppose you're right, Alec."

A log fell in the fireplace, sending up a shower of sparks. The wind howled softly in the chimney. "Why did you want to see me, Ellen?" asked Alec.

"My grandfather is getting old. The palsy seems to be getting worse. The HF is too big a ranch for him to handle now."

"Yes?"

"Parker seems to think he can handle the HF. I wanted your opinion on it."

"It's not my decision."

She came close to him. "I've been so lonely. These killings and the brutality that have gained control around here frighten me. Even the men of the HF seem to be different from those I remember as a girl. I feel as though we're all sitting on a powder keg waiting for the fuse to be lit."

Alec looked down at her. All the old memories came back—the rides they took as kids, the time he pulled her from a maddened horse, the square dances in the big barn on the HE. He recalled the angry face of Dance Ives as he watched the two of them together.

Suddenly he placed his hands on her slim shoulders and drew her close. He bent and kissed her. Her hands went up about his neck and then as swiftly, drew back. She pushed him away.

"I've decided to marry Parker," she said quietly. "He's stable and ambitious. I've got to do it, Alec!"

He shrugged. "Do as you think best."

"It won't be easy. Seeing you more often now."

"I'll keep to myself, Ellen."

"Yes," she said bitterly, "I know you will. You always did when things went against you."

He walked to the door. Someone rapped on it. The door opened and Parker Prince stood there, looking angrily from Ellen to Alec. "What are you doing here?" he demanded of Alec.

Alec pushed past him. "Business, Park. Just business. Good night, Ellen."

Parker closed the door behind him and came close to Alec. "I don't like this," he said.

Alec rolled a smoke. "So?" he asked quietly. "You haven't kidded that girl into marrying you yet, Parker."

The handsome face flushed. "Listen here! I stuck it out round here. I made a good sale on the Bar M. I've worked to pile up money. What the hell have you done with your time?"

Alec lit up. "I haven't been gambling or trying to throw a rope over a girl like Ellen Forrest."

Park gripped Alec by the front of the jacket.

Alec took the cigarette from his mouth. "What are

you trying, Park? You haven't got the guts to start anything."

Park let go of the jacket and stepped back. "You can't bully me anymore, Alec. Remember that!"

Alec spat. "Look, Park: I want three thousand dollars in cash by tomorrow to pay a down payment on the Bar M."

"You're loco! Strang wouldn't sell, anyway."

"He already has."

"God damn him!"

Alec looked at Parker curiously. "What difference does it make if he did sell?"

"He had no right to. Not to you, anyway!"

Alec looked closely at his half-brother. Parker's petulant mouth was drawn down, a sure sign that what Alec had said had disturbed him deeply. "I want three thousand by noon tomorrow."

"I'll give you a thousand. No more, you conniving bastard!"

Alec reached out his left hand and gripped Parker by his silk scarf. He drew the younger man close and slapped him hard across the mouth. "Damn you! Talk of *conniving?*" Alec shoved the younger man hard against the log wall. "I'll expect that money tomorrow. Another thing: Why did you gyp Strang out of that south water hole?"

"It wasn't on Bar M land."

"You're a liar!"

Parker slid his left hand inside his coat. Alec dropped his hand to the butt of his Colt. "Don't you draw a gun on me, Park!"

Parker withdrew his hand and settled his scarf. He touched his mouth. "I'll leave the money with Baldy Roscommon," he said quietly. "Then leave me alone, Alec."

Alec stepped down to the ground. "See that it's there."

Parker came to the edge of the porch. "Don't try to

get back that south water hole if you know what's good for you," he said. "The Ives boys will kill you if you try."

Alec turned slowly. "I'm worried sick about the Ives boys," he said. "Now go in there and put on your best manners. Stick the knife between my shoulders. Keep working, Park. You'll be a big hand around here someday."

Alec strode to his horse and swung up. He was all the way to the gate before he looked back. Park had the inside track, all right. A sickness seemed to grip Alec as he thought of Ellen Forrest in Park's arms. With a muttered curse he set the steel to Spade and rode hard for the creek trail.

CHAPTER SEVEN

The moon was covered by low clouds when Alec reached the road fence of the Bar M. A cold wind blew down from the heights. The ranch house was dark. Alec rode to the water hole and dismounted, looking through the dimness towards the far end of the blind canyon behind the ranch. There was no sign of life. Alec dropped the reins and padded silently through the scrub trees, looking for Joe Vestal. The moon drifted out from behind the clouds. There were no cattle visible in the canyon. Alec looked down the slope. The soft earth was churned by the passage of many cattle. A sinking feeling came over him. He ran silently through the timber, loosening his Colt in its holster. Where the hell was Joe? Maybe he had made a bad mistake in letting the former HF hand stay with the cattle.

Alec's right spur caught in something on the ground, and he pitched full length. He reached down and touched a blanket. There was another blanket and a piece of tarpaulin lying in front of him. Beneath a low bush was a dark shape.

"Joe!" called Alec. He disentangled the blanket from his spur and got up, walking to the dim shape. It was Joe

Vestal. He rolled the man over and dragged him out into the clearing. Blood stained the pale face, but the man was still alive. Alec felt the back of Joe's head and his hands met blood.

Joe moaned. He opened his eyes. "That you, Alec?"

"Yeah. What happened?"

Joe sat up, gingerly feeling his head. "Damned if I know, I was bedded down, watching the cows. Suddenly something whacked me. I went out cold. Seems to me. I heard the cattle bellowing and then I went under again."

"How long ago?"

"What time is it now?"

Alec took out his repeater watch. "It's after ten."

"Musta been about two hours ago."

Alec helped the injured man to his feet and down the slope. He helped him to the ranch house, lit the harp lamps and the kitchen stove. While the coffee was boiling he washed and bandaged the ugly gash on the back of Vestal's head.

Vestal wiped his mouth with a shaky hand. "All the cows gone?"

"As far as I could see."

"You're wiped out, then."

"Looks like it."

Joe looked up at Alec. "By hell, Alec, I'm sorry. Musta been a damned 'Pache come up behind me. I was wide awake, I tell you!"

Alec shrugged. He went into the kitchen. It was possible that Joe was in on the deal. Someone had been watching the ranch. There had been over a hundred head of fine steers in the canyon. He went into Joe, carrying the coffee pot and two cups. They drank silently. Joe eyed Alec. "What now?"

"It was my own damned fault. I shouldn't have left."

"They mighta got you, too. These rustlers are slick, Alec."

Alec stood up, "I'm trailing them," he said quietly.

"Not alone, you ain't."

Alec nodded. "Stick here, I'm staying on the trail tonight. I'll be in Tonto Wells tomorrow. I'll be back here tomorrow afternoon."

"If you're alive."

Alec shrugged. "I'll take that chance."

He got food from the pantry and placed it in a bag. He left the house by the rear door and tied the bag to Spade's cantle. He mounted and rode slowly towards the gate. The road was plainly marked with the passage of the cattle. The trail led across the main road and into the woods beyond, heading towards Clear Creek. Within half a mile of the creek, the trail turned west, following the general course of the creek. At the line shack, the trail was still plain, trending now to the northwest. Beyond the line shack, the herd had traversed a wide expanse of soft bottomland. The ground rose steadily towards Saddle Mountain. Then the trail cut sharply to the left, back towards Clear Creek, rounding the base of a huge spur of Saddle Mountain. Here the creek washed against a wall of rock fifty feet high. The far shore was rocky and extended into a narrow canyon cut through the living rock by the rushing stream. Alec swam Spade across, cursing at the icy contact of the water. On the far side, he found marks of the exit of the herd. It was well after midnight when the trail and the moonlight petered out together on a wide plateau of rocky eight miles to the west of the Bar M.

Alec dismounted and cast about, searching the ground like a questing hound. There were no dislodged stones, no broken stems of grass, no droppings of dung. Alec squatted on his heels and looked up at the sober bulk of Saddle Mountain. It was wild country in there, broken by tremendous upheavals of rock, tortuous canyons, dense thickets, and sheer drops of hundreds of feet where the frost-loosened rock had plunged far below in years past. Once it had been the haunts of the Tontos before the Cavalry had driven them out and penned them on the reservations to the southeast. He had hunted in there as a boy, and once had been lost for three days. Old Patched Clothes, a breed Tonto who had been a friend of his father's, had trailed Alec and had brought him out. Patched Clothes knew those mountains like the palms of his dirty hands.

Alec led Spade along a dim trail that led to the east. Somewhere ahead of him was the Ridge Trail that led over the mountains to the Mormon Lake country. There was a branch trail that led down into Tonto Wells.

It was close to dawn when Alec realized he was being followed. On a dim ledge of the trail, he distinctly heard a soft rush of cascading earth and rock behind him. He spurred Spade on and rode out onto a small mountain meadow. The first showing of grey light came from the east. Alec crossed the meadow, tethered Spade in the brush, and then lay down to wait, cuddling his cheek against the cold stock of his Winchester. Minutes drifted past. The shrill, blood-curdling scream of a hunting mountain lion came to him from across the great gulf to his left...

The sun was rising when at last Alec gave up his vigil. He mounted Spade and rode east, looking back over his shoulder as the buckskin carefully picked its way along.

Alec was far down the great slope of Saddle Mountain with the sun driving the night chill from his bones when he saw a flash high up the slope behind him. Someone was using field glasses. Alec shrugged. He was too far away to be shot at. He fashioned a smoke and thought of the huge breakfast he would buy in Tonto Wells. "The works," he said to Spade. "What'll you have, you damned old jughead? Oats? Maybe oats with some corn for good measure." Spade whinnied and increased his pace.

It was late morning when Alec rode slowly into Tonto Wells. He left Spade at a livery stable and walked to the Rancher's Friend, a small beanery set just off the main street. He ate well and then went into the barbershop for a haircut and shave. It was noon when at last he walked slowly to the Juniper.

Baldy Roscommon was polishing the mirror behind the bar when Alec came in. There was no one else in the saloon. Baldy waddled to the safe and brought out a cash bag. He placed it in front of Alec, "Rye?" he asked.

"I'll settle for a beer." Alec hefted the bag.

Baldy placed the bottle in front of Alec. "How's it going?" he asked.

"All right."

"Heard you bought back the Bar M."

"I did."

"Planning to stay put a while, hey?"

"Looks like it."

Baldy leaned on the bar. "Enos Strang sure was in a hurry yesterday. Pulled out for Winslow right after seeing Lawyer Danby."

"So? Guess he's headin' for California."

Baldy nodded. "Good thing he did, too. Dance and Pitzer Ives came in town right after him, looking for Ike."

"Ike took the Ridge Trail."

Baldy scratched his bald head. "Things moving too fast around here lately."

"They may move a lot faster."

"You'd better watch your cows. Steers been vanishing around here like snow on the south slope of Saddle Mountain when the spring sun gets at it."

"I'll be all right, Baldy."

Baldy leaned close. "Dance and Pitzer are still in town. They was talking war—war on the Strangs and you."

"I'm still here, amigo."

Baldy looked past Alec and paled. "Yeah. You sure are, and so are they."

Alec looked over his shoulder as the batwings were pushed open. Dance Ives stood there with his arms folded across his chest. His face was battered and out of shape. Behind him was the hulking Pitzer, staring coldly at Alec with his piggy eyes. Alec sipped his beer.

Dance walked slowly past Alec with a soft jingle of spurs. He leaned on the bar facing Alec. Pitzer stood near the door. "All alone, MacLean?" asked Dance.

"Looks like it, Dance."

"You stuck your nose into something it won't be easy to get out of."

Alec looked up at the angry man. "Looks like you stuck *your* nose against something. Seems to me it was Ike Strang's fist."

Dance stood up straight and looked past Alec at his cousin.

Baldy slid his hands below the bar. "Look," he said quietly. "I run a nice place here."

"Keep out of this, Baldy," warned Dance.

Baldy was not looking at Dance. He was looking past Alec at Pitzer. "I got a sawed-off double-barreled Greener under here, loaded with Blue Whistlers. Split wads. I could hardly miss at this range, Pitzer."

"Go to hell," growled Pitzer.

Dance wet his lips. "I'm going to kill Ike Strang," he said thinly.

Alec yawned. He tensed himself for a sudden movement. "Hit the trail for the coast, then," he said. "Ike is well on his way."

"So? But you're still here."

Alec shoved back his beer bottle and picked up the cash bag. "Yes, and I'm staying, Dance."

Dance stepped back. His hands slapped down for a double draw. Alec swept the cash bag across the bar. It hit Dance on the chest. Before he could draw, Alec was close to him, prodding him in the gut with a cocked Colt. "What did you have in mind, Dance?" he asked mildly. "A little target practice?"

Dance paled. "Put up that gun," he said. "I was only

joshing. I want Ike, not you."

"Then go look for him."

Dance stepped back slowly. He raised his hands. "I'll go," he promised. He circled past Alec and stood by his glowering cousin.

Alec placed the Colt on the bar and leaned against the mahogany, eyeing the cousins. "Another thing: I own the Bar M. That south water hole is legally mine. I'm taking it over."

Pitzer stepped forward. "You are like hell!"

Alec placed his hand on the Colt. "You won't stop me."

Dance touched his cousin on the arm. "Come on," he said quietly. "He's got all the aces—*today*."

Baldy wiped his round face as the two Ives men left. "Damn you, Alec," he said. "Why'd you rile them boys?"

Alec looked at Baldy in mock surprise. "How you talk! I'll buy you a rye, Baldy. I think you need it."

"Sure do," said Baldy hastily. "Sure do."

Later Alec walked down to George Danby's law office.

The lawyer eyed the cash bag that Alec dumped on his desk. "There should be three thousand in there," said Alec. "For Enos Strang."

Danby took the bag. "Enos was in a hell of a hurry to get out of here, Alec. I'll make up an agreement and forward a copy to Enos at Sacramento."

Alec stood by the window. He saw Park Prince leave the hotel and go into the Tonto. "The terms should include possession of the south water hole, George."

"As I understand it, Parker didn't sell it with the ranch."

"He didn't sell it to the Ives boys, either."

"Seems to me Parker said something about the water hole actually being on the Lazy L."

"It's part of the Bar M and always has been."

"The Ives boys consider it part of the Lazy L. Maybe

you'd better let it stay that way, Alec."

Alec turned. "It's Bar M land! Look into it for me, George."

Danby lit a cigar. "Why did you come back, Alec?"

'Tired of roaming."

"Things have changed. Parker is going to marry Ellen Forrest."

"So?"

"Everyone knows Ellen never forgot you. She was a lovesick girl when she went away to school."

"She's a woman now."

"Yes. She'll inherit the best ranch in the area before long. Do you think Parker can run it?"

"Frankly, no."

"Neither does anyone else. Old Harley can handle men like Mustang Roberts, the Ives boys, and anyone else that tried to bother the HF. But Parker hasn't got the guts."

"I know that."

Danby puffed at his cigar. "Seems to me you might still be able to horn in there, Alec."

Alec walked to the door. "George, you make up that agreement for me. Check into the property lines on the Bar M. Beyond that, please mind your own business."

The lawyer rose as Alec stepped off the boardwalk in front of the office. He shook his headland went back to his desk. There was no use arguing with Alec MacLean once he made up his stubborn mind. He swiftly penned a letter and sealed it in an envelope. He addressed it to Mr. Harley Forrest, c/o Lawyer Andrew Barker, Globe, Arizona Territory.

Alec walked down the street towards the outskirts of town. He saw a nondescript *jacale,* patched with flattened tin cans and pieces of dry hide. Smoke wreathed up from a crazy, wired-up arrangement of rusty stovepipe that clung to the patchwork wall. He crossed the littered yard and looked in at the sagging doorway. He wrinkled his nose at the stench of unwashed clothing, greasy food, stale tobacco, and general filth. A short figure was seated at a rickety table, drinking from a battered tin cup. "Brother," said Alec. "Patched Clothes."

The breed slowly put down his cup and stared at Alec. "My brother," he said. "Come in." There was the slurring inflection of the Tonto in his speech.

Alec sat down on a chair made from a barrel. He watched the breed as he swallowed the coffee. "Head bad," said Patched Clothes. "Stomach bad. No squaw. No money. All bad. *Danjuda.*"

Patched Clothes wore a greasy huck shirt hanging out over a pair of patched overalls. His long hair hung over his eyes. "You got *nato?* asked Patched Clothes.

Alec nodded. He took his tobacco sack and papers and tossed them to the breed. Patched Clothes shakily rolled a smoke and lit it with a splinter from the wood box. He inhaled deeply. *"Nato* good."

It was as though Alec had never left the Clear Creek country. It had been years since he had spoken to the breed. Patched Clothes watched the blue tobacco smoke lift and waver in the draught and then flow slowly out of the doorway. "You got whisky?" he asked.

"No whisky."

"You buy?"

"Later."

Patched Clothes rolled another smoke and lit it. "White-eyes call Patched Clothes bum! Get away, they say. You stink! You lazy! You no good!"

Alec reached for the tobacco and fashioned a smoke. "The town is no place for you, Patched Clothes."

"No. Mountains fine. Plenty deer. Talk with brother bear. Shoot panther. *Yah-tats-an,* I say when panther die! Here no good. Squaws get sickness. Patched Clothes get sickness. No good. All bad. *Danjuda.*"

"Danjuda," echoed Alec.

Patched Clothes suddenly looked at Alec as though

seeing him for the first time. "What you want, Alec?"

"I have a job for you."

"No one give Patched Clothes job. He stink. He lazy."

"You know Saddleback better than any man."

"Yes. Better than any man."

"Will you work for me?"

"What do?"

Alec leaned back in his chair. "I've lost some cattle. I want them found."

"Everyone lose cattle. No find. No one asked Patched Clothes. He find. No more, though. No more look for cows. Go away. Get squaw. Beat with stick. Do no work. Lie in sun and smoke. Drink *tulapai*. Play with fat babies."

Alec grinned. "I'll give you thirty dollars a month to work for me, Patched Clothes."

"Tobacco?"

"All you want."

The breed peered through his greasy hair. "Whisky?" he asked slyly.

"Sometimes."

"No. I stay."

Alec stood up. "My father knew you well. You hunted with him. You camped with him. He used to say to my mother, 'There is no man of the woods like Patched Clothes. His eye is keen. His death stroke is sure. He runs like the deer with little winds about his strong legs.'"

"You were but a baby then, Alec."

"My mother told me."

"The *estune* with the yellow hair?"

"Yes."

The breed placed his head on his arms. "They are all gone to the House of Spirits. Only Patched Clothes is left."

Alec walked to the door. "The Bar M is mine again. There's a place for you. I need the help of my father's old hunting friend. His blood brother."

The Indian's head jerked up. "Wait. I come." The

breed pulled himself up from the table. He staggered a little as he came to the door. He paused and looked back, ran to the sagging cupboard at the rear of the shack, and pulled out a jug. He drank deeply, wiped his mouth on the back of his hand, and threw the jug into the corner. He walked back to the door and followed Alec, never looking back.

Alec paused at the road. "Here is money. There will be no whisky, or the job is not yours. Buy some clean clothes. Go to the ranch and tell the white-eye there you will wait for me. He will feed you."

"It is understood." Patched Clothes took the money. He straightened up. "A man of the Shis-inday, I. I will go, Alec." The breed walked unsteadily across the road and entered John Springer's general store.

Alec walked down the street and into the Tonto. Parker was at the same table he had been at when Alec had seen him there before. He walked up to his half-brother. "Thanks for the money," he said quietly.

Parker scowled. "You've no right to it."

"Maybe you'd like to take it to court?"

"Forget it. One thing: stay away from Ellen."

Alec nodded. "I don't think she wants to see me, Park."

Parker lit a cigar. "You'd better let the Ives boys keep the south water hole, Alec."

"It's part of the Bar M."

Parker smiled coldly. "Go ahead, then. It's your neck."

"It's my water hole."

"Stubborn as ever, aren't you?"

"As ever."

Parker shrugged. "Just keep out of my way. I've got big plans, and they don't include you. I've spent a lot of time organizing my life, Alec. Just don't get in my way."

Alec turned on a heel. Parker followed him with his eyes. His slender hands gripped the edge of the table until the knuckles turned white.

CHAPTER EIGHT

Alec busied himself for several hours in town, ordering supplies. By the time he was ready to leave, it had turned cold, and a dismal fall rain had begun to drizzle down. "Tough winter coming up," observed John Springer.

"I expected it," said Alec. "I'll take one of those sheepskin coats, John."

Springer handed one of them to Alec. He shrugged into it.

"This will do. I'll send one of the boys in after those supplies tomorrow."

Springer nodded. "I hope you know what you're doing, Alec, taking up ranching again. Outside of the HF and Lazy L, there are none of the boys making it. I look to see the whole damned range around here divided up between the HF and the Lazy L. Yavapai County is getting as bad as Navajo County."

"How so?"

"Rustlers. The Hashknife outfit is losing a thousand cattle a year in Navajo County. They say they're losing a hundred and fifty thousand dollars a year. Still, they've been putting so damned much pressure on the long loopers over there that a good many of them are now operating in this area."

"I'll take my chances."

Springer shrugged. "I hate to see an old friend go under, that's all."

Alec looked up quickly. "I won't go under, John."

Springer leaned against a glass case. "You know something, Alec? I don't think you will, either."

Alec hunched his collar higher on his neck as he stepped out into the street. A thin paste of mud had begun to form. Yellow lamplight showed through the streaming windows of the stores and houses. A cowpoke splashed by, heading for the Tonto. Alec went to the livery stable for Spade. He mounted inside the building after paying the liveryman and touched Spade with his spurs, riding out into the rain. He glanced up at distant Saddle Mountain as he rattled over the loose plank bridge spanning the dark rushing creek. A wreath of fog hung about the rugged crest.

The rain beat down as Spade made steady progress along the rutted road. The trees thrashed in the moaning wind. Alec was thinking of a hot meal and a warm bed when Spade whinnied sharply. Alec raised his head, cursing as the rain slanted down against his face. It was almost as dark as evening. To his left, the road skirted a steep drop towards the winding creek. To his right the slope continued sharply, covered with brush and trees. Alec placed his hand on his Winchester. Spade was skittish.

They trotted on. Suddenly there was a quick movement in the brush. Alec jerked his Winchester free just as a bush seemed to blossom orange. The slug smashed the saddle horn, driving it back against Alec's thigh. The report of the shot echoed dully across the creek. Spade reared, and Alec raised his saddle gun as the hidden marksman fired again. The slug creased the left side of Alec's head. He went over sideways, his left boot caught in the stirrup. Spade raced down the road, dragging the unconscious Alec behind him. Then the boot broke free. Alec's momentum rolled him over and over, tumbling him over the lip of the road. He crashed down through the brush, hung for a moment on the steep escarpment of the creek, and then dropped heavily to lie just at the verge of the cold, rushing waters. His hat fell into the water and turned slowly, resting against a rock.

There was a crashing in the brush, and a tall man looked down towards the creek. Alec was out of his view, but the black hat freed itself from the rock and whirled slowly in the current, bobbing a little as it drifted away. The tall man spat and went back across the road. A few minutes later came the dull thud of hoofs on the muddy road and then nothing but the ceaseless drilling of the cold rain through the grey shroud of the creek mist.

A bedraggled figure rose from beneath an overhanging shelf of rock, peered down the road where the tall horseman had gone, and then slid down the greasy slope to the water's edge. The man stared down at the bloody face of Alec MacLean. With a grunt, he opened the buttons of the coat and withdrew the heavy Colt. He thrust it through the rope he wore for a belt and then picked up the unconscious form, heaving it to his shoulders. Patched Clothes grunted, gripped the tough branches of the bushes, and painfully hauled himself and his burden up to the road.

Spade trotted back, shying and blowing as he picked up the rank odor of the breed. Patched Clothes spoke soothingly to the buckskin and then gripped the bridle. He placed the unconscious form over the saddle and led the buckskin west through the driving rain.

———

ALEC OPENED his eyes and winced as his head throbbed. He was lying on a cot in the big living room of the Bar M.

Joe Vestal was stirring a pot of broth at the edge of the fireplace. Emmett Adams was seated at the table watching Alec. Patched Clothes squatted in a corner, sucking at a stump of a pipe. Emmett smiled. "You've got a damned thick skull, Alec," he said.

Alec closed his eyes. He could hear the steady beating of rain on the roof. The water murmured from the dripping eaves. "What happened?" he asked.

"The breed says he found you at the bend five miles up the road. Someone dry-gulched you, Alec."

"When?"

"Yesterday evening."

Alec touched the thick fold of bandage about his head. "Who did it, Patched Clothes?"

The breed shifted. "Tall man. Black coat. Black hat. Hair on upper lip. Thick. Shoulders bent. Riding grey cayuse."

Alec shifted a little. "You get a good look at him?"

"Dark. Rain. No see good."

"It's a good thing the breed saw it happen," said Joe.

"Sounds a little like Mustang Roberts," said Emmett.

"No," said Patched Clothes. "Not Horseface. Other man."

Emmett caught Alec's eye and tapped his shirt pocket. He glanced at Joe Vestal. He stood up and passed close to Alec, pushing a fold of paper into Alec's left hand.

"Get me some coffee, Joe," said Alec.

Vestal left the room. Alec could hear the old coffee grinder whirring away. He looked at the paper. It was printed on a pale buff telegraph form. "Use your own judgment. Glad you have Bar M back. However, you're still one of my boys. Swear in your new man. Have record of man named Robert Robertson. Wanted in New Mexico for murder. No record of nickname. Mossman."

Alec wadded the paper up and threw it into the fire,

watching the flames lick up about it, char it, and then devour it quickly.

"What next, boss?" asked Emmett.

"Joe can go into Tonto Wells in the morning for supplies. We'll sit tight until he gets back. Has Patched Clothes a gun?"

"There's an issue forty-five-seventy trap-door carbine in the bunkhouse."

"*Bueno.* You'll find a short-barreled Colt in the kitchen. Enos forgot it. Give the guns to Patched Clothes."

The breed came close to Alec and squatted beside him. His rank odor sickened Alec for a moment. "What I do?" asked Patched Clothes.

"Tomorrow follow the creek west. Where the creek makes a sharp bend, several miles from the line shack, you'll find a place where the cattle have crossed. See if you can pick up the trail from there."

"Rain. Trailing no good. I go anyway."

Alec lay back. Joe gave him his broth and later a cup of coffee. Alec fell into a deep sleep.

IN THE THREE days that followed Alec's brush with death, he kept close to the ranch, until he felt his strength return. The breed reported back. He had lost the trail because of the heavy rains. Emmett Adams had been duly sworn in as an Arizona Ranger, with a handwritten commission made out by Alec. Lawyer George Danby appeared with the information that the south water hole was still part and parcel of the Bar M. Alec made his plans to get it back.

It was a cold morning when Alec swung up on Spade. Patched Clothes and Emmett Adams rode with him as he headed towards the south water hole. Joe Vestal stayed at the ranch with instructions to watch for any intruders, although Alec expected none, for there were no cattle to be stolen.

Alec drew rein on a rise overlooking the south water hole. It lay across a grassy meadow below a sharp rise in the ground. The meadow was Bar M land. At the edge of it, closing off the water hole, was a triple row of barbed wire stapled to stout cedar posts. Alec followed the line of the fence with his eyes. There was a noticeable hump in the fence line, enclosing the water hole.

"Patched Clothes," he said quietly, "go into the woods where you can watch the water hole. If there's any trouble, you shoot when I shove back my hat. Don't shoot to kill. Shoot over the heads of the men who might try to stop what I am doing."

"Why, Alec? This is your water hole."

"Do as I say. Stay hidden. I want no one to see you."

"It is understood." Patched Clothes touched his horse with his heels and rode into the woods.

"Come on, Emmett," said Alec. He rode towards the water hole, drawing rein at the fence. He looked at the little man. "Cut it," he said quietly.

Adams was nervous as he unhooked the heavy wire cutters from his saddle. "You sure you know what you're doing?"

"Perfectly."

"Okay. Okay." Adams slid from his horse and attacked the taut wire. The first strand twanged loose. In fifteen minutes, there was a wide gap in the wire. Alec took his lariat and cast a loop over one of the posts, drawing the lariat tight and snubbing it about his saddle horn. At a command Spade pulled back. The post resisted and then pulled free from the soft earth. Alec was on his fifth post when Adams raised his head. "Riders," he said. He dropped the cutters and placed his hand on his Colt.

"Mount. Keep your hands from your gun unless they start a war."

"No need to worry about their not starting one."

Three horsemen drew rein on the rise. One of them cursed. He slid his big black down the slope, followed by the others. The lead man was Pitzer Ives; the other two were Lazy L hands. "Kurt Jones and Phil Lacey," said Adams. "Hardcases, both of them."

Pitzer drew rein thirty feet from Alec. "Damn you," he said, "this is Lazy L land."

Alec coiled his lariat. "You know damned well it isn't."

Pitzer placed his hand on his Colt. "Put it back up," he said thinly.

Alec swung his lariat. It looped about the next post and drew taut. Spade pulled away. The post flew out of the ground. Pitzer cursed. He started to draw his Colt. Alec shoved his hat back.

A rifle cracked from the woods. The slug whipped into the soft earth five feet from Pitzer. He withdrew his hand from his Colt as though it had suddenly burned him. Jones and Lacey looked nervously towards the silent woods. A wreath of powder smoke hung low in the trees.

Alec grinned. "I've got five men in those woods," he said quietly. "Now pound leather out of here, Pitzer."

Pitzer Ives glanced at the woods and then looked at Alec. "You can't get away with this!" he bellowed.

"I've got proof this water hole is mine. You string more wire here and I'll cut it down."

"You'll get cut down, you damned troublemaker!"

Alec dropped his lariat and leaned on his saddle horn. "Pitzer, I owe you something. Remember the time you and Dance jumped me years ago? You were aiming to cripple me for life. I stored that incident back in my memory. Someday you'll pay for it. Maybe you'd like to settle it now?"

Pitzer gripped his reins tightly. "You been throwing your weight around, MacLean. You got the drop on me and Dance at the line shack. You had Baldy Roscommon back you up at the Juniper. Now you got riflemen in the woods. I ain't stupid enough to buck your play now, but someday you'll run outa luck, and then I'll finish the job I started years ago!"

Alec shoved back his hat again. The rifle spat. Pitzer set spurs to his horse and galloped up the rise, followed by the two Lazy L hands. Alec looked at Emmett. "Keep cutting, amigo."

Emmett wiped the sweat from his face. "By hell, Alec. You ain't aimin' to live long, are you?"

Alec shoved back his hat. "Long's I can," he said. He ducked as Patched Clothes fired from the woods. The slug sang thinly over Emmett's head.

"Blast it!" Emmett yelled. "Watch what you're doing with that goddam hat!"

In an hour they had cleared the land of the cedar posts. Emmett started a fire with some dry squaw wood he found beneath an overhanging slab of rock. He threw the cedar posts atop them. When these were ablaze, he hurled the coils of barbed wire on the roaring flames.

Alec walked to the water hole and filled his hat with the water. He held it under Spade's mouth and watched the buckskin drink. "I'll keep what's mine, Spade," he told the horse.

Then the three of them rode away, leaving a pall of smoke hanging against the sky. Patched Clothes patted the butt of his carbine. "Shoot good," he said quietly. "Patched Clothes could have got three white-eyes. Why not?"

"This isn't war," said Alec.

"Not yet, anyways," said Emmett. "But it will be. Look for trouble, Alec. *More* trouble."

———

TROUBLE HAD COME to roost on the Bar M while they were gone. They rounded a turn in the road to see a pall of thick, greasy smoke hanging low over the smoldering barn. A sprawled figure lay in the road with the end of a lariat looped about one ankle. It was Joe Vestal. A thin drizzle started as Alec knelt by the squat puncher, who looked up at the leaden skies with sightless eyes. A bluish hole between his eyes oozed sticky matter. Beneath the battered head was a small rock. An empty gun was clenched in the right hand. Alec pried it loose. "Thirty-two-twenty," he said. It was the same caliber as the Winchester that had been dropped at the line shack the night it had been fired upon by the two mysterious horsemen.

"They fired the house," said Emmett. "Guess it was too wet to burn good."

Patched Clothes quested about the trampled earth. "Three men," he said. He scouted up the hill in the drizzle. He came back down again and looked about the house, picking up a bucket that lay behind the kitchen. It was drilled cleanly on one side with a bullet hole, while a larger, ragged hole showed on the other side.

Alec stopped beside the breed. Patched Clothes scratched his head. "Two men up on hill," he said. "Joe come out for water. Bullet go through bucket. Joe run. Not get far. Pow! Bullet in head. Three men here. Two on hill. Other one behind barn. Fire barn and house. Drag Joe with rope. Very bad."

Alec touched his throbbing head. "Bury him," he said quietly. He walked into the house, which stank of charred wet wood. A bullet had smashed the waggle-tail clock. He sat down at the table in the cold kitchen and rested his face in his hands. He hadn't been so smart going to the water hole.

CHAPTER NINE

A light snow had fallen during the night, shrouding the countryside in white. It mounded over the fresh grave of Joe Vestal. Patched Clothes vanished on some mysterious errand of his own, and Emmett Adams busied himself making the burned corner of the log house weathertight.

It was almost noon when Alec saw four riders pass through the gateway at the road and ride slowly towards the house. With a start, he realized one of them was Ellen Forrest. With her was horse-faced Mustang Roberts, the skinny puncher Alec had seen attending to Mustang's injuries the morning Alec had beaten him up, and a burly man, muffled in a blue sheepskin coat.

Roberts drew rein in front of the house and looked at Alec. "We got some questions to ask you, MacLean," he said.

Alec ignored the foreman. "Hello, Ellen," he said.

She smiled. "Hello, Alec. What happened to your barn?"

"Somebody held a burning bee yesterday," he said.

"I was talking to you," said Roberts.

Alec eyed the foreman. "So, you were."

"I said I had some questions to ask."

Alec leaned against a porch pillar. "Shoot," he said.

Roberts jerked a thumb at the burly man. "This here is Deputy Sheriff Norris Minnigh."

"Pleased to meet you," said Alec.

Minnigh nodded. "Seems as though the HF was hit again last night," he said. "Thirty head of prime beef missing."

"So?"

"Lanky Mages here says he followed the rustlers—there were three of them, to the fork of the Clear. He got a shot at one of them and dropped the rustler's horse. A bay lobo with a Bar M brand."

"Meaning?"

"I'll have to look over your herd."

Alec grinned, and then he laughed out loud.

Minnigh flushed. "What's so funny?" he demanded.

"Go take a look at my herd."

"Where is it?"

"You tell me. I had over a hundred head run off last week. Their trail petered out beyond Long Bluff on the flank of Saddle Mountain."

"He's a damned liar," said Roberts.

Alec rolled a smoke. "Go ahead. Look," he said. "While you're looking, Minnigh, you can also look for three men who hit this place last night, killed Joe Vestal, and burned my house and barn."

Minnigh leaned forward. "What'd you say?"

"Joe Vestal was shot between the eyes. We buried him last night."

"Why didn't you notify me?"

Alec eyed the lawman. "From the activities that have been going on around here, it wouldn't be much use."

"Now, you be careful," blustered Minnigh. "I got an ironclad complaint against you, MacLean. The Ives boys claim you cut the wire and fence about their north water hole yesterday and shot at Pitzer Ives and two of his boys."

"Their *north* water hole? You mean my *south* water hole."

"It's Lazy L land."

"Not according to Lawyer George Danby."

Minnigh looked uncertainly at Roberts. "I thought you said—" he blurted.

Roberts spat. "Shut up," he said.

Minnigh looked at Alec. "Maybe your cows are gone," he said, "but you haven't accounted for the bay lobo with the Bar M brand."

Alec shrugged. "There isn't a cayuse on this ranch you could mistake for a bay lobo."

"Not now there isn't," said Roberts.

Alec raised a hand. "Wait a minute," he said. He went into the house and got the .32-20 Winchester he had shot out of the rifleman's hand the night he had gone to relieve Emmett Adams at the line shack. He walked out to the porch and threw it at Roberts.

Roberts caught it. "What the hell is this?"

Alec looked at Minnigh. "Some bushwhacker dropped that last week near my line shack out on the creek bottom. Take a good look at it, Roberts. Tell me it isn't yours."

Roberts inspected the weapon. "It used to be," he said. "I lost it three months ago on the line between the Lazy L and the HE"

"Do tell," Alec said politely.

Roberts looked at Minnigh. "Well?" he said.

"I'll look around," said the deputy sheriff.

Roberts followed the lawman. Lanky Mages wandered behind the house to talk with Emmett Adams.

Alec looked at Ellen. "Why did you come along?" he asked.

"I was afraid there might be trouble between you and Mustang."

"There will be, but not right now."

She looked past the house. "Minnigh is no good," she said. "He's afraid of Mustang."

"Maybe Minnigh is on your grandfather's private payroll."

She flushed. "It's not easy to be friendly with you, Alec. You've changed a great deal."

"I'm sorry, Ellen."

She lowered her voice. "I want to get rid of Mustang, but Grandfather hired him. Parker says I should keep him on. He's rough, Alec, but he's done fine work on the HF."

"Parker's an expert on character," said Alec dryly.

"You must admit he's done well."

"Parker will always do well."

Minnigh and Roberts came back, and Minnigh lit a cigar. "You file a complaint on the burning, MacLean, and I'll investigate it."

"What about Vestal?"

"You should have saved the body for an inquest."

"We can exhume him."

"Well, I'll get in touch with you. Rustling is my big problem right now."

"Yeah. So, I see."

Mages came back to his horse. Minnigh leaned forward in his saddle. "You'll have to replace that fence at the water hole, MacLean."

"I'll see the Ives boys in hell first."

Minnigh shrugged. "It'll have to go to court, then."

"It will."

They rode towards the road. Ellen looked back and waved.

Emmett Adams came through the house. "Alec," he said, "I was just talking with Lanky Mages. He told me he wanted nothing to do with this deal. He knew your father years ago. Said he always liked him, and you were just like him. He told me something that might give us a lead."

"Keep talking."

"Roberts sent him out west a day before your herd was run off. He was on Long Bluff studying the country with field glasses when he saw a herd being driven past the bluff, with three men riding herd. He put the glasses on them. He didn't get a good look at two of the men because of the trees in the way, but he got a good look at one of them. Tall hombre with a black dragoon mustache. Stoop-shouldered, wearing a black coat and hat. Riding a grey horse."

Alec turned quickly. "Sounds like the hombre that bushwhacked me."

"Yeah, but I didn't say so to Lanky."

"Did he see where the herd went?"

"Over the talus slope into Crooked Canyon."

Alec scratched his jaw. "Crooked Canyon opens into Dark Valley."

"Yeah, and Dark Valley comes out on the Canyon Diablo Trail."

Alec looked at the puncher. "A herd could be driven into Winslow from there."

"Keno."

Alec slammed a fist into his other palm. "Get your horse. Take the Ridge Trail into Winslow. Poke around. See what you can learn."

"Right away, Alec." Adams went into the house and got his grub bag. He filled it and then went out to the corral. Ten minutes later he was on his way.

Alec went back into the house. Emmett had done a good job of patching the burned corner. He had torn a partially charred cupboard from the wall and had set it aside to get at the inner side of the roof. A boxful of papers lay beside the stove. The fire had scorched one end of the box. Alec idly pawed through the papers. His father's Army discharge was there, some letters from Aunt Helen, Alec's mother's younger sister, some old supply lists. A letter fell from the box. The bottom half was burned away. Alec picked it up and read it.

"Dear Parker," he read aloud. "Thing's ain't going so well here. You remember the deal I talked to you about in Holbrook? You don't have to worry about anything but keeping the old man from getting too nosy. I can rig everything from this end, and no one don't have to know I'm in on it. The way you go through money, you'll need every dime I can pay you for working the inside while I do all the rest. I take the risks.

"A friend of mine, Ed Short, will meet you in Holbrook about the middle of June. He's writing this since I banged up my hand. Eddie is one of the best and can be trusted. Used to know R in New Mexico. They worked together in the Magdalena country before R cut a man down and had to leave. The whole thing is as sure as a pig in a bag. The only thing is getting the Ives boys..." Alec swore as the letter ended in a ragged charred line.

Alec re-read the letter several times. Parker had always had a leaning towards dirty deals, but nothing so big as to get him involved with the law. Alec spread the contents of the box on the table and carefully read each item. There was nothing else that tied in with the partially destroyed letter. He took an unused envelope and placed the letter in it, hiding the letter behind another cabinet.

Alec heard Spade whinny from the corral, and he walked into the living room. A horseman was riding up towards the house. There was something familiar about him.

"Hello, the house!" the man called.

Alec stepped out onto the porch as the man circled his sorrel. "I'm looking for Park Prince," he said over his shoulder. He turned the horse to face the house, took a close look at Alec, and then set the steel to the sorrel. It was the little man who had been following Alec in Globe that rainy night when Alec had his meeting with Harley Forrest. The man reached the road and raced west, looking back over his shoulder as though the devil were riding herd on him.

Alec ran towards the corral, but then stopped. The stranger would be long gone by the time Alec could reach Spade and ride to the road. Alec rubbed his jaw. "Parker is somewhere under this mess," he said. "I might have known it." He went to the corral and saddled Spade, riding to the road and turning east towards Tonto Wells.

Alec tethered Spade outside of the Juniper when he reached the town and walked down the street to Springer's general store. John Springer greeted him. "What can I do for you, Alec?"

"Fresh box of forty-five-seventies and two boxes of forty-four-forties."

"Got two letters for you, Alec. Came in this morning from Holbrook."

Alec took the cartridges and the letters. He walked back to the Juniper, ordered a beer from Baldy, and opened the first letter. It was from Burton C. Mossman, captain of the Arizona Rangers.

Dear Alec:

I've checked into this man by the name of Robert Robertson. He was involved in a murder in Magdalena last year. Him and a man named Eddie Short. Robertson is described as being long-faced, nose bent to one side, slight limp. Grey eyes. Top cowman. I will be in Holbrook for some time, and you can contact me there. Write and let me know how you are progressing.

Mossman

The second letter had no return address, either. The address was written in a copper-plate hand. Alec opened it and saw that the letter was written in a different hand from that of the person who had addressed it. It was shaky and almost illegible in places. Alec glanced down at the signature: Harley Forrest. He read it swiftly.

Dear Alec:

Information has come to me that you did not get work at the HF. Perhaps it is just as well. I also have learned that you are now owner of the old Bar M. A damned good spread with great possibilities. In fact, I had my eyes on it some years ago. However, Parker sold it to Enos Strang, who was never suited for ranching. Frankly, I don't think Parker is, either. Consider yourself as still working for me. I will deposit your two hundred a month as agreed. Watch Mustang Roberts. I will have help for you before long. At present, I am still in bad health and may soon leave for Phoenix for further treatment. I rely on you, Alec.

Harley Forrest

Alec placed the two letters in his wallet and finished his beer. There was no doubt in his mind now that Mustang Roberts and Robert Robertson were the same man. The tie-in between Parker and Robertson was sure, as well as with the man known as Eddie Short. The enigma was the writer of the partially burned letter to Parker which Alec had found in the box.

Baldy placed another bottle of beer in front of Alec, "Bert Jepson was seen near town yesterday morning, Alec," he said quietly.

"Bert Jepson? I'd like to get my hands on him."

"I heard from Lanky Mages about the trouble he caused you. Hell of a note, leaving that running iron in your gear."

Alec touched his throat. "He damned near had me strung up."

"Yeah. Mustang Roberts is a fast man with a rope in more ways than one."

"Does Bert still work for the Ives boys?"

"He used to. They say he left here over a month ago because the HF *corrida* had a rope reserved for him."

"Let me know if he's seen again. Try to find out where he's holing up."

"You're damned right I will. But be careful, Alec. Ain't many men as fast on the draw as Bert. Uses every dirty trick in the book. They say he could cut five notches in his six-shooter if he had a mind to. Used to run with the Seven Rivers gang in New Mexico some years ago. He's mean."

Alec finished his second beer and left the saloon. He had a score to settle with Jepson, but right now he had other things on his mind.

CHAPTER TEN

It was snowing again when Alec returned to the Bar M. The woods were shrouded in white, and great moist flakes cut visibility to practically nothing. A thread of smoke rose from the ranch house and Patched Clothes' horse neighed from the corral. Alec walked into the kitchen. The breed was seated beside the fire sucking at his ancient pipe.

"No good," he said. "Snow. Cover tracks."

"Did you learn anything?"

"Yes. Find shack in mountains. One man living there. He not home. Old place for my people to hunt. Food there. Man live there for some time."

"A hunter or a prospector."

"No. Cowman. Find branding irons. Leave there."

"What irons?"

"Funny ones. No brand. Short straight. Short curved. Find this in brush behind shack." Patched Clothes handed Alec a piece of hide.

Alec studied the brand. "BB. Never heard of it." He held it close to the lamp. Barely discernible, the vertical and horizontal letters were burned a little deeper. The top arcs of the first letter B did not quite curve smoothly to meet the vertical lines. The second letter B showed a deep vertical line, and the two cross lines in the middle and at the top were deeper than the bottom curved line. "By hell," said Alec, "this is an HF brand blotted into BB."

"What is BB?"

"I don't know, but I'll bet this piece of hide against that stinking pipe of yours that BB cattle are being sold in Winslow!"

Patched Clothes grunted. "Find also funny iron. Like so." The breed traced a line on the dust of a shelf. Alec studied it. It was a curious design. Almost like a B without the center horizontal line. Patched Clothes looked at Alec. "Maybe so blot the bar in Bar M. Make brand BM."

Alec rubbed his jaw. "The three outfits operating here now are the HF, Lazy L, and Bar M. We've accounted for two brand blots. HF into BB. Bar M into BM. That leaves the Lazy L."

"Maybe Lazy L does not have cattle stolen."

"They've lost some."

"So?"

Alec filled the coffee pot. "Learn anything else?"

"Man at line shack near creek. Holed up because of heavy snow. Little man. Riding sorrel."

Alec dropped the coffee pot. "Get your horse and mine. We've got work to do."

"No like to work at time of Ghost Face. Cold. Wet. Stay by fire and smoke. Drink *tulapai*."

"Get those horses. You can smoke and drink all you want once I get my hands on that man!"

"Dan *juda*. All bad. No good." The breed shuffled out of the kitchen.

Alec put out the fire and followed the breed. They mounted in a great swirl of flakes.

A wisp of smoke trailed low from the line shack as Alec and Patched Clothes halted on the rise. Alec turned to Patched Clothes and indicated that he should circle about behind the cabin. Alec dismounted and took his rifle from its scabbard. His feet made no noise in the deep snow. The sorrel nickered from the lean-to shed behind the shack. Alec stepped behind a tree as the door opened. The little man from Globe looked out. He closed the door again. Patched Clothes moved like a ghost through the brush and stopped behind the cabin. Alec crossed the gap to the front of the shack and flattened himself against the wall. The sorrel whinnied sharply. The door swung open again and Alec moved quickly, poking the man in the back with the muzzle of his Winchester. "Calf rope," he said quietly. "Grab your ears."

The man raised his arms. "What the hell is this?" he demanded.

"Get into the cabin."

Alec followed him into the cabin. A fire roared in the potbellied stove. A sheepskin coat steamed behind the stove. A saddle, with a Winchester across it, was in one corner. "Sit down," said Alec as he deftly removed the Colt from the man's holster.

The man paled as he recognized Alec. He stared at the breed as Patched Clothes came silently in and grabbed a piece of raw bacon from the table and stuffed it into his mouth.

Alec kicked the door shut behind him. "Now," he said. "Who the hell are you?"

"The name is Short. Eddie Short."

Alec grinned. "Well, this is a surprise, Eddie. What are you doing in the Clear Creek country?"

"Looking for work."

"You were looking for Parker Prince."

"Never heard of him."

Alec leaned on his rifle. "You asked for him at my ranch."

Short looked sullenly at Patched Clothes. "I did like hell!"

Alec poked the little man in the gut. "You lie in your teeth! You were following me in Globe the night I was there. Why?"

"I never been in Globe."

Alec leaned back against the wall. "Patched Clothes," he said offhandedly, "how does a Tonto make a prisoner talk?"

The breed picked up a piece of bread and wolfed it down. His bloodshot eyes peered through his stringy black hair, still wet from the snow. "Easy. Slivers under fingernails. Light ends."

Short shifted uneasily.

"Anything worse?" asked Alec as he inspected his fingernails.

Patched Clothes picked at his nose. "Hang upside down over fire. Very nice."

Short went green. "Say," he blustered, "I ain't done nothing."

"Why did you follow me? Why did you want to see Park Prince?" asked Alec.

Short was silent. Patched Clothes took out his long-bladed knife and began to whet it on the leathery palm of his left hand. His eyes never left the little man. Short eyed the impassive breed. "You ain't going to let him get at me with that sticker?" he asked Alec.

Alec did not answer. The blade swept back and forth.

Short wiped the sweat from his face. The wind howled about the cabin. A stick snapped in the stove and Short jumped six inches from his chair. Patched Clothes never stopped honing. Short loosened his collar. "I'll talk," he said, "but you've got to promise to let me go."

Alec nodded. Patched Clothes tested the edge of the blade by paring a fingernail. *"Enju,"* he grunted.

"I was sent to Globe to keep an eye on Harley Forrest," said Short sullenly.

"Who sent you?"

"Park Prince."

"Why?"

"Park wanted to know when Harley left there for the HF"

"Why did you follow me?"

Short scratched under his left arm. "I happened to be in that saloon when you asked for Lawyer Barker's address. I knew Forrest was there. I figured I might learn something."

"Such as?"

"How the hell should I know?"

Alec straddled a chair. "You knew Robert Robertson in Magdalena. Is that the same man as Mustang Roberts, foreman of the HF?"

Short's eyes widened. "How did you know?"

"What's the connection between Roberts and Park Prince?"

"I don't know!"

Alec looked at Patched Clothes. The breed stood up and yawned. Suddenly he gripped Short by the hair and bent his head back. He placed the edge of the blade against the curve of the throat. Short gagged. "I'll talk! I'll talk!" he spluttered.

Patched Clothes let the little man's head come back up. But he kept hold of the hair.

"What's the connection?" demanded Alec.

"Mustang has something on Park. I don't know what it is."

"What have the Ives boys to do with Roberts and Park?"

"Something about the trail over Saddle Mountain."

"Is Roberts in with the Ives boys on this rustling that's going on?"

"I'm not sure."

"One more thing: you wrote a letter to Parker Prince from New Mexico for a man who had a damaged hand. Who was that man?"

Short swallowed hard. "I can't answer that."

"You will."

"I don't know!" Short almost screamed. He jerked free from Patched Clothes and stood up. A horse nickered and Alec turned. Above the howl of the wind, he heard a metallic noise. Short broke for the door. A shot flatted off. Glass smashed as Alec hit the floor. Patched Clothes dropped behind the stove. In the doorway, Short gripped his throat. He tried to scream and then collapsed over the hot stove, carrying it over against the wood-box, the crazy chimney-pipe arrangement breaking loose from the rusty wires and showering the room with soot. Short moved spasmodically and lay still.

Alec crawled to the door. The rifle sounded again. The slug ripped through the thin door inches from Alec's face, driving a splinter into his nose. Tears blinded him. Another shot smashed through what was left of the shattered window, and then came the muffled beat of hoofs in the deep snow. Alec opened the door, striving to see through the tears. He made out a tall man, bent low over his saddle horn, urging a grey up the slope.

Fire had caught the wood-box. Alec dragged Short from the stove and almost retched as he saw the gap where Short's tongue had been. A finger of flame licked up the wall.

"Go now," said Patched Clothes. "Too much light. Man with rifle kill easy. Go now!" The breed smashed a rear window and climbed through, ripping a hole in his greasy trousers.

Alec looked at Short and then at the fire. No use in saving a corpse and making two others. He snatched up his rifle and climbed through the window, dropping into the drifted snow. Patched Clothes led Spade to him. He swung up and set the steel to the buckskin. They rode towards the slope. Alec looked back. The sorrel was following them. The shattered windows of the shack showed leaping flames in the interior. Then Alec was over the rise and hammering towards the drifted road.

Alec looked up and down the road. There was no sign of life. The flakes coated his face. Patched Clothes grunted. "No see. No tracks. Better we go to ranch. Ghost Face no let Patched Clothes track. All bad. We go to ranch. Smoke. Drink *tulapai*. Think."

Alec nodded. The fire was an orange glow in the woods behind them as they rode east. He had been so damned close to getting a big piece of the puzzle into place. His stomach churned as he thought of Eddie Short lying back there in the blazing cabin.

CHAPTER ELEVEN

The snow had let up by ten o'clock, and it began to get cold. That night the old ranch house cracked and groaned in the grip of the wind that howled down from Saddle Mountain and gibbered at the eaves.

Alec stayed close to the ranch house, trying to fit the pieces of the puzzle together. He had Parker Prince and Mustang Roberts implicated now on the word of Eddie Short. There was no connection as yet between them and Dance and Pitzer Ives, but there was a tenuous thread because Parker Prince, who had never been friendly with the owner of the Lazy L, had given them the south water hole. There was no question about whose land the water hole was on.

Emmett Adams showed up two days after the killing of Eddie Short. His face was blue with the bitter cold. "Damned unseasonable," he said as he belted into hog belly and Mexican strawberries. He ate three pieces of apple pie and grinned at Alec. "Now, where the hell did you get apples this time of year?"

"Flavored soda crackers," said Alec. "Mother's recipe. She could cook anything out of nothing."

Emmett rolled a smoke and poured his fourth cup of

coffee. "I went into Winslow as you ordered. Didn't find any trace of Bar M cattle or HF either. There was a lot of cattle in pens at the Santa Fe yards. Brands I never saw."

"Like BB and BM, Emmett?"

Emmett took his cigarette from his mouth. "Now how the hell did you know that?"

"Those were blotted Bar M and HF cattle."

"They *were* sloppy brands. I was climbing into a pen to get a good look when a mean-looking hombre warned me off."

"Describe him."

"Burly bastard. Green eyes. Dragoon mustache. Seems to me I seen him somewheres before."

"Bert Jepson?"

Emmett slapped his thigh. "Hell, yes! I knew I knowed him!"

"See anyone else?"

"No."

"Any Lazy L cattle there?"

"Some. Maybe forty head."

"Any other information?"

"Hombre told me they been getting cattle from the Saddle Mountain area pretty regular. BB and BM brands. Mostly BB."

"That figures. Harley Forrest has been losing stock steadily."

"What do we do now?"

Alec stood up. "First I'm going to have a talk with my brother."

"You think he's in on this deal?"

"I know he is."

"Alone? He hasn't got the guts to run a deal like this, Alec."

"You're right there. Mustang Roberts is in on it, too."

"Still lacking brains in the deal, Alec."

"Yeah. I have a feeling the tall man with the black coat and hat could tell us the rest of the story."

"Who is he?"

"Never been able to find out."

Emmett rubbed his jaw. "He's the key, Alec."

"I'm going to put the squeeze on Park."

Emmett was worried. "Look, Alec. Park ain't one to fool with. He's got a toehold at the HF with Ellen Forrest.

He'll kill before he gets shoved out of that set-up."

Alec shrugged into his sheepskin coat and put on his hat. "Send Patched Clothes to take a look at the Lazy L spread. Boot him out of the house if you have to. He's a good man once he gets moving, but he likes his stove, tobacco, and liquor too much."

"He'll go, Alec, if I have to take him myself."

Alec saddled Spade and took the road for town. It was almost dark, and the wind keened down from the heights. The crusted snow crackled beneath Spade's hoofs. It was too early for such weather, but the game was afoot and there could be no waiting now.

The yellow lights of Tonto Wells shone through the darkness as Alec rode across the frost-gripped bridge. The streets were cut with frozen ruts. There were no horses standing at the hitch racks. Alec stopped at a livery stable and left Spade there. He took his Colt from the holster and slid it inside the front of his coat, leaving three buttons unbuttoned. He stopped at the Juniper for a warming drink. Baldy told him that Bert Jepson had been seen in town late that afternoon. Alec left the over-heated saloon and walked down to the Tonto. There was a broken pane in one of the frosty front windows. The place held only a few men. Park wasn't there. Alec plodded down to the Bell House, at the corner of Second, and walked into the brightly lit lobby. A drummer dozed in an overstuffed chair.

"Can I help you?" asked the clerk.

"What room does Parker Prince have?"

'Two-eleven. But he's busy now."

Alec smiled. "He's expecting me. I'm his brother."

"In that case, go right up. Turn right at the top of the stairs. Corner room, overlooking Second Street."

Alec padded up the stairs and walked to the door of the room. He heard a low murmur of voices. He gripped the knob and turned it. The door was locked. "Who is it?" called Parker.

"Clerk with a message."

"Shove it under the door."

"Can't. It's verbal."

There was a scuffle of feet. Then the key turned in the lock. The door opened and Alec pushed inside. Parker jerked his head in surprise. "What the hell is this?"

Alec looked past him. A bottle was on the marble-topped table. There were two glasses partially full beside it. But there was no one else in the big corner room. Alec looked at the closet. It was open and there was no place for a man to hide. He looked at the window. It was open a few inches. "I want a talk with you, Park," said Alec.

"I'll not give you any more money."

Alec kicked the door shut. "I don't need any."

Park glanced nervously at the window. Alec leaned against the wall. "Who was here?" he asked.

"No one."

"You always use two glasses?"

"One of the boys was up here a little while ago."

"I see." Alec shoved back his hat. "I won't take up much of your time, Park."

"I've got a game due to start in the Tonto in half an hour."

"You'll make it."

Park sat down at the table. "Drink?"

"Don't mind if I do."

"Sit down." Park jerked his head towards a chair with its back towards the window.

Alec sat down on the edge of the bed and took the

whisky glass from his half-brother. He eyed Parker as he sipped it.

"What is it you want?" asked Parker.

"Eddie Short is dead, Park."

Park never batted an eyelash. Alec knew the information was old. "Who's Eddie Short?" he asked.

"He was a running mate of Mustang Robertson's."

"You mean Roberts."

"Robertson."

"Maybe."

Parker shifted a little in his seat. Alec hooked a thumb over his coat belt, close to the butt of his Colt. Out of the corner of his eye, he caught a shadowy movement on the other side of the frosted window. There was a second-story porch built on the Bell House, running clear around the hotel.

Parker shifted again, gripping the neck of the bottle. "What has all this got to do with me, Alec?" he asked.

"I wonder if Harley Forrest would consider you a good prospect for a son-in-law if he knew you had put a man to watch him in Globe."

Parker's mouth pulled down. Alec stood up. Suddenly Parker rose, hurling the bottle sideways at Alec's head. Alec ducked and the window shattered behind him as the bottle crashed through it. Alec hit the floor, rolling over to free his Colt. A pistol was thrust in through the broken window. It flashed. The detonation and glare blinded Alec. Parker yelled and Alec jumped to his feet, warded off a blow from Parker, and neatly clipped Parker with a left jab. Parker went down cursing.

Alec jerked at the bottom of the window. It went up easily despite the frost, scattering shards of glass out on the porch. Alec stepped through. A thick-bodied man fired at him from thirty feet up the porch. Alec dropped flat. Parker ran to the window, jerking out a short-barreled pistol. Alec raised his Colt, but Parker leaned out of the window and fired directly at the shadowy figure. The man grunted, dropped his pistol, and spun about. For one moment he was poised at the railing, and then with a muffled sob he pitched over and crashed on the frozen earth below.

Alec got to his feet, but Parker was too fast for him. The pistol swung in a short arc, connecting with Alec's skull. He staggered back, dropping his Colt. He hit a post and fell forward in time to feel the crushing weight of the pistol behind his left ear. He hit the ice-covered boards and lay still.

————

"HE'S COMING TO," a voice said. It seemed far away. Alec opened his eyes. He lay on the bed in Parker's room. Deputy Sheriff Minnigh was standing over him. Alec's head throbbed. Park was seated at the table. Half a dozen other men were in the room looking at Alec.

Minnigh handed Alec a glass of whisky, and the liquid seemed to scorch his throat. He sat up and swayed dizzily. Minnigh looked down at him. "Alec MacLean, I hereby arrest you in the name of the citizens of Yavapai County, Territory of Arizona, for the murder of one Bert Jepson. I must warn you that anything you say may be used in evidence against you."

Alec shook his head. He looked at Minnigh. "I didn't shoot anyone," he said. "Look at my pistol. It hasn't been fired."

"Smell," said Minnigh. He shoved a pistol muzzle under Alec's nose. It brought the bitter stench of burned powder to him. He drew back his head. It was the short-barreled pistol that Parker had used. His own pistol lay on the table near Parker. "That's my pistol over there," he said.

Parker shook his head. "It's like I said, Minnigh. Alec butted in here while Bert and I were having a sociable drink. Alec accused Bert of leaving a Lazy L running iron in his camp, along the Clear. Bert swore he had never seen Alec anywhere before in his life. Alec attempted to buffalo Bert with that short-barreled pistol there. Bert put up a fight and crashed through the window when Alec tried to get a sight on him. Alec fired from the window and killed Bert. I knocked Alec out."

In the silence that followed, Alec stared at his brother. Minnigh snapped a pair of irons about Alec's wrists and touched him on the shoulder.

Parker stood up. "I'll hire a good lawyer for you, Alec," he said cheerfully. "You may get out of this yet."

Alec was pushed towards the door. He went slowly down the steps and out into the frosty street. A crowd was gathered about the body of Bert Jepson, sprawled in the gutter of Second Street. Alec noted that Bert's spurs were not mates. They crossed the street to the jail. It wasn't until the cell door clanged shut behind him that he fully realized how skillfully Parker had operated, shutting Bert Jepson's mouth forever and placing the guilt on Alec.

CHAPTER TWELVE

It was late in the afternoon of the day after Alec had been jailed when Charlie Bascom, the jailer, came down to Alec's cell. "Yuh got a visitor, MacLean," he said.

Alec sat up. "Who is it?"

"Miss Forrest."

Ellen came down the line of cells where Alec was the only prisoner. Her face was pale and drawn. "Alec," she said quietly. "Why did you do it?"

"Believe me, Ellen, I didn't do it."

"Then who did?"

"It doesn't matter right now."

She gripped the bars. "Was it Parker?"

He nodded.

"But why?"

He came close to the bars. "Listen, Ellen. Have you ever suspected that Parker had anything to do with the rustling that's been going on?"

She hesitated. "Not until now."

"What makes you think so now?"

She looked along the line of cells. Charlie was engrossed in cleaning a shotgun. "The day we went to the Bar M with Deputy Minnigh, they talked quite a bit

before we left the HF, Parker was there. He refused to go
along with us. Later, as we were riding to your ranch, I
overheard Minnigh say to Mustang that Parker was
getting worried. Roberts told him to keep his mouth
shut, that Parker was in too deep to pull out. That night
Parker wanted me to go to Holbrook and marry him the
next day."

"Can you reach your grandfather?"

"It will take a few days."

"Listen. Tell him everything that has happened. Send
a man to Holbrook. Tell him to contact Captain Burton
Mossman of the Arizona Rangers. Mossman can telegraph to Globe and reach your grandfather."

"The Rangers?"

He leaned close to her. "Yes. I'm a Ranger, sent here
to break up this rustling ring."

"Why don't you tell Charlie?"

He shook his head. "Six lawmen have been done away
with in this area in the last six months. I don't trust
Minnigh, and Charlie may be just as bad. Who can you
trust on the ranch?"

"Lanky Mages."

"Send him, then. Can you let Emmett Adams at the
Bar M know what's happened?"

"Yes."

He smiled. "It seems as though we're beginning to
understand each other at last."

Her eyes held his. "I always wanted to, Alec." She
turned and left the jail.

SHORTLY AFTER DARK, Charlie Bascom brought Alec's
dinner to him. He unlocked the cell door and passed in
the tray. He looked over his shoulder. "Alec," he said, "I
think you're innocent. I'm leaving this cell door
unlocked. About ten o'clock I'll leave here to get some

hot coffee across the street. I don't expect to find you here when I get back. Good luck." The turnkey shuffled away.

Alec ate slowly, digesting Charlie's startling information along with the food. He lay back on his cot. Charlie was a drunken sot, the town ne'er-do-well, a man who would sell his mother's Bible for the price of a drink.

It was after nine o'clock when someone tapped on the window of the cell. Charlie was dozing in his cell chair. Alec reached between the bars and eased up the window. The mournful face of Patched Clothes looked in at him.

"Alec, this for you," the breed said. He passed a Colt between the bars. Alec gripped it and slid it under the blankets on the cot.

Patched Clothes came close to the bars. "Men watch this place from across street. Patched Clothes go."

"Who's watching

"Dance and Pitzer Ives. No good. Hide in shadows. Watch all the time. Go for drink. Patched Clothes wait for chance. Have horses ready at empty warehouse near bridge. You come?"

"How do you know I can get out?"

"Hear Charlie Bascom talk with Parker Prince. No good. Charlie say he leave cell open 'bout ten o'clock. No good, my brother. Parker give money to Charlie. All bad."

"All right. Get out of sight."

Patched Clothes vanished silently. Alec checked the loads in the handgun. He slid it back under the blankets. There was a cold feeling up his spine.

Precisely at ten o'clock, the turnkey shuffled out into the night. Alec waited a little while and then took the Colt. He padded to the front office and got the key for the back door and walked back through the building. He eased the key into the lock, turned it, dropped the keys on the floor, and eased the door open. A cold draught blew about him as he stepped into the dark alleyway. He cocked the Colt and flattened himself against the wall.

Someone crunched by in the street that ran alongside the jail.

Alec crossed the alley and stepped into a shed. He crossed to the back of the shed and climbed through a window. He paused in the darkness, listening. A woman laughed somewhere on the street. Alec stepped two paces forward and froze. A shadow at the corner looked too solid. He turned slowly.

"There he is!" someone said. It was the deep voice of Pitzer Ives.

Alec sprinted for the shelter of a building. A pistol flared in the darkness. Alec crouched and fired at the flash. He darted between two buildings as a pistol cracked. The slug smacked into the wall at his side. He fired once more. and ran deeper into the alley between the two buildings. A man stepped out into the alley and fired twice. One of the slugs ripped through the slack of Alec's coat. He jumped up on a box, clawed at the low roof, pulled himself up on it, and rolled to its end. Boots crunched on the frozen mud.

"Where the hell did he go?" called Dance Ives.

Alec looked down into the street. It was empty. He dropped to the ground and darted across the street just as Pitzer Ives rounded the corner. Alec whirled and fired. Pitzer cursed and dropped his handgun. Alec ran up a flight of stairs on the side of a dark building. He pulled himself up on the flat roof and crossed it, pausing to look down into the street. Pitzer Ives was on his knees, pawing for his pistol.

Alec walked softly to the back of the roof and looked down into another dark alley. A man yelled from Main Street, "Jailbreak! Charlie Bascom says MacLean is loose!"

Alec hung from the edge of the roof and dropped. He hit hard on the frozen mud, dropping the Colt. He scrambled for it in the darkness. A man hammered up the alley and stopped as he saw Alec. A pistol flared, revealing the taut face of Dance Ives. Alec snatched up the Colt and fired from his knees. Dance grunted, dropped his pistol, and gripped his stomach. He took a few queer reeling steps towards Alec and then fell with a smash. Alec sprinted for Bennett Street, rounded the corner, and ran towards the bridge. Men yelled in the streets. "He got Dance Ives! Where the hell is he?"

Alec reached the creek. Patched Clothes stepped out of the shadow of the old warehouse. "Here," he said. He was holding the reins of two horses. Alec swung up on one of them and then Patched Clothes mounted and drummed his horse's flanks with his heels. They thundered over the bridge as a rifle spoke flatly from Main Street.

Alec turned and fired twice into the air, emptying the Colt. Then they were in the shadow of the trees, the horses full out.

Twenty minutes later Patched Clothes drew his horse to a plunging halt. "Emmett waits at creek with supplies. We hide in mountains. No go to ranch! Men wait there for you!"

They left the frozen road and cut towards the creek. Patched Clothes found the trail and they rode west through the cold night. At the bend of the creek, they saw Emmett Adams waiting for them with a horse and a pack mule. He gripped Alec's hand. "All hell is to pay," he said. "Mustang Roberts and some of the HF boys are at the Bar M. Get into the hills."

"What about you?"

Emmett grinned. "They've got nothing on me."

"They had nothing on Joe Vestal, either."

"I'll hole up somewhere. One of us has to be around."

"Maybe you'd better go to Holbrook and tell Mossman what's happened. Ellen Forrest has already sent Lanky Mages there to get Mossman to send a wire to Harley Forrest, but I'm not sure he can be trusted."

"Why Harley Forrest?"

"He'd better come back before he hasn't a steer left. Tell Mossman to investigate those BB and BM cattle at Winslow and attach them if he thinks they're actually HF and Bar M cows. Tell him also that I'm accused of killing a man, and that I think I killed Dance Ives."

Emmett whistled softly. "I know damned well you didn't kill Bert Jepson, but you'll have a hell of a time explaining killing off Dance Ives while you were on a jailbreak."

"Dance Ives no good," said the breed. "Patched Clothes go to Lazy L. Look in woods. Climb hills. In hills behind ranch, hidden way back, find cow pens."

"That's a blind alley up there," said Alec.

Patched Clothes shook his head. "Trail there. Not very wide. Lead to creek. Cows go across creek past Long Butte to Dark Valley. Canyon Diablo Trail. Into Winslow. Many signs of cattle near pens, even in snow."

Emmett looked at Alec. "The pieces are beginning to fit together."

Alec nodded. 'Take me there, Patched Clothes," he said.

Patched Clothes led the pack mule through the trees. Alec gripped Emmett's hand and spurred his horse.

Alec followed the breed. They crossed over on to Lazy L range and picketed the pack mule while they scouted the ranch buildings. Yellow light showed from the windows of the bunkhouse. Patched Clothes drifted down the slope towards the ranch and then came back as silently. "Four men down there. No one else around," he said.

"Show me the pens."

They led the pack mule between two rugged hills. Patched Clothes moved with a sureness that amazed Alec. In half an hour the breed stopped on an icy slope. "Look," he said.

Below them, Alec could see the squared pens of peeled poles. There were enough of them to handle a hundred head easily. Patched Clothes led the way past the pens and into a dark slot in the hills. In an hour they could hear the rushing of the ice-choked creek. Patched Clothes set his horse at the stream, hauling at the reins of the reluctant mule. They gained the far shore. Alec followed them on the black *grullo* that Patched Clothes had brought for him. The breed led them across the littered talus slope, slippery with ice and drifted snow.

An hour before dawn he stopped before a narrow offshoot of the canyon, dismounted, and led his horse in. Alec followed with the *grullo* and the pack mule. Patched Clothes stopped at a sagging stone shanty. "Patched Clothes hunt here," he said. "Make fire. Eat. Safe now."

They made a fire and ate. Alec rolled up in his blankets and dropped off to sleep as though he had been pole-axed.

CHAPTER THIRTEEN

The days that followed Alec's escape from the Tonto Wells jailhouse changed from cold to warm. The sun loosened great sheets of snow and sent them plunging down from the heights. The streams overflowed their banks, and the hard earth became a morass, but gradually the trails dried out. Patched Clothes scouted each day, coming back to report that he had seen no one in the area. He made a trip up to the old cabin in the mountains where he had been before and came back to report that he had found the ashes in the stove warm, but no sign of man about the place.

Patched Clothes left Alec one moonlit night and headed back towards the valley to contact Emmett Adams. Alec climbed up on a bald bluff to look down into the valley, silvered by the moon. It was unseasonable weather, with a warm wind blowing. Far below Alec could see the silvery loops of a branch of the Clear. It was then that he saw the lone horseman riding hard to the north. The man was too far away to identify. Alec slid down the slope and got his *grullo*, slipping the Winchester rifle Adams had packed with the supplies into the scabbard on the saddle. He spurred the *grullo* out of the canyon offshoot and rode down towards the trail that followed the stream.

He crested a rise and saw the lone horseman far ahead, riding slowly towards the mountains. Alec went on. For an hour he did not see the horseman and then he found a place where the ground was marshy. Here was a distinct trail of hoofs leading up a long, brushy draw. He led the *grullo* up the draw and came out on a small plateau fringed with tall pines. The trail led straight across the moonlit area, but Alec led his horse into the shelter of the trees and skirted the open place until he reached the trail again on the far side. He was about to mount when the bitter odor of wood smoke came to him. He tethered the bay in a hollow and took his Winchester, working his way through the brush until he reached a small clearing. Set back against a rock face was a cabin. Dim yellow light shone through the dirty windows. A black horse, similar to the one ridden by the strange horseman, was sheltered in a small lean-to fifty feet from the cabin.

Alec slipped behind a tree and watched the cabin. A man came out of the cabin and walked to a spring that was cupped by a wall of rocks. He filled the bucket and started back towards the cabin. Alec stared. There was no mistaking Mustang Roberts, foreman of the HE Roberts went into the cabin. Soon the odor of frying meat came to Alec. Twenty minutes later Roberts came out of the cabin and wiped his mouth, looking down the trail as though he were expecting someone.

Alec crawled through the brush and tried to look into one of the windows, but it was too dim to see anything. He was working his way back to where he had been hidden when he heard the dull thud of hoofs on the trail. He lay flat. Brush cut off his view of the newcomer, but he heard voices and then the slamming of the cabin door. He crawled to the edge of the clearing. A dun horse was tethered beside the black.

Alec sat up and pulled off his boots. He left his Winchester with his boots and padded round to one side of the cabin. He could make out two men in the cabin, but the window was too dirty for a clear view.

Alec inched his way towards the cabin. A low mutter of voices came to him. The window was closed tightly. Behind the cabin, there was a gap between it and the rock face just wide enough for him to work his way in. He stood up and padded to it, easing himself between the cabin and the rock. He placed his ear against the thin wall.

"I've had a hell of a time with Pitzer," said Roberts. "Ever since MacLean cut down his cousin in Tonto Wells the man has been out of his mind. Ain't paying any attention to business at all."

"He'd better," said the other man. "We got too much at stake now to have him fail us."

The voice was familiar, but Alec couldn't place it. He pressed against the wall.

"MacLean has vanished," said Roberts. "Some people think that stinking breed Patched Clothes gave him that six-gun he had for the jailbreak. By hell, you'da thought them Ives boys would have cut him down easy. He didn't have a damned chance against them, but he got clean away. I don't like it."

"Park handled his part all right. He's smart, even if he's yellow. He shoulda cut down MacLean too on that damned porch. But it was always like Park to be slick. This time he was too damned slick. A bullet is the answer, Mustang. Neat. Between the eyes."

"Yeah. I got Lanky Mages that way last week. He was heading for Holbrook with a message for someone. I think Ellen knows too damned much. I think she was sending a message to the old man."

"She can send another, can't she?"

Roberts cursed. "You don't expect me to kill her too, do you?"

"If Park had worked faster, he would have had his brand on her by now."

"She's got too much sense to marry him."

"She will."

Alec shifted. His right foot caught between the rock and the cabin. He leaned down and gripped it with his hand and tried to free it. The men were speaking again, but he was too tense to listen. He jerked at the foot, but it was wedged tight. He straightened up with cold sweat trickling down his sides.

"I wonder how much Eddie Short spilled to MacLean," said Roberts.

"Damned if I know. I cut Eddie down in the middle of a sentence. Eddie always did talk too much."

"MacLean knew that Eddie had something to do with me and Park."

"He didn't mention me, did he?"

"Hell, no!"

"Something's going on. Two hombres been hanging around the shipping pens in Winslow, playing dumb but watching everything that goes on."

"What do we do now?"

"Play it smart! We've cleaned up enough now to wait for a while. We can lay low until spring. By that time Park will have married Ellen and will have the HE"

"What about old Forrest?"

The other man laughed. "That old swine has made enough enemies in this country to rate a bullet. We can get him some dark night."

"That still leaves MacLean."

"He can't hide out forever."

"You think he's a Ranger?"

"I'm positive."

"Then we've got to get him."

"He's slick. He damned near got you the night you were shooting up that Bar M line shack. He bluffed the Ives boys more than once. I thought I got him that night

at the creek, but he lived through it. I don't often miss.
He got wise to Ed Short somehow. He shot his way out
of Tonto Wells when Minnigh had him all set for a
killing."

"There's only one answer, then. We'll have to hunt
him down."

"You've got bait."

"Who?"

"Ellen Forrest. He always was soft on her. Get
moving."

"What about you?"

"Back to Winslow for me. I've got to get those cattle
out of there."

Feet scraped on the floor, water hissed into the fire,
and the light went out. Then the door banged shut. Alec
stood stock-still with cocked Colt ready. He heard the
soft thuds of hoofs, and he was alone.

As Alec worked to free his trapped foot, he puzzled
over the strangely familiar voice of the man who had
been talking with Roberts. The man seemed to know
him well enough, but the voices had been slightly muffled
through the wall of the shack.

Alec braced himself and slid his foot out, leaving his
sock and part of the skin of his foot in the cleft. He
picked up the sock and eased himself out of the narrow
space. He padded down to the trail and listened. He
heard nothing but the wind soughing through the pines.
He waited half an hour, and then went into the cabin,
lighting matches to look about. A bunk was in one
corner, covered with rumpled bedding. A cupboard held a
supply of food. Lying in one corner were the odd running
irons that Patched Clothes had mentioned. There was
nothing to identify the mysterious stranger.

Alec went back to his boots and pulled them on. He
picked up his Winchester and went back to the *grullo*,
leading him slowly back to the plateau. He circled it
again and led his horse to the creek. Hoof marks led off

to the northeast. Other hoof marks followed the trail beside the stream heading southwest. Alec mounted and went back to his hideout.

It was almost noon when Patched Clothes returned. He gravely handed Alec a message from Emmett Adams.

Alec read it swiftly:

Lanky Mages dry-gulched near Tonto Wells. I contacted Mossman in Holbrook. He has two Rangers working in Winslow on those cattle. Mossman left for the Blue River country on a tip that Agustin Chacon was there. You been made Ranger sergeant. Full charge of this deal. Minnigh has sworn in five HF men as deputies as well as Pitzer Ives for a posse to hunt you down. Move your camp every night! Mossman says not to worry about any killings of these sticky loopers. He has a wired message from the territorial governor to the effect that he'll have a pardon for you on any shootings before the ink is dry on the indictment. That goes for any Arizona Ranger. I have been lying low since you left, for they have been hunting me down as an accomplice in your escape. It's a damned risky business, Alec, but I'll do my best.

Alec burned the letter in the fire. He sat down and wrote out a full report on everything he had learned and then made another copy of it. He secreted one of the reports in a niche behind the fireplace. The other one he gave to Patched Clothes. "Take that to Winslow," he said. "Give it to the marshal there with instructions to forward it to the governor if anything happens to me."

Patched Clothes grunted. "Nothing happen. We sneak about. Kill Mustang Roberts. Pitzer Ives. Kill all. No more rustling. No more trouble. Easy way. Tonto way."

Alec shook his head. "We've got to nail all of them, my brother."

"Where you go now?"

"Down into the valley."

"Very bad."

"I can't sit up here forever."

"Why? Hunt. Drink coffee. Smoke."

Alec grinned at the serious breed. "Take the message to Winslow."

"Where I find you?"

"Down in the valley. I'll have to keep moving."

"All right. No good. Patched Clothes no like."

After Patched Clothes left, Alec mounted the *grullo* and headed back towards the Clear. He had no definite plan, but things were beginning to shape up for a showdown.

It was late afternoon when Alec reached the creek trail. He rode with his Winchester across his thighs. He was barred from most places in the valley. He couldn't go back to the ranch. Tonto Wells would be a death trap. Men would be watching for him everywhere in the Clear Creek country. Suddenly he raised his head. There was one place they wouldn't think of looking for him—the HF spread.

He turned off the road and took a little-used trail across a low ridge and down the other side, emerging from scrub woods to look down on the sheltered valley behind the HE The lights from the ranch buildings shone through the darkness.

Alec watered the *grullo* at a rock pan and then picketed him in a sheltered place. He took his Winchester and worked his way slowly down the rocky slope until he stood on the floor of the canyon. The wind shifted, bringing the bawling of cattle to him from farther up the canyon. Faintly he heard the music of a harmonica played by one of the herders. He followed a fence line to a place where he could look over the ranch houses. The sky was lightening to the east, where the moon was rising. A door banged at the bunkhouse and a man yelled for someone named Benny.

Alec waited until there was no sign of activity about

the ranch buildings, and then walked softly up behind a shed a hundred yards from the ranch house. The kitchen door opened, the cook threw out a panful of water, and the door banged shut again. A little later the light in the kitchen went out. Suddenly Alec realized why he had really come to the HF He wanted to see Ellen.

Alec went into the shed and crawled up into a low loft full of hay, watching the house through a partially opened hay door. Now and then, someone moved past a light, throwing a shadow on the window, but he could not distinguish who it was. The moon now sailed through a sea of dotted clouds, and it began to get colder. Alec looked at his watch. It was after nine o'clock. He slid down from the loft and walked swiftly to the back of the ranch house. The sound of a piano came to him faintly. He skirted the house and stopped outside the window of Ellen's room. The window was partially open, and the room was dark. He eased it up, cursing under his breath as it squeaked protestingly. He stepped in. The faint odor of heliotrope enveloped him. He eased the window down again. A dog barked from near the bunkhouse. The dog barked again, this time closer to the house. Another dog took up the noise, barking repeatedly from near the big barn. A door opened at the bunkhouse. "Shut up, Buster!" a man yelled.

Alec placed his Winchester in a corner of the room and padded across to the door of the bedroom. He gripped the knob and turned it slowly. The door opened into a hallway that led to the living room. The kitchen was the other way. The piano was still being played. Suddenly it stopped. "That must be Parker, Grandfather," said Ellen clearly.

"I was afraid of that," said the voice of Harley Forrest.

Alec eased himself into the hallway and padded towards the living room. There was a little alcove to one side with a window looking out towards the bunkhouse. Alec stepped into it, between the curtains that shut it off from the hallway. He could see Harley Forrest seated near the fireplace with a blanket across his legs. Ellen crossed to the door and opened it. Park Prince stepped in, taking off his fine white Stetson.

"Evening, Ellen," he said. "Evening, Mr. Forrest." The old man nodded sourly.

Park took off his overcoat and hung it on the coat rack. "Turning cold again," he said.

Forrest raised his head. "What's the news from town?"

"They caught Emmett Adams," said Prince. "He won't talk."

"You didn't think he would, did you?" snorted the old man.

Parker smiled thinly. "Pitzer Ives is questioning him," he said.

"God help Adams, then."

Parker sat down and took his silver cigar case from an inside pocket. "Mind if I smoke, Ellen?" he asked.

"You know damned well she doesn't mind!" said Harley Forrest. He wore an ill-disguised look of dislike for the handsome man seated across from him.

Parker lit up. "We'll run Alec to earth before long," he said. "He doesn't dare come around the valley. We've got men watching the Bar M. Men are watching for him in town. Minnigh is camped at the Lazy L line shack near the bend in the creek. Mustang has been scouting Dark Valley. I expect a report from him soon."

"Mustang ought to be here working, where he belongs!"

Parker inspected his cigar. "There's a killer loose, Harley," he said quietly. "No one is safe until he's caught."

"There were a hell of a lot of killings going on around here before Alec MacLean came back to Clear Creek!"

"We have it on good authority that Alec was seen skulking around here long before Mustang caught him near the creek."

"That so?" Forrest spat into the fire.

"You don't believe me?"

Forrest shook his leonine head. "No! In fact, I think someone around here is trying to pin a lot of crimes on Alec to clear himself."

Parker flushed. "You seem confident that Alec wasn't around here. Yet he was seen around the Lazy L a week before Mustang captured him. Dance Pitzer saw him. Some people think he killed Dance to cover up his tracks."

"That's a damn lie if I ever heard one!"

Parker eyed the old man through a cloud of blue smoke. "Why do you always stick up for Alec?" he asked.

Forrest jerked his head. "Alec MacLean is an honest man! I can't say that I like him personally—he was always too fast with his sharp tongue to suit me. But he's a man clear through, which is more than I can say for some around here who know a hell of a lot more about the thieving and killing going on than they let on." Forrest looked into the crackling fire as though he hated the sight of Parker Prince.

Parker's dark eyes studied the old man. Ellen went to her grandfather. "You're exciting yourself," she said quietly. "It's time you went to bed. Dr. Phillips said you were to rest; he was against your coming back here."

"I had to! What's happened to this country, anyway?"

"It's all right, Grandfather."

"The hell it is! By hell, if I was only on my feet again, I'd get my boys together and keep going until I strung up every rustler between here and Holbrook!"

Alec flattened himself against the wall as Ellen helped her grandfather through the hallway to his room at the end of the hall. Alec could hear the old man talking on and on and the calm voice of Ellen trying to quiet him.

Parker Prince got up and stood by the fireplace. There was an unholy urge in Alec to walk into the living room and smash the handsome face of his half-brother to a pulp.

Someone tapped on the front door. Parker opened it and Pitzer Ives came in, looking quickly about the room. "I got to talk with you," he said.

"Then talk."

"Anyone around?"

"Ellen's with the old man in his room. Talk quick and get out of here. I don't want them to see you."

Pitzer's big hands opened and closed. "Adams is dead," he said.

"What the hell happened?"

"He wouldn't talk."

"So?"

Pitzer looked stupidly at his huge hands. "I only hit him a few times."

"You damned fool! We've got enough trouble as it is without something like this happening!"

Pitzer scowled. "That ain't all. Look at this." He pulled a paper from his coat pocket and gave it to Parker. Parker read it swiftly and then hurled his cigar into the fire. "Adams was an Arizona Ranger!" he said.

Pitzer nodded. "I found it sewn in the lining of his coat."

Parker rubbed his jaw. "This is handwritten."

"What difference does it make?"

Parker looked up at the big man. "That's Alec's handwriting."

"So what?"

Parker spat into the fire. "Don't you get it? Alec must be a Ranger too!"

Pitzer paled. "What do we do now?"

"Find Roberts. Tell him. Send a man to Minnigh and warn him. We've got to get rid of Alec. Then we'll have to lay low."

"If we get Alec, why worry? Ain't no other Rangers round here."

"You damned idiot! There will be! They'll put every available man on the job. The whole organization will blow up. We've worked too long to blow the thing now. Get going! We've got to get Alec's scalp!"

Alec gripped the butt of his Colt. Poor Emmett had been a Ranger to the last. There was a blood debt to be paid now. Pitzer Ives, for Emmett Adams.

Pitzer left just as Ellen opened the door of her grandfather's room. She went into her room for a few minutes. When she came out there was an odd look on her face. She entered the living room. "I thought I heard you talking with someone," she said.

"One of the boys came in to talk with me."

"Grandfather is badly upset. You'd better leave."

He took her by the hands. "Why don't we get married, Ellen? He's too old to handle the HF, I can do it. I've got money to invest in the place. We can make a kingdom here."

She shook her head. "I told you before I can't do it as long as he's ill."

"We can take care of him together."

She looked up at him. "He doesn't want me to marry you, Parker."

He bit his lip. "Maybe we ought to tell him what *we* want to do instead of letting him tell us what to do."

She pulled away from him. "We? I'm not sure, Parker. There are too many strange things going on here."

He shrugged into his overcoat. "You'd better reconsider," he said. "Your grandfather has many enemies in this country, men who think nothing of shooting from ambush."

She looked steadily at him. "Yes," she said, "I know."

Parker took his hat. "I've got things to do," he said. "Think it over, Ellen. I'm not a patient man." He left the house.

Ellen closed the door and stood with her back against it. She closed her eyes and shook her head as though it were all a nightmare. She put out the harp lamp and came through the hallway.

"Ellen," said Alec softly.

She stopped and turned quickly. "Is it you, Alec?"

Alec stepped into the hallway. She shook her head again. "I saw the rifle in my room. Somehow I knew it was yours." She took his hand and led him into her room, closing the door behind her. She looked up at him. He swept her into his arms and held her close, kissing her forehead. She slid her arms about his neck, and he kissed her again and again. Then she placed her head against his chest. "I'm afraid," she said. "They've been scouring the country looking for you. Can't you get help?"

He shook his head. "Minnigh is in on the deal," he said. "Pitzer Ives was just here talking to Parker while you were with your grandfather. He killed Emmett Adams in the Tonto Wells jail. They know Emmett was a Ranger, and now they know I'm one too. They'll try to kill me on sight."

"Run away."

"No. You must come with me."

She shook her head. "I can't leave grandfather."

"We'll take him along."

"It would kill him."

In the silence that followed a dog howled mournfully. Alec shook his head. "They'll kill him anyway to get him out of the way. Parker wants the HE. He means to get it."

"I'm afraid of him, Alec."

"He isn't the brains behind this rustling. There's someone else. I've got to find that man!"

"Then leave here. If Parker finds out you're here, you'll be shot down like a dog."

Alec closed his big hands. "There will be some shooting before long," he said quietly. "Maybe someone else will be shot down like a dog."

"But you're all alone!"

He kissed her. "Not anymore, Ellen. Now go back to

your grandfather. He must stay in the house. Let no one in. Do you have a gun?"

"Yes."

"Then keep it with you. If anyone tries to get in, you must shoot to kill. I'll be back as quickly as I can." He kissed her and picked up his rifle.

For a moment she clung to his hand and then he left her, moving silently through the dark house to the back door. He ran across to the shed and worked his way through the brush. The moon was high as he reached the *grullo*. He rode down towards the trail and headed north. He had no definite plan and he wished to God he had Patched Clothes with him. There was a feeling of intense loneliness in him. The Rangers usually worked in pairs, but this time he was solo, his only allies being his Colt and his Winchester and the skill he had in their use.

CHAPTER FOURTEEN

The moon silvered the ranch houses of the seemingly deserted Bar M. Alec left the *grullo* in the thick woods across the road and circled behind the buildings. He closed in on the barn and was startled to hear a horse whinny. He slid in through the partially open back door. In the rays of the moon, streaming through the gaping front door, he saw a black horse tethered in a stall. He spoke softly to the black and moved close to it. It bore an HF brand. Alec was sure it was the same black Roberts had been riding when he had the rendezvous with the unknown man in the lonely cabin overlooking Dark Valley. Alec looked out at the silent ranch house. Not a wisp of smoke came from the chimney. The moonlight shone on the white-washed logs. There was an eeriness about the place that sent a cold chill up his spine.

He left the barn by the back door and ran crouching to a shed, passing behind it to go behind the bunkhouse. He crawled up behind the silent house. The back door gaped open. Alec leaned his Winchester against the wall and eased in through the door. The kitchen was deserted. He crossed to the doorway leading into the living room. The house was as cold as death. Alec stood there a long

time with the cocked Colt in his hand listening to every
slight sound. He stepped into the living room and
snapped the Colt up quickly. A man lay on the couch, his
booted feet hanging to the floor. He did not move. Alec
walked silently across the wide room and looked over the
back of the couch into the staring eyes of Mustang
Roberts. The dead man's hands gripped a knife that was
sunk to the haft in his heart. Alec recoiled with shock.

A shutter banged in the rising wind. Alec crossed to a
front window and looked out on the moonlit ground.
There was no sign of life. He crossed to the couch and
touched the pale face of the dead man. It was cold.
Roberts had been dead for some time.

Alec walked out of the house and stood for a long
time looking at the moonlit area. He walked into the
stable and untethered the black. There was a rustling
noise in the hay in the loft. Alec leaped back as a dark
form dropped from the loft and grappled with him. A
familiar sour odor filled his nostrils. "For God's sake,
Patched Clothes!" he yelled.

The breed stepped back. "No see clear," he said. "I
wait for evil men."

Alec wiped the cold sweat from his face. "I thought I
sent you to Winslow."

"No go. Patched Clothes think about friend all alone.
Many against him. I say: Go back, Patched Clothes. I
come back. Hide in loft. Horse-faced man sneak in barn.
Go and wait in house. Wait for you. Patched Clothes
creep to house. Man sit on couch. Patched Clothes can
kill easy from behind. No good. Patched Clothes want
man to see who kill him. Evil man see. I wait for others.
No come. What we do now?"

Alec leaned back against a post. "I wish to God that I
knew."

The breed smiled evilly. "Easy. Trail enemies. Kill
from dark. Like Tonto. Finish all. All!"

Alec reached inside his shirt and touched his commission in the pocket sewn inside the shirt. "We'll start gathering the sheaves," he said. "Pitzer Ives. Park Prince. Deputy Minnigh."

'Tall man too."

Alec nodded. "Tall man too."

They left the ranch after turning the black loose. Patched Clothes had hidden his horse up the canyon. Alec headed for the Lazy L. He wanted Pitzer Ives first, and deep in his heart, he hoped the big man would resist arrest so mat Alec would have an excuse to shoot him down in revenge for the death of Emmett Adams.

The moon had died when they reached the hill overlooking the Lazy L. Patched Clothes, at Alec's suggestion, dismounted and disappeared in the darkness like a great lean cat, his stringy hair hanging in his eyes. He was back in an hour. There were only a few men at the ranch, and Pitzer Ives was not one of them. Alec led the way to the bend of the creek towards the camp of Deputy Minnigh and his posse.

They picketed their horses and went in on foot, downwind so as not to alarm the horses. There were four men asleep on the ground with their feet towards the smoldering fire. A fifth man leaned against a tree with a rifle cradled in his arms. Alec studied the sleeping men. Not one of them was big enough to be Pitzer Ives.

Alec shook his head wearily. He and the Tonto returned to their horses. The only other place Pitzer could be was in Tonto Wells, unless he had returned to the HE, Alec led the way east. It was getting colder, and he was having difficulty keeping his eyes open. At the place where the creek trail branched to go south, he drew rein. "Go to the HF, Patched Clothes. Watch the house. The *nahlin,* Ellen Forrest, is there with the old man. Keep an eye on them."

"It is understood."

Alec rode through the silent woods towards Tonto Wells. He was cold and hungry, but there was an inner drive in him now that would not let him rest until he had Pitzer Ives under arrest.

———

THE TOWN WAS SLEEPING when Alec rode over the bridge. A sharp chill was on him. He led his horse to the back of the Juniper. Baldy Roscommon slept in a room at the back of the saloon. Alec tethered the *grullo* in the shed and tried the back door of the saloon. It was locked. He tapped on the window of Baldy's room. He heard a muttered curse and the shuffle of feet. "Who the hell is it?" called Baldy.

"The bar is closed, you damned souse! Go home and sleep it off!"

"Shut up, Baldy. It's Alec. Alec MacLean."

"God's sake!"

The door creaked open, and Alec stepped into the dark-room. Baldy pulled down the shade and lit the lamp. He shook his head. "You're either the gutsiest man I ever met or the biggest fool," he said, "coming in here. They're looking all over for you."

Alec fed the potbellied stove. "Get a bottle," he said. "Pronto!"

Baldy shuffled into the saloon and came back with a bottle of rye and two glasses. Alec downed two hookers and collapsed in a chair. "Is Pitzer Ives in town?" he asked.

"Saw him at closing time. He was damned near drunk. He ain't been the same since you killed Dance. You're in a hell of a mess, Alec."

Alec poured another drink. "I want Pitzer," he said.

"For God's sake, why? He'll kill you with his bare hands."

"I'd like to see him try, Baldy. He murdered Emmett Adams in the jail with those bloody hands of his. I'm going to arrest him."

"You? A wanted murderer?"

Alec opened his coat and leaned back, closing his eyes. "I'm an Arizona Ranger, Baldy. Sent down here to clean up this rustling mess. Pitzer Ives, Park Prince, and Deputy Minnigh are all involved. I'm going to round them up."

"You're either drunk or loco!"

Alec opened his eyes. "Where does Pitzer stay when he's in town?"

"He's sleeping in the livery stable right now. Raised hell because I wouldn't sell him a bottle after closing hours. Rammed a fist through a front window. Blood all over the floor. I had to threaten him with my Greener before he left."

"Let me sleep here for a couple of hours. What time do you open?"

"Nine o'clock."

"You think he'll be back?"

"Probably."

Alec nodded. "I'll be waiting," he said. He closed his eyes and was almost instantly asleep.

It seemed only a few minutes before Baldy shook Alec awake. The saloon keeper was fully dressed. "Wake up," he whispered hoarsely. "It's seven o'clock. Pitzer is at the bar. I let him in to keep him from raising hell."

Alec stood up and shook his head. He slopped water on his face from a bucket and then peeled out of his coat. He checked his Colt. Baldy wet his lips. "What are you going to do?"

Alec smiled thinly. "Do? Arrest Pitzer."

Baldy wiped the sweat from his face. "I've got to get out of here," he said. "I can't stand this. I locked the front door behind him. The shades are drawn. No one stirring in the streets yet. You're on your own, Alec." Baldy snatched up his coat and hat and scurried out the back door.

Alec walked softly to the door that opened into the

saloon. He eased it open. Pitzer stood at the end of the bar, gripping a bottle in a big fist. He was talking to himself. One harp lamp was lit at the far end of the bar. Alec stepped into the saloon.

"Baldy!" yelled Pitzer. "You got anything to eat?" Pitzer poured another drink, slopping the liquor all over the bar. "You hear me, Baldy?" he yelled.

Alec walked forward. "I heard you," he said.

Pitzer stiffened. He raised his head slowly. Then he turned and looked Wearily at Alec. "You," he said softly. "I been looking for you."

"I'm here."

Pitzer licked his thick lips. He glanced down at Alec's holstered Colt. Then he looked up at Alec again. Suddenly he jumped sideways, still gripping the bottle. Alec's hand dropped for a draw, but Pitzer was too fast. The bottle sailed through the air, striking Alec on the chest. He staggered at the impact. Pitzer swept up a chair and hurled it at Alec. Alec ducked and the chair smashed against the door behind him.

Alec edged towards the bar, watching the big man like a cat. Pitzer lowered his head. "Draw," he said. "Go ahead."

Alec reached for his Colt. Pitzer snatched his hat from his head and sailed it at Alec's face. Involuntarily he ducked. Pitzer closed the gap. One big hand clamped down on Alec's right wrist. The right hand drove in short and hard, rattling Alec's teeth in his head. He brought up a knee into Pitzer's gut. The big man grunted and released his hold. Alec's Colt hit the floor and Pitzer kicked it to the far end of the bar.

Pitzer stepped back and grinned. "Now," he said softly, "I'm going to break you in two. Look!" He snatched out bis Colt and threw it towards Alec's.

Alec watched the grinning giant in front of him. Pitzer opened his huge hands and came forward. Suddenly he lunged at Alec. Alec side-stepped, threw a left that shook the big man and drove in a short right to the gut. Pitzer grunted. He lowered his head and began to stalk Alec. Alec bumped against a table. He gripped a chair and hurled it at Pitzer. The impact staggered the big man. Alec closed in and hit hard with three blows before Pitzer backhanded him, driving him back.

They circled slowly, the only sound was their harsh breathing and the shuffle of feet on the dirty floor. Pitzer lunged at Alec and wrapped powerful arms about him. Alec moved swiftly, thrusting both hands up underneath Pitzer's block of a chin, driving the head back. Pitzer went off balance and fell back against the bar, releasing his hold. Alec slashed in two blows to the eyes before Pitzer threw him back. Alec jumped behind a table. Pitzer gripped it with both hands and upended it towards Alec. Alec threw a chair against the legs of the oncoming giant and came off the floor with a well-timed blow that caught Pitzer behind the ear as he fell forward over the chair. The chair smashed beneath him. He shook his head and got up slowly, breathing hard.

Alec measured him with a straight left and threw a right jab that shook the big man. He bellowed like a bull and charged recklessly in. Alec stepped to one side and snatched up a chair, bringing it down on Pitzer's head. The giant sank slowly and hit the bar rail with the back of his head. He lay still.

Alec wiped the blood from his face and picked up the two Colts. He slid one into his holster and kept the other one in his hand. Pitzer didn't move. Alec rolled him over and got a piece of rope from the back room. He trussed the big man up and gagged him. His breath was harsh in his throat as he leaned against the bar. He walked behind the bar and grabbed a bottle, opened it, and drank deeply.

The back door opened, and Baldy Roscommon peered in. He stared at Pitzer and then at Alec. "I don't believe it," he said.

"I don't either," said Alec thickly.

Baldy looked at the wreckage. "It's worth it," he said, resignedly.

Alec drank again. "Keep him in the back room until I come for him."

"God help me," said Baldy. "If he ever gets loose he'll kill me."

Alec looked at the saloon-keeper. He handed him Pitzer's Colt. "If he breaks loose, shoot to kill."

Baldy took the six-gun. "What are you going to do now?"

"Look up my brother," Alec said. "He's next on the list."

CHAPTER FIFTEEN

A lec headed west along the creek trail in the early afternoon. Baldy had learned that Parker Prince had been in town early that morning and had left for the HF spread. Alec reached the hills overlooking the ranch just before dusk. Patched Clothes had made a camp hidden among a jumble of rocks where he could watch the sprawling ranch buildings. He handed Alec a pair of battered field glasses. "Men ride towards creek," he said. "Only few men left here at ranch. Your brother at ranch house."

Alec nodded as he scanned the buildings. Farther up the darkening valley he could see the HF herd, guarded by two men. Smoke drifted up from a shack at the far end of the valley, but there was no smoke coming from the big bunkhouse. Alec cased the glasses. "Go up the valley, my brother," he said. "Watch those men. If any of them come towards the house, you must get to me ahead of them to warn me. If you can't reach me, shoot three times into the air." Alec eyed the breed. "There will be no more killings, my brother."

Patched Clothes nodded. "It is understood." The breed hid his blankets and camp gear and got his horse. He vanished into the woods.

Alec led his horse down the slope, keeping to the cover of the scrub trees. He tethered the horse in a gully and took his Winchester, approaching the house behind the buildings. He walked up beside the house. A horse was tethered to the fence. It was Parker's horse. Alec walked to the back of the house and looked into the kitchen. It was deserted. He let himself in through the door and padded towards the living room, peering into Harley Forrest's room. The old man was asleep on his bed.

Voices came from the living room. Alec stopped just inside the hallway. Parker was leaning against the fireplace, talking swiftly to Ellen, who was seated on the couch.

"This is a dangerous place for you and your grandfather, Ellen," Park said. "There have been some mysterious killings. I want you and your grandfather to come with me to Holbrook. I'll come back here and take charge of the ranch until things settle down."

"We're safe enough here," she said.

"I feel that I'm responsible for you both."

"We'll be all right. Grandfather can't travel."

Parker shook his head in exasperation. "Maybe I'll take you away from here for your own good!"

Alec leaned his Winchester against the wall and walked into the living room. "Hello, Park," he said easily.

Parker Prince whirled and clawed his hand down to his Colt.

"Don't draw," said Alec. "You know better than that."

Parker paled. He said, "You've got a nerve coming here."

"No more than you. I'm arresting you, Park, for complicity in rustling... and murder."

"By what authority?"

"Arizona Rangers."

"A likely story."

Alec reached inside his shirt and ripped the lining

open. He took out his commission and extended it towards Parker. "Read it," he said. "Pitzer Ives is under arrest. Mustang Roberts is dead. You're next on the list. Will you come quietly?"

Parker crossed the gap between them and snatched the commission from Alec's hand. He scanned it and then looked up at Alec. "This is phony," he said. "You can't arrest me on the strength of a piece of paper."

"It's authentic, Park. There might be a break for you if you turn territorial evidence and help clean up this mess."

Parker swallowed. "What do you want to know?"

"Many things. Who killed Eddie Short? Who tried to dry-gulch me on the creek road? Who is the tall dark man who seems to be the brains behind this rustling?"

Parker raised his head. "I don't know who you're talking about!"

"Then you'll have to come with me."

Parker looked at Ellen. "He's loco, Ellen. I know nothing about these things."

Alec took the commission from Parker's hand. "HF and Bar M cattle have been brand-blotted and taken to Winslow to be sold as BB and BM cattle. Arizona Rangers are checking on them now. You're up against a wall, Park."

Parker loosened his collar. "You're just trying to turn Ellen against me. You never liked me, Alec, because I was the favorite at home. You were jealous because my father left me the Bar M. Most of all, you're jealous because I took Ellen away from you!"

Alec shifted a little and glanced at the girl. She stood up and came to Alec, looking back at Parker. "You never took me away from anyone, Parker. You'd better do as Alec says."

Parker shrugged. He reached down to place a piece of wood on the fire. "All right," he said, "I'll go. I'll prove easily that I had nothing to do with these killings and the rustling."

"I hope you do," she said. She walked to the hallway to listen. "Grandfather is getting restless," she said. "You must go before you awaken him."

Parker picked up another piece of wood. Suddenly he whirled and threw the faggot at Alec. Alec warded off the missile with his left arm. Parker snatched up a poker and swung it. It clipped Alec alongside the head. He fell against Ellen, driving her back against the wall. Parker was on him like a cat. He drove home a boot to Alec's jaw. Alec grunted in agony as the spur raked his face. Alec rolled over and Parker drew his Colt, cocked it, and jammed it against the back of Alec's head. "Now move," he said softly. "Move and I'll scatter your brains all over the floor."

Ellen remained backed against the wall, her hands at her throat.

Alec felt the blood run down his face. He cursed himself mentally for a fool. The muzzle of the Colt shoved against his head.

"Lie still," said Parker. He ripped Alec's Colt from its sheath. He stood up. "Get up," he said coldly. "Hands over your head. Against the wall!"

Alec did as he was told.

Parker laughed. "My brilliant brother! For once I've got the upper hand. How does it feel, Alec? What are you going to do now?"

Alec turned his head a little. "Put up that pistol, you damned idiot," he said. "You haven't got a chance. I've got a man watching the house."

"Who? Joe Vestal? He's dead. Emmett Adams? He's dead. You're still wanted for the murder of Dance Ives and Bert Jepson. They had friends in Tonto Wells. I can take you back there. Judge Lynch will take care of you and your big mouth, Ranger!"

A door creaked open down the hall. Feet shuffled in

the hallway. Harley Forrest came into the living room. "What the hell is this?" he demanded.

Ellen went to him. "Alec came to arrest Parker."

"So? It looks like Parker has the upper hand."

Parker laughed. "I can handle him. He's wanted for two murders. He's behind the rustling. Not me as he says!"

Forrest gripped his shaking hands. "Put away that Colt, Parker. Alec has been working for me to clean up this mess. I didn't know then he was still with the Rangers but learned since then that he is."

Parker jammed the muzzle of the Colt between Alec's shoulder blades. "You move towards me, Forrest, and he'll get it."

Forrest wet dry lips. "Ellen," he said quietly, "talk to that madman."

Ellen went to her grandfather. "Please, go back to your room."

Harley Forrest moved swiftly, surprisingly. He slashed a hand down on the Colt. It exploded, driving a slug into the floor. Parker cursed and leaped back. Alec whirled as Parker fired again. The slug whipped through the slack of Alec's coat. Parker darted for the door, and Alec hurdled a stool and closed in on his brother. He ducked as Parker fired again. There was a startled exclamation behind him. Alec snatched up a chair, but he was too late. Parker slashed at him with the Colt. The barrel struck Alec's temple. He went down hard, striking his face against the floor. He tried to get up and couldn't make it. A wave of darkness swept over him.

———

THE STENCH of burning wood and cloth came to Alec. He opened his eyes and coughed in the veil of smoke that filled the big living room. He pulled himself to his feet and wiped the blood from his battered head. The room was filled with smoke and the crackle of flames. The whole wall near the fireplace was ablaze. Alec staggered back towards the hallway and stumbled over something soft. It was Harley Forrest, lying across a twisted rug. Alec gripped him under the arms and dragged him through the hallway to the kitchen. He kicked open the back door and dragged the old man out into the cold night air. Smoke hung low over the burning ranch house.

Harley Forrest coughed harshly. "Forget about me, Alec," he said. "I'm done for. Slug in my chest. Parker has Ellen."

Alec picked the man up, carried him to the shed, and placed him in the straw. Three shots broke the quiet of the valley. Hoofs drummed on the soft earth. Forrest gripped Alec by the sleeve. "I'm not sorry," he whispered. "Rather die this way than lying in bed. Get that girl!"

Alec jerked a horse blanket from a hook and covered the rancher.

Patched Clothes drew rein just outside the shed. "Men come," he said. "See smoke and fire."

Alec ran into the house and snatched his guns. He raced back through the doomed house and saw Patched Clothes leading up Alec's horse.

Alec glanced at the old man. His sightless eyes were open; he was dead. Alec swung up on his mount and set the steel to it. He followed the breed down the road as a pistol cracked down the valley.

A cold wind swept the creek road as they hammered north. Alec looked back. A tongue of flame licked redly at the roof of the house.

Patched Clothes looked curiously at Alec. "Where go?" he asked.

"My brother has Ellen Forrest."

"The *nahlinl* Why?"

Alec touched his battered head. "He's loco," he said. "I gave him his chance."

They reached the trail that turned west. Alec drew rein. "Look for tracks," he said.

Patched Clothes slid from his horse. He crouched and looked at the ground. "No new tracks on town trail," he said. He padded to the west, studying the ruts. He skirted the road on both sides and suddenly dropped to his knees with an exclamation. "New tracks!"

Alec dismounted and crouched beside the breed.

"Deep tracks," said the breed. "One horse. Heavy load. Maybe carry two people."

"You sure they're fresh?"

Patched Clothes raked brown fingers through a pile of manure. "Horse pass little while ago."

"We'll take a chance," said Alec.

They mounted and followed the west trail. The wind was colder now. It soughed through the bare trees and whispered through the brush. To their left, they could hear the swift rush of the creek.

They reached and passed the burned shell of the line shack where Eddie Short had died. Beyond that, they passed a large meadow. Saddle Mountain was a huge brooding bulk to their right. Patched Clothes drew rein as they reached a place where the trail skirted the rushing creek. "Hear something," he said quietly.

Alec raised his head. "Nothing but the wind," he said.

"No! Hear something!"

Alec shook his head impatiently. He spurred his horse ahead.

Two hundred yards down the trail they saw something in the trail. Alec cursed. The breed had been right.

"Men," said Patched Clothes. He kneed his horse into the brush. A rifle spat orange flame and the slug buried itself in a tree. Alec turned his own horse and spurred it towards the brush. The rifle spat again. "Get 'em!" a man yelled. It was Deputy Sheriff Minnigh. Rifles roared. Alec crashed through the brush, cursing as the branches slashed at his face. The breed had vanished. Alec came out into a clearing and raced across it. Men yelled on the trail. Hoofs thudded. Slugs whined through the trees. Alec crashed through brush again and came out beneath a long, high ledge of rock and followed it. The shouting finally died away.

Alec eased the blowing horse. He sat for a long time in the saddle with his Winchester ready, listening to the night sounds. He touched the horse with his spurs and rode west, curving back towards the creek trail. When he reached it there was no sign of life. He rolled a smoke as he sat there. Where the hell had Parker gone with Ellen? Odds were that he had headed into the hills. The night was cold and getting colder. There was a smell of snow in the damp air. "The shack in the mountains," said Alec. "It's my only bet."

He followed the creek, crossed it, rode down the south bank, and recrossed it to follow the bulk of Long Butte. He reached the valley just as the first flakes of snow touched his face.

Alec reached the hide-out cabin in the valley offshoot in a whirl of thick flakes. It was dark and deserted. He unsaddled his horse and picketed it in the shelter of a rock overhang. He started a fire in the shack and made himself a meal. There was no use trying to trail anyone in the white world outside...

Patched Clothes showed up in the cold light of dawn, wrapped in his blanket. He staggered a little as he came into the shack. "No good," he said. "Ghost Face has come to stay. Patched Clothes nearly freeze."

Alec watched the breed wolf the food he had prepared. "Did you see anyone?" he asked.

"Only snow. Snow everywhere deep. No good for horses."

Alec sat and smoked while Patched Clothes slept. Now and then he looked out on the white valley. Snow was beginning to drift deeply.

Alec was worried. If Parker had not got to shelter, he

and the girl might have been caught in the blizzard. But he knew there was nothing he could do until he was able to travel.

THE SECOND MORNING after Alec's arrival at the hide-out, the snow finally blew itself out, leaving a vast white world deep in snow. He went in to talk with Patched Clothes. "You must go into Winslow," he said. "Deliver that report I gave you. Try to find an Arizona Ranger." Alec wrote out a description of Parker, Ellen, and the mysterious man who had never been identified. "Give this to the marshal at Winslow. Have him contact Captain Mossman of the Rangers. The address is written here. I want Mossman to send men to Tonto Wells. Everything is written down."

"No go! Snow too deep. Horse can't ride through deep snow."

Alec spat. "Go on foot. Keep to the high ground. We've got Parker on the run. We can't let him get away."

Patched Clothes took the message. "I go. Not like."

Alec gripped the breed's shoulder. "I'll make it up to you, Patched Clothes. Plenty *tulapai,* tobacco, and food. Good money."

The breed shrugged, and then made up a packet of food. He took two blankets and made a pack, slinging it over his shoulder. "White men loco. All the time have to move around. Time of Ghost Face is for sleep, squaw, food, tobacco, and plenty *tulapai.* Lie around fire."

Alec couldn't help grinning as he saw the breed trudge off through the snow. Maybe Patched Clothes had something there.

Alec busied himself making up a pack. He cleaned his guns and reloaded them, then slung his pack from his shoulders and left the shack. He released the horses, hoping they might find some forage, and then took off up the steep rocky slope behind the shack, slipping and sliding in the drifted snow.

He stopped at the top of the ridge, leaning on his rifle, looking down into the snow-choked valley. There was no sign of life below him. Behind him, the cold wind lifted a streamer of dry snow from the heights of Saddle Mountain. He started along the ridge.

CHAPTER SIXTEEN

The sudden cold had crusted the deep snow, but even so, it was hard going for Alec as he trudged the ridge route, plunging at times hip-deep. The one satisfaction he had was that Parker must have holed up somewhere with Ellen Forrest, for the young woman could never have made it through the snow.

He made only five miles that day, camping for the night under a shelter of spruce branches, huddling close to his fire, listening to the wind moan through the snow-caked trees high above his head.

He rested until late morning and bound strips of blankets about his worn boots. The land was locked in a bitter cold. He trudged on, bucking against the wind that swept down from the heights. By late afternoon he was at the bottom of the plateau on which the lonely shack was perched. He made his camp in a shallow cave at the base of the plateau, making his fire from the dry lower branches of the towering pines.

The cold drove him into movement at dawn. His food was running low. He made up his pack and started up the icy plateau side. It was a dreary white land he moved in, dotted by the dark boles of the large trees. Now and then he plunged into deep drifts, at times forced to crawl flat on his belly, thrusting his Winchester out ahead of him. Another time he was stranded on an icy ledge with no way to advance and was forced to descend again, to find an easier ascent.

Three times he was forced to backtrack, and in the middle of the afternoon, he was deadbeat, shivering, and beginning to feel the cold hands of death closing about him. There was no choice but to camp in a deep cleft with a roaring fire, despite his fears of discovery. He spent a cold night, huddled close to his fire, feeding it all the wood he could find. He melted snow for water and ate the last of his food.

In the cold light of early morning, he fought on, dragging himself painfully up to the lip of the plateau. It was a blanket of unsullied white, broken here and there by the dotted trails of rabbits. His strength was almost drained, but his natural stubbornness drove him on through the deep snow of the woods until he dropped into a hollow where he could see the cabin. For a desperate moment he thought it might be deserted, but he could see the rump of a horse in the lean-to shed. He was sure it was the horse Parker Prince had had the night he had taken Ellen from the ranch house.

Alec rested his head on his arms. The trip had taken more out of him than he had realized. A lethargy seemed to come over him. He wanted to drift off into sleep and forget about the whole thing. Suddenly he raised his head. The door of the shack had opened. Parker Prince stepped out into the tracked snow and began to gather firewood from the lower branches of the trees that ringed the little clearing. Then he hurried into the cabin.

Alec forced himself to his feet. He skirted the clearing, plowing knee-deep through the crusted snow. He came out behind the cabin and peered in through a window. Parker was feeding the potbellied stove. Ellen Forrest, pale and with dark circles under her eyes, was seated in a chair close to the fire, warming her hands.

Alec stepped back and levered a round into his Winchester's chamber. The action worked stiffly because of the cold. He walked softly to the front of the cabin and paused to listen. He heard the lid of the stove grate into place. Alec walked to the door, leveled his rifle at the hip, and booted the door open. He stepped into the cabin, pointing the rifle at Parker. "Stay where you are," he warned quietly.

Parker's face was a mask of fear. "It can't be you," he said.

Alec grinned, wincing as his frostbitten face drew up. "It is, Park. Half frozen, but it's me. Throw that Colt on the bed. Take it, Ellen. Point it at him. Shoot if he makes a break!"

Ellen took the six-gun and cocked it. She stood up and walked behind Parker. Alec leaned his rifle against the wall and took some leather thongs from a hook on the wall. He lashed Parker's wrists behind him and guided him to a chair. He lashed his ankles to the legs of the chair and then stood up, shaking his head wearily. She came to him and kissed him on his cracked lips. "I knew you'd come," she said quietly. "We just made it through the snow."

He held her close. "Your grandfather is dead," he said. "Another crime for Park to answer to."

She bowed her head. "I knew he shouldn't have returned, Alec."

Alec dropped into a chair. He looked at Parker. "What did you expect to do?" he asked. "Stay here? Try for Winslow? You would have been picked up the minute you walked into town."

Parker swallowed. "Look, Alec. I'm not the brains behind this thing. Let me go. You've got Ellen. You've got Pitzer Ives. Dance Ives and Bert Jepson and Mustang are all dead. I'm your brother! Give me a fair chance!"

"Like you gave me when you killed Bert and had it hung on me? Remember the scheme you had to have me

killed by the Ives boys when I stepped out of the Tonto
Wells jail? You think you can talk me out of taking
you in?"

"Look," said Parker quickly, "I'll tell everything. You
promised me a break if I turned territorial evidence."

Alec unbuttoned his coat. "That was before Harley
Forrest was shot down in his own house and before you
left me to die there. It's too late!"

Parker bit his lips. He looked at Ellen. "You talk to
him," he said. "Didn't I treat you all right? What's to be
gained by turning me in?"

She looked at him. "You'll have to answer for yourself,
Parker," she said.

A terrible lethargy settled over Alec. "I've got to rest,"
he said.

"I'll make coffee," said Ellen. "Lie down."

Alec took off his coat and staggered a little as he
walked to the cot. He dropped on it, watching her fill the
coffeepot. He closed his eyes and was instantly asleep.

————

WHEN ALEC OPENED HIS EYES, the cabin was in
darkness except for the winking red eye of the stove
draft. Ellen was asleep in a chair close beside the cot.
Parker was still in his chair, sitting still. Alec couldn't
make out his face. Cold moonlight shone in through the
dirty windows.

Alec closed his eyes again. He wanted to get up, but
he felt too weak. Finally, he sat up and bent his head.
Weariness broke over him like a great wave. He stood up
and swayed a little. He picked up the girl and placed her
on the cot. She opened her eyes and smiled and then was
asleep again.

Alec went to the stove and opened it. The fire was
low, and the wood box empty. He glanced at Parker. His
eyes were closed, and he hung forward against his lash-

ings. Alec went outside, wincing as the cold night air met him. He walked across the crisp snow and into the woods to gather branches. He piled them in front of the cabin and went back for more. He worked steadily for an hour gathering the squaw wood.

He checked the horse. There was plenty of feed in the lean-to. He covered the horse with a blanket and broke the ice in the water bucket. The moonlight shone down with a glittering light that gave an unearthly silver glow to everything.

Alec went back into the cabin and filled the stove from his wood supply. In the cupboard, there were a few cans of beans and embalmed beef, some coffee, flour, sugar, and dried beans. Not enough to keep them fed for more than a day.

He glanced at Parker, who was still asleep. Alec yawned and placed the coffee pot on the stove. He turned to cover the sleeping girl with the blankets. Feet scraped on the floor. He turned in time to meet a crashing blow to the jaw. He staggered back against the wall as Parker drove in with insensate fury, throwing well-timed punches that gave Alec no time for defense. Ellen sat up and screamed.

Alec drove Parker back with a left and smashed home a right to the jaw that set Parker back against the front wall of the shack. The whole structure shook at the impact. Parker cursed and closed in, gripping for Alec's throat. Alec drove him back. Parker screamed like a woman as he smashed back against the wall. He raised a leg as Alec bored in, caught Alec in the gut, and clawed at his face.

Alec was breathing hard. Parker darted for a gun, but Alec stepped in front of him, clipped him from under the jaw, and whirled him about with his left hand. Alec ripped in a right that sent Parker back against the door. He yelled in fury, gripped the door handle, and jerked the door open. Alec hit him behind the ear as he stepped out into the open. Parker went down and Alec dived on top of him. Parker met Alec with a raised knee. Alec rolled free, covered up his face, and got up on his knees. Parker snatched up a thick piece of firewood and smashed at Alec. Alec went underneath it and grappled with his frenzied brother. They swayed back and forth, pitting their strength against each other.

Alec began to feel the toll of his hard trip. Sweat soaked through his clothing as he grappled with the younger man. He threw Parker back. Parker rushed in, butted Alec with his head, and kicked savagely as he went down. Alec gripped Parker's ankle and upset him, gripping for his throat with a grunt of satisfaction. They rolled over and over to the edge of the clearing. Alec came out on top. He gripped Parker by the collar and smashed his head down against the frozen earth, again and again.

"Don't!" screamed Parker. "I'll tell the truth! My God, Alec, you're killing me!"

The blood craze left Alec. He staggered to his feet and dragged Parker up with one hand. He set himself, shoved his screaming brother back, and unleashed a right. Parker went down, striking his head hard against the earth.

Alec wiped his face and seemed suddenly to become aware of the pain that shot through him. He gripped Parker by the arm and dragged him into the shack. He said nothing until Parker was lashed back in his chair.

"He almost had me," he said to Ellen. "When he comes to, he'll talk. It won't be a pretty sight, Ellen. I warn you."

Alec felt for his makings and rolled a smoke as Ellen lit the candle lantern and poured the coffee. Alec sat down astraddle a chair and rested his chin on his folded arms. His eyes never left the battered face of his half-brother.

CHAPTER SEVENTEEN

Parker Prince groaned as he opened his eyes. He stared at Alec. "You've won again," he said, "damn you! I might have known."

Alec threw down his cigarette and stepped on it. He rolled another and lit it. "Park," he said, "I want you to talk. You can't gain anything by keeping quiet now."

"I'll wait for my trial."

"If you get there."

"What do you mean?"

"I'm taking Ellen out of here tomorrow. There's not enough food to last more than another day."

"So?"

Alec shrugged. "I don't intend to take you unless you tell me all you know."

"You're bluffing. It would be murder to leave me here tied up."

Alec grinned. "I won't leave you tied up, Park. I'll cut you loose before we leave. You can sit here and listen to the winter wind howl about the cabin. No food. No gun to drop game. You can't make it out of here without food."

"You wouldn't dare!"

Alec shrugged. "It'd be safe enough. When they find

your body in the spring there won't be a mark on you. Died of exposure, they'll say."

In the silence that followed, a branch snapped in the stove. Park looked at Ellen. "You won't let him do it, will you, Ellen?"

"You left my grandfather wounded, to die in a burning house. Can you expect any sympathy from me?"

Parker swallowed hard. He looked at Alec. "If I talk, how do I know you'll let me go out of here with you?"

"My word, Park."

The younger man hesitated. "Yes... I think you would."

"Who killed Andy Fairweather?"

"Roberts."

"Who wounded Bill Hoskins?"

"Dance Ives."

"Who killed Hash Melrose, the foreman of the HF before Mustang Roberts got the job?"

"Mustang. He wanted the job."

"Why?"

"To be on the inside of a rustling deal we cooked up."

"Who did the shooting up of the Bar M cabin at the creek?"

"Sometimes Mustang Roberts, other times the Ives boys. They wanted to drive any Bar M man from that area so it would be easy to rustle the rest of the Bar M cattle."

"Why did you gyp Enos Strang out of the south water hole, when you sold the Bar M?"

"You knew the Ives boys always wanted that water hole. They talked me into it. I had to let them have it because they knew too damned much about the rustling."

"Who killed Carl Adams, Emmett's brother?"

"That I don't know. It could have been Pitzer or Dance Ives."

Alec rolled another smoke. He stood up and thrust it

into Parker's mouth. He lit it and sat down again. "Who tried to kill me on the creek road?"

"I don't know."

"You're lying."

"I said I didn't know!"

Alec shrugged. "Who killed Joe Vestal and fired the Bar M?"

"That I don't know either."

"Who wrote you that letter mentioning Eddie Short and Roberts?"

"A friend of mine who wanted some cattle cheap."

Alec rubbed his jaw. "What was his name?"

"You wouldn't know if I told you."

Alec tried another tack. "Who dry-gulched Eddie Short?"

"It could have been any of them."

"I saw the man—tall, dark, riding a grey. The same man who tried to kill me."

"It could have been any of them, as I said before."

"Who was the man who met Mustang Roberts up here?"

"How should I know?"

Alec leaned back. "It seems to me you don't know too much. Once I figured you were the brains of this gang."

"Think what you will."

Alec yawned. "You ever seen the territorial prison at Yuma, Park?"

"No."

"Rotten place. On a bluff overlooking the Colorado. Cells hewn out of solid rock. Cold in the winter, hot as Hades in the summer. A man rots there, mixed in with the worst border scum you ever saw. You wouldn't like it, Park."

Parker swallowed hard. "You said you'd help me at the trial."

"I will. Talk a little more, Park."

"What do you want to know?"

"One thing: the name of the man behind this rustling ring. You haven't got the brains to organize the foreman of the HF, the Ives boys, and Deputy Sheriff Minnigh. Now, who was it?"

"I can't say. He'd kill me if I talked."

"It'll be cold up here, Parker. You'll freeze and you'll go hungry. The wolves will get your corpse. Come on, now. Tell me!"

Parker shifted uneasily. A wolf howled in the rough country behind the cabin as though backing up Alec's words. He raised his head suddenly and then lowered it.

He glanced past Alec at Ellen. Alec turned. Ellen drew her blanket about her.

"What's bothering you, Park?" asked Alec. "The wolf?"

"Yes, the wolf."

"Then you'd better talk. Who was the man?"

Glass shattered behind Ellen. She screamed. Alec whirled, drawing his Colt. He kicked his chair away. He could see a rifle barrel thrust through a hole in the shattered window. A gloved hand was visible. "Don't move, Mac-Lean," a muffled voice said, "or this filly will get it in the back!"

Alec stared at the shattered, frosty glass. He was sure it was the same voice—the voice he had heard in the cabin, the man who had been talking with Mustang Roberts. Cold sweat trickled down his sides. He stared at the gloved hand and the rifle barrel.

"Cut Park loose," the muffled voice said. "Pronto!"

Alec dropped his Colt and cut Parker loose. Parker was staring at the gloved hand. He wet his lips. His head jerked a little as he picked up the Colt. He backed to the door and opened it. He held the Colt on Alec. The rifle barrel was withdrawn through the window. Feet grated on the crisp snow. Parker's lips drew back from his even white teeth. "You'll see the man now," he said thinly. "You won't like it, Alec."

Parker stepped aside. The man stopped outside the door and then moved again. He stepped into the doorway cradling his Winchester in his arms. Hard, dark eyes studied Alec with the look of a wolf. Alec felt amazement and fear at the same time. There was no mistaking the aquiline nose, the thin mouth, the heavy black dragoon mustache.

"Sam Prince," he said. "You!" Instinctively he raised his left hand to touch the scar at the edge of his left eye — the eye that Sam Prince had nearly put out when Alec was eighteen.

Sam Prince jerked his head at Parker. "Shut the door," he said. "Get some grub." His eyes never left Alec.

Parker crossed to the stove and placed a pot on it. He got food from the cupboard and placed it on the table.

Clumsily he began to work the can opener. Suddenly it occurred to Alec that Parker was just as afraid of his father as he had always been.

Sam Prince pulled the muffler from about his thin neck and threw it on the cot. "You've changed, Alec," he said coldly. "You've just about spoiled my whole game, but it's not too late to get out of this mess."

"You haven't a chance," said Alec. "This country will be full of Rangers within a week."

"Yeah. Who knows I was behind this? I've got money in three different banks. I can be over the border in a week. You think I didn't figure on having trouble like this?"

"No, I guess you did."

Sam Prince looked at the girl. "Park," he rasped, "this was a damned fool stunt, bringing her here."

"What did you expect me to do?"

"Shut up! You haven't got the guts of a fish. Alec would have been more of a help than you if he had used his head and stayed around the old place."

Parker dumped the beans into the pot. "You'd better use your head now," he said. "We're in a hell of a fix."

Sam Prince grunted. "We? *I'm* in the clear."

The wind moaned about the shack. Alec studied his stepfather. There always had been a coldness about Sam Prince. He had the flat-eyed look of a killer. Alec felt a chill that was not brought on by the winter night. He knew now that what had happened up until this time was nothing —he faced the greatest test of all now. Sam Prince had always been a man to reckon with. Alec knew that his chances of leaving that shack alive were practically nonexistent. Cold fear had come into the shack.

CHAPTER EIGHTEEN

S am Prince ate his meal with a cocked Colt lying on the table close at hand. He ate swiftly. For all his bravado, there was still a hunted look on his narrow face. Parker sat on a chair holding a Winchester on Alec and Ellen, who sat on the cot. Now and then, Parker got up and put wood in the stove, but he still held the rifle in his hands. There was a nervousness about him. He constantly glanced at the silent man who had joined them.

Sam finished his meal, slowly rolled a cigarette, and lit it from the candle lantern. He tilted his head and turned it slowly. "Damned smart, wasn't it, Alec," he asked, "playing dead? No one would ever suspect Sam Prince would come back from the dead." He laughed without mirth.

"It's been done before," said Alec.

"Yeah. It ain't nothing new. But it takes a smart hombre to really work out the deal."

"Like you," said Alec dryly.

"Yeah. Like me."

Alec studied his chances. His Winchester leaned by the door, too far away for a quick dash. His Colt was on the table in front of Sam, while Sam had his own pistol in its holster. Parker had Sam's Winchester across his lap and his Colt was thrust through his belt.

Sam shifted a little. "If you're thinking of making a break, Alec, it'd pleasure me to shoot you. Now sit tight!"

"What are you going to do, Sam?" asked Parker.

Sam Prince picked at a front tooth with a dirty finger-nail, thoroughly enjoying the situation. "Get out of the country for a time. There's good land to be had down in Mexico for a song. Live like a king down there with plenty of cattle, a big hacienda, plenty of good Baconora mescal, and your choice of young senoritas."

"Sounds good," said Parker.

"Yeah, you'd like that, wouldn't you? Letting your old man do the planning, the dirty work, and the killing."

"I helped!"

Sam scratched his bristly chin. "Yeah. You were all right for a time. If you'da killed Alec off like I told you, none of this woulda happened."

"It was only a matter of time before the Rangers would have come in anyway."

Sam spat. "It was up to me to figure out when we'd pull out. Now we got to go."

Parker fiddled with the lever of his rifle. "What about them?" He nodded his head towards Ellen and Alec.

Sam leaned back in his chair and took the Colt, rubbing the barrel with his sleeve. "There's only one answer, Park."

The wind scrabbled at the thin walls. The wolf gave tongue again, closer this time. "We can take her with us," Park said.

Sam shook his head. "Get smart. It took me over a year to organize things here. Every way I figured; I won the deal. We got rid of the cattle, got money into the bank, shut up any wagging mouths. The rest of the deal is to go to Mexico."

"She couldn't talk down there."

Sam looked at his son with disgust. "Maybe this will come as a surprise, but they got police in Mexico too."

"They won't bother us."

Sam spat again. "Maybe you don't know Burt Mossman, captain of the Arizona Rangers. Tough as whang leather and teethed on a six-shooter. Seems as though Burt Mossman swung a deal no one else was ever able to swing. Made a deal with Colonel Emilio Kosterlitzky, head of the *Guardia Rural* in northern Mexico. Kosterlitzky escorts American criminals wanted in Arizona over the line. Mossman, in turn, sees to it that Mex criminals go south over the line about the same time. Very nice. No papers. No treaties. Nothing but an even trade. Kosterlitzky is tough as nails. Ain't he, Alec?"

Alec nodded. He knew Kosterlitzky well. *Juez de los Cordados,* he was called by the *campesinos.* Judge of the roped ones. His prisoners stood before him, bound with ropes, and answered his probing questions as though he were Satan himself. He was cold-eyed, stern, and unrelenting in his pursuit of the criminal element.

Sam polished his Colt. "Now, if we was to take this filly over the line and Mossman got news of it, we'd have Don Emilio hot after us with his men, and believe me, Park, he'd hunt us down clear to the Guatemalan border."

"Do we have to go to Mexico?"

Sam turned slowly. "That's where *I'm* going."

Parker was frightened of his father. He looked at Ellen. She turned away.

Sam raised the Colt and aimed it at Alec. The bore looked as big as a Sharps fifty. Alec did not move, but cold sweat began to soak through his shirt. It was like the time he had awakened out in the desert to a side-winder poised a yard from his head, eyeing him with a flat basilisk stare. Until the rattler had slithered off, Alec had been on the flaming brink of hell.

Sam held the big handgun steady as a rock. Then he smiled thinly. "You always had guts, Alec, which is more than I can say for *my* kid." He lowered the gun and began to polish it.

Sam was enjoying himself. Alec suddenly remembered that he had once seen him beat a half-broken pony almost to death because the pony had broken a fence. Alec realized that Sam Prince was a sadist, delighting in his reign of terror.

Ellen dropped her hand into her lap and then took out a handkerchief. She wiped her lips with it and then placed her hand close to Alec's. He placed his hand on hers. She removed her hand, leaving the handkerchief on the cot.

Alec's hand rested on a short, hard object, curved and rounded—a derringer. A ray of hope came to him.

Sam looked at the shattered window. "Gettin' light," he said, "Park, you gather all the food and them blankets together. Load them on our horses. My grey is down the slope a piece. Wore out, but he'll last to get us out of here. We can buy another on the way." Sam Prince laughed. "Could steal one," he said, "but I got to be careful now. I'm an honest man."

Parker placed the small supply of food in a sack and took it from the cabin. He came back and shoved Alec to one side, ripping the blankets from the cot. Alec slipped the derringer into the side pocket of his coat. It was a single shot. One shot between the two of them and merciless death.

Parker made up two bedrolls and carried them outside. Hoofs thudded on the frozen earth as he brought up Sam's grey. Sam rolled another smoke and looked about the cabin. "Can't leave no traces. That's the smart way, Alec. No traces. Hit hard and clear out. Learned that with Quantrill during the war."

"I thought you might have been with him," said Alec.

Sam grinned. "Your old man was a fool, fighting for the Union. Why, hell! I made plenty with Quintrell."

"It figures."

Parker came back into the cabin. "All set," he said. He hesitated. "Let's take her with us," he said. "Maybe we can get some ransom."

Sam whirled. "Damn you! I'm running this show!"

Alec eyed the two of them. It would be better to get Sam first, as he was the more dangerous of the two of them.

Sam slid Alec's Colt beneath his belt and picked up a Winchester. "Outside," he ordered.

Parker waited outside as Alec and Ellen came through the door. The two horses were tethered to a tree. He looked at Alec. There was stark fear in his eyes. He was as afraid of Sam as he was of Alec.

The cold light of dawn lightened the sky. A wisp of smoke hung low from the chimney of the shack. Sam suddenly kicked over the stove. The embers scattered across the floor. He shut the door and rubbed his narrow chin. "No traces," he said.

"Someone will see the smoke!" protested Parker.

"Yeah? Who? Ain't no one within twenty miles of here. If they did investigate the smoke, we'd be miles away by then."

Parker looked at Alec. Sam walked into the shed and scattered forage on the floor. He touched it off with a match and waited until the flames took hold. He came out through the wreathing smoke like a lean devil straight from hell. "Let's go," he said. He jerked his head at Alec and Ellen. They trudged through the crusted snow. Ellen came close to Alec and gripped his hand. "Very touching!" jeered Sam. "See, Park? The filly likes your lawman brother!"

They climbed a slippery slope and came out on the top of the sharp-edged ridge that stretched behind the cabin. The pall of smoke from the burning shed and shack drifted over them with a bitter stench. They kept walking, Alec momentarily expecting the crash of a gun close behind him and the shocking impact of lead.

Ellen stopped fifty feet from the edge of the ridge. It dropped over two hundred feet to the valley below. Snow was drifted thick along the edge, scalloped by the cold winds. She looked up at Alec. "I never thought it would end like this," she whispered.

"It isn't over," said Alec softly. He slid his hand into his coat pocket and worked the derringer up his left sleeve beneath the knitted wristband.

Sam stopped and slowly buttoned up his coat. He looked out over the valley. "Snow is crusted hard," he said. "We can be out of the valley by noon. Cut through Pine Pass and come out near the East Verde. Camp there tonight. Then we can make Prescott leisurely-like, get another horse, and ride down to Phoenix. After that, we can take our time into Sonora."

Parker shifted his Winchester. "We ain't going to kill them," he said. "I can't do it, Sam."

Sam turned slowly. "You gutless fish," he said. "Leave the dirty work to me, like always. You sat in style in the Bell House in Tonto Wells, playing the gentleman, while old Sam did the killing. If you'd killed Alec when you got rid of Bert, we'd have been in the clear. But you had to play it fancy. Throwing Alec in the jailhouse and letting Dance Ives do the dirty work. Well, all he got was a slug in the guts, and Alec got away. Now you'll play along with me.

"I will like hell!" Parker raised his Winchester and centered it on his father. Sam grinned. He crossed the gap between them with measured steps and placed a hand on the barrel of the rifle. He jerked it away from Parker. "See? You're gutless!" He slapped Parker across the mouth and stepped back. "You got a Colt. Draw it. I'll show you how tough I am!"

A worm of blood trickled from Parker's mouth. He slowly raised his hand and touched his bleeding mouth. His eyes never left his grinning father.

Alec slipped the derringer into his hand. He moved

swiftly, shoving Ellen behind a tree. He cocked and raised the gun. He squeezed the trigger. Flame and smoke spat just as Sam jumped to one side. The soft-nosed .41 slug rapped into Sam's left sleeve, raising a puff of dust. Sam fell back against a tree. He snapped up the Winchester, levering it with one hand, and dropped it to cover Alec. Alec closed in. The Winchester slug tugged at Alec's left sleeve. Sam grinned and levered another round into the saddle gun.

Parker yelled harshly and launched himself at his father. Sam went down and fired from the ground. Parker screamed as the slug caught him in the left thigh. He went down, gripping his leg with his hands. Sam rolled up and leaped to his feet, but Alec was on him like a tiger. He hurled the derringer into Sam's face and jerked the Winchester free. He slipped and dropped the rifle. Sam kicked it into a drift. The rustler backed off, fumbling with the buttons of his coat. His eyes were narrowed slits as he watched Alec.

Parker moaned as he thrashed on the ground. "Your Colt!" called Alec.

Sam was still backing away, working awkwardly at his coat. His left arm dangled helplessly. Alec glanced at Parker. His brother had rolled down the slope, groaning like a sick child. Sam ripped at the buttons, scattering them across the snow. Alec rushed the older man. He closed, driving a left to Sam's face. Sam broke away and slashed a backhander across Alec's eyes. Alec drove in a punishing right, and caught the rustler with a left uppercut, snapping back his head. Sam grunted in pain. He swept his hat from his head and slashed it across Alec's eyes, half blinding him. Alec slipped on the ice and went down on one knee. Sam booted him on the jaw and shouted as Alec sprawled flat. Sam ripped the Colt from inside his coat. Alec uncoiled like a spring and gripped the gun wrist, shoving it up high.

Alec drove in short hard blows to the gut. His stepfather's rank breath filled his nostrils. Sam turned away quickly, dragging Alec off his feet. His knee came up in a punishing drive to Alec's groin. Alec grunted in pain. He fought to his feet and pushed Sam back. Sam broke free and cocked the Colt. The snow beneath him sank a little. He looked down and Alec gripped the gun wrist again. Alec felt the snow give beneath him.

Ellen screamed and ran forward, gripping the slack of Alec's coat. She dragged him back as the snow sank again. Sam was up to his knees in it, scrabbling desperately at Alec's legs.

Suddenly the snow gave way altogether with a soft rushing noise, burying the rustier up to his waist. He screamed like a frightened woman. The Colt cracked flatly, sending a slug whining harmlessly up into the air. Then with a roar the whole snowbank gave way, pouring down the side of the cliff, covering Sam Prince in a thick white blanket. There was one more muffled scream and then nothing but the cascading roar of tons of snow pouring down into the rocky valley far below, sending up a powdery cloud that drifted off before the bitter wind.

Alec lay back on the very brink of the chasm, breathing harshly. Ellen had wrapped her arms about his neck and held her head close to his. The avalanche had awakened the valley echoes. The dull roaring noise seemed to bounce back and forth between the steep crags of the valley and then died away.

Alec rolled over and got to his feet, pulling the white-faced girl to her feet.

Parker lay back against a log, gripped his leg, his eyes wide with horror. "He's dead," he said. "He'll never order me around again."

Alec limped up the slope and stopped beside his brother. "Let me look at that leg," he said.

Parker whipped out his Colt with a bloody hand. "Get back!" he said thinly.

Alec stepped back. "Put up that gun, Park. There's been too much bloodshed as it is."

"Get back!"

Alec backed away.

Ellen came to stand beside him, looking down on the pale-faced man. "Park," she said, "do as he says."

Parker struggled to his feet. "Ellen," he said, "come with me. We can make Sonora. We'll live like a king and queen down there. I'll let Alec go."

"No."

Parker swallowed hard. "I'll kill him," he said.

"Parker," said Ellen. "Sam is gone. You can live your own life now. Go with us. Turn yourself in. We'll help you."

For a long moment, Parker eyed his brother. Then he lowered the hammer of the Colt. "You always win, don't you, Alec?"

"Not always, Park."

Parker backed away, limping painfully. He went down the slope to the horses. Alec and Ellen followed him, Alec carrying the Winchester he had dug out from the drift. Parker stopped at his horse and leaned against it, placing his head on the saddle.

"Park," said Alec, "let me look at that leg."

Park raised his head. "The bone isn't broken. I'll live to make Sonora. Alone."

They watched him struggle painfully into the saddle and grip the reins. For a moment he looked at them. "I would have had you, Ellen," he said quietly, "if Sam had left me alone and Alec had stayed away. Isn't that true?"

"Yes, Park."

"You can still come with me. I'm sick of killings."

She shook her head.

Park leaned over in pain and then got hold of himself. He touched the horse with his spurs and circled it on the forehand, kneeing it towards the trail.

Alec leaned on the Winchester. The smoke from the burning buildings hung about them.

"Where will he go?" Ellen asked.

Alec shrugged. "He'll be picked up," he said, "either in the territory or in Sonora." He almost added *If he lives to make it*.

Parker disappeared down the trail.

Ellen turned to Alec. "We'd better start for home," she said.

Ellen mounted Sam's tired grey. Alec took the reins and led it down the trail. The tracks of Parker's horse showed, cutting across the small plateau. They reached the top of the steep trail. Far below them, they could see Parker riding slowly at the foot of the trail. Now and then he bowed his head as the pain hit him. Suddenly a picture came to Alec —Parker, a kid of nine, sitting on a corral fence watching Alec break his first horse. "You can do it, Alec!" he had yelled in excitement. "You can do anything!"

Alec looked back at Ellen. "Maybe if I had stayed with him he would have been all right," he said.

She shook her head. "He took the wrong fork in the trail," she said. "He has himself to live with now. It's punishment enough for any man."

The sun tipped the eastern mountains, sharp and clear, glittering from the high snowfields. Alec looked back at Ellen. "It will be a long trail for us going back." She smiled. "Not so long," she said.

———

THEY SAW a strange sight as they reached the cold rushing waters of the creek. A stout man was trudging through the snow, his hands bound behind his back. A stick was thrust under the elbows. A bedraggled figure was riding a fine sorrel, with a rifle resting across his thighs. Lank black hair hung over the broad flat face. It was Patched Clothes. He turned, resting a hand on the cantle of his saddle, eyeing Alec and Ellen. "My brother," he said. "Is all well?"

"Yes, my brother, all is well."

The stout man turned. It was Deputy Sheriff Minnigh. His fat face was drawn and pale. "For God's sake, MacLean," he said, "get me away from this crazy breed!"

"Where'd you find him?" asked Alec.

Patched Clothes jerked the line that was attached to the lawman's wrists. "Fat man come to Winslow. Tried to arrest Patched Clothes. Patched Clothes arrest *him*. Rangers at Winslow deputized Patched Clothes. Say I take him back to Tonto Wells to stand trial. Patched Clothes do. Fat man pull gun and shoot Patched Clothes' horse in valley. Patched Clothes beat him on head. Make walk. All the time talk about what he do to me."

Minnigh raised his head. "By hell, you won't get away with this, MacLean. You and that dirty breed!"

Patched Clothes jerked the line hard, throwing the deputy off balance. "All the time talk."

Alec grinned. "Minnigh," he said, "Sam Prince is dead. Parker Prince may be dead. Pitzer Ives is cooling his heels in the Tonto Wells jail. I don't know what you had to do with this mess, but you'd better sing like a bird when the time comes."

"You got nothing on me. You're nothing but a saddle bum. I've got influence in this country."

Alec shrugged. "You *had*," he said. "I was detailed to clean up this mess by Captain Mossman of the Arizona Rangers."

Minnigh paled. "You ain't no Ranger!"

Patched Clothes scratched himself. "Yes. Alec is Arizona Ranger. Patched Clothes is deputy. Dirty breed help Alec clean up mess. All right. Rest of Ghost Face time Patched Clothes and Alec sit beside fire. Eat. Smoke. Drink *tulapai*. Good time. Eh, Alec?"

"Right!" said Alec.

Patched Clothes jerked the line. Minnigh shambled through the snow. Patched Clothes began to hum softly.

Ellen placed a hand on Alec's shoulder. "Can I sit beside that fire too?"

"Where else?'

Alec led the grey on. A man had to put down roots sometime. Spring was coming; he had work to do, rebuilding, buying stock. Somehow his years of drifting seemed to be off in the dim past. He looked at Ellen. "It's good to be home again," he said and met her with a kiss as she leaned towards him.

TAKE A LOOK AT TOO TOUGH TO DIE AND THE VALIANT BUGLES:

Two Full Length Western Novels

Gordon D. Shirreffs was an award-winning author of incredible tales of the old American West. In this volume, readers will be delighted with two such action-filled stories.

In *Too Tough To Die*, Buck Ruffin, a righteous gunfighting lawman on a mission, stalks four vicious outlaws across the desert and through an abandoned mining town where snares and pitfalls threaten around every corner. Even against the odds, Ruffin is determined to see justice done for their victims —even if some of the dead might have deserved their fate. In Ruffin's mind, no man was above the law—or above the swift justice of death.

In *The Valiant Bugles*, Captain Holt Downey had vowed upon pain of death to kill the Apache brave known as "The Butcher," the unconscionable savage who had murdered Downey's brother and subjected his fiancée to a fate worse than death.

It takes time and many miles, but eventually Holt catches up to The Butcher, setting up a showdown between two able and determined fighters that will leave one victorious and alive, and the other dead in a shallow grave...

"Gordon Shirreffs, who has written extensively both for teen-agers and adults, does a professional job of merging history, Americana, and virile action..." — **Kirkus Reviews**

AVAILABLE NOW

ABOUT THE AUTHOR

Gordon D. Shirreffs published more than 80 western novels, 20 of them juvenile books, and John Wayne bought his book title, Rio Bravo, during the 1950s for a motion picture, which Shirreffs said constituted *"the most money I ever earned for two words."* Four of his novels were adapted to motion pictures, and he wrote a Playhouse 90 and the Boots and Saddles TV series pilot in 1957.

A former pulp magazine writer, he survived the transition to western novels without undue trauma, earning the admiration of his peers along the way. The novelist saw life a bit cynically from the edge of his funny bone and described himself as looking like a slightly parboiled owl. Despite his multifarious quips, he was dead serious about the writing profession.

Gordon D. Shirreffs was the 1995 recipient of the Owen Wister Award, given by the Western Writers of America for "a living individual who has made an outstanding contribution to the American West."

He passed in 1996.

9 781639 773176